Four Minutes to Save a Life

Anna Stuart has wanted to be a writer ever since she sat up in her cot with a book. For years she wrote short stories and serials for women's magazines before being published by Pan Macmillan as a historical novelist under the pseudonym Joanna Courtney. Her *Queens of the Conquest* series, set in the pre-1066 years, has been published to acclaim in all formats, including audiobook, and has been translated for European markets. She is delighted to now return to the contemporary world for *Bonnie and Stan* and *Four Minutes to Save a Life*.

Also by Anna Stuart

Bonnie and Stan

Four Minutes to
Save a Life

Anna Stuart

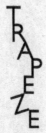

First published in Great Britain in 2020 by Trapeze
an imprint of The Orion Publishing Group Ltd
Carmelite House, 50 Victoria Embankment
London EC4Y 0DZ

An Hachette UK Company

1 3 5 7 9 10 8 6 4 2

A CIP catalogue record for this book is
available from the British Library.

ISBN (Mass Market Paperback) 978 1 4091 7766 1
ISBN (eBook) 978 1 4091 7767 8

Typeset by Born Group
Printed and bound in Great Britain by Clays Ltd, Elcograf S.p.A

MIX
Paper from
responsible sources
FSC® C104740
FSC

www.orionbooks.co.uk

For Maggie and Jacky –
We all need friends and I'm very lucky to have these two

Prologue

'More,' Charlie muttered. 'It needs more.'

He shoved the last few items on to the bonfire, pushing them so deep into the flames that his hands burned with them. Good. If he was brave enough, he'd step right into the heart of it and let the heat scorch all his skin off so he could grow a new one. A better one. If he was brave enough.

But then, if you asked his parents, he'd always been useless.

Charlie grabbed a fork and stabbed at those bits of his belongings threatening to catch the breeze and escape the fire. It had to go, all of it. He couldn't change his past but he could burn it away, scrape it clear, wipe the board – all those metaphors and more besides.

The binding of a book caught the flames and the pages, suddenly released, went fleeing up into the air. Charlie watched them go then took the last item out of his pocket. The burgundy leather shone in the light of the fire and slowly he opened it up and looked down at the picture – a goon of a young man, curly-haired, ruddy-cheeked, clean-shaven. What a twat!

Charlie thrust the passport into the heart of the fire. It was consumed instantly but he stared at the spot where it had landed until his eyeballs felt like red-hot coals. It was gone. He was gone. He'd once read a quote from George Sand: 'We cannot tear out a single page of our life, but we can throw the whole book in the fire.' That's what he'd finally done and now all that was left was to stand here until the flames were spent and he could rise up like a phoenix from the ashes.

'Phoenix!' Charlie scoffed into the spark-lit night.

He was no phoenix. A phoenix was a bold, beautiful, bright-plumaged bird and he was just a run-of-the-mill idiot going to seed before he hit thirty and with enough mistakes under his sagging belt to last a lifetime. He really should just step into the flames with everything else and be done with it but, no, he still wasn't brave enough.

His parents had been right.

It was time to take a different path. Once the bonfire was burned out, he would start again, not as a phoenix but perhaps as a sparrow – a little dull, a little ordinary but, pray God, harmless.

WEEK ONE

WEEK ONE

Chapter One

Charlie pushed his bike up to the railings and peered through. His heart was hammering against his chest and he was glad of his shapeless corporate fleece to keep his nerves hidden. He was working in the 'yard' now. It would be a place of muscles and banter and cruel practical jokes, or so his family had told him.

'You'll be one of the lads, Charlie,' his brother had roared.

He'd found it hilarious. They all had. Remembering, Charlie almost turned away but a voice stopped him.

'Mornin'. You the new bloke?' He blinked. Striding towards him was a petite girl in a purple fleece like his own but teamed with shimmering leggings. Her chunky plait swung to her waist in a rainbow of colours as she tipped her head curiously to one side. 'Charlie, is it?'

'Oh. Sorry, yes. Charlie, that's me.'

'You coming in then?'

'Er, sure. Course.'

Charlie gripped the handlebars of his bike and forced himself through the big steel gates towards the girl, hoping she'd blame the slight shake in its frame on its obvious age and not Charlie's pounding veins. She didn't even seem to notice.

'I'm Bri.' She stuck out a hand. 'Welcome to Turner's Super Supermarkets!'

'Charlie,' he said. 'Oh, but you know that.'

'Sure do. Sean's been giving us the management speak – we're to be welcoming and helpful and all that. So here I am welcoming you.' She spread her hands wide. 'Let me show you where to go.'

With that she grabbed his bike from him and set off at a sharp pace across the yard. Charlie rushed to follow, sneaking looks around as he went. Some twenty purple Turner's delivery vans were lined up in front of the vast warehouse like carthorses waiting patiently to be loaded. An army of people, also in corporate purple, were wheeling baskets out, supervised by a slim, white-haired man with a large clipboard who raised a hand to Bri as they passed. She waved cheerily back.

'Mornin', Jack. Lovely day for it.'

Charlie glanced to the sky – resolutely grey with a light drizzle forming on the chill air.

Jack laughed. 'Ever the optimist, Bri. This the new lad?'

'Charlie, yeah.'

'Hey, Charlie!'

Charlie waved a tentative hand.

'Hey, er, Jack.'

'Welcome to Turner's.'

Charlie's heartbeat slowed a little. He could do this. They were just normal people, not the gang of thugs so fondly conjured up for him by his nearest and supposedly dearest. His family were all set for him to fail – to prove as useless at this as he had been at everything else.

'At least he can't do any harm delivering bananas,' his sister had crowed when he'd told them his plan, sneering at him as if he were still a teenager and not a man approaching his thirtieth birthday. But, then, that's how his family had always treated him – the little one, the afterthought, the joke. This time, however, although Annabel had meant it with calculated malice, Charlie had held on to her words as a core truth. He didn't want to harm anyone ever again.

'Charlie? You OK?'

Bri had parked his bike and was peering at him in concern. Charlie noticed a luminous tattoo winding down her slim neck.

'That's a beautiful dragon.'

Her fingers went to it and she flushed.

'Thanks. It's new. It marks . . . Oh, never mind me. Here comes Sean. Look sharp!'

She gave him a quick dig in the ribs and he felt himself snap to attention as the team leader came striding over, smoothing his gelled-down hair and proudly brandishing a clipboard.

'Charles Sparrow?'

'Charlie,' Charlie muttered. He'd never been a Charles, however hard his parents had tried.

'Charlie, right. I remember. Got your training manual, Charlie?' Charlie lifted it out of his bike basket and Sean beamed. 'Good, good. You'll be wanting to refer to that regularly, I'm sure.' Behind him, Charlie thought he heard Bri snort. Sean glared at her. 'Don't you have a van to check, Briony?'

'They've not been assigned yet, Sean.'

'Ah. No. True. I have the papers here.'

Sean tapped the clipboard, holding it close to his chest as if it contained state secrets.

'How exciting,' Bri said mildly.

Charlie looked to the ground, trying not to smile, but the next thing he knew Sean was tugging officiously at his fleece.

'So, Charlie, let's have a look at you then. Hmm. Bit tight but you'll soon trim down on this job.'

Charlie bit his lip. He knew he'd put on weight. He despised the roll of flesh that sat around his middle these days but he also loved the fact that no one looked at a podgy man in a fleece. The same went for his beard. It was a bit itchy and sometimes he didn't recognise himself in the mirror but that suited him down to the ground.

'Name badge,' Sean was saying, jabbing at it. 'Very good. Very important is the name badge.'

Charlie drew himself up a little.

'So they said on the course, Sean. Gives the customer the personal touch.'

He pictured the pompous woman who'd told him that, pointing proudly to her own nondescript monosyllable: Sue.

'Quite right, Charlie. Very good. Now, what's the most important thing to remember on your first run?'

Sean looked expectantly at him and, despite being twenty-nine years old, Charlie felt instantly as if he were at school again.

'The customer is always right?' he tried.

Sean tipped his head to one side.

'That *is* important, Charlie, but it's not what I meant.'

Charlie racked his brains.

'Be polite and respectful?'

'Again, Charlie, a good point but . . .'

Bri groaned and Charlie looked across.

'I think Sean is referring less to the way you treat our customers than to how fast you do it,' she said.

'Oh, of course!' This Charlie did remember. He'd been stunned by it. And not in a good way. 'We have four minutes per house.'

'That's it, Charlie boy! Four minutes.' Sean stroked the words around his mouth as if they were a particularly delicious sweet. 'Four minutes is the gold standard. Any less and the customer feels rushed, any more and you're robbing someone else of a premium service. Remember that. Some of our softer drivers . . .' he paused to look pointedly at Bri, '. . . are unable to tear themselves away efficiently.'

'Because some of our "softer drivers" don't like to hassle shaky old ladies into an early grave, or stop them from telling us about their grandsons' hundred-metre swimming badges. We're the only person some of our customers see the whole day long, Sean, the whole bloody week even.'

Sean gave a slow shake of his head. 'I appreciate your sentiment, Briony, truly I do but . . .' he jabbed his clipboard at her, his voice hardening, 'we are not social services. If you want to play nursemaid, then take your bleeding heart off to the NHS. If you want to drive for Turner's, speed up. End of.'

Charlie felt Bri bristle at his side so her words, when she finally found them, surprised him. 'I will. Sorry, Sean.'

Sean bounced a little on the toes of his impractical brogues. 'Good. Now then, Team West, where's Ryan?'

He moved away and Charlie edged closer to Bri.

'Team West?' he asked in a low voice.

'Cos we do the west of the town. Brilliant, isn't it? He's genius, Sean.'

'You were very nice to him then.'

'Have to be, don't I? I need this job. I got people relying on me.'

'That's nice. Who . . .?'

But now Sean had found the third member of 'Team West' and was coming back over, a lanky, thin-faced man swaggering at the boss's side.

'Charlie,' Sean said, 'this is Ryan.'

Charlie held out his hand but Ryan just gave him a sharp nod.

'Morning, Charlie. Hope you're up to speed training-wise.' Charlie tapped half-heartedly at the manual and Ryan gave a snide laugh. 'Oh, that thing's all well and good but it's out on the road that you'll really learn your stuff.'

He made it sound like an American coming-of-age movie. Charlie glanced to the line of purple vans, each one emblazoned with a gigantic fruit. They didn't look quite the vehicles in which to capture the zeitgeist of a generation but he chose not to say so.

'Ryan Sharp is one of our most experienced drivers,' Sean told him. 'If you need to know anything, ask Ryan.'

Ryan puffed out his scrawny chest.

'Two years on the road,' he said proudly, then added, 'Don't you worry, Sean, I'll keep my beady eye on him.'

Instantly, Charlie heard his family laughing again and felt an all-too-familiar panic rising. This wasn't his world. What on earth was he doing here? His hands felt clammy against the cheap plastic cover of the training manual and he caught a smell of ash on the air. He looked frantically around but it was nothing more than exhaust fumes as the first of the vans – presumably Teams East, North and South – headed out of the yard.

'Right,' Sean was saying, 'your runs, team. We've reallocated with the new staff pattern but, as you know, Turner's are unique in working to keep the same driver on the same run for that personal touch.'

'Personal touch!' Bri scoffed.

Sean glared at her.

9

'Therefore, Briony, you have the Sharman Street area again.'

'Course I do,' Bri said wearily, taking the sheet. 'Rough end,' she told Charlie. 'It's Sean's subtle way of pointing out where I belong.'

'Nonsense, Briony. It's all allocated by the computer, as well you know. Ryan, you've got Chestnut Hill and the Green.'

'The posh bit,' Bri said to Charlie.

'Yummy mummies,' Ryan confirmed gleefully as he accepted his list. 'At least half of them live in yoga gear. Lovely.'

Bri groaned.

'And Charlie, you've got between the station and the marketplace along Hope Street. Here.' He thrust the list at Charlie, who took it and peered at the endless run of names. The number of deliveries was huge. 'That's the morning run,' Sean said. 'Back here for one p.m. to reload.'

Charlie's eyes widened. Hope Street ran all the way through town so he supposed a lot of people must live on it, but you'd have to be Santa Claus to get through this lot on time.

'Told you you'd soon trim up, Charlie boy. Can you cope?'

'Course,' Charlie said automatically, still scanning, and that's when he saw it.

That name.

The bustling yard froze around him instantly. The name on the sheet was the only thing that mattered. He'd recognise it anywhere. It had haunted his sleep for too many months to ever forget. He looked to the sky for some sign of divine retribution, then remembered he didn't believe in God. But still, what were the odds? Turner's must cover a huge number of houses and somehow he'd landed this one.

'You OK, Charlie?' he heard Bri ask. 'You've gone a bit white.'

He forced his eyes off the page. 'I'm fine. Sorry. Just, er, a name I recognise.'

'Really?'

Ryan was at his side instantly, leaning over to see. Charlie longed to press the list to his chest but didn't dare in case somehow that name disappeared. So *this* was why he was here – not divine retribution but maybe some sort of karma at play.

'Greg Sutton!' Ryan exclaimed suddenly and now Charlie did snatch the sheet away.

'Who's Greg Sutton?' Bri asked.

Ryan rolled his eyes.

'He's famous, Bri. Candy Drew has been tweeting about him non-stop for the last week.'

'Candy who?'

'Candy Drew. Lead singer of the Mardy Cows. Rear of the year.'

'Not for me, thank you very much. I like my asses real, not stuffed with bloody silicon.'

'How pious of you. But, actually, Candy's ass is neither here nor there. Point is, she's got a disabled sister and this guy – Greg Sutton – is disabled too and he writes a blog about travelling.'

'Travelling?'

'Yep. *Don't let disability disable your life* – that's his slogan. Candy thinks he's inspirational and he is too. See.'

Ryan tapped at his phone and held out a striking photo of a very good-looking young man – all sharp jawline and designer stubble.

'*Very* inspirational,' Bri said. 'Fancy him do you, Ryan?'

'No!' Ryan snatched his phone back. 'Course I don't. We're not all batting for the wrong side thank you very much, Bri.'

'*Wrong* side, Ryan? I hope you don't say that to the customers. Turner's drivers show respect for people of all colours, creeds and sexual orientations, don't they, Sean? It's in the manual.'

Ryan coloured furiously.

'I know that. I'm not homophobic. I'm not anything phobic. I fancy a girl in a wheelchair, that's how not phobic I am.'

Bri glanced at Charlie, who wasn't sure whether to laugh or be sick. Maybe it was both. His head was starting to spin and he took a couple of steps back and looked down at the sheet in his hand. The name pulsed out at him, as if it were shouting for his attention. *This* was why he was here; *this* was his purpose. He wasn't sure how yet but it had to be his chance to make amends, to redeem himself. Not fully — that wasn't possible — but maybe he could reach out and . . .

The thought dried up in his head. Reach out? Make amends? Now who was talking crap? He could never make up for what he'd done but, even so, he felt a fierce need to at least try.

'Right,' he said as decisively as he could. 'Which one's my van?'

Sean turned to point but Ryan stepped between them. 'Hang on a minute. Why does new boy get Hope Street, Sean?'

Sean looked back, confused. 'The computer does the allocations, Ryan.'

'But we can swap, right?' Ryan planted his feet a little wider. 'I can take Hope Street instead. It's very long, very busy — better for an experienced driver, right? Right, Sean?'

He reached for Charlie's sheet; Charlie held on to it.

'It's my round, Ryan. Look, it says so on the top and we have to keep the same rounds for — what was it, Sean? — the personal touch?'

'But we're reallocating anyway, so we can change. Right, Sean? Please?'

Sean swallowed and glanced at his clipboard but after only a moment's consultation he looked up again.

'Charlie's right, I'm afraid, Ryan.'

'What?'

'It's the computer, you see.'

'Screw the computer.'

'Ryan! Swearing is a sackable offence.' Ryan stared at Sean, aghast, but Sean just clutched his clipboard to him like a shield and said tightly, 'Best get going, team.'

Still Ryan was glaring and Bri grabbed Charlie's arms and hustled him off towards the vans.

'Good Lord, Charlie,' she hissed, 'that was amazing. Sean usually bends over backwards for bloody Ryan so I've got no idea how you did that. But I tell you what, I like it!'

Charlie swallowed.

'Ryan didn't,' he said, glancing over his shoulder.

The other driver pointed two fingers to his eyes and then towards Charlie. That guy really was stuck in B-movies. Charlie just hoped they weren't horror ones. His first day at work, his first bloody minutes, and already he'd made an enemy. What an idiot!

But then he looked down at the list and saw the name again, still shouting out at him, and he blocked Ryan from his thoughts. Jumping into his van, he revved the engine as assertively as he wished he felt. Next stop, Hope Street.

Chapter Two

Number 95 Hope Street:

Onions
Garlic
Ginger
Coriander
Mint
Pomegranate
Okra
Green chillies
Amchur powder
Spaghetti hoops x2
Weetabix
Milk

Vikram Varma added cardamom to his raan musallam, stirred gently and tasted it. A touch more salt perhaps? He reached for the pot, sprinkled a good pinch in and stirred again. Better. Once the mint and pomegranate arrived it would be perfect. And the dhal was good too. It could sit while he made the bhindi masala. Dhal was better with a few hours to sit.

'Just like me,' Nika had always said, settling down into the sofa as if she were a part of it.

She'd always been so good at settling down; so much better than Vik. He looked to the lounge door as if she might, even now, be sitting in there, but it was resolutely shut and quite right too. That damn room was best avoided these days.

Gripping his wooden spoon tighter, he stirred the curry again just as the doorbell shouted out. Grumpily, Vik laid the spoon down and shuffled the length of the kitchen to answer.

'Delivery?'

The man on the doorstep was young, about his son's age, Vik thought instantly, though his squishy tummy and scruffy beard gave him none of Sai's suavity. His feet were shuffling nervously against the tarmac of the drive and Vik stood hastily back to let him in.

'Where do you want it, sir?'

'Could you take it up there? It's a bit of a squeeze, sorry.'

They both looked at the thin passageway down the side of the dining area. The table was too big for the room really, but Nika had insisted they needed it.

'The family that eats together, stays together,' she'd always said.

How right she'd been.

'No problem,' the driver said and lifted the baskets high to slide his portly frame past.

Vik followed awkwardly, realising too late that all the surfaces were covered with ingredients.

'Could you just put the baskets on the floor?' he asked. 'I'm cooking.'

'So I see,' the lad said. 'Someone's in for a treat.'

Vik looked to the stove where his pots were bubbling like something in a magician's den. 'Er, yes. Hopefully.'

'Hopefully?'

'Well, you never know how they'll turn out, do you? It's not, you know, an exact science.'

Vik heard his own words with a groan. He sounded old. Old and confused. Which he wasn't. Definitely not. Sweat prickled on his temples and he lifted the hem of his apron to dab at it, before noticing the bold red and orange fabric and feeling ridiculous. What must this young man think of him?

'My wife's,' he said, dropping the fabric. 'She is – *was* – a little rounder than me.'

The driver's blue eyes clouded instantly. 'I'm so sorry for your loss.'

'I miss her every day,' Vik said, like some terrible cliché. 'Sorry. That's what everyone says, isn't it?'

'Doesn't make it any less true.' The lad set the baskets of shopping on the floor and looked to his paperwork. 'You've just got one substitution, Mr Varma.'

Vik jumped at the formal address. 'It's Vik,' he said quickly.

'Vik, right.'

'Short for Vikram but no one calls me that since . . .' He swallowed the self-pity. 'And you are?'

'Er . . .' The lad fumbled for his name badge, almost as if he had to check it himself. 'I'm Charlie. Charlie Sparrow.'

'Pleased to meet you, Charlie Sparrow. So, what's missing?'

Charlie squinted at the paper.

'It says here that there was no okra so they've sent mangetout instead.'

'Mangetout?' Vik stared at the little pack of greens in disbelief. 'How am I meant to make bhindi masala with mangetout?'

Charlie coughed awkwardly. 'I don't know. Sorry.'

'It's my son's favourite.'

'Is that who you're cooking for? That's nice. And I'm sure he won't mind. It looks as if you have all sorts of delicious things on the go.' He gestured to the stove but Vik couldn't take his eyes off the mangetout. 'I can take them back, sir.'

'Vik.'

'Sorry. Vik.'

'I got sick of people calling me "sir" at work,' Vik explained. 'I vowed when I retired that I wouldn't be "sir" ever again. Nika, that's my wife, well, *was* my wife, said I shouldn't worry. It showed respect, she said, but to me it just felt blank. Do you know what I mean, Charlie?'

Charlie nodded.

'The mangetout?' he asked, shaking them a little and Vik realised with a jolt that he was holding him up.

'They're fine,' he said, taking them from him and shoving them onto the side.

He was getting overexcited at the company, that was the problem. He truly *was* a cliché, but days went by sometimes when he spoke to no one save Rickets, his wizened tortoise. He could talk to Sai, *should* talk to Sai, but his son was so busy he didn't like to bother him. There were Fridays of course, Family Fridays, but these days they felt few and far between.

Stop jabbering, Nika would say if she was here. He could almost hear her.

Vik bit back grief and set himself to unloading his groceries. He wanted to tell this quiet young man that he hated being 'sir' because he hated the man work had turned him into. He wanted to tell him that he hated how far he'd let it permeate his life, how much of a bloody 'sir' he'd turned into.

Nika had wanted him to retire at sixty-five but he'd got all wound up in final salary pensions and what that meant for their 'twilight years'. He'd actually called them that, but Nika hadn't been having any of it. 'We're comfortable enough, Vikram,' she'd insisted and she'd been so right, but it had been hard to know what 'enough' was. It had been hard to know when to stop. So he'd done one more year and then another and, in the end, he'd only been retired two years when . . .

Bloody waste.

Vik glanced to the lounge door, as if he could see through the crack into the past that had once been beyond. She'd sit in there for hours, his Nika, with magazines, or sewing, or a silly sitcom. He'd hear her chuckling away as he went about his business and know that all was well with the world. She used to apologise to him for being lazy but he'd seen the stillness as a gift. These days he sat a lot but he wasn't still, not as Nika had been. And there was no chuckling wife in that room any more; far from it. He went quickly to the door and slammed it shut. Charlie winced.

'Sorry,' Vik said. 'I, er, felt a draught. From the lounge.' He pointed vaguely to the door. 'I don't go in there much. It's . . . cold.'

'Right.'

Charlie stood a moment, a box of cereal in his hand, and then put it on the table. It caught on the packet of mangetout and tumbled to the floor.

'Sorry. Oh God, I'm sorry.' They both bent to retrieve it and almost banged heads. 'Sorry,' Charlie said again.

'Not your fault,' Vik told him firmly. 'I'm holding you up. But I've got everything now, thank you. Better get on. Lots to do.'

He picked up the wooden spoon and waved it towards the bubbling pots in what he hoped was a purposeful way. Charlie slotted the baskets together and lifted them easily into his arms.

'OK. Bye then. I hope you have a great meal tonight, Vik. Your son's very lucky.'

'If he . . .' Vik stopped, took a quick breath and went on, 'if he brings his family I'll need it all.'

'Lots of them, are there?'

'Not really. Just his wife and daughter, but that little Aleesha . . .'

He paused, thinking of his granddaughter. She was three now and a bundle of energy, from her dark curls to her never-still feet. She chattered non-stop, a revelation to Vik after having only a son, and she seemed to radiate love. Whenever he saw her, which hadn't been nearly often enough recently, Vik was left feeling in equal parts exhausted and energised.

'She's great,' he finished, feeling as if he'd let her down with such a lukewarm phrase, but Charlie was edging towards the door anyway.

Stop jabbering, Vikram.

'Good job you've got plenty of space then.'

'You think so?' Vik looked around, startled. Sai always said how cramped the house was.

'I do. Well, enjoy your meal. I hope your family like it.'

'Me too. It can be . . . hard. It's not the same without Nika, you see. Sai and I, we . . . Anyway. The family that eats together stays together, right?'

'I wouldn't know.'

'Oh?'

'I'm quite a bit younger than my brother and sister so I usually ate before everyone else. I hadn't "got the conversation" for the dinner table.'

Charlie's face twisted and Vik sought frantically for something comforting to say, but before he could find it the lad had offered him a funny little wave goodbye and gone. He slowly closed the door and leaned back on it for a moment, catching his breath. Charlie seemed nice and friendly. A little guarded, perhaps, but who wouldn't be with Vik gabbling on at him?

Stop jabbering!

Nika's voice would have been sharp but softened by her smile. Her lovely smile. Vik closed his eyes. She'd smiled at him that last, beautiful night just over a year ago. Then she'd fallen asleep smiling and so had he. But, come the morning, only one of them had woken up.

Vik's eyes flew open again and he marched over and slammed the packet of cereal into the cupboard. He lived on cereal these days. Cereal and spaghetti hoops. Except on Fridays. Fridays were curry day, family day, and somehow he had to keep it that way. Somehow he and Sai had to keep it that way. If he came, of course.

Vik picked up his spoon and stirred the spiced onions hard and fast. Of course he'd come. He'd been busy last week, that's all. He was a very busy man. He was at a very busy point in life. But this week, surely, he'd be here?

'Keep cooking, Vikram,' Nika had always said. 'Everyone gets hungry so just keep cooking and he'll come.'

Closing the cupboard door more gently, Vik returned to the stove. Carefully he stirred the bhindi base then looked at the mangetout. Mangetout for okra? Who at Turner's Supermarkets made those decisions? Despite himself, he smiled. Nika would have sent him out to comb every shop until he found okra but Nika wasn't here now and Vik wasn't going out. Vik rarely went out. No, mangetout masala it would be and if Sai didn't like it, he didn't have to eat it.

With a last glance to the closed lounge door, Vik picked up the little greens and tumbled them into the spice mix.

Keep cooking, Vikram. Keep cooking and he'll come.

19

Chapter Three

Number 112 Hope Street:

Value wholemeal bread
Baked beans, 4 cans
Value ready salted crisps, 6-pack
Bacon bits
Pasta
Value pasta sauce
Lamb mince
Rice
Lemons, 3
Vodka, 1ltr
Tonic, 2x 1ltr
Paracetamol x2

'OK there?'

Ruth Madison, once Clarke (still Clarke officially, but so what), tipped her head on one side as she addressed the food processor. It didn't answer. They never did. Not unless she'd really hit the vodka. She reached for her glass without taking her eyes off the machine and took a quiet sip, just to steady herself.

'Now then,' she told it kindly, 'let's see if we can get you working.' Replacing the glass on the side, she flicked the switch and the food processor leaped obligingly into life. Ruth clapped her hands, then glanced around self-consciously in case she'd been seen, before remembering that no one ever saw her any more. And a good job too. 'Well done,' she told the machine.

She turned it off and watched the blade spin slowly to a halt, the euphoria of the repair dissipating with it. What was there to do with the day now? It wasn't even lunchtime and already she was wishing for darkness. She really should go back to work but every time she reached for her uniform she'd shake so badly that she had to crawl into bed. That or find the vodka.

Her hand crept back to her glass as she glanced around the cluttered kitchen. She could do a jigsaw, she supposed. On the kitchen table sat a completed one of a Monet painting that she'd found in a charity shop last week for £2.50. A quarter of a pence for each of the one thousand pieces and all of them there too. Bargain. But she'd done it three times already and wasn't sure she could face taking it apart just to start it all over again.

There must be something else she could mend. She scanned the appliances covering almost every available surface but as far as she could remember they were all fixed. Well, all bar one. She glanced to the deep-fat fryer sat sulking in the corner. She should never have brought it back from the tip. It should just go in the bin, except that the bin was down the side of the house and it was raining. Well, drizzling. But either way, she wasn't getting wet for that; for *him*. It could just stay there for now.

Ruth turned back to the food processor. Whoever had chucked it out had been thorough, throwing all the fancy attachments into the bag with it. She had no idea what most of them did and no inclination to find out. You didn't need a food processor to mix cheap bacon with cheap pasta and shove it into your gob. She did feel a bit sorry for it though – all mended and no one to play with!

Honestly, Ruth, she told herself. *It's a machine. It doesn't have feelings.*

Lucky machine, she thought bitterly.

She paced the kitchen but there was no outrunning her own discontent and it was a matter of moments before she returned to her glass. Empty. Damn. She glanced to the chopping board where half a lemon sat invitingly, just waiting to dive into ice-cold liquid, but then her eyes snagged on the clock. Only

11 a.m. She shouldn't have had that first one so early, but it was Friday, wasn't it? And, besides, her hands had been too shaky to manage the fiddly screws on the processor without a drink.

She looked around again, willing one of the myriad other machines to leap up and reveal itself as broken, but none of them did. She'd have to go back to the tip. Frank was bound to have something good for her. He looked out for her now, saved her the 'treasures' from among the dross of people's lives. He was an angel in a high-vis vest and the only person Ruth really spoke to from week to week, except Maureen and Sanjeed at the corner shops and the Turner's driver. All three of them kindly provided her with a litre of vodka a week. None of them needed to know about each other. And Frank needed to know about none of them.

He was a good kid, was Frank. Funny name for someone who couldn't have turned twenty yet but it suited him – solid, open, straightforward. She'd met him when she'd taken a load of Tony's crap to the tip after he'd left. He'd steadied her when she'd nearly tipped herself into the giant skip with her husband's old shoes, and when she'd spotted the poor, abandoned appliances sat on the 'electrical goods' shelf at the bottom of the ramp, he'd been more than happy to let her take them home.

She'd brought back a kettle and a veg steamer that first time. Mending them had kept her a step back from the chasm of black emptiness that was for ever threatening to swallow her up and she'd returned to the tip just three days later looking for more. The problem, of course, was what to do with the machines once they were mended, but at least they kept her company now that there was no one else to do so.

And just like that, there they were: two big, blue eyes looking at her straight from the past, accusing her. Libby. She put up her hands to ward her daughter away but still she stared, piercingly bright from the centre of the darkness that seemed to rise up all around. She stumbled towards the vodka bottle but when she picked it up there was nothing but a viscous slick around the bottom. Shit. She upended it frantically over her glass but it caught the edge and the glass tipped off the side.

Acting with an agility she thought she'd long since lost, Ruth caught it halfway to the hard tiles and crouched there, breathing heavily, trying to fight the shakes that those eyes always brought. And then, as if by way of cosmic reward, a sturdy Turner's van edged on to the drive alongside her long-neglected yellow work one.

Gathering herself, Ruth rose slowly and shoved both glass and bottle on to the side between a toasted sandwich-maker and a milk frother. She edged to the window and watched a man getting out of the van. He was youngish, a little chubby and with one of those thick beards people seemed to favour these days. She hadn't seen him before and was glad of it.

The last one had taken to plonking her vodka down on the table in a very pointed way, as if he was less a delivery driver and more some sort of moral guardian. Ridiculous. She didn't drink that much. Or, at least, he didn't know she did. She was always careful to dispose of the corner-shop bottles before he came. It was a routine – Turner's on Friday, Maureen on Sunday, Sanjeed on Wednesday. People needed routine, didn't they? Everyone knew that.

But now the driver was approaching the house and as she went to open the door, she caught her reflection in the van's window and winced at the mess that stared back. She was a big woman – Amazonian, Tony had used to call her, back in the day when he'd liked her – so she was used to struggling for elegance, but at least she'd always kept herself tidy. Now, though, her top was stained with what looked like baked beans and her anonymous black leggings were baggy at the knees. Worst of all was her hair – once a shiny metallic-red bob, it now had long, grey roots that made the colour look as if it was oozing on to her hunched shoulders.

She yanked her eyes away as the young man held the single basket out to her.

'Come in.'

He shuffled past her and looked around.

'Where should I . . .?'

For a moment, Ruth saw the kitchen as it must look to him – like some bonkers workshop. He probably thought she was losing it; he was probably right. She waved to the table but he frowned.

'I can't put it on that, it would ruin it.'

Ruth looked down at the Monet jigsaw. 'Oh don't worry. I've just got to break it up anyway.'

'I hate that part.'

The response surprised her and she looked at him more closely. 'You like jigsaws?'

'I do. They're . . . straightforward.'

'They are,' Ruth agreed. He'd put his finger right on the very thing she liked most about them – straightforward, undemanding. Just one piece after the next, sorting chaos into order without all the jumbles and confusions of life. 'But I'd have thought you were too young for them . . .' she peered at his name badge, 'Charlie.' He touched it self-consciously. 'You *are* Charlie?'

'I am, yes. Charlie Sparrow.'

'Like the bird?'

'That's right.'

'I like sparrows. Sweet little things. Always twittering away busily.'

'I suppose so.' He set the basket as carefully as he could on top of the jigsaw and grabbed the paperwork out of it. 'Now, Mrs Clarke . . .'

'Madison.'

'Sorry?'

'It's Mrs Madison. Or Ms Madison, maybe.'

'I see. Ms Madison. Lovely.'

She realised with a start that he thought she'd got married. How sweet – and how very wrong. Her fingers twitched for her glass but it was out of reach. And empty anyway.

'Ruth,' she said quickly. 'That's better, isn't it? No one uses surnames any more, do they?'

She leaned forward to check for her vodka but the young man was already reaching into the basket and pulling out a yellow bag.

24

'Substitution,' he said, holding it out. 'Says here that they didn't have any lamb mince so they've sent chops instead.'

'Chops? Lamb chops? Aren't they expensive?'

'I think so. Yes, look – they should be seven pounds fifty.'

Ruth's heart started to race. She hadn't got that sort of money to waste. Not until she went back to work.

'I can't afford that.'

'You don't have to.'

'Why have they done that? I asked for mince, not chops. I can't afford chops.' She pushed the bag back at him but he was too slow and it fell to the floor tiles with a thwack. 'You have to take them back.'

Charlie bent slowly, his eyes trained on her as if she were some sort of dangerous animal, and picked them up.

'It's OK, Mrs . . . Ruth. It's a substitution, you see, so Turner's covers the difference. Look . . .' He held the paperwork out. 'The mince should have cost four pounds so that's what you pay.'

'What about the other three fifty?'

'That's our loss. You don't have to pay it.'

'Oh, right. Thanks.' Charlie held the chops out but she didn't take them. 'Even so – chops? What am I meant to do with chops?'

'Have them for tea? I bet Mr Madison would . . .'

'There's no Mr Madison.'

'Sorry. Er, Mrs Madison?'

She gave a half-smile.

'I'm not a lesbian, Charlie. Did you think I was?'

In front of her, Charlie swallowed. She knew she was being confrontational but the vodka was coursing around her veins now, warmed up by her panic over the chops, and she wanted someone to challenge. She wanted someone to challenge *her*. It seemed, however, that Charlie was not going to do that. He'd gone nearly as purple as the funny little van outside and suddenly all the fun dropped out of the exchange, leaving Ruth feeling mean and empty.

'Sorry. I'm making you uncomfortable. Ignore me, Charlie. I don't get out enough. I've forgotten how to talk to people. Madison is my maiden name. There *was* a Mr Clarke but he's gone.'

'Gone?' Charlie asked, his voice hoarse. 'You mean . . .?'

'God, no. He didn't die. Just, you know, left. Over a year ago now.'

'Right.'

The poor young man was still holding the chops out, as if they were some sort of sacrificial offering, and Ruth forced herself to take them. Tony liked chops. Chops and chips had been his favourite things. Libby had groaned at him and told him he should eat more vegetables and he'd looked at her as if she was some sort of guru, not an upstart teen. He'd always been like that with her, encouraging her crazy ideas as if she was cleverer than him. And, of course, she *had* been cleverer, but she hadn't needed to know that. It had only fuelled the fire. Mind you, that's what he'd wanted, wasn't it?

Biting back stupid tears, Ruth peeled the yellow carrier away and looked at the contents. Four plump chops, like meaty apostrophes, looked back from their cellophane packaging and she felt bile rise in her throat. She thrust them at Charlie.

'You have them.'

'What?'

'Take them, from me. For your tea.'

He held up his hands. 'Oh no, I couldn't.'

'Why not?' She just wanted rid of the wretched things. 'Why couldn't you?'

'Well, I . . . It wouldn't be right.' He took a step back. 'I bet they freeze nicely.'

'Freeze?' Ruth looked down at the fat little slices of flesh. 'Yes, yes I bet they do. Good idea. I'll freeze them and then when I have a friend over I can get them out.'

She stared at Charlie, daring him to laugh at this frankly ridiculous suggestion, but he just looked a little desperately at the still full basket. Ruth sighed, threw the chops on to the table and began quickly decanting her mindless array of value products, wedging them between her appliances.

'That's a nice coffee machine,' Charlie said as she sat a pack of pasta up against it.

'Is it? I suppose it is. Thank you.'

'Is it new?'

'New? Lord, no. Do I look like the sort of person who buys new coffee machines?' He shrugged unhappily. 'No, I take them from the tip and mend them.'

'Really?' He stared at her as if she'd said she took bodies from the morgue and got their hearts going.

'Usually it's just a quick fix,' she said. 'Sometimes nothing more than a fuse.'

'Right. But how on earth do you know what to do?'

'Oh, I'm an electrician. Well, I was. I had − have − my own company. Sparkly Sparkies. It's an all-female firm. People seem to like it.'

'I bet.'

'Yeah. It did well. Still does. It's just that right now I'm not, you know, practising.' She gave a little laugh. It was meant to sound jolly but came out more manic. Charlie shifted.

'So you mend things and sell them on?' he asked, reaching for a bag of satsumas.

'Do I? Oh, no. I should, of course. That would be sensible but I haven't really got past the mending bit.'

'You could sell them online,' he suggested. 'eBay and that.'

'I could, couldn't I? How would people get them though?'

'Post, I suppose, if you wrapped them up well. Or you could do them for collection.'

'Collection? From here?' She looked around, horrified at the thought of strangers coming into her hideaway. 'Oh, no. I don't think so. I don't want people coming here.'

'*I'm* here.'

'You are, aren't you?'

Ruth tried to summon up a smile but it sat awkwardly on her weary lips. But now her fingers closed around her litre bottle of vodka, fat and sparkling and assured. The urge to open it was almost overwhelming and she shoved it hastily on to the side.

'Would you like a cup of tea, Charlie?'

'No, I—'

'I've got three kettles, look. There's this light-up one, or this shiny upright, or this one pretending to be a stove-top fancy thing. They all boil water in exactly the same way, of course, but people like their kitchens to look good, don't they?' She glanced around and added, 'Well, some people do.'

'I'd love a cup of tea,' Charlie said.

'Oh good. Let's—'

'But I can't, I'm afraid. I'm on rather a tight schedule.'

His words hit her like a punch in the heart. She put her hand back on the vodka bottle.

'Of course you are. Silly me.'

'It's not silly. It's just that we only have four minutes per house, you see.'

'I see,' she said. 'Of course I see. I used to be exactly the same. People were always offering me tea and I just wanted to get on and fix their electrics.'

'Why don't you . . .?'

'Please. Don't let me hold you up or you'll lose more time.'

He looked flushed. The pale skin of his neck was mottled red and his fingers, when he picked up the basket, were white with gripping too hard. He looked at the broken jigsaw beneath and visibly winced.

'I hope no bits are lost.'

'Doesn't matter if they are. I've done it three times already this week.'

'Three times?'

'Bugger all else to do.'

'You should—'

'Get a new one? Not made of money, am I? You should be able to borrow jigsaws from libraries, right? Like books.' Charlie winced. 'What's up with you? Don't you like books?' He shook his head and made for the door. She followed him. 'Why? What's wrong with books?' She was being confrontational again, tormenting this mouse of a driver, but she couldn't stop herself.

'I just don't like them,' came back the answer, surprisingly fierce. 'They lie.'

Ruth jumped as if he'd pulled out a gun and shot her straight through the heart. She stopped, rested her hand on the table, drew in a deep breath.

'They do, Charlie Sparrow,' she agreed. 'They really do.'

And then, thank heavens, he was gone, and she could turn back to the sparkling promise of the vodka. It was the one thing that might soothe. The one thing that might keep her from the pit full of uselessly mended appliances and broken jigsaws and the yawning, gaping hole where once her family had been.

Chapter Four

Number 80 Hope Street:

Chicken thighs, boned
Basil
Shallots
Lemongrass
Rice noodles
Galangal root
Roasted peanuts
Green papaya
Jasmine rice
Lime leaves
Nam pla
Dried shrimp
Pork tenderloin
Pork liver
Mint
Spring onions
Tamarind paste
Singha lager, 4-pack
Nail-tail Shiraz, 2 bottles
Multivitamins for men

Greg Sutton sat staring at the counter on his Twitter feed. Any minute now he was going to top 100,000 followers. It was a ridiculous number. All those people couldn't possibly have an interest in him. He knew this was what marketing folk would call a golden opportunity – the perfect platform to take his blog, and therefore his life, to the 'next level' – but Greg had been awful at climbing steps since his accident and this one was no exception.

99,929.

It was close. It seemed hard to believe that seventy-one followers would just appear in the next few minutes but that's what had been happening all week, so logic dictated that they would, and Greg had always been a man for logic. Order, discipline, rigour – those had been the driving principles of his life since he'd chosen sciences for GCSEs all those years ago and headed happily down a smooth track into ecological research. But all order had been thrown away when he'd been chewed up and spat out by an industrial winch two years ago. The return to some semblance of it had taken every ounce of his strength and now the world was going mad on him again.

99,952.

He stared at the numbers, still struggling to believe them. It wasn't him that they were interested in, he reminded himself. They were Candy Drew's fans and followed her like sheep all over the internet. Why on earth she had decided to single Greg out as 'inspirational', he didn't know, but suddenly his carefully constructed online persona was coming under massive attention and he had no idea whether to be pleased or terrified.

He glanced to the mantelpiece on the far wall of his open-plan house. Sat there, above the funky fake log-burner (he'd have liked a real one but he wasn't fetching logs in a wheelchair), was a large, gold-embossed card announcing him as a shortlisted candidate in the 'Inspirational Blog of the Year' awards. Candy had timed her interest to perfection, picking up his blog just two days before the shortlist was announced. Now the awards publicity was covered with pictures of her and her wheelchair-bound sister, almost every one showing Candy looking soppily concerned and her sister downright bemused. Her hypocrisy made Greg furious but somehow he'd still let himself get caught up in it.

99,981.

He didn't even know why he was looking. He didn't care. What made 100,000 a better number than, say, 99,999 or, indeed, than the 432 he'd been happily plodding along with for the last year? All those big fat zeroes just looked smug to Greg, though his sister kept sending him excited screenshots of his profile from her fancy office in America, so at least it was pleasing her. Something cold ran down Greg's spine.

I'll come over for the awards, Rachel had texted him last night. *No way am I missing seeing my gorgeous brother onstage.*

There'd been a run of celebratory emojis after the words and Greg appreciated her joy, really he did, but it terrified him too. He didn't deserve this damn award. There was nothing 'inspirational' about him. He was just a grumpy bloke, writing about his travels to distract himself from the inherent emptiness of his once-useful life. And mainly in clichés too, though perhaps it was the clichés that had caught Candy's eye? The Mardy Cows' lyrics ran along much the same lines.

99,995.

Greg felt a jolt of excitement as the counter headed towards those fat zeroes and hated himself for it. Writing his travel blog had given him a purpose in life at a point when it had seemed there was none, but he hadn't done it for fame. He'd done it to escape the bitter, miserable git of a man he'd become. And it had worked. That first trip had been like magic.

It was almost a year to the day that his parents had nervously dropped him off at the airport and he'd stepped out on his own. The first photos he'd sent them of India had provoked such an outpouring of pride and happiness that he'd finally been able to pick himself up and get on. There'd been five more trips since and every one of them had made him a progressively better man. He'd even started liking himself again, or at least his travel self. Problem was, his home self could still be pretty gittish, and if he went to these awards everyone might see that.

Greg stared at the screen. For a moment the numbers seemed to settle, as if the cosmos knew that he'd reached his ceiling, but then they went again.

99,996.

99,997.

Briiiinng!

The doorbell buzzed and Greg looked up, annoyed. Not another journalist? There'd been several doorstepping him this week, dragging him and his stupid bent leg out to hear his 'story'. Well, they weren't having it. He knew what they were like, taking people's words and twisting them as much as his damn spine to suit whatever agenda they were currently peddling. He'd had enough of them after the accident when they'd prowled around as if he was some sort of zoo exhibit, wanting his 'side' of the case.

He'd nearly given it to them, mind you. He'd been so angry back then that he'd longed to out the bastard who'd got him into all this, but his father had quietly suggested that a dignified silence was the better approach, and his father was pretty much always right about things like that, so he'd submitted. He'd sat back and refused to talk to even the most persistent journos and once he'd started his blog he'd been able to tell his story his own way. His own words, his own pictures, his own careful presentation – organised, logical, controlled. He might not work as a scientist any more, but he still liked his life in scientific order. Which is why all this rush of interest was so unsettling.

Brrinnng!

God, but they were persistent. Reluctantly, Greg reached for his stick and pushed himself out of his big computer chair.

100,003.

Shit – he'd missed it. Not that he cared but, you know, it would have made a good Twitter post. He could have added something gushing like 'you guys are amazing' and people would have believed he meant it. People believed pretty much anything if you said it with confidence and an appropriate GIF.

Greg stomped to the door, rapping his stick on his faux-oak flooring. It must have cost his parents a fortune to get this house converted but it had clearly been worth it to get him out of theirs. He didn't blame them. They'd been angels to put up with him for as long as they had.

33

'Yes?' he demanded, yanking the door open.

The chubby man outside took a hasty step back. He was wearing a purple fleece and had three baskets balanced precariously in his arms.

'Delivery?' he asked hesitantly.

'Course. Yes. Sorry. I thought you were someone else. Come in, please.' Greg stood back and let the Turner's driver into the house. He'd ordered the ingredients for a big Thai cuisine re-creation for his 'enjoy travel from your own home' feature, but in the excitement of the damn Twitter-fest he'd forgotten all about it. 'If you could take it through to the kitchen that'd be great. I'd help you, but . . .'

He braced himself for the look of pity as the man clocked the unnatural curve of his once-strong back and the helpless skew of his left foot but he didn't even flinch. He looked more curious than anything and Greg realised with a shiver that he might already know who he was. This man might be a Candy Drew follower. He might be a 'fan'.

'Are you on Twitter?' he asked.

'Twitter?' The delivery driver paused halfway across the lounge area. 'Er, no.'

'Right.'

'Should I be?'

'No. No, of course not. I just . . . Oh, never mind. This way.'

Greg brushed past him and bumped into the mantlepiece. The fancy invitation fell off and floated to the floor.

'You've dropped something,' the driver said.

'It doesn't matter.'

'But it might be a slipping hazard. It—'

'It doesn't matter!'

'OK. Fine. Sorry. Where shall I put this?'

Greg heard the man's voice tighten and hated himself all over again. He had to stop being such a miserable bastard. It was his home self. Trapped in here, he tended to brood, to magnify everyday difficulties and to look back, like an addict succumbing to temptation. The past was his alcohol, his gambling, his hard

34

drugs. He was drawn time and again to remembering the handsome, successful self he'd once been and, like all addictions, a
binge session never ended well. That's why he needed the trips
– his travel self was a sunnier, funnier and altogether nicer man.

'Here.'

He forced a smile as he reached out to the side of the breakfast
bar and released a catch so that a lower counter dropped smoothly
into place. The man carefully set the three baskets on the floor
then lifted the top one on to the counter. Greg was touched.

'Thanks, mate. I'm Greg, by the way. Sorry for all the grumpy
shit.'

'No problem. I'm Charlie.' Charlie put a hand to his name
badge and gave a sideways grin. 'Can I do anything to help?'

'If we could unload this lot, I'll put it all away later. It takes
me an age and I'd hate to hold you up.'

'Oh it's fine. Take your time.' Charlie winced as he said this
but began helping Greg unload. 'What on earth's this?' he asked,
pulling out a small packet of pale brown root.

'Galangal,' Greg told him. 'It's a bit like ginger. Perfect in
Thai curries.'

Greg unloaded some jasmine rice and lime leaves and the other
man lifted out a little bottle of nam pla and a green papaya.

'I didn't even know Turner's had fancy stuff like this,' he said.

'It's not that fancy. Well, not in Thailand, anyway.'

'You've been there?'

'Is it so hard to believe?'

Greg heard the snap in his voice and longed to pull it back.
He needed to stop being so bloody defensive with anyone who
asked about his travels. They were just interested, that was all.
Well, most of them anyway. Every so often he got trolls telling
him he was a fake who got a kick out of being noticed for his
deformity and he had to fight to stop himself agreeing with
them. There'd been a few of those this week.

'Of course not,' Charlie stuttered. 'Sorry.'

Greg took a deep breath and banished the trolls and their
insidious brand of truth from his mind.

'Don't apologise, please. I'm not your obvious adventurer.'

'Adventurer?'

'Sorry. Again. Stupid term. Makes me sound like an Enid Blyton book. You get used to talking crap on a blog.'

'Right. I heard something about that actually. Not the talking crap, that is. Just the blog.'

'You did?' Greg was on instant alert. 'Where?'

'Bloke in the depot. He wanted this delivery run to meet you but, you know . . . I got it.' He gave a funny little shrug. 'You must inspire a lot of people.' Greg's eyes shot to the invitation lying on the floor in the middle of the oak boards and Charlie's followed. 'You've got an award? That's amazing. You must be so chuffed.'

'Chuffed?' A sudden burst of sunshine caught at the gold edges of the invitation as if mocking him. 'I'm not bloody "chuffed". A year I've been blogging with no one paying the slightest bit of attention, save those in a similar situation to me, which is fine, exactly as it should be. But then along comes Candy frigging Drew with her utterly abled legs up to her armpits and says I'm "inspirational" and suddenly everyone's at it.'

'Right.' Charlie looked a little stunned. 'Candy . . .?'

'Drew. She's a pop star, so God knows what makes her an expert on disability. I mean, she may be a very good singer. I don't know. It's not my sort of music. But it doesn't give her a right to hijack other people's stuff for her own callous ends, does it?'

'No, er . . .' Charlie switched the baskets over. Greg barely even noticed.

'I've looked back down her social media, you see, and do you know how many pictures of her sister she posted before last week? Three. Then in the last fortnight there have been *ninety*-three. Where did they all come from all of a sudden? That must have been some photo shoot, I can tell you! The poor kid must have been exhausted. And all just to make Candy bloody Drew look like a caring human being. And now . . . now she's dragged me into it. It's sick. It's sick and . . .' He trailed to a halt as he saw poor Charlie staring at him, open-mouthed. 'Sorry. It's, er, got to me a bit.'

'So I see.' Charlie offered him a wry smile. 'Couldn't you just forget about her and enjoy the ride?'

'The ride to some poncey award I don't deserve?'

'The ride to some poncey award with a free dinner, all the champagne you can drink and a whole load of celebs wanting to be your friend . . .'

Greg was forced to laugh.

'OK, OK, it doesn't sound so bad put like that. But I'd feel a fake, Charlie. There are people out there who've been dutifully blogging about all sorts of amazing stuff – dutifully *doing* all sorts of amazing stuff – and then there's me just putting up my travel diary.'

'But that's what it's about, isn't it? Getting on and doing things. It doesn't all have to be "worthy". What you're doing is showing people how to *live* and maybe they like that.'

Greg stared at the driver, stunned at the eloquence of his words. Then he felt like an idiot for imagining that just because someone wore a fleece and carried baskets of groceries around for a living they didn't know how to express themselves. He was a snob. A grumpy, ungrateful, fake of a snob.

'Thanks, Charlie. It's nice of you to say so.'

He looked at the invitation again. What red-blooded male wouldn't snatch at the chance of a free night out with the stars? There'd be women all over him. He'd seen it already on Twitter this week. So many of them had been sliding into his DMs, sending cute messages and pictures – so many pictures. It had been almost like the old days. Almost.

'Even so,' he said, as steadily as he could manage. 'I don't think I'll go.'

'Right. Well, fair enough. It's your life.'

Charlie moved to the door with the now empty baskets and opened it. He was chubby and slightly unkempt, but Greg envied the easy way he walked and the swing of the baskets in his hand. Such little things. It was all very well being positive and going 'adventuring' but sometimes – a lot of the time, actually – he just felt frigging robbed.

'Catch it!' The voice shot out of his past, his addictively gorgeous past, and almost he put his hand up to snatch the tennis ball out of the air.

It had been summer, a park somewhere. Him and Tia and the gang playing rounders, with empty beer cans for bases and a carefully chosen stick for a bat. Rachel had hit a hell of a whack. He hadn't caught it straight but he'd stopped it with his foot.

'Throw it back!' Josh had called, his voice squeaky with excitement. 'Quick!'

He could picture his sister charging round the cans, her legs bare and brown and moving fast towards the all-important fourth base. He could see Josh leaping up and down, ready to dob her out, and Tia ducking around in front of her on third, holding her up. He could hear Rachel protesting – 'Cheat!' – and feel himself flinging the ball with all his might. He could see Josh leap but miss and Rachel scramble forward and then the ball, by some hundred-to-one chance, bounce up and hit the can a second before she passed it.

His team had gone wild. They'd charged him, bringing him to the ground and piling on top until he'd been almost suffocated by their delight. He could feel it now – the weight of them, the musky smell, the hearty slaps and the voices: 'You lucky bastard, Greg Sutton. You lucky, lucky bastard!'

Well, he wasn't so lucky now, was he? He'd been well and truly dobbed out of the game. People thought of 'disabled' as a state of being, but it was nothing so passive. It was an active verb – dis-abled: a forcible ripping away of all you'd had. And you felt it that way day after day after . . .

Greg stopped his thoughts right there: no looking back. However hard that was.

'See you, Charlie,' he managed.

The man was staring at him in concern. 'You OK?'

'Course.'

'Good, right. It's just . . .' Charlie lingered in the open doorway. 'For what it's worth, I think you should go to the awards ceremony.'

'And for what it's worth,' Greg shot straight back, still caught in his lost rounders game, 'I think you should mind your own business.'

Charlie flinched and his head dropped. 'You're right. Nothing to do with me. I'm meddling. Sorry.'

He shot across to his lorry and leaped into the cab like the driveway was on fire. Greg stood there watching the funny purple van bump off his drive and feeling like the shit he knew he was. All those Twitter followers had no idea what he was really like, God help them.

He turned and limped into the house. The counter on his Twitter feed was at 100,124 now but it wasn't that that caught his eye so much as his recently updated profile picture. He was standing on a beautiful Thai beach, his scar snaking round from his back and heading into his shorts, like a lover's hand. He'd put the scar proudly on view because that's what you were meant to do. Princess Eugenie had even done it on her wedding day. He'd written a blog praising her for it and he'd meant it, truly – or at least his travel self had. Sat here in the lonely splendour of his converted house, however, it was easy to see that scars were just life art – *jolie-laide* cool. The constant struggle to walk or lift things or even just stand up straight was not so appealing.

Greg shuddered. He had to stop this; he was letting himself get depressed and it was foolish. A new trip, that's what he needed. Something to focus on. He'd been fancying Iceland for a while and he'd had a nice sponsorship offer from North Face two days ago. Where better to show off their designer thermals than in Iceland? Volcanos, hot springs, healing spas – perfect stuff for the high-profile disabled adventurer.

It was the closest he'd have been to the Arctic since the accident, but he'd go anyway. He *had* to go, for his own self-respect if nothing else. And, of course, if he was out of the country then he could hardly make the stupid awards ceremony, could he? Definitely perfect!

Chapter Five

Charlie drove into the yard a little after five, exhausted but quietly proud. He'd done it. He'd survived the first day on the job and it had been OK. Good even. He wasn't sure what he'd expected but it turned out that all sorts of people ordered all sorts of things.

There'd been the design studio on the marketplace, crammed full of hipsters who'd led him and his laden trolley around a maze of 'communal spaces' – at least two of which seemed to have Lego in them – to a chrome kitchen where they'd all eagerly decanted more bottles of Prosecco than a socialite's wedding. They'd made certain to get the delivery receipt off Charlie 'for accounts', button noses wrinkled at the inconvenience of this, and Charlie had left in awe of a workplace with so much cause for on-expenses celebrations and wishing he'd paid more attention in art. His parents, he'd reflected bitterly, would have hated that even more than the 'fluffy' subjects he'd opted for.

'Do you have to do something so damn caring?' they'd asked him when he'd finally braved telling them what he wanted to do in life.

'What's wrong with caring?' he'd demanded.

'Nothing, nothing at all,' they'd gushed. 'Of course nothing's wrong with caring. It's just, surely, best left to other people – less able people.'

Charlie had walked out then. Told them he was pursuing his own path whatever they thought, but in the end they'd been right. Not about him being more able; quite the reverse. But it had amounted to the same thing anyway. Not that it mattered. That path was closed to him now. He was a delivery driver these days. A nice, safe delivery driver.

Charlie parked up, turned off the engine and sat a moment. He could see Ryan swaggering across the yard and wasn't sure he could face him. He'd seen more people today than in the last six months put together and he was worn out. He'd delivered to harassed mothers with toddlers dangling from the rips in their jeans; to retired couples and self-employed workers; to people on their days off and people who looked like they never had days on; and to people who clearly had trouble getting out of the house. He'd even delivered to one man who'd answered the door in nothing but a pair of briefs in a hard-to-miss canary yellow. He'd clearly been looking for a reaction but Charlie had had no idea what that reaction should be so had just unloaded his shopping as fast as he could and scarpered.

So very many people, but it was the three in the middle of Hope Street who stood out in his mind as he ran through his day. He'd been expecting to be affected by one of them, of course, but the others had also tugged strings in his heart that he'd thought were severed and he couldn't get them out of his mind. Three identical houses but so different inside – Vik cooking for his son in his cosy yellow kitchen full of spice jars; Ruth doing her huge jigsaw in the middle of all those broken machines; and Greg with his high-tech adaptations and his shiny invitation lying discarded on the floor. So different and yet all three so identically alone. It didn't seem right.

'Not your problem, Charlie,' he told himself out loud.

'What isn't?' demanded a perky voice and Charlie looked down to see Bri bobbing about below his half-open window.

'Doesn't matter.' He stepped out of the van.

'How was your first day?'

'Fine, thanks. Not bad at all. Few odd ones.'

'There's always a few odd ones. Did you get pants-guy?'

'Yes! What's that all about?'

41

'God knows. When he tried it on me, I told him I had no interest in what was in his pants unless it was a pair of socks hiding a nice fanny. He hasn't tried it again.'

Charlie laughed. 'I'll say the same.'

'You should. Got a girlfriend then, Charlie?' He shook his head. 'Shame. I can—'

'I'm not interested at the moment. Thanks, anyway.'

'Fair enough. Bad bust-up?'

'Nope. I just . . . I just don't think I'd be good for anyone right now.'

Bri frowned but said no more until they got to the warehouse doors, where she turned.

'I felt a bit like that for ages,' she said. 'Then I met Harper and, oh my God, I tell you my world exploded. She's just, like, the best thing that ever happened to me.'

Charlie stared down at his tiny fellow driver. Her eyes were aglow and even her multicoloured hair seemed to shimmer with joy.

'That's good.'

'It is, Charlie. I'm so lucky. I was going a bad way. A really bad way, and Harper saved me.' She leaned in. 'She's pregnant now. Eighteen weeks. I'm going to be a mum.'

'Wow.'

'Yep. That's why I can't rile Sean. I need this job. I need to provide for Harper and the baby. That's the most important thing now so even if the little prick—'

'Ah, Charlie, you're back. All go well?'

Bri clamped her mouth shut as Sean Cooper strode up to them, brogues clicking on the warehouse floor.

'Very well, thank you, Sean.'

'You're just about on time at least. You were a bit late to the lunch pick-up, I believe?' He ran an officious finger down his clipboard. 'One fifteen.'

'Yes, Sean, but I cut my lunch break short to catch up.'

'Good, good. That's the spirit.' He sounded like somebody's grandpa praising him on resilience at the wicket in the face of an older fast bowler and Charlie half expected a pat on the head, but thankfully Sean just put an exaggerated tick in some clearly important box and said, 'See you tomorrow, then. Bright and early.'

'Tomorrow,' Charlie agreed and turned gladly away.

Bri came with him to the bike racks.

'You cycling too?' he asked her.

'Nah. Harper's picking me up. We're going to Mothercare.' Charlie looked down at her, trying to picture this miniature woman with her tattoo and her dyed hair and her metallic leggings among the Babygros, and she giggled. 'Mad hey? This time last year I was in juvie and, let me tell you, Mothercare is a helluva lot nicer – though the drug supply is crap!'

She threw him a wink and strode off towards the gates, her pace quickening to a half-run as a little blue hatchback pulled up outside. Charlie watched her leap in and suppressed a sigh as he turned to wrench his bike out of the rack.

'Good day, Charlie boy?'

Somehow Ryan made it sound more a threat than a question.

'Yes thanks.'

Charlie hurriedly mounted his bike but Ryan stepped in front of it and put both hands on the handlebars, trapping him. 'Any questions?'

'No questions, Ryan, thanks.'

'Hope Street OK, was it? You coped with hobnobbing with the stars?'

Charlie pulled his bike backwards. Ryan held on.

'Greg Sutton's just a bloke, Ryan. Nothing to get worked up about.'

'Why did you want the run so badly then, hey? I saw you. Desperate for it, you were.'

Charlie could feel his heart starting to pound again. 'Please, Ryan, I'd like to go home.'

'Would you now? And you're used to getting what you want, are you?'

'No. I . . .'

Ryan leaned in, so close Charlie could smell cheese and onion on his breath.

'What have you got on Sean, Charlie boy?'

'Nothing. I've got nothing "on" Sean. Don't be ridiculous, Ryan.'

'Bent over backwards for you, didn't he?'

'He did not. He—'

Ryan let go of the bike so suddenly that Charlie lost his own hold on it and it clattered sideways, the pedal banging painfully against his calf. Ryan watched dispassionately.

'I've got my eyes on you, Charlie boy. OK?'

Charlie looked at him in astonishment. This was ridiculous schoolboy bullying of the most pathetic kind. He should laugh. He *would* laugh, except that his stupid heart was beating time too vigorously against his lungs to let enough air in.

'OK?' Ryan demanded again, doing his stupid fingers-to-eye thing for good measure.

'OK,' Charlie said wearily and at last Ryan was gone, leaving a stench of stale sweat, onion and low-level corruption that made Charlie's gut wrench.

The ride home cleared both his stomach and his head and it was with huge relief that he tethered his bike to the stair-rail in the communal hallway at Hazel Road and made for the lift. A red sign informed him that it was 'out of order right now', as if it ever wasn't, and he turned wearily to the stairs. Two flights up was his flat – his lovely flat. In truth, it wasn't so lovely since he'd burned everything in it two months ago, but it was still his and he craved its simple blankness.

His legs were tired after a long day heading in and out of houses, apartments and artistic damn workspaces, but he took the first flight at pace. On the first-floor landing, however, stood an obstacle – a grey-haired obstacle in bifocals and a leather-buttoned cardigan.

'Charlie, just the man!'

The jollity was false and they both knew it.

'Mr Graham – what a lovely surprise.'

Charlie leaned against the banister and prayed to the gods of patience to be with him. First Ryan and now this.

'Been at work?'

'Yes.'

Mr Graham eyed his purple fleece. 'Somewhere new, I see.'

There were a thousand acerbic replies Charlie could have made but he was too tired. 'That's right.'

'Very good. Important to get out.'

Charlie couldn't resist this time. 'And to get back in again.'

'Yes, well, this won't take a minute. It's about my greenhouse, you see. You did promise you'd clean it after, you know, your little bonfire.'

'I did promise,' Charlie agreed, gripping the banister tighter, 'and I did clean it.'

'I'm sure you tried but, Charlie, it's not clean.'

'What?'

'It's all green inside.'

Charlie stared at Mr Graham. The bare-faced cheek of the man!

'That's algae, Mr Graham. There's no way it can have been caused by the fire.'

'Ah, but that's where you're wrong.'

'Explain.'

Mr Graham rubbed his hands together. He'd clearly been working on this. 'It's the ash, you see. It blocked the light and so the algae grew.'

Charlie closed his eyes. Clearly the gods of patience were off having a cheeky Friday-night pint because they certainly weren't helping him. The algae had been building inside that pathetic plastic greenhouse for at least three lazy years and a light dusting of ash two months ago couldn't have made an iota of difference.

Mr Graham leaned in. 'I know you went through a lot, young man, with the inquest and the press and all, but I do feel that we at the residents' association were very tolerant about that. Other groups might have been tempted to ask you to leave back then but we stood by you, even when the journalists were trampling the flower beds.'

'They didn't—'

'Even when you then coated the place in ash, burning all those lovely books that, frankly, would have been better given to a charity shop and—'

'OK, OK, I'll clean your greenhouse.'

'Oh.' For a moment Mr Graham was wrong-footed, but he wasn't a man to let a little capitulation get in the way of a good lecture. 'It's my seedlings, you see, and . . .'

'I said I'll clean it. On my next day off.'

'Right. I see. Well, thank you.'

'My pleasure. Now, please, can I get to my flat?'

'Of course.' Mr Graham bounced aside, jollity pulled back on like a second cardy. 'Lovely to chat.'

Charlie didn't bother replying. He took the second flight even faster than the first and at last he was inside. He threw his fleece on to the hook and all but fell on to his sofa. He'd made it. Day One – tick. So now there were just . . . Charlie called up the calculator on his phone: five working days in a week, fifty-two weeks in a year, thirty-eight years until retirement – 9,880 days. And at an average of thirty deliveries a day that was . . . 296,400 deliveries.

The weight of the number overwhelmed Charlie and he dropped his head into his hands, driving his fists against his eyes to stop tears from falling. What use were tears? This was all his fault and there was nothing to do but get on with it, one delivery at a time.

Eventually, boringly, his stomach rumbled and he forced himself to look up. The walls were resolutely blank and the huge rack of shelves he'd so lovingly installed for his many books were empty of all but a single jam jar. Charlie pushed himself up and went across to pick it up. He unscrewed the lid and inhaled. The grey ash inside swirled and a little went up his nose, scratching at his nostrils. He turned the jar to read the inscription he'd stuck around the edge:

We cannot tear out a single page of our life, but we can throw the whole book in the fire.

'No meddling,' he whispered to himself. He wasn't trying to be a phoenix; just a harmless little Charlie Sparrow.

Carefully, he replaced the lid and returned the jar to the shelf. It was Friday night and down below he could hear the town revving its collective engine to accelerate into the weekend, but that wasn't for him. Not now. He turned towards the kitchen but something else caught his eye. The only splash of colour in the white room was provided by his little pile of jigsaws.

It was the counsellor who'd suggested them, back in January when he'd decided he had to try and get his life back on some sort of track, however rough. He'd laughed at her but it had turned out to be her most useful advice. Far more useful, certainly, than all the 'you mustn't blame yourself' crap.

'Why mustn't I?' he'd asked. 'It's my fault.'

But she'd just produced a run of platitudes about guilt being a negative emotion, which he knew, damn her. What he'd needed to know was what to *do* with it and 'forgive yourself' had not been the answer.

At first he'd thought the jigsaw suggestion was equally silly but he'd been desperate, so when he'd seen one in the window of a charity shop, he'd bought it, muttering something utterly untrue to the saleswoman about how much his granny would like it. She'd just smiled and said, 'Oh, I love a good jigsaw' and he'd looked at her in surprise and felt as if a whole new world – albeit not a desperately exciting one – was opening up.

He'd googled it that night and found that, far from being the premise of grannies (even imaginary ones), jigsaws were leading the digital counter-revolution. Feeling just a teensy bit cooler, Charlie had opened the box and from the first piece he'd been hooked.

He'd sat and done that jigsaw in one go. Hours it had taken him. Blissful hours, in which he'd thought of nothing more taxing than where the next piece went. When he'd finally slotted the last one into place he'd looked up, blinking, and realised it had gone dark and he was starving. He'd gone out and bought five more puzzles the very next day and there they were now, looking at him as if they were trying to speak.

You should be able to borrow jigsaws from libraries.

The voice floated into Charlie's head and he pictured, as clearly as if she were there before him, Ruth from number 112 with her leaking hair and her big, hunched shoulders.

You should be able to borrow jigsaws.

He half-reached out for the top one, then stopped himself.

'No more meddling, Charlie Sparrow,' he repeated, louder this time. Then he made for the kitchen to the echo of his own admonishment around the blank walls of his flat.

WEEK TWO

Chapter Six

Charlie looked down at the jigsaw wobbling in his bike basket as if excited about the trip out and wondered again what he was doing. He hadn't meant to bring it, really he hadn't, but last night he'd dreamed of Ruth Madison's face on a thousand-piece jigsaw and when he'd woken up, taking one of his puzzles with him to Hope Street had felt like the obvious thing to do. Now, though, it just seemed bonkers.

He parked his bike in the rack, relieved to see that he'd beaten Sean in, and made for the common room just inside the warehouse doors. It wasn't so much a room as a roughly partitioned area, noisy and only faintly heated by cowering convector radiators but with reasonably comfortable chairs and a little kitchen with a kettle and a microwave. After a week on the job he felt settled enough to walk in without thinking too much about it. Indeed, he felt almost relieved to be back. It had been his day off yesterday and he'd spent it up to his elbows in lukewarm suds scrubbing algae off Mr Graham's damn greenhouse.

This had led less to the owner's thanks than to a lively debate about the effect of detergent on seedlings but, really, if Mr Graham had been that bothered he should have moved the wretched things. Charlie figured he could confidently expect a bill from some overpriced nursery in the coming weeks, but he'd been too tired last night to stand his ground. It had, all things considered, been a pretty rubbish day off and he'd pulled on his Turner's fleece with something approaching enthusiasm this morning.

'What the hell is that?'

Charlie sighed at the now-familiar voice and turned reluctantly to his fellow driver.

'Isn't it obvious, Ryan?'

'Looks like a jigsaw.'

'Correct.'

Ryan gawped at him. 'A jigsaw? Seriously? What are you, some sort of big kid?'

'Jigsaws aren't just for kids, Ryan. They're leading the digital counter-revolution.'

'The what?' Ryan looked over as Jack came in. 'Charlie says he's staging a revolution, Jack. Over jigsaws.'

'No, I . . .'

Jack, however, meandered over and picked up the box. 'My wife loves jigsaws.'

'Really?' Ryan asked, as if he'd said she liked wrestling with worms.

'Oh yes. Always has one on the go does Mary. Keeps it on the dining-room table and sits there for hours some evenings.' He smiled. 'Makes eating tricky but she looks so cute with her head bowed over it that I can't really object. She has this funny way of tapping the pieces against her teeth that I could watch for hours.'

'All fun in your house!' Ryan scoffed but Jack didn't even seem to notice.

'Gorgeous, she is. I used to spend ages trekking around shops looking for new puzzles but it's a doddle nowadays with the internet. Mind you, you can't always tell what you're getting. I bought her this one for Christmas called Cocks and Chicks. Thought it was going to be a henhouse – how wrong was I?' He chuckled. 'Didn't matter though – she loved it. Said she wished she'd had it for her eighteenth as it would have saved a whole lot of time and worry.'

He winked at Charlie, who smiled and offered him a cup of tea.

'No thanks, lad, just dropping my cup off from earlier. Vans to load to get you shining grocery-knights out on the road. See you outside.'

And with that he was off again.

'Did he just say his wife has a smutty jigsaw?' Ryan asked, staring after him.

'Sounded like it,' Charlie agreed.

'Is that what this one is then?'

He snatched up the box with new interest.

'No!'

'You sure?' Ryan opened the box and looked inside. His nose wrinkled. 'It's just a load of flowers.'

'I told you.'

'OK, weird. But even weirder – why've you brought it into work?'

There was no way Charlie was going to tell him about Ruth Madison and the jigsaw library. It sounded mad enough in his own head, let alone spoken out loud.

'Keeps me busy at lunchtime.'

'You? Freak. And you never make it in time for lunch anyway.'

Charlie headed for the kettle, trying to ignore this unsettlingly accurate statement. He seemed to be even worse than Bri at getting away from customers. Some were OK – they'd just unload and see him on his way, as keen to get on as he was – but with others he got the uncomfortable feeling he was the highlight of their day. He wasn't much of a highlight, God help them, but if they wanted his pathetic company then he found it very hard to tear himself away.

'Morning, team!' Sean burst in, very chipper this morning. 'Nice to see you keeping an eye on Charlie, Ryan.'

'Certainly am,' Ryan agreed. 'And he needs it too. D'you know . . . Oh.'

Ryan trailed off and Charlie turned from his tea-making to see Sue from the training course stepping incongruously into the common room in an off-puttingly purple suit.

Sean semaphored something to Ryan with his eyes as he said, 'This is Ryan Sharp, Sue, my senior operative. He's looking after Charlie.'

'Good, good. Ah, Charlie, there you are. All well?'

Charlie stared in astonishment as she came tapping up to him.

'Fine, thanks,' he stuttered.

A few of the drivers from the other teams were looking over curiously and he felt himself flush as Sue reached out and gave him a pat on the arm.

'Good, good. We at Turner's like to keep up with how new drivers are settling in.'

'But you never . . .' Ryan started until Sean's eyes signalled wildly to him again and he shut himself up with a limp, 'How lovely.'

'New directive,' Sue said breezily, but Charlie felt Ryan's eyes boring into her and hated it.

What had this Sue been told about him? Why was she here? And, more to the point, who was she reporting back to? Bri had arrived now and was standing in the doorway gawping at their guest.

'All is very good, thank you, Sue,' he told her hastily.

'Excellent, excellent. That's what we like to hear. Vans OK?'

For a moment, Charlie was tempted to ask her about the carburettor as it was quite clear she had no idea what might be required to make the vans 'OK,' but he hadn't the nerve.

'The vans are very comfy.'

'Good, good. Route easy to work out?'

'Oh yes. Hope Street is long but very straightforward, thank you.'

Ryan still looked confused but he wasn't slow to spot a management opportunity.

'I recommended he had that route,' he told Sue, stepping up next to her. 'It's easier than around the Green.'

'Is it? That's very kind of you . . . Ryan. Nice smart name badge.'

Ryan puffed out his scrawny chest. 'I clean it every weekend.'

Bri snorted from the doorway and Sue spun round.

'Is there a problem?' she asked.

'No, no, not at all.' Bri sized the situation up in an instant. 'I was just, er, surprised that Ryan only cleaned his badge once a week that's all. I like to give mine a daily rub.'

Ryan's eyes narrowed, as did Sue's, but she took in the rainbow badge pinned alongside Bri's distinctly grey name one and chose not to pursue the matter.

'Yes, well, I should be off now but, Charlie, here's my card – let me know if you have any problems. Anything at all. Here at Turner's we pride ourselves on looking after our staff.'

She pushed a card at him and was gone, Sean on her heels. Bri stared at Charlie.

'What was that all about?'

Charlie shrugged. 'No idea. She said something about a new directive.'

'New directive, my arse,' Ryan growled. 'What's so special about you, Charlie Sparrow?'

Charlie looked to Bri but she was staring at him too.

'I told you, I've got no idea. I guess I'll just have to be on my best behaviour.'

He knew he was as red as the strawberry on the side of today's van so, snatching up his jigsaw, he made for it, leaving his tea stewing in its mug.

'I'm going to find out,' Ryan called after him. 'I'm going to google you, new boy, and the devil help you if I find out something bad.'

'The devil, Ryan?' he heard Bri ask as he went, but there was nothing funny about the threat.

The devil, frankly, had been after Charlie for a while now and it wouldn't surprise him if he caught him up sometime soon. Forcing himself to breathe slowly and calmly, he collected his list from a flustered Sean and checked for the name he'd been waiting for all week. Seeing it safely on there, he made for Hope Street at pace.

Chapter Seven

Number 80 Hope Street:

Cod fillets
Emmental cheese
New potatoes
Gullskifur fish bites
Black lava salt
Langoustine
Lemons, 2
Omega-3 fish oil
Einstok white ale, 4 cans
Nail-tail Shiraz, 2 bottles

Greg was ready for the Turner's delivery this morning. He'd been horrible to the poor driver last week so was all set to be charming this time round. Charlie did not deserve to take the brunt of his endless tantrums and, besides, he was the only person Greg would see in the flesh all week so it was a waste not to have a pleasant chat with him.

He really ought to make more effort to see his parents. They loved coming over between trips but these days they always waited for him to invite them. At first they'd just turned up but he'd given them such short shrift they'd soon stopped doing that, thank God. It wasn't that he didn't want to see them, just that he needed time to prepare so as not to be caught still in bed, or wearing the crappy scruffs that were comfy against his scarred skin but made him look like a layabout. He'd never been a layabout before.

'How much further?' a voice asked from the past – Rachel's. 'My legs are tired. It's not fair. They're littler than all yours.'

He could see her now, sat stubbornly on a rock to the side of the final ascent up soggy Snowdon, legs held indignantly out in front of her.

Greg, aged fourteen and in the middle of a growth spurt that had seen him overtake his mum, had stopped, considered. She'd had a point. He'd been at the age where he'd done his best to ignore his little sister most of the time, but up here on a misty Welsh mountain with only a handful of other ramblers around, cool hadn't seemed to matter. He'd gone back and sat down next to her, stretching out his own legs. His feet had reached half a metre past hers.

'You *are* a bit of a titch, aren't you?'

'Oi! I reckon I've done at least twice as many steps as you lot.'

'Hardly twice, Rach. And nowhere near as many as Billy.'

They'd both looked at their spaniel as he'd bounded out of the mist, considered them quizzically and then shot off again.

'But Billy's got four legs. And he's . . .'

'Bonkers,' they'd finished together and laughed.

'Come on, then,' Greg had said. 'We'll have four legs too.'

'What?'

'Here.' He'd stood up and crouched in front of her. 'Piggyback.'

'Greg, you can't!' his mother had objected, but he could and he had, all the way to the top.

In truth, his legs had been burning by the end but having made his heroic gesture there'd been no way he was going to stop. And just as they'd got there and he'd set Rachel down for the final scramble up the cairn to the summit, the mist had cleared and all of Wales had been laid out before them.

'We did it!' Rachel had cried. 'We made it!'

'You didn't,' he'd told her and she'd nudged him and grimaced and then Mum and Dad had come up beside them and for a moment it had been just the four of them there, at the top of the world.

Greg furiously shook the memory away. He'd never make the top of Snowdon again, not unless he took the train and there was no way he was doing that. His 'adventures' had to be very carefully chosen to challenge just enough without being impossible. People liked it that way. He used to have quite nice chats with them about access ramps and airport security and the best foreign pharmacies. In this last week, though, it had all got so much more personal. Since Candy Drew had decided he was 'inspirational' everyone seemed to want to know about *him* – what he ate, how he slept, who'd converted his house, whether he had a girlfriend, what he looked like naked. Especially what he looked like naked.

He hadn't realised until now how intrusive other people could be. It was different with his trips. He always picked faraway places, where people were still curious to know about you but not so determined to *share* you. And with the blog he could control what he released. The mornings when he stayed in bed with the sheets pulled over his head, or the nights where he raged at the stars that had twinkled uncaringly down on the moment his life had been chewed up by a winch, never made it on to the screen. Now, though, they seemed to be exactly the bits people were after.

Even the big boys were at it, he reflected as the Turner's van pulled up at his door. North Face were keen to sponsor him travelling to Iceland but they wanted to send their own photographer along and he wasn't up for that. Greg Sutton did his own photography, just like he did his own words. Iceland felt important to get his travel self out there again but not with company. He couldn't do it with company.

The doorbell rang and Greg pushed all the grumpiness determinedly aside and stepped up to answer.

'Good morning, Charlie,' he cried, super-cheery. 'Great to see you again.' The driver looked at him and then surreptitiously checked his paperwork. Had he been so awful last week that one simple greeting made him seem like a different person? 'Come in, come in,' he rushed on. 'How's your day been?'

Charlie sidled inside. 'Fine thanks. Just, you know, deliveries.'

'Course. Anyone interesting?'

Greg rolled his eyes at himself. He sounded like someone's gran making polite conversation with the reluctant kid next door. Charlie put the baskets down next to the counter and lifted the first one up for him.

'The hipster designers ordered red this week,' he offered eventually.

'Sorry?'

Charlie gave him a sideways grin. 'There's a graphic design company on the marketplace that seem to order extraordinary amounts of wine. It was Prosecco last week but it was all red today. Loads of bottles of some fancy Rioja and a huge amount of cheese. I'm guessing some sort of wine and cheese evening.'

'You should be a detective, Charlie.'

Charlie grinned again. 'I'm very astute, me. Shall I help unload?'

'Oh. Yes. Thanks.'

Greg limped over to help. Poor Charlie had a job to do and it wasn't to pander to Greg's pathetic need for human contact.

'Ever had a dog, Charlie?' he asked, as he lifted the first item out of the basket.

'A dog? Er, no. I wanted one when I was a kid but my parents . . . Let's just say they weren't keen. They said pets were messy.'

'Messy but fun, right?'

Charlie grunted. 'Fun wasn't very high up their list of priorities.'

Greg looked at the man across the counter from him as they unloaded the Icelandic food he'd ordered to get himself up for the trip ahead. Charlie's neck had flushed red and he was focusing extraordinarily hard on lifting a small tub of lava salt from the basket.

'That's a shame,' he said lightly.

At least he got on with his parents, he reminded himself. His sister too. Well, he did when he wasn't tearing strips off them for trying to help. He had to count his blessings. It was just that, stuck at home, they were so much harder to remember than the curses that tripped him up every minute of every day.

'I got a tortoise in the end,' Charlie said quietly.

'A tortoise?'

'Yeah. He was kind of cute but not great at cuddling.'

Greg felt a jerk of sympathy at the look of sadness on the delivery driver's face. 'Any siblings?' he asked.

Charlie grunted again. 'Two – a brother and a sister. Both older than me. Both perfect.'

'Perfect?'

'In my parents' eyes, yes. Did all the right subjects at school.'

'*Right* subjects?'

'Science, maths – useful stuff.'

It seemed Greg's attempts at charming Charlie were not going well. He was rusty. Back in the day he'd have been able to charm anyone but then, back in the day, he'd been tall and straight and had done interesting things, instead of sitting around waiting for some sucker to sponsor him to limp across foreign countries spouting 'inspirational' stuff about how great life is. *Don't look back*, he told himself firmly and focused on Charlie.

'You didn't like science?' he asked.

'No. Well, not for itself. I liked – *like* – what it can do. I like how it can help people, but my parents only like the way it makes money.'

'You don't get on with them?'

Charlie gave a harsh laugh. 'Can you tell? No, I don't, but that's OK because they don't get on with me either. We don't speak much.'

'I'm sorry.'

'Please don't be. *You* were a scientist, right?'

Greg shifted. 'You've seen my website?'

'I had a look, yes. I thought it was great.'

'Thanks.'

'Your blogs are beautifully written.'

'They are?'

'Oh yes. Your description of sunset over the Ho Chi Minh trail made me feel as if I was right there. That's hard to do.'

'Especially for a scientist?'

60

Charlie gave the tiniest smile. 'I didn't say that. You were on research trips before?'

Before, Greg noted, but he forced himself not to comment. 'Yep. Surveys into fish populations mainly.'

'So you were using your science to help the world.'

Greg thought about that. 'I'm not sure it was anything so altruistic, Charlie.'

'But you were tackling global warming.'

Greg shrugged. 'True, but what mainly drew me was how amazing it is up there in the Arctic. The sun's so bright off the snow it makes every line of the landscape razor-sharp. And it's so peaceful – nothing but the creak of the ice and the odd splash of a hunting seal. And it's going. It's melting away.' He felt a long-forgotten urgency spike through him and reached out and grabbed Charlie's arm. 'We're killing it. Literally killing it centimetre by painful centimetre and in return, one day, it will kill us all. And we'll deserve it.'

He could hear his voice rising and see Charlie's poor arm going red under his grip. He dropped it hastily, though, God, it was good to feel so passionately about something again – something other than his own misfortune. He definitely had to get to Iceland.

'So, yes,' he finished more calmly, 'I do believe in the issues but I think I mainly took the job because I loved the work and the people I was working with. I wish . . .'

He cut himself off again.

'You wish you were still out there?'

Greg shrugged. 'Still doing something important, yes. But, hey, no point in wishing the impossible, is there? I got . . . injured. It happens.'

'Not as badly as it did to you.'

'Not usually, but, then, I shouldn't have been there.'

Charlie fiddled with a packet of Emmental. 'Why not?'

'I was in "no fit state". Well, that's what my mates said. My girlfriend had dumped me. The old Dear John letter all the way to the icy Arctic. It shocked the hell out of me, though Lord knows why. I should have seen it coming. She'd been complaining for a year about me working away and I'd just put her off and off. I loved the work. I loved being on the ships and I loved that she was there waiting for me when I got home again. Selfish bastard!

'Then, that day, I got a letter saying she couldn't take it any more, that we were over, and I lost it a bit. Well, a lot. I hit a few walls, threw a few things – not great behaviour on a ship miles above the ice line. My manager sent me straight to occupational health but the idiot bloke didn't think being dumped was a valid mental health issue. And, to be fair, it shouldn't have been.'

'Shouldn't have?' Charlie's protest squeaked into a cough. 'Mental health isn't about "should haves", though, is it? No one "should" be depressed, just like no one should have a broken bone. But sometimes things just break.'

Greg smiled gratefully at him. 'I was certainly broken back then, though not as badly as when the winch got its teeth into me.'

Charlie flinched but kept his eyes tight on him. 'Can you tell me about it?'

'Have you got time?'

Charlie shrugged. 'Probably not, but I'll make it up later.'

'If you insist, I'll give you the edited highlights. It was two years ago and I was on night shift, pulling up tanks full of fishes to count them every three hours. Exciting stuff. When the occupational health git said I was OK to work, my manager wanted to switch me to days but like a twat I said no. Figured I wasn't sleeping anyway so I might as well let some other bugger do so. And I loved the Arctic at night.'

He closed his eyes, picturing it. He could see the stars, the ice, the boat – the winch. He waited for the contrast between then and now to punch him in the face but for once it didn't. If anything, it felt good to put himself back there – perhaps because he was focusing on the place rather than himself. He could almost feel the cold against his nose, almost sense it frosting in his beard. He could feel the rock of the boat beneath his feet and hear the creak of the ice shifting.

'That's when I saw the polar bear,' he told Charlie. 'It was a large female out on the ice edge. I thought she was hunting but there was none of the muscle tension of a creature on high alert. She was just sitting there, looking out across her domain in magnificent profile against the starry sky. She was perfect and for a moment it was like she'd been sent to remind me of all I loved about that wild place. For a moment she brought me peace.

'I took this fabulous photo of her – white ice, black sea, silver sky, and in the middle this stunning creature at one with her environment. I was giddy with the joy of it and went straight to the share button. A split second later I realised I couldn't send it to Tia any more and I folded – like grief had whacked me, cartoon-style, right across the midriff. I dropped the phone and I wailed. Or I thought I did. But it must have gone inwards not out, because my colleague Max never heard it. If he had, he wouldn't have sent the tank down to collect the fishes. But he did.'

Greg could hear it now, the winch whirring into action as he stood there full of this ice-white pain. Tia was deleting his number, she'd said, so if he sent the beautiful, perfect polar bear up to the satellites wedged in the stars, it wouldn't bounce back to her but just keep on going, for ever and ever, into the layers of space above. The connection was severed and Greg was well and truly isolated in his stupid Arctic idyll.

'I was so caught up in my own emotional drama that I didn't even notice the chain. I didn't do the safety checks and I didn't stand back as it uncoiled and somehow it caught in my foot and lifted me into the cogs of the winch. It shouldn't have happened. That's what everyone said, time and again – when the red alert team ran to me, when the helicopter came, at my bedside, at the inquest. Over and over: "it shouldn't have happened". There were so many safety measures in place, so many guards and backstops, but one of those measures – and a fair one – was the competency of the staff and that's the one that failed.

'I told them that, once I could speak again. I told them it was my fault, all mine. Not the manufacturers, not the team, definitely not Max. Just me. Well, me and the occupational health bastard who said I was fit to work.'

Charlie, he noticed, had gone very pale. 'It must have been agony,' he stuttered.

'Not for long. I passed out pretty quickly. It's merciful, the body, when faced with extremes of physical pain. Sadly, it's not so merciful with the emotional stuff. We rarely get to pass out over that; quite the reverse, in fact.'

'I didn't realise,' Charlie said.

Greg squinted at him. 'Didn't realise what?'

Charlie coloured. 'Your blog post about it. It's very well-written but hearing you talk about it here in the, er, the flesh . . .'

'The broken flesh.'

Charlie looked as if he might be sick. 'Yes. It's much more . . . vivid. How on earth did you survive?'

'I really don't know. Max got to me first and had the sense not to try and pull me out. The cogs that had broken my bones were also keeping the wounds sealed and just about enough blood inside me to keep me alive. Luckily my arms were free. My head too. Small mercies. If I'd landed head first, bits of my skull would have shot across the Arctic instantly and I'd be long gone.'

'Don't!' Charlie said. 'It's so tragic.'

'So *neglectful*.'

'By the, er, occupational health guy?'

'Yeah. Tosser. God knows how he'd got on to the ships. He was fresh out of training and I reckon he'd only gone to see the world. Probably had some romantic idea of cruising the Arctic with little more to do than the odd plaster and paracetamol. The irony is that on most trips he'd have been dead right.'

Charlie fiddled with a carrier bag. 'You didn't like him?'

'I hadn't really noticed him, though I remember a couple of the others saying he was a funny one. He loved reading. Not that that's a problem, obviously, but on a boatful of scientists it was unusual. He'd filled the medical room with books and he was always trying to get people to a book club. Tosser! He'd have been better reading his "mental health at sea" book more often and *Moby* bloody *Dick* less. All he did when I was sent to him was give me some frigging novel and tell me it would help me calm down.'

'Novel?' Charlie squeaked.

'Yep. Some old thing – *Jane* Somebody.'

'*Jane Eyre*?'

'That's the girl.'

'Did you read it?'

'Not a word. Never got the chance. That night was winch-gate . . . boom!' Charlie jumped back, the baskets rattling in his hands, and Greg felt instantly awful. 'God, Charlie, I'm so sorry. You should never have asked. I should certainly never have explained. It doesn't matter.'

Charlie squinted at him. 'It obviously does.'

'Not any more. Seriously. You can only live forwards, right?'

Charlie gave a weak smile. 'Very inspirational.'

Greg groaned. 'Don't! I spend half my life looking back, wishing things were different. Addicted to it, I am.'

'Me too.'

The words came out so low that Greg wasn't sure he'd heard them right and by the time he'd decided he had Charlie was almost at the door. His plan to charm the poor man hadn't gone very well but, then, he probably didn't want charming. Greg limped hastily across the living room after him but at that moment the letter box opened and an envelope floated down to land at Charlie's feet, stopping him in his tracks. It was small and yellow with Greg's name written on it in a careful, rounded hand and the address added by someone else. He tried to pick it up but bending wasn't his strong point and he slipped.

'Steady.' Charlie had him by the arm instantly. 'Allow me.'

He swept up the envelope and handed it over. Greg wanted to snap, 'I can do it,' but he patently couldn't so he took the letter passively and turned it over. In a childish hand were the letters SWALK. Goodness!

'A fan?'

'It seems so.' Greg undid the flap and lifted out a single sheet. The words seemed to crowd in on each other but the gist was very clear indeed. 'Oh no,' he said.

Charlie turned back from stashing baskets in his van. 'What's wrong?'

Greg looked over to the shiny awards invitation he'd reluctantly restored to the mantlepiece. All week long he'd been meaning to contact them and say he'd be in Iceland so couldn't make it, but with North Face banging on about photographers it had felt like a lie and now it was too late.

'It's the awards. I bloody have to go now.'

He wafted the letter in front of him and Charlie came back to the door. 'Is that from Candy Drew?'

'Candy?' Greg laughed. 'God no. She probably can't write this well. It's from a girl called . . .' he checked the careful writing, 'Holly Adebayou. She's eleven years old and she's a carer for her sick mother.'

'Poor kid. But what's that got to do with you?'

Greg sighed. 'She's been selected to escort me on to the stage at the awards and she's very excited about it. Like, *very*.'

Greg turned the letter towards Charlie to show him the run of enthusiastic words and parade of excitable exclamation marks. Little Holly was full of the dress she was going to wear and the taxi that was going to come to her house to fetch her 'like a princess' and how it would have a special fitting for her mother's wheelchair so she could come along. Her mother, it seemed, was very excited too. It was, in fact, the most exciting thing that had happened to them 'ever'.

'How can I let her down, Charlie?'

Charlie scanned the letter slowly and finally looked up at him. 'You can't.'

'Great.'

'It might be fun,' Charlie offered, shuffling his tablet from hand to hand.

'It might be hideous,' Greg snapped. He slapped his hand over his mouth. 'Sorry. I'm sorry, Charlie. I meant to be nice to you today, really I did.'

Charlie squinted at him. 'Why?'

'Why not?'

'I'm just a delivery driver, Greg. You don't have to be nice to me. In fact, it's probably better if you're not.'

'What d'you mean?' Greg asked, but Charlie was swinging himself up into his van and clearly didn't hear him.

Puzzled, Greg watched him drive away, then looked down at little Holly's letter full of colourful exclamation marks, before retreating into his house. He took the letter across to the mantle-piece and sat it next to the invitation. The jaunty simplicity of it looked touching next to the glossy card and he almost smiled before he remembered what this actually meant. He'd have to go to the damn ceremony now. He might be a horrible man but he wasn't horrible enough to wreck a little girl's dreams.

Another memory hit – of his little sister running into his room in a Cinderella dress someone had passed down to her.

'Look at me, Greggie. Look at all my skirts. Look at my tiara! Will you be my prince? Will you? Please.'

He hadn't wanted to, but Rachel had been so excited and no one had been there to see, so he'd let her dress him with straps round the bottom of his trousers and one of Mum's big puffy shirts then he'd paraded her around the house on his arm. Truth be told, he'd felt a million dollars. Would it be like that again? Fat chance! He'd be the one resting on this poor Holly's arm and not the other way round. But still, it was a chance to do good. A chance to let 'cool' go to hell and make someone else happy and, God knows, he didn't do that enough these days.

Iceland could wait. He'd go to the fancy hall, hold Holly's hand and pray that no one found out exactly what a horrible bastard of an 'inspiration' he truly was before the clock struck midnight and he could escape, glass disability boot intact.

Chapter Eight

Number 95 Hope Street:

Ginger
Mixed chillies
Asafoetida powder
Dried fenugreek
Popadums
Tomatoes
Okra
Greek yoghurt
Spaghetti hoops, 2 cans
Alpen
Milk

Vik sat cross-legged in the garden watching Rickets poke through the grass for whatever it was tortoises liked to poke through grass for. It was a bit chilly but he'd sat down here to tempt his pet with a dandelion some time ago and couldn't seem to find the energy to get up again. His bum was cold and he'd probably catch a chill if he wasn't careful, but he didn't really care. What even was 'a chill'? It sounded like the sort of thing that had been eradicated with TB and rabies but maybe that was just because people weren't stupid enough to sit around on wet grass these days.

He ought to be cooking really. The papad ki sabji wouldn't make itself, after all, but right now he was feeling that perhaps Rickets' approach to life was the more sensible one. You didn't catch tortoises sweating over a hot stove, did you? They chomped down a juicy dandelion leaf if it was on offer and if it wasn't, well, they just poked through the grass until something turned up. You didn't see them looking up recipes. You didn't see them poring over lists of ingredients and ordering endless exotic items in plastic packages to be delivered in purple vans and . . .

'Charlie!'

Vik looked guiltily at his watch. It was way into his delivery slot; the poor driver might even now be hammering unheard on the front door. With a last nod to Rickets, Vik jumped up and sprinted for the house. At least, in his head he did. In reality, he creaked upwards by dint of tipping himself awkwardly sideways and levering himself on to his knees from where he could lean on the garden table and finally find his feet in order to hobble inside. The whole stupid performance must have taken him even further into his Turner's slot and it was with huge relief that he saw the purple van pulling on to the drive as he finally reached the kitchen.

'Made it,' he told Nika.

In his head she laughed but then, in his head, she'd been laughing the whole way through his undignified rise from the grass.

'We're so old now, Vikram!' she used to say, as if it was the funniest thing ever.

She'd never had a problem accepting how things were, his Nika, not even when she'd got ill. It had been him who'd railed against fate, who'd raged and pleaded and tried to make bargains with every cosmic force he could think of while she'd just sat there and let nature take its course. Well, until the end of course. Why she'd suddenly found the energy that night, just when he didn't want her to, he would never know.

Vik batted a tear away as Charlie, spotting him looking out of the window, gave a little wave. He waved back and went to the door. His bum was still cold and he had a horrible feeling it might be damp so he carefully kept his back to the wall as he ushered the delivery driver inside.

'Not cooking yet, Vik?' Charlie asked.

Vik looked to the stove where the pile of onions he'd chopped earlier were quietly sweating on the board.

'I was just about to make a start. I've been, er, feeding my tortoise.'

'Tortoise!' Charlie's dark eyes lit up at the word. 'I had a tortoise when I was a kid.'

'You did?'

'Yep. In fact, I was just telling . . . Doesn't matter. My parents wouldn't let me have a dog, or a cat, or even a hamster. They said they were too much mess. But even they couldn't say that about a tortoise, so a tortoise it was. I bought him myself with the proceeds from my paper round.'

'Very impressive. How old were you?'

'Nine.' Charlie must have seen the surprise in Vik's eyes because he gave a self-conscious shrug and said, 'We lied to the newsagent. Said I was eleven. I was quite tall for my age back then so they believed us.'

'*Us*? Your parents lied for you so that you could work aged nine?'

'Yep. Working was very important to my father. And to me – because it meant I got my tortoise.'

Vik decided not to push the matter any further. It was hardly abuse, was it? And hardly any of his business either.

'What did you call him?' he asked instead.

'Huckleberry Finn.'

'Great name.'

'Thanks. It was a bit of a mouthful to shout down the garden, though, so he pretty much became Huck. What's yours called?'

'Rickets. Because he looks like he's got really dodgy knees. My wife thought it was funny.'

Charlie laughed. 'It *is* funny.'

There was a pause and they both turned their attention to Vik's shopping, transferring it from the baskets on to the side next to the raw onions. Vik felt his eyes start to sting and looked to Charlie but he didn't seem to have noticed.

'Okra!' he said suddenly, pulling a pack triumphantly out of the basket.

'Thank heavens.' Vik took it from him. 'Not sure I could cope with another weird substitution.'

They gave each other small smiles.

'How *was* the mangetout bhindi?' Charlie asked.

Vik set a tin of tomatoes carefully on the table. 'Interesting.'

'Did your son like it?'

Vik thought about that one. 'No,' he said, eventually.

It was kind of true. Sai hadn't liked it because Sai hadn't tried it. Sai hadn't even turned up. Again. The excuses were starting to wear thin. So thin that Sai didn't dare call with them any more but just fired them off by text:

Sorry, Dad, Aleesha's ballet show taking up all our time. Can't make it this week.

Surely it would save you cooking, son, Vik had sent back.

We'll just have to get a takeaway, had been the reply and then, swiftly afterwards, as if even Sai was aware how hurtful that sounded, *Won't be the same but we'll make do till things are a bit freer and we can come again.*

What were these '*things*'? Vik had found himself wondering over and over as he'd cleared away all his carefully prepared curries last Friday. The surface implication was that they were small child and work 'things' but Vik suspected it was more than that. He suspected that Sai blamed him for Nika's death; that he couldn't look him in the eye these days without seeing him for the useless husband and father he was. Or maybe he'd always seen him that way but Nika had papered over the cracks between them well enough for them both to pretend they weren't actually there. It was only now that she was gone, taking the paper of her kindness and love with her, that they gaped so clearly.

'Vik? Vik, are you OK?'

Vik stared at Charlie, momentarily stunned to find the young man in his kitchen. Goodness, he really was getting old, standing here like an idiot as the poor lad waited patiently for him to sign for a load of groceries he didn't really need.

'Sorry, Charlie. I was thinking of my wife.'

'I'm sorry you lost her.'

Something in the young man's hangdog tone dug at Vik's already smarting flesh. 'Lost?' he snapped. 'Oh I didn't lose her, Charlie. She left me.'

Charlie froze halfway to the door and stared at Vik. 'Left you?'

'Morphine. She stored it up. A whole week's worth. I didn't know.'

Charlie visibly swallowed. 'Was she ill?' he asked nervously.

'Bone cancer. Last stages.'

'Ah. Right. I see.'

Again the slightly mournful tone. Vik hated it.

'Last stages, Charlie, but not the end.' His voice rose angrily and he caught himself. 'Sorry. I'm sorry. What am I doing?'

'Not at all. It's—'

'You get along,' Vik interrupted him before he filled the awkward space with some horrific platitude. 'There'll be people waiting for you.'

'Yes, but—'

'And I've got curry to cook.'

'Right. Delicious curry.'

'I hope so. Thank you, Charlie.'

Charlie made it to the door but didn't seem able to tear himself away. He turned back to Vik. 'You don't blame yourself?'

'Oh I do.' Vik insisted. 'And I should. I got worn out, you see. That's what Nika called it: "worn out", as if I had only a certain store of care to give. How could I, who was perfectly healthy, have got worn out?'

'It happens, Vik. You're not Superman.'

'No, but I was her husband. I should have cared for her. I shouldn't have got worn out, not by her. I *loved* her.'

He stopped, waited for Charlie to leave but the lad just stood there and it was so tempting to tell him. So tempting to talk about it in case doing so took even just a tiny bit of the load away. Was it any wonder that he couldn't get up from the grass with all of this on his back? He put his hand to his bum and felt it cold and damp. What an old fool. And still Charlie stood there, looking at him so compassionately.

'It was her idea,' he blurted out.

'The morphine?'

'No! Well, yes, but the care home first.'

'Care home?' Charlie's voice was oddly sharp.

'That's right. "Respite," she called it. Just for a week, she said, so I could get my strength back. Insistent, she was. "Just for a week," she said again and again, so I agreed. Fool. It was there that she stored up the pills, you see, so that she could kill herself once she got home. Care home, ha! The chap in charge couldn't have cared less. He had this book-trolley thing going. He was some sort of readaholic. That's what he called himself, as if it was a good thing – a readaholic – and he took this trolley around and handed out books to people as if they were prescription medication.

'"I think this romance would do you good, Marge."

'"Why don't you give this thriller a try, Jack?"

'"How about a nice bit of crime, Nika?"

'Oh, she lapped it up, thought he was wonderful. "Don't you worry about getting in again tonight, Vikram," she'd say to me when I went at midday, "the Bookman will sort me out. You rest, my love. You rest and the Bookman will take care of me." But he didn't, did he? He was so busy with his stupid books that he didn't bother to watch her swallow her pills, so she came home with a death-sized stash of them. He was her carer, Charlie, but he didn't – bloody – care.'

'I'm sorry,' Charlie said, his voice shaky. 'Oh my God, I'm so sorry.'

Vik saw little beads of sweat on the lad's temples and felt terrible.

'It happens,' he said wearily. 'She could be very determined, my Nika, when she wanted to be.'

'But even so . . . Did you, you know, take action?'

'Sue them, you mean?'

'Well, prosecute them certainly. Or him – the carer.'

'No. There was an inquest of course, but no more. They said I couldn't prove she'd got the pills from the care home and not from our own bathroom cabinet – which was true, except that I always kept the key to that cabinet. Always. It was that man that did it, that bloody Bookman.'

'I'm so sorry.'

'Thank you. Sai wanted to pursue a case but, in the end, I couldn't face it.'

'Might you yet?'

'It's been a year, Charlie. Best left to lie, isn't it? Or do you think I should?'

'No! That's to say . . . No. Sign here, please.'

He shoved the tablet under Vik's nose and, surprised, Vik scrawled his signature on to it with his shaky old finger.

'Thank you, Charlie,' he managed. 'It's, you know, good to talk.'

Charlie peered at him in concern. 'Are you sure you're all right? Is your son coming later?'

'Of course,' Vik said, forcing certainty into his voice. 'Of course he is. Don't you worry about me. Have a good day, Charlie.'

Then he bundled him out of the house before the young man saw through lies as thin as his wrinkled old skin. It hadn't been good to talk at all. All it had achieved was to bring up the sort of painful memories he normally tried to keep shut behind the lounge door with his other shameful secret.

Vik banged his head back, once, against the wall. Pain juddered through his skull and he welcomed it. How had he slept so soundly that night? How had he missed her waking? Or maybe never sleeping; he didn't even know that much. How had he not woken up to see her taking those damn pills? She'd always been surprisingly dainty for such a wonderfully fulsome lady but, even so, had she truly been calm enough about ending her life to do it in such perfect silence? Had she simply swallowed them down and curled back into his arms? Or had she sat, staring into darkness for a long time, while he snored like a fool beside her? He'd never know. After all they'd shared, she'd kept those final moments – hours? – for herself. Why?

He knew the answer, of course. It had been so he wouldn't stop her. That and, perhaps, to spare him. She couldn't have known they'd do a post-mortem; would have thought he'd just assume she'd died peacefully in her sleep. She'd been protecting him, caring for him, as she'd strived to do throughout their forty-nine years of married life.

Vik stomped back into the kitchen and began putting his shopping away with barely contained fury. Forty-nine years. One more to be golden. One more to say 'Oh yes, we were married fifty years, you know.' He was angry they hadn't made it and even angrier that it mattered to him. Their marriage *had* been golden, every bit of it, and he didn't need some tomfool-imposed anniversary to celebrate that. He had, however, needed more of it, of her. He hadn't been ready to lose her and sometimes, despite it being over a year after he'd woken to find her cold in his arms, he felt that he was still every bit as shocked as he'd been that dark morning.

Chapter Nine

Number 112 Hope Street:

Value wholemeal bread
Baked beans, 4 cans
Value ready salted crisps, 6-pack
Bacon bits
Pasta
Value pasta sauce
Beef mince
Potatoes
Lemons, 3
Vodka, 1ltr
Tonic, 2x 1ltr
Paracetamol x2

The doorbell pierced Ruth's sleep like a scream. She sat up in bed and stared around her, unable to see past the relentless eyes of her nightmares. They were staring through the darkness at her, bluer than a thousand oceans and every bit as deep – deep enough to be lost in for ever. She blinked desperately, trying to force them away, and a voice bleated in protest.

Mummy!

Ruth grasped the sides of her head, trying to shake the voice off, though she knew already that nothing she could do would drive it away. It was almost a relief when the doorbell went again and she dragged herself up, pulled on her once-pink dressing gown and stumbled down to the door.

'Oh, it's you, Charlie, sorry. I was . . .'

She didn't bother completing the sentence. It was gone eleven. What sort of dosser was still in bed at gone eleven? The sort who was afraid to go to work, that's who. The sort who'd been draining Sanjeed's finest 'Russian White' at 2 a.m. as she pored uselessly over red mortgage statements. She felt shame run over her like the hot wash her dressing gown so badly needed and tugged it tighter.

'Oh, don't worry about it,' Charlie said lightly, if a little too late. 'Why shouldn't you be in your dressing gown in your own home?'

'Because it's not very nice for you.'

'I don't mind. I see all sorts. There's a bloke a few streets away who comes to the door in his pants. Tight ones and always in very bright colours.'

Ruth tried to process this all-too-vivid image. '*Just* his pants?'

'Yep.'

'Maybe he fancies you.'

Charlie glanced down at himself. 'Unlikely,' he said dully. 'He just seems like the sort of man who enjoys shocking people.'

Ruth wondered what that must feel like. She'd always gone out of her way to avoid scrutiny or attention. It was one of the reasons why everything had hit her so hard.

'What do you do?' she asked Charlie.

'Ignore it completely. Very British of me, hey?'

A laugh burst out of Ruth, surprising her. It tickled at her throat and she put a hand up, feeling as if the evidence of it might have flushed across her skin. Charlie shifted from one foot to another.

'Come in, please. Look at me, holding you up again.'

'It's not a problem really. Er, where . . .?'

He looked around and she looked with him. If anything, her kitchen was even more crowded than last week. Screamingly bored of her jigsaws, she'd gone to see Frank at the tip on her way to Sanjeed's on Wednesday and, bless him, he'd kept her several new 'treasures'. They were all in here now, half mended and pushing up against the existing ones for space. Ruth snatched a dismembered microwave off the table and shoved it on to the floor, wires spewing behind.

'There you go. Sorry, I meant to clear it off before you came but I, er, slept in.'

'That's OK. Everyone needs a lie-in sometimes.'

'All the time,' Ruth muttered as she began grabbing her shopping from the basket. 'I need to get back to work.'

There was an awkward pause. Charlie seemed to be considering whether he should agree with her, but in the end he just said: 'I had a while off last year. I wasn't myself, if you know what I mean?'

'Oh, I know.' Ruth stopped unpacking and looked at Charlie. His cheeks were flushed and his eyes over-bright – it was a look she knew well from the mirror. 'I'm so not myself that I don't even know what that self used to be like any more. I mean, look at me – I was the sort of person who thought a pink dressing gown was a good idea. Pink! I keep meaning to dye it a sensible colour, navy or black or something, but, well, you lot don't do fabric dyes.'

'Sorry. Bit specialist. There's a good hardware store just—'

'I know where it is.' Her voice came out bullet-sharp and she tutted furiously at herself. 'Sorry, Charlie, rude of me. As usual. I didn't used to be rude. Well, not *as* rude. It's just that the hardware store belongs to my husband. Ex-husband. That is, he's still my husband technically, but not actually. My ex-partner, perhaps.'

'I'm sorry.'

'Not your fault.'

She reached for the vodka bottle, running her fingers up and down its smooth coldness as she remembered the start of it all – the magic of meeting the man who now lived and worked just two hundred metres down Hope Street. His shop was in the opposite direction to Maureen's and Sanjeed's stores – the direction she never, ever went in any more. She couldn't bear the contrast between the ridiculous happiness of then and the black despair of now.

She'd been eighteen when she'd first met Tony and working as an electrical apprentice for her uncle. She'd had to fight to get him to take her on and had been on a mission to prove she was up to it. But then one day she'd gone charging into the hardware shop for supplies for an urgent job and there he'd been, Tony, standing behind the counter. God, he'd been gorgeous. He'd been serving someone else but he'd looked over their head and given her the cheekiest wink and suddenly she'd not been in a rush at all. Suddenly she'd felt like she could wait in that shop all day long. Ha!

Ruth looked down at herself and picked angrily at a bit of dried egg yolk on her lapel, wondering nervously where she'd left Sanjeed's empty bottle last night. She didn't want Charlie thinking she was an alcoholic. Not that she was. Not really. It was just a temporary thing to get her through the blackness. She'd stop once she went back to work and that would be soon. Very soon. She just had to somehow banish these constant thoughts of Libby. Libby and Tony. And why they weren't with her any more. *How had it gone so wrong?* she asked herself. But, in truth, she knew. Libby, that's how, with her cleverness, and Tony with his stupid hero-worship.

She looked up from her reverie to see Charlie carefully unloading the last of her baked beans on to the table, stacking the cans one on top of each other in the limited space.

'Thank you.'

He gave her a little smile. 'Sign here, please.'

He held out the tablet and she tried, but her fingers were so big and strong that she only got two strokes in before she hit the edge of the little screen.

'It's fine,' Charlie said. 'No one checks anyway.'

'So I could have put an X.'

'I suppose so.'

'Like an illiterate.'

'Well, now, I—'

'My daughter thought I was illiterate.'

'Sorry?'

'Libby. My daughter. Got very into reading, she did. Books everywhere. Fancy ones. You know – famous writers, the sort who don't make sense but everyone bangs on about anyway. That's how I saw it anyway. My daughter wasn't impressed. Called me illiterate, and that was on a good day.'

'I'm sure you're not.'

'I was to her. She'd look at me with her big, blue eyes and all I'd see was contempt. She had this English teacher, a young man who gave her all this strange stuff to read. It gave her ideas, you know, sent her places she shouldn't have been going at that age. He thought he was so clever but he wasn't. He was an interfering, self-inflated bastard.'

'Right.'

Charlie fiddled with his tablet and glanced to the door. Ruth knew she was being self-indulgent but, oh God, she could imagine that bloody teacher now. He'd sent such a patronising report home telling them what a 'little star' they'd got, as if he'd discovered her himself. Smug bastard. He'd had no idea. None. And Tony had been no help either. Lapped it up, he had. Gone in for a 'special' meeting with the damn man and been all pious with Ruth when she'd refused to join them.

'Tony was illiterate too,' she told Charlie, 'but he was happy to admit it so that seemed to be OK. He got on far better with her than with me.'

She could picture him and Libby sat at the table now, their heads locked together as they whispered away over some stupid book. Tony had had no more idea what he was talking about than Ruth, but he'd solved this by asking Libby question after question and she'd loved it.

'You're encouraging her,' Ruth would snipe at him.

'Good,' he'd fire back. 'Isn't that what parents are meant to do? Isn't that what the teacher suggested we did?'

And, of course, it had been. Only she'd seen the darkness and they hadn't. And then Tony and Libby had been gone and the darkness had been all hers.

'Er, Ruth . . .' She pulled herself out of the blackness to blink at Charlie. 'There's, er, one more item.'

She looked down to see he was holding out a large, flat box. 'What is it?'

He'd gone very pink but he nudged it determinedly towards her. 'Jigsaw. On the house!'

'From Turner's?'

He flushed even deeper. 'No. No, not from Turner's. It's, er, one of mine. You said you wished you could, you know, borrow jigsaws, so I thought maybe you'd like this.'

Ruth stared at him, absurdly touched. Her chest pinged as if someone had stabbed a pin into her heart and prodded it back into life.

'I don't know, Charlie . . .'

'It's all there. Seven hundred and fifty pieces.' He nudged it towards her again and when she didn't take it, he bent and set it carefully on top of the discarded microwave. 'I'll, er, leave it with you.'

He backed out of the kitchen, catching his knee on a steamer as he stumbled into the hall, barely suppressing a yelp.

Ruth snatched up the jigsaw and rushed after him. 'Are you OK?'

'Fine. I'm fine. Best get on. Hope you like it. The jigsaw, that is. I can get it back next week. If, you know, you have a delivery. If not, well, it doesn't matter. It's just a jigsaw. It's not—'

Ruth put up a hand to stop him.

'It's really very kind of you, Charlie. I appreciate it, truly I do, but I can't keep your jigsaw, not for a whole week.'

'I don't mind. I've got other ones.'

Ruth stared at him. Why was he being so kind? Was she really such a wreck that even delivery drivers felt sorry for her now? Or was he just a nice lad? He seemed nice. He was backing towards his van, the giant strawberry on the side framing his head like a scarlet halo. Tony had always had a van – a big, red one, not like the little yellow Sparkly Sparkies vehicle rusting on her drive now. They'd taken their first holiday in it, back when they'd barely enough money to make it to the end of the month.

Ruth blushed, recalling the three-week tour of France. Lord knows why they'd decided to try and cross the Alps in that battered old thing but those nights sitting on their squashed mattress with the doors open to a flaming Alpine sunshine had been worth every slope they'd had to coax it up. She'd lost count of the number of times they'd made love in there, the oranges and pinks playing across their bare skin like the finest film effect possible.

Don't think about the bastard, Ruth, she told herself.

She didn't mean to think about him. She didn't even like thinking about him. Or about Libby. It hurt. Stupid that, wasn't it? Those were the happy memories. They shouldn't hurt; they should amuse, touch, comfort. Just because they could never happen again didn't mean they hadn't been good at the time. People weren't just bones and organs and flesh but memories and experiences. Every day they lived weaved itself into their DNA and became as much a part of them – more, maybe – as the shell encasing them. No wonder it was hard work being human.

Ruth shook her head. She wasn't usually one for philosophising. She wasn't clever enough, as Libby had so often pointed out. Little cow!

'Please.' She pushed the jigsaw towards Charlie. 'It's very kind of you but you don't need to bother.'

The young man straightened a little. 'But I *want* to bother.'

She was stunned. 'Why?'

He shrugged. 'I dunno. Common humanity? Jigsaw lovers unite?'

He gave her another uneasy little smile and she couldn't help but smile back. The pin in her heart dug around and she squirmed.

'But a whole week . . .'

Charlie set his shoulders. 'Tell you what, then – how about I come and get it tonight? And maybe have that cup of tea? If you're in tonight, that is?'

'If I'm in?' Ruth glanced back at the starkly blank calendar on the wall. 'Oh yes, as luck would have it, I'm free of social engagements this evening.'

'Good. I mean, not good, but . . . Look, I'll fetch it later. Right?'

'Er . . .'

'About five thirty. See ya.'

He was gone before she could formulate a proper reply and she was left standing alone in the hallway, jigsaw in hand. Eventually, she went back into the kitchen, swept her shopping off the table and set the puzzle down in its place. She paced around it, her thoughts as jumbled as the ridiculous machines crowding her work surfaces. She looked longingly to the vodka bottle. The only decision vodka demanded of you was when to pour the next glass, but it wasn't really an answer, just a way of keeping the questions at bay.

'Not yet,' she told herself and sat decisively down at the table with her back to its tantalising promise.

Slowly, she lifted the lid of Charlie's jigsaw and peered in at what seemed to be a mass of chopped-up flowers. So simple. All she had to do was take them out of the box and put them together in the right order. If a minute or two were used up for every piece located, a whole hour could be usefully dispatched. A whole hour closer to bedtime and another day ticked meaninglessly but successfully off the calendar.

Ruth reached inside and dug out a straight-sided piece, then another and another. Slowly the frame of the picture began to form and, gratefully, she sank into the simple world of the puzzle and, for a few moments at least, forgot the far spikier edges of the real one.

Chapter Ten

Bri was in the common room at lunchtime but, thankfully, there was no sign of Ryan.

'Jumper on the ring road,' she informed Charlie cheerfully. 'All the traffic's stopped while they talk down the poor git and Ryan's right there in the middle of it all. His yummy mummies will have to wait for their organic hummus today.'

Charlie sat down abruptly. 'Whereabouts is the jumper?'

'On Queen's Bridge.'

'In the middle of the day?'

'Couldn't take it any more, I guess. When you crack, you crack. There's a negotiator talking to him.'

'Poor man.'

'Yep.'

They both sat silently for a moment. Charlie tried to imagine the unknown man clinging to Queen's Bridge. It was an ugly seventies structure with no soul or poetry, not that that mattered. If you'd chosen to exit the world, presumably you thought it was all ugly. Either that, or you noticed nothing but your own ugliness. Charlie knew how that felt and for a moment he admired the jumper. At least he was doing something. At least he wasn't standing around flinching at the smallest burn.

'Penny for 'em?'

He blinked. 'Sorry. I was just imagining the man on the bridge. Wondering if he'll go through with it.'

'God, I hope not.'

'Oh, me too. Course.'

'Life's a gift, right?'

'Right.'

'Charlie?'

He forced a smile. 'I guess maybe sometimes it's just a gift you don't want.' Bri was staring intently at him and he fought for levity. 'Like, you know, the dodgy socks your aunt gives you at Christmas.'

Bri laughed. 'My aunt gave me a cushion-decorating course for Christmas last year.'

'Do you like cushion decorating?'

'No! What sensible human would? I think it's cos I'm "gay". That's how she says it, with her fingers up in pantomime inverted commas – "gay". Bless her. I thought I'd save the course up for next year's work Secret Santa and pray Ryan gets it.'

Charlie smiled but still the jumper played on his mind. He'd been looking forward to a bit of downtime after what had felt like a pretty intense morning but it seemed there was no let-up yet.

'He must be very sad to stand up there and, you know . . .'

'Jump?'

'Yeah.'

'Well, let's hope he doesn't. Don't dwell, Charlie, it's lunch-time. Forget it for a bit.'

'I find that hard.'

'You're too sensitive, mate. Look – let me show you something to cheer you up. Making life, like, not ending it.'

Bri unzipped a pocket in the side of her combat trousers and drew out a small blue card, very well-thumbed. She shoved it at Charlie.

'What is it?'

'Look!'

Charlie looked. On the front, written in a circle around what seemed to be a tadpole were the words *St George's neonatal unit* and when he opened it, he found a grainy black-and-white photo.

'Is that . . .?'

'Yep!' Bri leaned in, pointing keenly. 'That's him, that's my son. Isn't he amazing?'

Charlie looked more closely. He'd heard people talk about scan pictures, laugh about them as things that only doting parents could ever fathom, but this baby was as clear as day. He was lying on his back, little arms and legs waving in the air. His one visible eye was closed but clear to see, as was his tiny nose and pursed-up lips.

'He really is amazing, Bri. He's so . . . complete.'

'Isn't he? He's twenty weeks. That's halfway through.'

'Only halfway? What's still to grow?'

Bri frowned.

'Dunno. Lungs and kidneys and that, I think. It's a miracle really.'

'It is.' Charlie looked sideways at Bri. 'How did you . . . you know?'

'Conceive?' She glanced around the room but the drivers from the other teams were all chatting among themselves. 'It was easy – just our good mate, Kyle, a few bottles of wine and a turkey baster.'

'No way?'

'Yes way. We only had to do it once. Harper must be, like, *so* fertile. We couldn't believe it when she got pregnant but there he is.'

She stroked the little picture fondly.

'That's great, Bri. I'm so pleased for you.'

She gave a funny little shrug. 'Cheers, Charlie. I'm so pleased for me too. I thought I was a lost cause to be honest, but it seems I got a second chance. That's why I got the dragon tattoo – it symbolises renewal.'

'Like a phoenix.'

'A what?'

'Doesn't matter. It's lovely, Bri.'

'Thanks. I've been lucky, Charlie, and I'm going to make the absolute most of it. I hope that man on the bridge gets a break, too. I hope someone makes him feel special enough to want to stay around.' Charlie stared at her. 'What?'

He shook his head.

'Nothing. I just . . . Nothing.'

'You OK, Charlie?'

'Absolutely. Here, don't lose your picture.' He handed the card back. 'Have you chosen a name yet?'

'Not yet, but Harper's bought a book. An actual paper book. We're going to make a shortlist.' She moved to tuck the picture back into her pocket but someone leaned over and snatched it out of her hand. She looked up and groaned. 'Ryan! What joy to have you back!'

'At last. This your kid?' Bri nodded. 'What is it then? Not a boy, I hope.'

'Why?'

'Well, you know – poor lad'll get the piss ripped out of him at school, won't he?'

'Why?'

'Cos of 'avin no dad and that.'

'Plenty of kids have no dad, Ryan.'

'Maybe, but not many have two mums, do they? It's pretty weird, right?' He saw Bri glaring at him and hastily handed the picture back. 'Not weird. I don't mean weird. Just . . . unusual.'

Charlie saw Bri fight for breath and felt fury rise at Ryan and his ridiculous, unkind opinions. He stood up.

'What *is* usual though, Ryan?'

Ryan squinted at him. 'Well, you know, one of each – a mum and a dad.'

'I see. And that's the ideal, is it?'

'Well, I guess. I mean, biologically it certainly is. Can't argue with that, can you?'

'Biology is no indicator of happiness though, is it?'

'Eh?'

'Is it better, do you think, to have a dad who beats the mum up? Is it better to have a dad who's out at the pub all the time? Or a mum who's shagging someone else?'

'Whoa, Charlie! Is this some personal shit?'

'Nope,' Charlie said. 'As a matter of fact, I had a mum and a dad and an older brother and sister. Very gender-balanced we were. Very "ideal". Except, of course, that both my parents worked so bloody hard I never saw them and when it emerged that I didn't have the same . . . ethos as the others, I saw them even less. I wasn't worth their precious time, see.'

Ryan's Adam's apple bobbed awkwardly in his skinny throat. Other drivers were looking over curiously and Charlie wondered what on earth had possessed him to talk about his bloody family. But Bri had been so excited and Ryan had popped all her happiness like a balloon and he didn't like it. It wasn't fair.

'So, personally,' he said, fighting to keep his voice low and calm, 'I would take two mums who love and care for me any day, because that, Ryan, is surely what matters and not what you've got in your pants.'

He sat down suddenly, worn out. Ryan stood over him like a dark shadow but from across the room someone called out 'Hear, hear' and under the table Bri reached out, took his hand, and squeezed it so hard he almost cried out in pain. Well, in something.

Ryan gave him a slow hand clap and spun away. 'Haven't you lot got vans to get to?'

Charlie looked at his watch. He'd still got fifteen minutes of his break but he couldn't stay here now. He got up and made silently for the door, then remembered something and turned back.

'Did they talk the jumper down, Ryan?'

Ryan's lip curled.

'Nah. He jumped. But he landed on the bike track so they could get the traffic going again, thank God. I was starving.' He moved over to the microwave and stuck a large Cornish pasty in to warm up. 'Maybe if he'd had two loving mummies he'd still be alive, right?'

Charlie's fist curled but Bri was up and leading him outside before he could unleash it on Ryan's smug jawline. Not that he would have done. Not brave enough, see, just like his dad had always said.

'I can't believe you said all that, Charlie,' Bri told him as they broke into the rare sunshine on the yard.

'I know. What an idiot!'

'Not at all. You were amazing. You . . . you stood up for me.'

'Course I did.'

'Yeah, well, you're the first to do that. Apart from Harper, that is. But still . . . it's, you know, appreciated, right? Right?'

'Right,' Charlie said. 'Er, thanks.'

''S'OK.' Bri rubbed at her eyes and made for her van. 'So, see you later, yeah?'

'Later,' Charlie agreed.

Touched, he watched her swing into her van and then looked back to the warehouse. Ryan was standing there, arms folded, his eyes locked on to him like a raptor sighting a meerkat separated from the pack. Charlie groaned to himself. He might have won this encounter but he was under no illusions about the next one. He really must try to be nicer to the damn man. For now, though, he had his afternoon run and then, God help him, he was heading back to Ruth Madison's house. Ryan would call him a total idiot if he knew, and Ryan would probably be right.

Chapter Eleven

Charlie had been hovering outside for a while now. Ruth had noticed him there when she'd poured her first vodka at 5.30 and had braced herself for him to press the doorbell, but by the – admittedly quite short – time she'd gone back for her second he still hadn't walked up the drive. She peered out from around the edge of the curtain to watch him standing a few doors down, bike propped against a low wall so he could pretend to fiddle about with the pedals.

It didn't fool Ruth. She'd spent years on a bike and there was nothing you could do with the pedals while out on the road. He was just pissing around, stalling for time, and it wasn't doing either of them any favours. Cross, she strode to the door and yanked it open. 'You coming in or what?'

He looked up, flushing scarlet. 'I am, yeah. Just, er, fixing my bike.'

'I can help you with that.'

'You do bikes too?'

'I know my way around a set of gears.'

Charlie stood up and gave the back tyre a little kick. 'It's fine, thanks. I think I've sorted it.'

She was tempted to ask him more but as he'd gone out of his way to do her a favour it would hardly be sporting.

'Great. Well done you. Come on in then.'

He wheeled the bike up the driveway, looked around uncertainly and then pushed it into the chaotic grasses of what had once been her lawn.

'Guess I should try and find a lawnmower to mend next.'

Charlie shrugged. 'I think smart lawns are overrated.'

'You do?'

'We have a lawn behind my block of flats. There's this bloke, Mr Graham, who seems to have appointed himself its keeper which suits me, really, because it means I don't have to do it, but a couple of months back I had a . . . a bonfire and . . .'

He seemed to run out of words all of a sudden and bent to fiddle with the bike again.

'You ruined this bloke's lawn?' All she got was a small nod. 'Well, you know what, Charlie – grass grows. In fact, grass never bloody stops growing.'

He looked up at her through the long blades and gave a slightly strangled laugh. 'Right.'

'By spring it will be as if your bonfire had never been there at all.'

'If only,' Charlie grunted, but he let go of the pedal and came to the door.

Ruth felt a disorientating rush of tenderness as he shuffled inside. He must be approaching thirty, this young man, but there was a nervous awkwardness about his movements that made Ruth feel like mothering him. And she didn't like that, not one bit. She'd had her mothering privileges revoked, and quite rightly too. It wasn't her place to start foisting herself on other waifs and strays just because they weren't as challenging as her own daughter. Libby had been her chance and she'd blown it. End of.

Mummy! a voice called deep inside her brain. *Mummy!* And there they were, the blue eyes.

'Vodka?' she blurted out.

Charlie looked at her glass with a raw longing that was all too familiar to her but then he shook his head. 'I don't drink.'

'You don't?'

'No!' It came out rather fiercely and he visibly swallowed back the word. 'I did. Too much. So I don't now.'

Three quick-fire half-sentences that so clearly contained a wealth of story behind them.

Ruth swallowed. 'I admire that. I should stop too. In fact, I *will* stop, when I go back to work.'

She pictured her uniform sat in a drawer in her room – clean, crisp and utterly terrifying. Mind you, the pile of red mortgage statements was getting pretty terrifying too. If she was chucked out of the house, she'd have to leave Libby's room and she couldn't do that. She couldn't leave Libby's room. She shuddered.

'You have to be ready,' Charlie said kindly. He lifted a hand as if he might touch her arm but then glanced at the table and instead said, 'Oh wow – you're almost done!'

He dropped his hand and moved to the nearly completed jigsaw. The flower bed burst out in a riot of colour and exuberant elegance and Charlie pored over it as if he'd never seen it before.

'You're fast,' he said and Ruth felt a silly little rush of pride.

She set her vodka carefully behind a toaster and stepped up next to him.

'I got on a roll,' she said. 'Just kept on hunting down the next piece.'

'That's good. That's the point of jigsaws, isn't it? There's always the next piece to find.'

She nodded. 'And while you're finding it, it's the most important thing in the world, which is . . .' she ran her fingers lightly over the jigsaw, 'a relief,' she finished.

Charlie nodded vehemently. He looked across at her and for a moment their eyes met, identically red around the edges, then they both looked quickly down again.

'I'll have to bring you the thousand-piecer next time,' he said.

'Is that a challenge?'

'Yep.'

Ruth grinned. 'You're on. Cup of tea?'

'That would be great, thanks.'

She saw him draw in a deep breath as he lowered himself on to a chair, being careful to remove a partially wired plug from it first. Hastily, she picked a kettle – the light-up one – and plugged it in. She watched intently as bubbles started to form in the blue water.

'Been doing jigsaws long?' she asked over her shoulder.

'Since the start of the year,' Charlie said, picking up a piece and slotting it into place.

'What started you off?'

'A, er, friend recommended it. I thought it was silly at first but I was hooked as soon as I started. There's something very soothing about them.'

'Do you need soothing, Charlie?'

He grabbed at another piece. 'Don't we all?'

'I guess so.' She poured water into the mugs. 'Milk? Sugar?'

'Just milk, thanks.'

She brought the teas across and sat down next to him, pointing to the bottom corner of the puzzle where a broken patch of peonies awaited completion. 'I got stuck here. All the pink did it for my eyes.'

Together they peered at the piece in Charlie's hand.

'It might go there,' Ruth suggested.

He nodded and for a few minutes they worked together on the puzzle. Ruth looked down at the pretty picture through the steam of Charlie's tea and listened to the heavy tick of her clock and felt suddenly relaxed enough to take a sip of her own without looking round for the vodka. Charlie completed two peonies and she filled in a small worm in the soil beneath and then suddenly they noticed at the same time that there was only one neat hole left and both gave a little squeal of triumph.

'Here.' Ruth handed the last piece to him.

'No, no – you did all that bit.'

'And it's your puzzle. You do it.'

She pushed it insistently forwards and he took it and pressed it into place with a little click. They both sat back to appraise the finished picture.

'Good work, pardner!' Ruth said in a mock-American drawl that sounded stupid the moment it came out of her mouth, but Charlie just laughed.

'You did most of it.'

'Yeah, well, I haven't been at work all day like you, have I?'

'Why not?' He clapped a hand to his mouth. 'Sorry, I . . .'

'No, it's OK. I should work. I *will* work. Soon. It was just, after Libby went I sort of lost my sense of purpose.'

'Went?' he asked tentatively.

Her throat constricted. 'Went, yes.'

Mummy, Libby called from deep inside Ruth's brain, but she shook it away.

'She didn't want me as a mother any more and can you blame her? I wasn't enough for her. I didn't "get" her. Tony didn't get her either, but at least he let her be whatever she was. At least he didn't try to change her like I did.'

'I'm so sorry.'

'Yeah, well. It was my fault.'

'That can't be true.' She stared at him and he flushed. 'I mean, how could it be your fault?'

They were both staring at the jigsaw. Ruth lifted it up by the corner and watched the edges of the pieces flex against each other, distorting the flowers.

'You're right. It wasn't me. And it wasn't Tony, not really. It was the books. They seduced her away from me.'

She stared at the flowers but all she could see now was Libby's face all lit up with a strange, dark joy as she dived into yet another novel, and then cut through with anger when Ruth dared to interrupt her, to suggest she might like to spend some time in the real world.

'Why?' she'd spit, her eyes burning blue. 'Why would I want to spend time there? The real world is shit.'

Ruth flexed the jigsaw further. The flowers nearest the corner rippled.

'It was all because of this bloody English teacher who arrived at the school and filled her head with "aspirational" stories. I had to look that word up when I read it on her report, that's how "illiterate" I was. And even when I did, it still didn't make sense. Libby was going on about Romeo and Juliet at the time and I just didn't get it. I mean . . .' She banged the jigsaw down and it cracked apart. 'How could two idiot kids killing each other out of a melodramatic sense of hormonal love possibly be "aspirational"?'

Charlie gave a funny little grunt. 'I don't know.'

Ruth groaned. There were pieces of jigsaw all over the place.

'God, I'm sorry. I've wrecked it. I wreck everything.' She felt tears threaten and grabbed for her drink, gulping it down before she realised it was tea not vodka. The heat scalded her throat and now the tears did come. She batted them furiously away. 'I'm sorry. I'm so sorry.' She leaped up and scrabbled for pieces, flinging them into the box. 'We'll find them all. I'll count them. I'll find them. I'll . . .'

'Ruth, stop!' Charlie placed a hand on her arm and she felt his quiet strength. Two angularly joined pieces in her fingers dropped to the table and she stood still. 'It doesn't matter,' he said. 'It's just a jigsaw.'

'But it's wrecked.'

'No, it isn't. It's broken up, as it's meant to be. That's what jigsaws are for – piece them together then take them apart again.'

'And again and again.'

'Exactly.'

She dared a look at him and saw no judgement, just concern. 'But we have to find all the pieces.'

'And we will. Come on.'

He dropped to his knees and started picking pieces up from the floor, placing them on the table one at a time. Ruth loaded them into the box but tears were still threatening and through their fug she saw the eyes again, Libby's eyes, driving into her. She couldn't bear it any more – the hiding, the fear, the silence.

'She died, Charlie.'

Charlie froze, one arm reaching up to the table. The jigsaw piece plopped down on to it. 'Who died?'

'Libby. Libby died. A year and a half ago. When she was thirteen. We were on holiday and she didn't want to come out with us because she was reading and so we weren't there and . . . and she died.'

She looked for the eyes, looked straight into them. Were they accusatory? Or just scared? Or both? Libby seemed to reach out a hand to her and she shrunk from it, but now Charlie was up on his feet and facing her.

'I'm so sorry, Ruth. That's awful. I mean . . . I'm so, so sorry.'

He looked distraught, as if Ruth had passed all the distress into him and for a moment it felt as if she had. For a moment, having said the terrible words out loud, she felt calmer. But only for a moment. She looked hastily away.

'It's getting dark, Charlie. I bet you don't have lights, do you? You'd better get off.'

'But I can't leave you here alone. Not now.'

She shook her head. 'I've been here alone for ages, Charlie. Tony left a couple of months after Libby . . .'

'Died?'

'Died. Yes. It's nothing new.'

'Maybe, but . . . Is there anything I can do?'

'No more than you already have. Thank you.'

She put the lid back on the jigsaw box and pushed it into his arms, shooing him gently towards the door. He moved reluctantly, darting nervous looks in her direction, but she stood firm and in the end he stepped out and yanked his bike from the grass. October was here now and it was getting dark fast. Shadows were stealing across the length of Hope Street and the street lights had come on, faint but warming up rapidly. Charlie looked small and young beneath them, burdened with his kind jigsaw and her reckless confession.

'I could look for some lights,' she offered, staring back into her chaos of a kitchen as if there might be some lurking behind one of the appliances. Which, indeed, there might.

Charlie, however, shook his head. 'It's fine. I'll push it. I don't mind the walk.'

He turned, head bowed, and behind her all her mended machines seemed to chatter a manic protest. She glanced back, spotted something. 'Charlie, wait! I want to give you something.'

'You do? But . . .'

'Wait!' she ordered again and dashed back into her kitchen to snatch up the fancy coffee machine. 'I want you to have this.'

'That! I can't, Ruth. It's too much.'

'Too much for what? Please.' Still he hesitated. 'I don't have anything else to do with it.'

'Oh. Right. But . . .'

She couldn't cope with any more protests; she just wanted him to take the damn machine. Stepping forward, she tumbled it into his bike basket next to the jigsaw box. He looked down at it in silence but when he finally looked back up his cheeks were pink and his eyes shining.

'That's very kind. *Too* kind. No one's given me . . . that is . . . you shouldn't have . . . Oh never mind. Just . . . thank you.'

''S'OK.' Ruth could feel herself going pink too now. 'You'll have to, you know, get the coffee for it.'

'I'll get the coffee.'

'Good. Great. Nice for it to get used.'

'Yes. Well, er, thanks.'

'Pleasure.'

'And, er . . . Well, night, Ruth.'

'Night, Charlie.'

Ruth retreated into her house, closing the door and leaning back against it.

'Libby died,' she said to the room and it hurt. Of course it hurt, but it hurt less for saying it. Less for sharing it. 'Libby died,' she said again.

She listened for the protesting echo of a reply in her brain but it didn't come, and as she glanced out the window at Charlie's retreating figure she remembered again the startled smile on his face when she'd given him the coffee machine and felt peculiarly faint. How strong had she made those bloody vodkas?

She knew, though, that it wasn't alcohol dancing a jig around her big body, it was something far, far more dangerous – it was happiness. Or, at least, a hint of happiness. It tingled across her, painfully bright, as if someone had poured hot water over frozen skin and it was all she could do to wait for it to pass and the familiar darkness of her usual dread to return. It would, she knew it would, but in the meantime might she, perhaps, enjoy the light?

She waited again to hear Libby's voice, but again it didn't come and in the end she edged her way back through to the kitchen and looked around at the remaining appliances. There must be people up and down Hope Street who would love these, who would make daily use of them instead of leaving them festering like kids stuck in cots in foreign orphanages. Maureen in the first corner shop was always moaning that her kettle was on the blink and here were three of the things sat in Ruth's kitchen. Perhaps she'd take her one on Sunday. Would she think it was weird? Did it matter?

Ruth felt giddy with the thought of it. For months now she'd hidden from other people, afraid of their scorn. What sort of mother couldn't even keep her own child alive, they'd say, and they'd be right. Perhaps that, in the end, was what she was actually afraid of – not their condemnation but their confirmation of her own. Maybe, after all, it was best just to stay out of the way.

Ruth went to the window to look out on to the bustle of Hope Street. As usual, she focused resolutely left, away from Tony's store, though it lurked in the corner of her eye wherever she stood and whatever she looked at. Rush hour was over now and the traffic was calming down. Across the road, a taxi pulled up and three girls in tiny dresses came spilling out of a house and tumbled into it, giggling. Ruth watched their pretty heads bobbing about in the back window as they headed off into town with no idea that life was about anything more than having fun. Lucky them.

The euphoria of her gift-giving was leaking out of Ruth fast.

'Libby died,' she whispered, the words slipping around on returning tears, but now something else caught her eye.

It was Charlie. He was still there on Hope Street, stood stock-still outside number 95, staring into the window as if frozen in place. It was a house Ruth had noticed before. Its front door was shiny, its drive immaculate and its lawn lined with an array of pretty flowers. Old-fashioned yellow light was spilling out of the window on to the perfect paving slabs and Charlie was leaning towards it, as if it was pulling him in. But then a shadow crossed the window and he jumped back, leapt on his bike and was off, wobbling precariously away into the darkness.

For a moment, Ruth was struck again with painful maternal tenderness, but then someone pulled thick curtains across the light at number 95 and she pressed a hand crossly to her heart and turned away. Her own kitchen looked even more chaotic than usual but at least somewhere in here was her vodka. She crossed to the toaster, stepping on something as she went – a piece of jigsaw. Damn. She lifted it up to see a worm staring at her from beneath a peony petal.

'Ah well,' she told it, putting it carefully into the tray of a vegetable steamer. 'He'll be back next week. Charlie will be back next week.'

WEEK THREE

WEEK THREE

Chapter Twelve

Charlie hated waking up before dawn. He lay in bed in the darkness playing time games in his head. Best scenario, it was about 3 a.m. – the sort of time he might be able to convince his brain to give up again. Worst scenario, it was about 4.30 – close enough to morning for his brain to refuse sleep but not far enough into the night to have had sufficient. He reached for the clock: 4.32. Brilliant!

Charlie was all too familiar with the dark crevices of the night these days. He hadn't been when he was younger. Even after bitter rows with his parents, his head had used to hit the pillow and check out almost instantly until the alarm for school drove itself fiercely into his sleep. Ever since things had gone wrong, though, his brain had refused to let go for more than a few hours at a time. It was doubt – creeping, insidious, nagging doubt.

As a kid he'd been so certain that he was on the right path that even his family's derision hadn't bothered him. In his early twenties, as he'd pushed on down that path despite their furious opposition, he'd been cushioned by his own sense of certainty, but not now. Now he questioned everything he'd considered so clear and interrogated his own choices again and again. His poor brain scratched its way through every night in a creeping, burning rash of 'if onlys'.

Tonight, though, tonight was different. Because tonight his mind was filled less with his own poorly constructed past and more with a single image – an image he'd seen last Friday night, that had been waking him up ever since. It was an image of Vik Varma sat at his too-big pine table, laid with red and gold mats on which stood all sorts of shiny pots of curry and rice. Fluffy naans had sat in a little basket and chutneys on a raised stand. It had looked beautiful but it wasn't the meal that had caught in Charlie's tortured brain. Oh no, it was Vik himself.

He'd been sat behind the biggest pot, all on his own, with a fork in his hand which he'd been tapping slowly against the rim in a sharp, persistent chime. As Charlie had watched, he'd looked up to the old-fashioned clock on the wall then back to the food. He'd checked his phone and looked at the clock again. Then slowly he'd pushed himself to his feet, picked up a plate and spooned a little of each dish on to it, moving with studied care, until eventually he'd sunk back on to his seat and again picked up his fork.

Charlie had stood transfixed, willing Vik to eat, but the old man had just jabbed his fork into his food, pushing it around his plate until the pretty dishes were all churned into one big mush before, with sudden ferocity, he'd flung the fork at the wall. Charlie had ducked instinctively and then moved swiftly away, leaving Vik to the privacy of his own pain. The bitter taste of it had stuck so tight in his own gullet, however, that this morning, a whole week later, he could taste it still. He had to do something to help.

'No meddling!' he shouted into the darkness, scattering the phoenixes before they could beat their wings at him.

Oh, but they were such pretty wings.

As he'd hurried away that night, he'd passed the blue glow of the house opposite and pictured Greg sitting at his giant computer screen writing about his exotic travels for those who could only experience such joys vicariously. He'd taken to reading Greg's blog every day, drinking in the tales of his various adventures around the world. It was amazing to see what he'd achieved out of such adversity, to look at how he'd pulled himself out of the mire of an awful accident and got on. It gave Charlie hope, but the problem was that seeing inside his house, seeing beneath his glossy persona, had made it uncomfortably clear that Greg was not as sorted as he looked.

He was a man who raged, and no wonder. His scars looked stunning on the screen but up close they were skewed and raw and painful and they twisted Charlie's heart. And last Friday the space-age glow of Greg's windows had stood in stark contrast to the warm yellow of Vik's – moon to sun – and a glimmer of an idea had formed in his mind. He'd tried to outrace it on his bike but it had been very persistent. So persistent that it was still here at . . . He glanced at the clock again . . . 4.36 a.m.

'Go to sleep,' he instructed his brain, but it wasn't listening.

It was leaping around, thinking of connections and possibilities and plans and, in truth, he couldn't shut it up because he *wanted* to listen. It seemed such a shame that Greg and Vik were so close to each other and both so very much alone. If only they could meet . . .

'Go to sleep!'

If only someone could find a way to get them together . . .

'Go to bloody sleep!'

If only someone had access to them both . . .

'Oh, for frig's sake!'

Charlie threw back his covers and got up.

Four hours later, Charlie skidded round the corner towards the Turner's depot and almost collided with the first of the purple vans heading off on their runs. He groaned. How had he managed this? How had he been up in the middle of the night and still made it to work late? It was doubt again, messing with him. He'd been up and down to his flat three times on his supposed way out – first to fetch his bike lights in case he was late home again, then to grab his waterproof because it looked like rain, and finally because Mr Graham had been in the hallway and he hadn't been able to face him.

He'd had a peak at the wretched man's seedlings on his day off and they'd looked fine but no doubt they were stunted or something. What on earth he was growing in October Charlie had no idea. Perhaps it was weed. The thought of prim Mr Graham growing his own drugs had been momentarily diverting, but now it had made him late. Sean would be furious.

Sure enough, the team leader was stood over the bike racks as Charlie skidded to a halt beside them. Bri was already in her van and gave him a supportive wave as she drove off, but Ryan was lurking, looking as smug as if he'd landed tickets to the FA Cup Final.

'Sorry, Sean.' Charlie flung his bike into the rack. 'Hit an awful hold-up.'

'On a bike?'

'Police were being very careful.'

'I see. Where was this, Charlie?'

'Near my place.'

'Which is?'

Charlie swallowed. Sean knew exactly where he lived – he had his HR records. 'Hazel Avenue.'

'Hmm. You see, the thing is, Charlie, that as team leader for all the Turner's deliveries in this area it's my job to monitor the roads. I have Google Maps running at all times ready to divert potential delivery disasters.'

Charlie fiddled with the strap of his bike helmet. Sean could join Ryan in his on-the-road coming-of-age movie. Armed with half a ton of other people's groceries, a clipboard and the Google Maps app, they'd be invincible.

'Charlie! Are you listening to me? You slept in, didn't you?'

'No, I . . .'

'Didn't you?'

Charlie sighed. 'Yes, Sean.'

'I knew it.' Sean tucked his thumbs into the top of his shiny trousers and rocked back on the heels of his brogues. Charlie glanced at his watch. He was only fifteen minutes off schedule, but Sean had clearly been looking for an excuse to have a go and he braced himself as his boss jabbed a finger into his face. 'I've got my eye on you, Charlie Sparrow. Don't think you can dick around on my watch. Don't think you're entitled to any bloody privileges just because you're Sue's little pet.'

'I don't, I—'

'I don't know what makes you so special, Charlie boy . . .'

'Nothing. Really.'

'. . . but it won't help you one bit if you violate procedures and the first one of those, the very first one, is good timekeeping.'

'I know. I'm sorry. It won't happen again.'

'Too right it won't. Consider this a verbal warning. The next level is a written warning and the third level . . .' A slow smile crept over his face. 'The third level is out. And nothing Management-Sue can say will help you then.'

'Of course not. I told you, I'm sorry.' Charlie hooked his helmet over his handlebars. 'Can I get on now? It's just that I don't want to be any later for the customers.'

'You better not be,' Sean shot back, still standing in his way. 'How many minutes per house?'

'Four, Sean.'

'Too right. Now, what are you still hanging about here for? Scram!'

He shoved the paperwork at Charlie and finally stood aside. Charlie dashed for the vans, trying to still his pathetically beating heart. Sean was a knob, he told himself, so why on earth did he care what he thought? But the problem was that Sean was a knob with power. Charlie needed this job. He needed it for his sanity and he needed it to make amends. He glanced down at the list and saw, to his relief, the vital name there again, alongside the two other residents of Hope Street who were fast becoming tangled in his consciousness.

'In trouble already, hey, new boy?' Ryan said as he sauntered past. 'What a pity.'

Charlie gripped his paperwork tighter and forced himself not to respond. Today wasn't about Sean or Ryan. Today was about his customers and he had a plan to get Greg and Vik together. It wasn't a very clever plan but it was worth a shot and it certainly wasn't worth messing up for a pathetic argument with his fellow driver.

'Don't let the bastards get you down, hey Charlie?'

Charlie felt a pat on his back and turned to see Jack. The older man threw him a wink and Charlie relaxed a little.

'I won't. Thanks, Jack.'

'There's no biggies today so you'll soon catch up.'

'The design studio not ordered?'

'Barely. Don't know what's up with them – only a single crate of Prosecco.'

'Slackers.'

The side was still up and Charlie peered into the orderly racks of baskets. Clearly marked alongside the rest were numbers 95, 112 and 80: Varma, Madison and Sutton. He looked around as Jack headed back to the warehouse, but Ryan was driving off and Sean was out of sight, presumably glued to Google Maps in his nice warm office. Hastily, he pulled out number 80's baskets, rifled inside until he found the green bag he was looking for and transferred it in one swift movement into one of number 95's. Job done!

Heart beating even more wildly than before, Charlie slammed down the shutter and made for the cab before he could change his mind.

Chapter Thirteen

Number 95 Hope Street:

Kidney beans, 2 cans
Dried fenugreek
Garlic, 1 bulb
Ginger
Green chillies
Mango powder
Chicken thighs
Tomatoes
Paneer cheese
Bell peppers
Double cream
Spaghetti hoops x2
Cheerios
Milk

'Morning, Charlie. Come in, come in.' Vik tried not to gush but he felt ridiculously excited to talk to someone other than Rickets, who'd been surlier than usual this week. 'Here, let me clear a space for you. I hope you've got my kidney beans. I'm trying a new recipe today – rajma masala. Well, it's not a new recipe, actually. It's a very old one. Nika used to make it for us when we were first married. I found a copy in her cooking file the other day and thought I'd try it.'

He was gabbling again, he knew he was, but Charlie wouldn't be here long and there seemed to be a lot of words inside him fighting to get out.

'Sounds great, Vik,' Charlie said, setting the baskets down on the table.

'I doubt I'll do it as well as she did but I can give it a go, right? And Sai will like it, I'm sure.'

Charlie smiled reassuringly. 'Don't worry, Vik, there's no subs this week so it should all be there.'

Vik dived into the basket and started unloading, searching for the beans. He didn't really know why he was bothering. He'd had a text from Sai yesterday saying: *Ballet Show preps hotting up. You'd never believe little kids could take so much effort.* It had had that jocular, isn't-parenting-hard tone that seemed to be obligatory these days and while Sai hadn't actually followed it up with *So I can't come over on Friday,* Vik presumed that was the subtext. Even so, imagine if he did turn up with Hermione and Aleesha and Vik hadn't cooked. Nika would be shaking the skies with fury.

Keep cooking, Vikram, and he'll come.

That's what she'd promised and it was what Vik was holding on to.

'Did your son enjoy last week's curries?'

Vik froze, his hand curled around the can of beans. He didn't enjoy lying, but he enjoyed looking like a friendless old git even less.

'He did, thank you,' he said, with only a small cough. 'Very much.'

Something flickered across Charlie's eyes and for a moment Vik wondered if the young man had somehow guessed that he'd been stood up by his family, but how on earth would he do that? He was a delivery driver not a psychic.

'Sai's doing very well in life,' he said as he set the beans down and carried on unloading.

'Your son?'

'Yes.'

'That's good. What does he do?'

'Business. I'm not sure exactly what. He seems to get promoted so often that I lose track.'

'Very good,' Charlie said absently. He'd taken a green bag out of the basket and seemed to be looking around for somewhere to put it. 'You must be proud.'

'Proud?' Vik turned back. 'Oh yes. It's what we wanted for him, Nika and I – a good, solid career. Security, you know?' Charlie nodded, though he seemed to be looking more under Vik's table than in his actual direction. 'It's important,' he pushed on. 'Sai used to complain so much about doing his homework but Nika would stand over him until it was finished and it paid off. No one needs a high score on a computer game. Exam results, that's what they need. A degree. A pathway. Education is so important, don't you think?'

'Erm, yes, of course.' Charlie had put the bag down somewhere. Vik looked round for it but already the lad was reaching for the baskets. 'All done here?'

Vik tried not to hear him. 'Sai's going to send his daughter Aleesha to private school. He has a trust fund set up already.'

'That's nice.'

'Isn't it? We'd have sent Sai to a private school but we couldn't afford it. It's very expensive.'

'So I've heard.'

Charlie was shifting from one foot to the other and casting surreptitious glances around the kitchen.

Vik's stubborn streak kicked in and he leaned on the basket edge. 'You didn't go? No. No, I suppose not. Well, we got Sai into grammar school and we made sure he worked. We gave him that and it paid off. Very proud we were when he got into university. Leeds. It's a good one. Russell Group.'

'I know,' Charlie said.

'Do you? Sorry. No reason why you shouldn't.' The lad coloured and Vik looked at him curiously. 'Did you go to university then, Charlie?'

'I did, actually. Wasn't much use to me, though. What about Sai? What did he study?'

'Economics. I suggested accountancy, like me. I wanted him to follow me into my firm but he . . . he had bigger ideas.'

111

'People have to choose their own path,' Charlie said with a funny strangled noise and then he made a grab for the baskets and headed for the door. Already Vik missed him.

'He was so grown-up suddenly,' he burst out, following him. 'It was like one minute he was skipping down the road to nursery holding my hand and the next he was a man with his own ideas about his life. And quite right. Ambition, that's what you want in this world, isn't it?' He looked at Charlie in his purple fleece and felt suddenly crass. 'Well, that and finding something that makes you, erm, happy.'

He wanted to snatch back the words the minute he'd spoken them – it didn't look as if delivering groceries made Charlie 'happy' any more than a fancy office job would. He attempted a weak smile but Charlie just shrugged.

'I'm doing this job because . . . Well, it doesn't matter why but it won't be for ever. I've got plans.'

Vik beamed. 'That's good. That's very good. You seem a very nice young man.'

Charlie looked as if he might cry at that. What had Vik done wrong? He'd only been trying to help and he *did* seem like a nice young man. Was that not something people said any more? Nika would know. Nika would know exactly what to say to young Charlie, but Nika wasn't here so it was left to Vik to bumble around putting his clumsy feet in it with the few poor sods who tried to be friendly.

'I didn't mean to offend,' he said desperately.

He saw Charlie take a deep breath, then he set the baskets carefully down on the floor and took Vik's hand between his two young, strong ones.

'You didn't offend, Vik. Really. Now, enjoy your cooking and I hope you have a lovely meal tonight. I'm sure you will.'

He gave Vik's hand a warm squeeze and then he grabbed his baskets again and was gone. Vik stared after him, feeling rather as if it might be him that cried now. Why on earth was Charlie so sure he'd have a lovely meal tonight when Vik was almost 100 per cent certain that he would not? Perhaps, he thought ruefully as he tore himself away from the door, he should stop farting around with old family recipes and start making dandelion-leaf curry – at least Rickets would like it.

He shuffled back into the kitchen and was heading half-heartedly towards the stove when his eye was caught by the green bag Charlie had been messing around with. He'd put it on the floor for some reason. As if Vik's back wasn't bad enough without poorly placed groceries! Grunting to himself, he leaned on the table and bent to pick it up. It was heavier than he'd expected and swung against the table leg with a sharp clang. What on earth was in it?

Hefting it on to the table, Vik pulled back the plastic and stared in astonishment at the bottle of red wine he'd revealed. The label was a jaunty orange and showed some sort of kangaroo-type creature staring at Vik in a most disconcerting way.

'What do you want?' he demanded of it then, coming to his senses, he snatched the bottle up and ran back to the door. 'Charlie!' he called. 'Charlie, this isn't mine!'

But the Turner's van was already halfway down Hope Street and there was nothing left to do but to carry the strange bottle back into his kitchen.

Chapter Fourteen

Number 112 Hope Street:

Value wholemeal bread
Baked beans, 4 cans
Value ready salted crisps, 6-pack
Bacon bits
Pasta
Value pasta sauce
Value sausages
White rolls
Ketchup
Lemons, 3
Vodka, 1ltr
Tonic, 2x 1ltr
Paracetamol x2

Steady now. Ruth bit her tongue and slowly, carefully, poured the precious remaining liquid from Sanjeed's red-labelled bottle into the purple-edged Turner's one. Stupid, really, but she didn't want Charlie noticing her extra purchase. Not that it stopped her from knowing how much she drank herself, but she was better at ignoring it than others might be. And she'd stop soon. Really, she would.

Yesterday, she'd actually managed to open her uniform drawer. She'd looked down at the smart blue combat trousers and almost put them on, but the cheery yellow polo shirts had been too much for her and she'd run away from their efficiency. She had, however, forced herself to ring Hayley, her second-in-command,

and tell her she'd be back soon. Hayley had been delighted and asked when, but dates had stuck in Ruth's throat and she'd had to pretend someone was at the door.

Carefully, Ruth screwed the lid back on to the Turner's bottle, forcing herself to resist the sharp, clean pull of the fumes, and took Sanjeed's empty one outside. She glanced at the clock: 10.15. At least this Friday she was up and about, but her delivery wasn't scheduled until the 12-to-1 slot and she wished she was back in bed. When she was asleep, the darkness felt right, even when the big blue eyes came.

Ruth shivered. What to do now? Her eyes were pulled to the deep-fat fryer. It was just a small one – a silver cube, nicely neat, save for a coating of yellow grease. Was it any wonder it had given up working, poor thing? She pulled it to the front of the work surface, edging two kettles aside to make space. The third one, she thought with a little smile, was now bubbling brightly away in the little kitchen behind Maureen's shop.

Hours it had taken her to pluck up the courage to give it to the shopkeeper when she'd gone in for her vodka on Sunday. She'd been too worked up even to have a drink and had nearly postponed the trip until Monday, but Sunday was Maureen's day and in the end the thought of breaking her routine had been more upsetting than the thought of taking the kettle. And thank heavens. Maureen had beamed so hard when Ruth had presented it to her that her whole face had seemed to stretch outwards.

'Oh, you dear,' she'd said, over and over. 'Oh, you absolute lamb.'

And then she'd hugged Ruth right there, in the middle of the shop, and insisted she stay for a brew. And when she'd seen the water light up blue and then yellow and then red, she'd laughed and laughed and called her a dear and a lamb all over again. Ruth hadn't known where to put herself but it had been nice all the same.

She glanced to the understairs cupboard where she kept her toolbox. There was a palette knife in there perfect for scraping off this grease but if she got that out all the other tools would clamour to see daylight as well and she couldn't quite face that. She tried scraping at it with her nails but it was sticky and resistant and clung to her skin. Why was she bothering anyway? Why would Tony want a knackered old fryer from her? He probably sold them in his shop so he could get himself a shiny new one at cost and without having to talk to her. He'd much prefer that.

Sod Tony. She pushed the fryer away. Sanjeed had grandchildren, didn't he? He was always going on about them, always trying to show her photos of them on his phone when she went in on Wednesdays. She hated the flashes of plump, happy young faces but that wasn't their fault, poor kids. Maybe there'd be something at the tip that she could fix up for them. Frank would know.

Ruth let herself out of the front door before she could change her mind and turned automatically right. She spotted the unmistakeable purple of a Turner's van sitting at the lights further down Hope Street and glanced at her watch, worried she'd got the time wrong, but it was definitely only 10.30 and when she risked a look back again it was heading off towards the marketplace. Towards Tony.

What, she wondered, did her ex order to his bachelor pad above the shop? Ready meals for one. Or two? Jealousy bit, twisting hard in her gut, and she snapped her teeth at it. An old couple passing by hand in hand leaped sideways and for a moment she hated herself. Or, rather, for a moment she hated herself even more than usual. Putting her head down, she strode out past Maureen's, past Sanjeed's, past the gym and the nursery and the run-down warehouses and finally turned into the tip. And relaxed.

All was order here. Cars were parked obediently in two rows of strong white lines and people were diligently sorting items and taking them up the clearly marked ramps: cardboard, garden waste, metal. If only life was so easily compartmentalised – work, romance, motherhood. If you could do them all one at a time they'd be a doddle. It was when they got jumbled together that things went tits up.

'Ruth!' Frank came leaping over and shook her hand. 'Great to see you.'

'Is it?'

He laughed. 'Of course it is. Oh, I've got some treasures for you today. Come and see.'

He still had hold of her hand and she looked curiously at her old fingers in his young ones as he tugged her across to the electrical goods area. There, he reverently lifted up a tarpaulin to reveal several items.

Ruth took a step forward. 'Is that an electric scooter?'

'Certainly is. At least, it's a non-electrical scooter at the moment but I bet you can sort that out.'

He was looking so trustingly at her that Ruth had to laugh. 'What makes you so sure?'

Frank shrugged. 'You look clever like that.'

'I do?' Ruth was stunned. 'Er, thanks. And thanks for saving these for me.'

'No problem. I hate seeing things go to waste. Obviously.' He put out a hand to indicate the whole recycling unit and Ruth smiled.

'You like your job then, Frank?'

The lad grimaced. 'It's OK sometimes, but it's not like I want to do it for ever.'

'No?'

'No way. I'm going to college as soon as I can afford it. Wanna be a nurse, don't I?'

'Do you?'

'Yeah. You can, you know. I mean, boys do.'

'Of course they do,' Ruth agreed hurriedly. 'It's a wonderful profession. Really. I'm very impressed.'

'Yeah, well, don't be. Not yet. I need to save loads so I can afford to do it full-time and it's slow-going.'

'I bet.'

'I live with my nan so I don't have to pay rent, like. That helps loads. And she can't, like, get about much so I mainly have to stay in and look after her. That helps too. Who needs to piss their money away in pubs, right?'

'Right,' Ruth agreed guiltily.

This lad was, what, twenty, and he had twice her self-control. Three times. Here he was working away at the tip every day and looking after his nan every night and she was just sitting around on a pile of mortgage demands, swigging vodka and doing jigsaws and mending machines she couldn't even be bothered to sell.

'That's great, Frank,' she said, but he'd already turned away to pull the other items forward. Ruth looked down at them. Next to the scooter was a cylinder vacuum cleaner and a foot spa. 'More treasures. Thank you. Only, how am I going to get them home?'

She should have come in the van but it was such a bloody cheery yellow and the Sparkly Sparkies logo on the side was so silvery and, well, sparkly. Besides, she hadn't been in it since that last terrible holiday. It was rusting away at home, just like her. Frank, however, wasn't fazed.

'I've thought of that!'

He ducked behind a big wire basket full of car batteries and re-emerged with a pram. Ruth gasped. It was the exact same model she and Tony had bought for Libby thirteen years ago. She could almost see her baby girl lying in it, little legs kicking beneath the blanket Ruth had lovingly crocheted when she was pregnant. In truth, she'd been rubbish at crocheting and the stitches had started unravelling within days, but Libby had loved to stick her little fingers through the holes.

'Ruth?' Frank's voice brought her back to the tip. 'Is it OK? It's a bit torn at the edges, like, but the wheels work. I checked.'

'It's great, Frank. Perfect. Thanks.'

She watched numbly as the lad laid the hoover and the scooter in the pram like weird, futuristic babies and sat the foot spa jauntily on top.

'There we go. All yours.'

'Just needs a blanket.'

'A blanket?'

'Never mind. Thank you, Frank.'

'All part of the job!'

He gave her a funny little salute and headed off across the tip to help an older lady with a mattress. Ruth watched him swing it up over his head and bounce up the ramp to the textiles skip, then shook herself and made for the exit, pushing her pramful of electrical goodies before her and fighting to ignore how painfully familiar it felt.

She was past her door almost before she realised it. Perhaps it was the pram. How many times had she walked Libby up the road to see Tony? How many times had she pushed her into the shop, humping the wheels over the sill, watching her baby girl laugh as the big bell jangled above her, seeing her little nose twitch at the unmistakeable smell of tangled metal, compost and paint. How many times had Tony come rushing over to meet them? *Where's my angel, then?* Libby had always been his angel, right from the moment he'd lifted her, red, greasy and screaming, into his big arms just minutes after she'd been born.

'My angel,' he'd said and she'd stopped screaming and looked at him with her tiny blue eyes and given a funny little gurgle. He'd have called her Angela, Ruth had always teased him, if it hadn't been so very eighties, but he'd said no, Angel was his own special name for her.

Ruth looked down at the tangle of broken machinery in the pram and saw, startlingly clearly, the great chasm between then and now. Was this, then, the pit that so often threatened to swallow her? Was this the darkness that those same eyes so often rose out of, older and deeper but still every bit as blue? Was it carved out by the unbearable gap between how her life once was and what it had now become? And if so, should she just step into it, accept it, let it take her?

The shop bell jangled as if calling to her straight from the past. She edged towards it, head low over her monstrous babies, wishing she had, after all, found a blanket to cover them. What if Tony looked out and saw her? She should turn around, go home, never come this bloody way up Hope Street again, but the bell rang for a second time, exerting a pull stronger, even, than vodka and she edged forward until she was level with the wire shelves outside the door. She leaned into them as if she might blend with the buckets and the plant pots and the handy storage tubs on display and looked through a small section of glass like a man at a peep show.

And there he was – Tony, her husband. Or, rather, the living memory of her husband. But, oh, for a memory he was so big, so solid. That's what Ruth had always liked about him. At a broad-shouldered six foot three, when he'd wrapped his arms around her at the end of their first date, she'd known that she'd found her place in the world. She'd known it deep in her gut, in her bones, in the very blood cells running through her veins.

So how, then, could she have forgotten?

Her body, it seemed, hadn't forgotten at all. Beneath her baggy leggings and oversized hoodie her skin was tingling as she watched Tony lift light bulbs down from the shelves behind him and patiently show them to his customer one by one. When he smiled, she leaned so far in towards him that she toppled against the buckets and set them rattling. He looked up and she cowered away, but he turned back to his customer without spotting her.

A tiny smile snuck on to her lips. How often had she fretted about this outdoor display? How often had she told him that someone could so easily steal from it? And how often had he simply said, 'So let them, sweetheart'? Buckets, he'd argued, cost very little compared to how blank the shop would look without them. And maybe, if it was a good bucket, they'd come back and actually buy something the next time. That had been Tony – ever the optimist. Until Libby.

Even Tony hadn't been able to find a positive spin on losing Libby and without that they'd soon fallen apart. Maybe throughout their marriage she'd just been riding on his warmth and positivity. Was it any wonder then, that in the end she'd ground him down?

The customer was leaving now, light bulb in hand. Ruth saw Tony wave, smile again, and a rush of anger surged up from nowhere. It seemed that he'd got his positivity back pretty quickly. It seemed that his world was bright again. He'd moved on, put Libby behind him, put Ruth behind him. She clutched the pram handle tighter as the man came out of the shop and he glanced at her and hurried away.

Above her, the clouds were clearing and the sudden light on the glass obscured the man inside, mercilessly casting up her own reflection instead. She was a wreck, a freak, an alcoholic bag lady with a broken scooter cradled in a pram. She scrambled back and knocked several long-handled brushes over, but she couldn't stop to pick them up. She had to get away. What a fool she'd been, blinded by pictures of a lost past from the stark, vicious view of the present.

Behind her, she heard the bell clang as Tony came out to pick up his wares and she broke into a half run. The wheels of the torn pram bumped against the cracks in the pavement, making the scooter inside it leap about in front of her. *Mummy!* her aberration of a baby protested on a high wail, but she just ran faster until finally she skidded into her own dump of a drive, her heart thumping and her breath coming in rough pants. God, she needed a drink.

She made for the door, but before she could even fumble for her key a jaunty purple van pulled up behind her. Christ – Charlie! Was it that late already? Ruth gave a half wave over her shoulder, rammed her key into the lock and tumbled inside, leaving the pram on the drive. She leaned against the wall, drawing in breath and trying desperately to compose herself.

'Ruth?'

'Hi, Charlie, come on in. Sorry, bit out of breath. I rushed back.'

'Thanks.'

He sounded distracted and when Ruth peeled herself off the wall to go to the door he was standing there, staring down the road towards the flower-lined house again.

'You OK?' she asked.

'What? God, yes. Sorry. I was just wondering . . . Oh, never mind. Let's get your stuff inside.'

He surged forward, squeezing past her and making for the kitchen. She trailed after him and peered into the basket as he edged it on to the table.

'No jigsaw?'

He jumped. 'Er no. Sorry. I was in a bit of a rush this morning. Damn. Sorry.'

He looked terribly upset.

'It's OK,' she said, smoothing her disappointment. 'You're a grocery driver, Charlie, not a jigsaw library. And it was a stupid idea anyway.'

'No, it wasn't. I did mean to bring one. I just . . .'

'Forget it. Please. I've got new machines to mend so I'll be far too busy for jigsaws.'

'Right.' He glanced to the door. 'Is that them in the, er . . .'

'Pram? Yes.'

'Right. Good.' He stood there a minute then asked, 'Shall I help you unload?'

He seemed nervy today. He glanced through the window to the van beyond and his hands twitched at the side of the basket.

'Are you running late, Charlie?'

'Late? Oh no. No, for once I'm on time. But, you know, Friday traffic . . .'

Ruth started unloading, deliberately slow. Charlie seemed eager to get away and she didn't like it. He might only have four minutes for her but she wanted every last second of them.

'I thought Fridays weren't so bad these days? That's what I'd heard. Everyone who can works from home, don't they?'

'I guess. I don't know. I haven't been doing this long.'

'Of course not. What did you do before, Charlie?'

'Do?'

'Before, yes.'

'Oh, this and that. Odd jobs.'

'Like?'

'Does it matter?' He fired the words at her and she recoiled.

'No. I, I . . .'

She felt a ridiculous urge to cry and delved hastily into the basket, but already Charlie was falling over himself to apologise.

'God, I'm sorry. That came out all wrong. I shouldn't have snapped, Ruth. I . . .'

'It's fine, Charlie. Really.'

The tears subsided and she put a hand on his arm. It was surprisingly strong, surprisingly nice. Human touch, it seemed, *was* nice and she'd had something of a rush of it recently. First Maureen hugging her and then Frank shaking her hand and now this. Before that it must have been weeks. Months even. Perhaps the last time had been the day Tony had left, and that had been more of a shove than a hug.

Ruth shivered and withdrew her hand. 'You'd better get on.'

She grabbed the last of her shopping and wedged it on to the table, all bar the vodka bottle, which she held on to. It was too big to fit.

'It's OK,' Charlie said. 'I've only got to go across the road.'

Now he had the empty basket he seemed reluctant to leave.

'Oh? Where?'

'Number eighty.' He edged towards the door. Pointed. 'That one.'

'With the wheelchair ramp?'

'Yep.'

'An old person?'

He gave a harsh little laugh. 'Not old, no. But hopefully slow on the uptake.'

'What?'

'Nothing. Really. Don't listen to me today. I'm a mess.'

Ruth looked to the mutant pram still sat outside the door and pictured herself as she'd been reflected in Tony's glass – a madwoman with eyes as red and wild as the ends of her neglected hair.

'You and me both, Charlie. See you next week.'

He shoved the basket into the van and slammed the side shut. 'Sorry about the jigsaw.'

'No problem, I told you. I've got things to mend.'

She waved at the pram and then marched back inside as Charlie, thankfully, got into the van. But she couldn't resist creeping to the window to watch as he pulled out into the traffic, only to indicate almost immediately and turn into number 80. Ruth felt a strange flash of jealousy. Looking down at the vodka bottle still clutched tightly in her hand, she twisted off the lid.

Chapter Fifteen

Number 80 Hope Street:

Cup-a-Soup mixed pack
Ready-to-eat lasagne
Ready-to-eat chilli and rice
Ready-to-eat chicken tikka masala
Ham, family pack
Granary bread
Eggs, one dozen
Assorted cereal bars
Satsumas
Bio washing powder
Ibuprofen gel
Lager, 12-pack
Nail-tail Shiraz, 1 bottle

'If you could just move your legs apart a little, sir . . .'

Greg glared down at the tailor crouched before him. 'Do you know how hard that is for me?'

'Of course, sir. Sorry, sir. This is a new experience for me too.'

Greg looked to the double-height ceiling for patience. It wasn't the tailor's fault; he was only trying to do his job. Leaning heavily on his stick, he forced his squint leg a little to the left and closed his eyes as the man took a tape measure to his groin.

'Just a moment more, sir,' he assured him, his voice quavering, and Greg wasn't sure which of them was more relieved when the doorbell went.

'I'll get that, shall I?' the poor bloke said and he went scampering off, tape measure in hand, to open the door.

'Er, hi,' Greg heard Charlie's voice say. 'Groceries for Greg Sutton?'

Greg edged sideways and waved. 'Come in, Charlie.'

Charlie did so, looking curiously at Greg as he stood there in his boxers and a dark suit jacket covered in rough white stitching.

'My DJ didn't fit,' Greg offered by way of explanation.

'So you're having one made specially?'

'Apparently. I happened to mention on Twitter that because of the stupid twist in my spine my DJ was all out of line and the next thing I know some fancy suit-maker is DM-ing me. Then this morning Marcus here turns up.'

'Fantastic!' Charlie said.

Greg saw Marcus shoot him a grateful look and hated himself.

'You're right, Charlie, of course you are. I'm very lucky and Marcus has been great, especially considering what a miserable sod I've been about it.'

'Not at all, sir,' Marcus said smoothly.

Greg laughed. 'Oh I have, and I'm sorry. It's not your fault. It's just all so weird.' He turned to Charlie. 'I tell you, Charlie, I don't know how famous people spend any of their millions because as soon as you get any sort of name people seem to fall over themselves to give you stuff for free. All you have to do in return is drop their name into your tweets. Which reminds me.' He leaned over and offered Charlie his phone. 'Could you snap a few pics of me and Marcus here doing our fitting? I promised the company I'd post them.' He looked around. 'Maybe take them from over there so you get my lovely lift in the background?'

Charlie looked a little disconcerted but did as he'd asked. Marcus stuck pins between his lips and waved his tape measure around, Greg gave his patient smile – the most deceitful one of the lot – and Charlie snapped away.

'You're good at this,' he told Greg, and Greg didn't know whether to be pleased or ashamed.

He *was* good at it, that was one of the problems. He'd always been a bit of a poser. He'd never really had to fret about his height or his weight or even his skin, and both friends and girlfriends had come easily. The accident was, he supposed, the ultimate irony. That, or some sort of cosmic vengeance. Either way, it had divided his life into a blissful *before* and an angry *after*, with no bridge between.

'Higher!' Tia's voice squealed out of the past. 'Push me higher, Greg!'

He remembered how he'd grabbed the big log swing they'd found in the middle of the woods and pushed. She'd gone flying across the river in a whirl of flowery dress and flowing hair and when she'd come swinging back towards him, he'd reached up and grabbed the log seat with both hands so that they'd both shot through the air, she sitting on top, him dangling beneath. Back and forth they'd gone, her bare feet by his face, toes wiggling a glorious fuchsia pink. And she'd leaned forward to look down at him, her pretty face full of joy.

'You're mad,' she'd giggled.

'Mad for you, beautiful,' he'd called back and then he'd dropped into the water and she'd gasped and, with barely a moment's hesitation, dropped in after him. They'd stood in each other's arms, waist-deep in freezing water with the swing still rocking crazily above them, and life had been perfect. He'd been able to push her, able to hold on to her, able to catch her – just *able*. But, then again, it wasn't his accident that had cost him Tia, but his obsession with his work. Why had he done that? Why had he thought science and acclaim and money were worth anything near as much as holding a laughing girl in his arms? Fool.

'Wait till you see yourself in the finished DJ,' Marcus said, yanking him back into the present. 'It's going to be fabulous. Our sales will rocket.'

Greg raised a sardonic eyebrow at Charlie. 'An influencer, that's me. Next thing you know everyone will be leaping into winches to get a cool spine like mine.'

'Now, sir, I don't think anyone would be that—' Marcus shut himself up just in time.

'Shall I unload?' Charlie suggested.

'If you don't mind, mate, cheers.'

But now Marcus was backing off, saying something about cutting the trousers and making for the long table he'd set up to the side of the living area, leaving Greg free to join Charlie at the breakfast bar. Charlie looked curiously put out and began unloading at some speed.

'You're going to the awards ceremony then?' he asked.

Greg nodded. 'I made the mistake of replying to Holly and yesterday she sent me a picture of her new dress.'

He gestured to the fridge where a dark-skinned girl beamed out at him from a froth of pink tulle, similar to the Cinderella dress he remembered Rachel wearing as a child. Or perhaps that was just projection.

'Sweet,' Charlie said mildly, adding, 'I can unpack, Greg. You should rest while you can. It looks as if Marcus is going to be here for a while.' He pulled one of Greg's funky orange stools out from under the bar and nodded to it. 'Go on, take a load off and I'll handle this.'

'Really? Thanks.'

'No Icelandic stuff today?' Charlie asked, as he took out a stash of ready meals.

Greg shook his head, looking at the dull, plasticky dishes with shame. He hadn't felt like anything more exotic. North Face weren't budging on the photographer and Greg knew what it meant – photographs of him battling to get up, of him looking harrowed and unshaven, of him falling over in gutters and having to be helped up by strangers – the 'real' Greg, as they kept enthusing down the phone, but couldn't they see that the 'real' Greg was rubbish? It was only the crafted version that was worth any sort of attention.

'Bit tired this week with all the awards fuss and that,' he told Charlie. 'Couldn't really face cooking and certainly not anything fancy.'

'Don't blame you. It'd be nice to have someone to cook *for* you, hey?'

Greg looked curiously at the delivery driver, but Charlie was focusing hard on unloading the rest of his boring shopping so he just edged gratefully on to the stool. His leg was aching from the unaccustomed standing and he stretched it out in front of him, massaging the crooked knee.

'It looks very painful,' Charlie said.

Greg grunted. 'At least it's here. I nearly lost it all. They thought they were going to have to chop it off above the knee but the surgeon worked some sort of miracle.' He prodded at the strange knobble. 'Doesn't look much of a miracle, does it?'

Charlie shook his head. 'The whole thing must have been awful.'

'Not my finest day's work, certainly. One minute I'm winching up fishes and the next, great big metal teeth are snacking on my spine.'

Marcus stopped cutting and stared. Greg felt his shock like a glug of wine, strong and heady. He was being a git again, he knew, but he had no idea how to stop. He was like Jekyll and frigging Hyde and if he wasn't careful the whole world would find out. He had to keep a lid on his bitterness somehow. He had to wear his pretty suit and churn out his pretty blog phrases and hold Holly's pretty hand and get through this awards ceremony without anyone knowing the real him.

For a while no one spoke and then Charlie said, 'I'd better get going.'

Greg shook himself. 'Of course. You've got a job to do.'

Charlie held out his tablet for signing but Greg reached for the paperwork instead. 'Just checking, mate.'

'Oh. OK. I'm sure it's all here though.'

'Scientist's habit. Rigour, that's what they drum into you. Rigour and attention to detail.'

Lord, he missed that sometimes, he thought as he grabbed a pen and ticked off his goods. He pictured the test tube rack he'd kept on his lab bench on the ship – six separate tubes with a different-coloured pen in each, always in the same order. His workmates used to swap them round just to wind him up. Such blissfully petty concerns! But he'd been good at his job. And he'd loved it. Cared about it too. What did he care about these days – camera angles and Twitter followers? He was a joke.

'Er, Greg . . .' Charlie was fidgeting, and no wonder. Look at him stood like a moron locked into a lost past.

'Sorry. Won't be a minute.'

He forced the pictures away and pushed on down the list until he got to the Shiraz. God, he could do with a glass of that right now. He looked around. Charlie shifted the tablet from one hand to the other.

'Everything OK, Greg?'

'I'm missing my wine. Look.'

He showed Charlie the paper. Charlie peered at it.

'Odd.' He made a rather ostentatious check of the sleek breakfast bar, then said, 'I'll look in the van.'

He'd gone very red and dived clumsily outside, where Greg could hear him rummaging frantically in his van. He began steadily putting things away, trying not to look like a man who was desperate for a drink, but when Charlie returned his hands were empty.

'No wine for me, hey?' he asked, trying to keep his voice light.

'I'm sorry, Greg. It looks like there's been a bit of a mix-up.' Charlie was even pinker now and kept tugging at a lock of hair behind his ear. 'I've had a message from HQ and it seems your wine went to number ninety-five instead of number eighty. Sorry.'

'Number ninety-five Hope Street?'

'That's right. It's just down there.' Charlie pointed out the window as if the wine might even now be walking up the road to find him, but clearly it wasn't. 'I can get it back for you, of course, but it'll have to be later, if that's OK? I'm behind schedule already.'

'Oh. Right.' Greg forced a little laugh. 'That's OK. I mean, it's not like I'm going to drink wine right now, is it?'

He glanced to the tailor, who looked as if he might rather like a glass himself but said nothing.

'It'll be at the end of my shift,' Charlie said. 'Five-ish? A bit later, maybe.'

'Pain for you, mate.'

'It's fine. Company's fault and all that. The picker must have put it in the wrong basket.'

'Did you have plans?'

'Oh no. I . . .' He tugged at the lock of hair again. 'That is, nothing that can't wait a bit. Unless . . . I mean, you could pop down and get it yourself if you'd rather?'

'Pop down?'

'To number ninety-five, yes. If you wanted.'

Greg edged to the window. 'Which one is number ninety-five?'

Charlie pointed. 'That one straight down there, with the flowers. It's not far.'

'No,' Greg agreed, trying to keep his voice casual, trying not to scream. 'It's bloody miles with a leg like this and all your neighbours staring at you.' Charlie would think he was mad. Marcus too. He was an adventurer, after all, a man who'd trekked the world, a man who'd coined the 'inspirational' phrase, *don't let disability disable your life*. Fifty yards down his own street was hardly a problem for that sort of a man, was it?

He glanced to Marcus who was stood, scissors frozen mid-snip, looking at him curiously. All he needed was the damn tailor reporting back that he was a chicken in his own home. He'd never been chicken; never. As a kid he'd always been the first to leap on to the dodgy rope swing, the first to climb the secret wall, the first on to any passing craze. And OK, so he'd had his share of soakings and scrapes, but he'd had so much fun.

'I'll be back later, of course,' Charlie was saying. 'If you need me to. It's Turner's fault, after all. I just thought . . .'

'No, it's fine.'

'It is?' Charlie looked hopefully at him.

'Sure. Number ninety-five?'

Greg fixed on the flowers. They were lined up in a scientifically meticulous colour pattern.

'Vik's a really nice bloke,' Charlie was saying. 'Makes amazing curries. Better than this one, I bet.' He tapped the plastic ready-meal with its shiny picture of a generic tikka masala. 'You should go later on and I bet he'll offer you some.'

Greg looked at him askance. 'You're suggesting I gatecrash this Vik's dinner?'

'Worth a try.'

'Right.' Charlie was neon pink now. This whole thing was getting weirder by the minute. 'Well, I do love a curry.'

'Who doesn't?' Charlie stuck the tablet out again. 'Sign, please.'

'Sure.' Greg scrawled flamboyantly across the screen and looked out the window again. 'Number ninety-five?'

'That's it. Will you be all right?'

Greg stiffened. 'Of course I'll be all right. Why wouldn't I be? See you, Charlie.'

He forced himself to give a jaunty wave – back to jovial Mr Jekyll again – and carefully shut the door on the purple-fleeced driver.

'Not much of a service,' Marcus said, his eyes appraising Greg with care.

'It's no big deal,' Greg told him firmly. 'The fresh air will do me good.'

He just hoped that was true.

Five hours later and the sun was going down over number 95 Hope Street, setting the dahlias aglow with dusky colours and presumably lighting up Greg's bottle of wine. His one, carefully controlled bottle of wine. Damn.

He turned from the window and looked hopefully around the big room. There had to be a bottle in here somewhere, huddling in a cupboard or under the stairs. Except, of course, he didn't have any stairs, just a shiny glass elevator like in *Charlie and the* frigging *Chocolate Factory*.

Charlie! Honestly. Why hadn't he just asserted himself and told the delivery driver he'd have to come back? Why had he cared what he thought of him? Or the poncey tailor for that matter?

'Beer would be nice,' he tried, but it wasn't true. He'd got his heart set on his Shiraz and an ice-cold lager just wasn't the same.

He looked again at number 95 but it seemed awfully far down the road. Shifting his aching hip, he forced himself to lighten his grip on his stick. The white-knuckle look might work when trapped in a Thai jungle overnight by an impending tornado but it didn't really cut it in your own home. He was tired, that was the problem – tired and gagging for a glass of Shiraz. Marcus had been here for hours, cutting and pinning and stitching. It had been almost like the early days of physio a year and a half ago, with people urging him to stand for 'one more minute' or to 'take one more step', as if he wasn't already burning up with the effort of doing something even the most determined couch potato could manage without taking his hands out of the crisp bag.

When the tailor had gone, taking Greg's half-made DJ with him and promising to return with it 'pronto', he'd collapsed on to the sofa and gone straight to sleep. He'd woken an hour later, cold and dribbling and even more eager for a drink than he'd been when he'd scanned that shopping list and seen it was missing.

He was just being perverse, he told himself. It wasn't as if he had wine most nights and so what if it was Friday – it was only some hangover (or not) from his days as a normal human being that placed any significance on that. If you weren't in work it didn't matter what day of the week it was, did it? But something about the thought of all those other people out there pulling corks and cracking cans made it harder to sit with an orange juice and count yourself blessed that your left leg was only turned 180 bonkers degrees and not lopped off.

Right, that was it. He was getting even more bitter than usual and that wouldn't do. He needed a drink and some food and something silly on telly. He still had those Icelandic beers in the fridge – they'd have to do. And if they were any good, he'd get straight on to North Face and agree to their damn photographer coming along with him. The company might be just what he needed to get his arse in gear and it was only three weeks to the awards ceremony, so he could go once it was over.

His heart quivered as if it were already in the snow and he tutted at himself. He was being ridiculous. He'd seen pictures of Iceland on the internet and the place looked nothing like the Arctic circle. Or like India or Vietnam or Thailand. It would be a good choice. Different.

Greg made it to the fridge and grabbed a beer. Sinking on to a stool, he cracked it open and drank. It was very cold and tasted of . . . well, of very little, actually. He slammed it down so hard on the breakfast bar that it frothed up all over his shopping, still sat there waiting to be put away. He looked at the Icelandic beer fizzing across the pallid English ham and felt unhappily certain that this was some sort of obscure metaphor.

He needed wine.

The sun was almost behind number 95 when he got back to the window. The days were closing in fast so if he waited just a little longer it would be dark, which would at least hide his pathetic limp. Although, of course, it might just make him seem sinister, the tap-tap of his stick like Mr Hyde again. Not that he was in a Victorian novel, of course. He was a perfectly modern man, with a perfectly understandable disability, going to retrieve his well-deserved Friday-evening wine. There was nothing sinister about that at all.

What would all his blog readers say, he wondered, if they could see him now? The man who could trek through the Thai jungle being stumped by a five-minute stroll up his own street. Some adventurer he was!

He glanced at his watch and saw it was ten minutes to six. Six was a good time for wine, right? He'd go at six. On the dot. It would all be fine once he put one slightly twisted foot in front of the other. He just had to get going, that was the key.

On the other hand, orange juice was really very tasty. And so much better for you.

Chapter Sixteen

The bottle of wine was sitting in the middle of the table looking oddly at home. Vik and Nika had never been big drinkers. They'd have the odd beer or champagne at celebrations, or a glass of white if they were invited out for dinner, but they'd never been 'Ooh it's Friday, crack open a bottle' type of people and Vik certainly wasn't in the habit of drinking alone. Now, though, he could see the appeal. Something about the seductive curves of the bottle and the dark purple of the liquid within seemed to be calling to him.

It was one of those modern screw-tops. All he had to do was pick it up, twist and it would be there for the taking. It was Ribena for grown-ups and he'd always had rather a soft spot for Ribena. He reached out a hand and then snatched it back. The wine wasn't his. It belonged to some man down the street. He'd had a curious call from Charlie apologising profusely for the mix-up and saying someone called Greg would come and pick it up later. But when was later? It was dark already and he didn't want strangers knocking at his door in the dark. And, besides, Sai would be here any minute.

Vik picked up the wine. 'Who am I kidding? Sai's not coming.'

It sounded bleak said out loud and Vic glanced to the lounge door, wishing for possibly the millionth time since she'd died that Nika was sat in there chuckling over some bit of rubbish TV. The door sat slightly ajar and the sliver of darkness taunted him. He went over and yanked it shut. Nika couldn't be here, bless her, but Sai could if he wanted to; he just clearly didn't.

He'd sent Vik another text an hour ago: *Up to our eyes in tutus! Won't make it. Sorry*. The sorry had been tacked on the end – an afterthought, a platitude, a sting in the tail.

What a shame, Vik had texted back. But then he'd thought about it a bit more and realised it was less a shame than a downright lie. Aleesha was three. Any 'extra rehearsals' would never go on past six o'clock at the absolute latest. It was just an excuse.

He sighed. He and Sai had once been so close. The first time Aleesha had slotted her little hand into his, he could swear his skin had vibrated with the memory of Sai's touch. Every morning when his son had been small they'd walked to nursery together, hand in hand. When had that stopped? Had it been when teenage pride had kicked in, or had it, in fact, been much, much more recent?

Vik tightened his grip on the top of the bottle. This Greg wasn't coming, so he might as well drink his brash Australian wine and see what all the fuss was about. At least it would be something to do.

I'd love to come to Aleesha's ballet show, he'd texted to Sai. *When is it? Wednesday week? How do I get a ticket?*

There'd been a long phone silence, unusually long. Vik had gone into the garden to wait it out with Rickets. The tortoise was phenomenally patient and Vik had tried to learn by his example.

Eventually, a reply had come: *Hermione's checked and it's sold out. Sorry*. Again the sorry, but he wasn't, was he?

'They should have asked me if I wanted to go right at the start, shouldn't they?' Vik had asked Rickets. Rickets had gone on eating his leaf but had looked understanding all the same. 'They'd have asked Nika,' Vik had said.

He'd known, though, without Rickets giving him a sceptical tortoise look, that Nika would have been in there finding out about these things long before they got to the sold-out point. She'd have been at the ballet lessons, chatting to the other parents and finding out how it all worked. In fact, she'd have been on the damned committee *making* it all work. He couldn't do that. He'd never thought of himself as shy but it seemed that, without Nika, he was.

Sod it. Vik twisted. The seal broke with a satisfying click and a rich, fruity smell hit his nostrils – blackcurrant, like Ribena, but also pepper and maybe apricots and even a hint of cumin. It would go very nicely with a curry. He glanced back to tonight's offering simmering on the stove – chicken madras, a kadhai paneer and, of course, Nika's rajma masala. Maybe tonight he'd eat some, just to go with his wine. He went to the cupboard for a glass but as he reached one down there was a knock at the door.

Vik froze, glass in one hand, open bottle in the other, feeling like a kid caught shoplifting. Heart racing, he shoved the glass back in the cupboard and grabbed the wine lid. Another knock. He fumbled the lid and it bounced off the side of the bottle and fell to the floor. Shit!

'Just coming,' he called, super-cheery.

He bent down, searching under the table, but he couldn't see the lid anywhere. His back protested and he stood crossly up again. Sod it. He'd got nothing to apologise about. Turner's had left him wine and he'd opened it. So what?

He marched to the door and pulled it open, prepared to brazen it out with the strange wine-drinker, but the man on the doorstep took all the wind out of his sails. He was young, about Sai's age, and with the sort of dirty-blond locks that would have made Nika say 'phwoar' if he'd stepped on to the set of one of her beloved sitcoms. But it wasn't his face that caught Vik's attention. The man was leaning his twisted body heavily on a stick with the sort of tight grip that Vik recognised from bad days with his own dicky back and he felt instantly terrible for keeping him waiting.

'You've come for the wine?'

'Yes. I'm so sorry. A pain for you, I know.'

'Not at all, not at all. Come in, please.'

Vik stood as far back as he could, his heart aching as the lad limped inside with a charming smile of thanks. It was as if some cruel child had ripped the wings off a butterfly. Vik ducked quickly round him to pull out a chair, making sure the lounge door was still closed on the way past.

'Take a seat, please.'

'Thank you.' The man sank on to the pine chair with a groan of relief and looked at the topless wine bottle, still releasing its tantalising aroma into Vik's kitchen. 'It's open.'

Vik felt shame clog this throat. 'Sorry. I didn't think you were coming.'

The man nodded slowly. 'Fair enough. Smells good.'

'Yes.'

'Could I, er, have a glass then?'

'God, yes. Of course.'

Vik opened the cupboard and took down the glass he'd hastily stuffed back in there a moment before.

'You'll join me?'

'I will? I mean, are you sure?'

'Of course I'm sure. It's your house.'

'And your wine.'

He gave a shrug. 'Wine is always better shared. Sorry, we haven't been introduced. I'm Greg.'

'Vikram — Vik.' Vik set two glasses on the table and took Greg's proffered hand. His grip was warm and firm. 'I'll pour, shall I?'

'Please.'

It was a beautiful sound — a sort of throaty gulp and then a slow glug like a guttural sigh of satisfaction. Vik sat down opposite Greg and raised his glass.

'Cheers.'

'Cheers.'

They clinked and drank as if it was something they did regularly. Vik supposed that was the value of rituals — they settled you, made you feel a part of something even when you weren't. Or maybe the ritual *was* the something.

Greg looked to the stove. 'Oh God, you're expecting people. I'll drink this up and get out of your hair.'

'No rush. They won't be here for ages.' They both drank. 'So, you live down the road?'

'Yep. Number eighty. Guess the deliveries got mixed up.'

'Apparently. The driver – Charlie – called me. Very apologetic, he was.'

'He's a nice lad.'

The choice of word made Vik smile. Surely Charlie was a similar age to Greg? But maybe whatever had happened to the poor man had aged him.

'Are you hungry?' he asked.

'Sorry?'

'Are you hungry, Greg? I've got loads of food.'

'Oh, I couldn't.'

'It'd be doing me a favour really. I don't think my son can make it now so it'll all go to waste if no one eats it.'

'That would be a shame,' Greg said cautiously.

'Yes. I've tried a new one today too – my wife's recipe. She was a very good cook, my wife.'

'She died?'

He liked the simple way Greg said it.

'Yes. Just over a year ago. Cancer.'

He left off the miss-her-every-day bit. Mawkish.

'You must miss her.'

'I do. Every day. Damn!'

'Damn?'

'I didn't mean to say that. It's so self-pitying.'

Greg gave a rough laugh. 'And God forbid we should pity ourselves, hey?'

Vik drank more of his wine. It was really very nice.

'You look to have had it tough yourself, Greg?'

'This?' The young man waved dismissively in the general direction of his twisted spine. 'It's not great but these things happen.'

'Not to most people.'

'No.'

A pause. Vik set his glass down. 'Curry then?'

'Great!'

Vik took his time serving. He got out the mats and the runner. He found his best dishes and nicest serving spoons. Greg offered to help but he waved him away.

'Thanks, but I like doing it.' He dished up with care – rice in the middle, curries round the edge. He didn't go as far as putting the rice in a fancy mould like on that *MasterChef* programme Nika had loved, but it looked pretty smart all the same. 'Dig in.'

'Fantastic.' Greg dug. He tried all the dishes with gratifying eagerness and Vik sat watching until he looked up again. 'These are amazing, Vik. I don't know about your wife but you, mate, are definitely a great cook.'

'Glad you like it.'

Vik felt himself blush like a schoolgirl (was he allowed to say that any more?). Hastily, he forked paneer into his mouth. It *was* quite tasty actually; he really should eat his own food more often.

'You know, I've been to India and I tasted nothing as good as this.'

'Recently?' Vik asked, surprised.

'At the start of the year.' The words were as fierce as Greg's stare as he added, 'It's possible, you know.'

'I'm sure it is. Of course. It's just . . .' He remembered the white pain he'd seen in Greg on his doorstep. 'It must be tricky.'

Greg shrugged. 'The things worth having are worth fighting for.'

'I suppose so. Do you have someone to travel with?'

'A girlfriend, you mean?' Greg's words were as chilli-laced as the madras.

'Or just a friend?' Vik said hastily.

'Neither. I travel alone. I prefer it that way.'

'Right.'

Vik drank the last of his wine and Greg gave an audible sigh.

'If you must know, I had a girlfriend, quite a serious one, but she dumped me.'

'Because of your accident?'

'No! Rather the other way round.'

Vik's eyes widened. 'This girl did that to you?'

Greg gave a bark of a laugh. 'God no. Her letter just sent me a bit loopy. She'd threatened to end it before but I hadn't believed her. No one had ever dumped me until then.'

'You'd, er, had a lot of girlfriends then?'

Greg grinned. 'I did my fair share of larking about before Tia, yes.'

Vik looked to the lounge door. He'd never 'larked about' with anyone but Nika. Did that make him dull? He had a feeling it did but he was used to being dull, liked it, even. He was an accountant who'd met his wife through family friends, proposed after six weeks and settled into domestic life with little more than a cranky tortoise to rock the boat. And he was OK with that. Wasn't he?

'Sounds fun,' he choked out.

'While it lasted. I was a bit wild at uni – scientists, contrary to their popular reputation, know how to get it on!'

Now Vik really did feel dull. He pictured Greg doing – what? Sex on lab benches? Sex with two scientists at once? He had a feeling he was too dull to actually imagine what wild was and then felt treacherous for worrying about that. He and Nika had had a lovely sex life. That is, they'd had a lovely life that had included sex. Did it have to be more?

'It was just transitory fun,' Greg went on. 'I thought I was so cool, Vik, but that's not cool. What's cool is having someone who means the world to you in your arms every night.'

A warmth spread through Vik – not so dull after all!

'I had that with Nika. We were in love.'

'Then you were a very lucky man. I had it with Tia too, but like a twat I let it go.'

'I'm sorry, Greg. And you're right, I was lucky. I just wish . . . No. I was lucky.'

'*Are* lucky.'

'Sorry?'

'I know she's not with you any more, but are you not still in love?'

Vik felt tears prick his eyes. It must be the wine. If so, he liked it even more than he'd thought.

'I am,' he said, raising his glass. 'I am still in love and it's wonderful. Thank you, Greg. I'm so glad you came over.'

Greg raised his own glass. 'Me too.'

Vik looked down at his texts. *Drowning in tutus*. What a load of nonsense. All Sai was drowning in was cocktails with his fancy friends and Vik was tired of fighting it. Maybe it was all his fault. Maybe he should have talked to his son after Nika had died, but whenever he'd tried tears had threatened. And tears just embarrassed them both.

'Same time next week?' he suggested to Greg.

There was a momentary pause, which seemed to expand with the weight of all that was missing in Vik's life, before a smile crept across his neighbour's face and he said, 'Same time next week, Vik. Great.'

Chapter Seventeen

'So, Charlie, the monthly results came in this afternoon and Team West won!'

Charlie blinked at Sean.

'Won?'

'Yep. Highest rate of on-time deliveries.'

'We won *that*?'

'Hard to believe, isn't it? The stats did drop off a bit in the second half . . .'

'When you started,' Ryan put in, appearing at Sean's side.

'So it'll be a hard fight next month.'

'Unless you pull your socks up, new boy.'

'Which I'm sure he will.'

Sean smiled at him, this morning's shouting apparently forgotten. It was very disconcerting.

'What have we won?' he asked cautiously.

It was bound to be something like a certificate or a badge or a mention in some poxy email. But Sean surprised him.

'Drinks.'

'Drink,' Bri corrected, coming up alongside Charlie. 'At the Peacock.'

She pointed across the road to a rather battered pub with a rusty 'saver menu' screwed to the wall and a big Sky TV logo over the door.

'I don't drink,' Charlie said.

'Typical,' Ryan scoffed. 'You don't drink, you like jigsaws. Are you vegan too?' Charlie squinted at him and he threw his hands up in the air. 'Just asking! Well, you can have a lovely lemonade then. No, hang on – if you have a pint on Turner's, I'll get you a lemonade and we can swap.'

'It's not Turner's, actually,' Sean said stiffly. 'It's me. Actual me. As your team leader.'

'Actual me?' Bri giggled behind Charlie, but Ryan looked at Sean with genuine astonishment.

'Wow. Right. Er, thanks Sean.'

'Leadership isn't all about gain,' Sean said primly. 'Now, shall we go?'

He marched off across the yard with Ryan in his wake.

Charlie looked to Bri. 'Do we have to?' he asked.

She laughed. 'It won't take long. And Harper's picking me up so you could meet her. If you'd like to, that is?' She suddenly looked shy.

'I'd love to. It might even be worth putting up with Sean for.'

'And Ryan?'

'Maybe not that, but I'll cope.'

They left the warehouse to good-natured ribbing from the other teams. Clearly, Sean's drink wasn't quite the motivational prize he thought it was and Charlie felt almost normal for the first time in far too long. Look at him – going for after-work drinks, indulging in a bit of banter. He remembered how terrified he'd felt when he'd first arrived outside the gates of the big yard, how easily his family had convinced him he wouldn't fit in. The truth was that these drivers and loaders had been far more accepting than his siblings ever had. This certainly wasn't the way he'd planned his route through life and he'd never forget that he'd taken an acutely, unforgivably wrong turn, but perhaps he could salvage something yet.

'Coming, Jack?' Bri called across the yard as they trailed after Sean.

'Yep. Be there in a minute.'

'Is Jack in Team West then?' Charlie asked Bri as she waved acknowledgement.

'Jack's in every team. He holds the whole place together and Sean knows it. Now, come on – you might not drink, but I sure as hell do.'

*

Inside, the Peacock more than lived up to its unpromising exterior. Charlie looked round at the mismatched tables, the worn stools and the dusty TVs playing lower-league football on silent and turned incredulously back to Jack, who'd caught them up at the door.

'You voluntarily come here every month?' he asked.

Jack grinned. 'The landlord keeps his beer well and what else matters? Pint of best, please, Sean.'

'Already in, Jack,' Sean said proudly, nudging the glass along the bar.

'Fantastic. Cheers.'

Sean loudly took all their orders and, drinks in hand, they settled uncomfortably around the nearest table. Charlie clutched his lemonade and looked around his workmates: Bri, with her highly coloured hair drinking a large gin; scrawny Ryan frowning into his lager; and slender Jack cradling his bitter. Sean had a cider of the lethal cloudy sort. Maybe this was a bit of an ordeal for him too. Certainly his smile looked forced as, after some painful small talk, he addressed the motley crowd.

'So, a toast. To Team West's new member. To Charlie!'

'To Charlie!' Bri chimed in, Jack right behind.

Ryan muttered something that sounded like agreement but then looked up and locked eyes with Charlie across the table, his own dark with intent.

'Why not tell us a bit about yourself , Charlie,' he suggested, dangerously lightly, 'seeing as you're part of the team now?'

Charlie took a glug of his lemonade and wished it was something stronger. 'Not much to tell, Ryan.'

'Oh come on – there's always something to tell. Where d'you live? Do you have a partner? What did you do before you got this glorious job as a delivery driver?'

Charlie looked to Bri for help but she just stared at him curiously. He cleared his throat.

'I live in town and I haven't got a partner right now.'

'And . . .'

'And what?'

'And what did you do before this, Charlie?'

'Oh.' Charlie could feel his skin burning. 'This and that.'

'Like . . .?'

It was Jack who saved him.

'Does it matter, Ryan? Leave the lad alone. Believe it or not, not everyone likes being centre of attention.'

Ryan glared at the older man. 'Just showing a friendly interest, Jack.'

'Well, now you've shown it, so enough. Going to the footie this weekend, Bri?'

'I wish,' Bri said, rolling her eyes. 'Harper's got me painting the nursery instead.'

She utterly failed to make this sound like a hardship and Jack smiled.

'When's the baby due?'

'February.'

'Fantastic. Hey, Mary . . .' He turned as an elegant lady approached them. 'D'you hear that – Bri's baby is due in February.'

'Wonderful.' Mary's eyes went to Bri's stomach. 'You're very neat, dear.'

Jack rolled his eyes. 'Bri's not having it, love. Remember, I told you – her wife, Harper, is.'

'Oh that's right!' Mary slid in next to Bri. 'Wise choice, sweetheart. It's a pain in the you-know-what having a baby.'

Bri grinned at her. 'I might give it a go next time.'

'How lovely to have the choice. And will you get maternity leave?'

Everyone looked to Sean, who furrowed his brow. 'Surely not?' he stuttered.

'Paternity leave then?' Mary pushed.

Charlie liked her enormously. He looked curiously back to Sean, who sank the last of his fancy cider in one big gulp.

'That's for HR to decide,' he mumbled. 'Now, who's getting the next one in?'

Everyone looked down. Accepting a drink from Sean was one thing; prolonging the agony at your own expense was quite another.

'I've got to get off, I'm afraid,' Jack said, taking Mary's hand and pulling her smoothly to her feet while downing the last of his pint. 'We're meeting our Paul in town. Got tickets to *Othello*.'

Charlie looked up in surprise. 'Shakespeare's *Othello*?'

'Is there another kind?' Charlie blushed and Jack set a kindly hand on his shoulder. 'I know what you mean. This one's a modern-day interpretation set on an airbase in Afghanistan.'

'Sounds great.'

'Doesn't it? Mary and I have got a goal to see every Shakespeare play in performance before we die, right, love?'

'Right,' Mary agreed. 'Though we're not doing all that well. This is our third *Othello* and God knows how we'll ever dig out a *Coriolanus*.'

'Or a *Henry VIII*,' Jack agreed. 'No one ever stages that.'

'Because it's crap,' Charlie said and now it was their turn to stare. 'You know it?'

Charlie gulped at his lemonade but it was all gone. 'This bonkers teacher at school once made us do it,' he mumbled.

'Right.'

Charlie stood up. 'I should go too.'

'Hot date?' Ryan asked.

'No, I . . . I just need to get back before dark.'

'Oh dear? Curfew?'

'No! Lack of bike lights.' Charlie clutched his rucksack close to his chest, hoping no one had spotted the lights in it. 'Thanks for the drink, Sean.'

'Pleasure, Charlie. Keep up the good work.'

Cider was mellowing the team leader. Already his eyes looked a little glazed.

'I'll get you another, Sean,' Ryan said, leaping up.

Charlie turned gratefully away, but a squeal behind him made him jump and he stepped sideways just in time to avoid Bri bowling past him into the arms of a young woman standing hesitantly in the doorway.

'Harper! You made it.'

As soon as she saw Bri, Harper's face lit up and she hugged her tight, then pulled back and kissed her squarely on the lips.

'Girl on girl,' Ryan muttered delightedly at Charlie's side.

Charlie looked at him. 'You can't say that, Ryan.'

Ryan glowered. 'I just did. And it *is* girl on girl.'

'Not in the way you're implying. It's just a couple greeting each other.'

'A couple who are both girls.'

'So? You wouldn't say "boy on girl", would you?'

'Well, no, but . . . God, what are you, new boy, the PC police?'

'No, I . . . Oh, forget it.'

Bri was tugging Harper over and Charlie wasn't going to let Ryan's stupid fantasies get to him. He stepped firmly away and held out his hand to the new arrival.

'Hi. I'm Charlie. You must be Harper. I've heard so much about you.'

'All good I hope?'

Bri batted at her arm. 'Of course it's all good. Drink?'

Harper shook her head. 'No, ta. It's rubbish without alcohol.'

'Couldn't agree more,' Charlie said.

Harper grinned at him. 'You pregnant too?'

'Sadly, science hasn't got that far yet. I'm just rubbish at drinking. Or, rather, at stopping drinking.'

Even as the words came out he regretted them. He was getting carried away with all his 'normal' after-work stuff and letting down his guard. He looked uneasily around but thankfully Ryan was at the bar and Harper didn't seem fazed at all.

'Been there, mate. Shitty. I stopped just in time, I reckon. That's to say, getting banged up stopped me just in time – and introduced me to this little darling. Every cloud, hey?'

She curled under Bri's arm and Bri proudly pulled her close. Harper was a little shorter than her wife and, with olive skin, almond eyes and liquorice black hair, she made a striking contrast to Bri's rainbow colours.

'Bri certainly looks like a silver lining,' Charlie offered and the pair giggled gratifyingly.

Happiness radiated from them and Charlie was drawn to its warmth but he didn't dare step too close. Even a gentle heat, he knew, could turn to flames with just a little foolish fanning and he was far better out in the cold.

'Lovely to meet you,' he said to Harper, 'but I have to get off now. Good luck with the nursery.'

'Ta, Charlie. It's going to be so cool. I've got this great paint and these transfers and this special stuff for doing floorboards. Bri's going to be very busy.'

'Slave driver,' Bri said fondly.

Charlie could take no more. It was great to see people happy, really it was, but if he stayed too much longer he might get jealous and jealousy wasn't pleasant. Look at Othello!

'See ya!' he called to Sean, who raised a hand in farewell.

Ryan had sat back down next to him with two new pints and two chasers.

'Sure we can't tempt you, Charlie boy?' he called. 'A few drinks relaxes a man, makes him less uptight.' He looked sideways at Sean. 'Less inclined to hang on to secrets.'

Charlie's gullet contracted. He looked to Bri but she was getting ready to leave with Harper and didn't see. Ryan kept his eyes drilled into Charlie. Soon he would have Sean all to himself and that's clearly exactly what he had planned. Charlie didn't know what his damn HR record actually said but it looked like Ryan was on a mission to find out. Should he stay? Probably. But he couldn't. He mustn't. Already the smell of alcohol was creeping tantalisingly up his nose and running amok around his brain.

One wouldn't hurt, it was saying. *It's Friday, after all. And you've worked so hard. You deserve it. Just one. Just one. Just . . .*

Charlie put his hands over his ears and backed towards the pub door.

'I have to go,' he spat out. He fumbled for the handle and felt it smooth and warm against his palm. 'Night,' he managed and then he was out and sprinting back to the Turner's yard.

He shouldn't have gone to the stupid pub. It had been madness. He didn't do pubs nowadays, didn't deserve their simple joys any more than he deserved to go to the theatre or paint a nursery or have someone put an easy arm around him. He was damaged. And the worst of it was that he'd damaged himself. He'd made his own cloud and it would have no silver lining.

Charlie leaped furiously on to his bike, not bothering to stop and fit the lights clattering against each other in his bag. He shot past the front of the Peacock, glancing in to see Ryan plying their boss with drinks. He should have given him Hope Street on that very first day at Turner's. Why had he fought him? What had he been hoping to achieve? All he'd done was see, first-hand, the misery he'd created. And more besides. He couldn't help any of his customers with his futile little plans, let alone make amends.

Charlie turned left and found himself on Hope Street, as if karma was messing with him again. He scanned the town map in his mind but he'd never had much of a sense of direction and could think of no alternative route home without going miles out of his way. Gritting his teeth, he set his eyes forward and pedalled faster. Hope Street blurred. Traffic became a dull roar, washed with waves of sound as people opened the doors of pubs or cafes and let laughter spill out. Ahead of him, a bus indicated left and he pulled out to pass it.

'Watch out!'

Charlie screeched to a halt as a 4x4, view hidden by the bus, pulled out of a side street and jerked to stop in front of him. Charlie braked barely two metres from the big wheels, gave a nod of thanks to the fellow cyclist who'd shouted to him and, breathing heavily, edged his bike on to the pavement out of the way of the chaos.

With a start, he realised he was two doors down from number 95. Familiar yellow light spilled down Vik's drive and as people shouted at each other across the road, Charlie edged towards it. Behind him, the 4x4 had moved on and the traffic was flowing again but Charlie didn't even notice. Leaning forward, he peered surreptitiously into the house and there they were: Vik and Greg, clinking glasses across a curry-laden table like lifelong friends.

Charlie's hands went to his mouth. He'd done it. His plan had worked. He felt wonder creep seductively through him and suddenly everything was forgotten. Suddenly it didn't matter that Bri and Harper were cuddling up at home, or that Jack and Mary were on their way to the theatre, or even that Ryan might be wheedling pathetic little secrets out of Sean. Suddenly all that mattered was that Charlie's plan – his ridiculously simple plan – had worked. Right at this moment, two of his lonely customers were *not* lonely and his beating heart gave a trill of long-forgotten delight at the quiet triumph. Maybe, in some small way, Charlie *could* make amends.

The bus pulled off, casting a shadow across Vik's drive and Vik looked out. Charlie ducked down, fiddling yet again at his fully functioning pedals. He remembered Ruth shouting out at him last week – 'You coming in then or what?' – and looked down the busy pavement to number 112. It sat cold and dark among the other houses. Was Ruth in there working her way through her new bottle of vodka? Should Charlie be delivering it to her when she was so clearly in a bad way?

Not your business, Charlie, he told himself. *You've done enough harm with your bloody meddling already.*

He yanked his bike lights out of his rucksack but as he stood again to fit them, his head crept inexorably back to Vik and Greg. The older man was saying something, waving his fork to illustrate a point, and the younger one was laughing. They were not alone tonight and all because of one neatly misplaced bottle of wine. Little Charlie Sparrow's meddling hadn't, it seemed, done harm this time round. Now, if only there was a way of getting Ruth there too . . .

Don't, Charlie told himself, but already his mind was racing and when he remounted his bike and made for home, his thoughts were as alight as the little lamps on his rickety bicycle.

WEEK FOUR

WEEK FOUR

Chapter Eighteen

First on to the yard! Not even Sean's maroon saloon was here yet and Charlie quietly congratulated himself for getting up and out this morning. As usual, he'd been awake from the early hours, but he'd filled the time before dawn testing and re-testing his plan.

He parked up his bike and felt in his pocket for the little plug. Still there. Excellent. It had taken hours on the internet to find this and he could only pray no accident would befall his block of flats while his browsing history read so strangely, but he had at least found what he was looking for. Certainly, when he'd tried it at home it had worked a treat. Of course, if it went wrong . . .

But he couldn't think like that. It wasn't dangerous. He'd checked that over and over this time and he just had to pray that everyone had placed their usual orders. Surely they would have done? People, he'd discovered since starting at Turner's, liked routine. Most households ordered on the same day at roughly the same time and, indeed, roughly the same goods. It was easy to tell if people were having guests or a special occasion or, in the case of the mad design lot, what wine-based event was planned this week. Turner's kept drivers on the same routes for just this sense of continuity and personal service. After all, four minutes a week amounted to, ooh, at least sixteen minutes a month – how much more personal could you get?

Charlie made for the common room, chiding himself for his cynicism. It was business, that was all. At the end of the day, the books had to balance and if that meant flinging goods on to people's work surfaces at top speed then so be it. Turner's didn't want to pay drivers to hang around chatting, but neither, to be fair, did customers. As Sean had put it with such mercenary precision on Charlie's first day, they weren't social workers. But they could, perhaps, help their customers to be that for each other.

Charlie felt again for the plug. The video had been most explicit – switch the earth and the live wires and you'd short-circuit the power and fuse the system. The fuse wouldn't be able to be switched on again until the plug was removed by someone placed conveniently nearby. A delivery driver, for example . . .

'Morning, Charlie. You're here bright and early.'

Charlie jumped guiltily as Jack came out of the warehouse, clipboard in hand. 'Thought I'd get a head start.'

'Impressive. You're not the first in, mind you.'

'Really? Who beat me?'

'Ryan. Been here half an hour. Something about his wife dropping him off so she could have the car.'

'His wife?'

'Apparently. Who'd have thought it. He's in the common room if you want to know more.'

The last thing Charlie wanted was a tête-à-tête about home life with Ryan. He'd got here early mainly to avoid the damn man.

'I'll get going thanks, Jack. Which is my van?'

Jack pointed. 'That one. But you can't go till Sean's here to sign you all in.'

'Really? Shit.'

'Looks like it's me-time with Ryan, hey?'

Charlie shook his head vehemently. 'No way. I'll sit in the van.'

'Suit yourself.'

Jack held out the keys and Charlie took them from him and made for his van. All week Ryan had been trying to get him on his own. All week he'd been giving him menacing sideways glances and doing his fingers-to-eyes gesture, with an added wink for sinister measure. Charlie kept picturing him cuddled up to Sean in the Peacock last Friday evening, on a mission to find out what he could about Charlie. Had he succeeded? Or was he bluffing? So far, Charlie had taken the only route he could think of by avoiding the damned man altogether but that couldn't last.

If Sean had told him anything it would be a disciplinary offence, he told himself, as the team leader drove in and parked smugly in his special slot, but now Ryan appeared in the common-room doorway and, spotting him stranded in the middle of the yard, was heading his way. Charlie looked frantically around for escape and he was hugely relieved when he spotted a blue hatchback pull up outside the gates. Bri bounced out, blowing a kiss at the departing driver, and Charlie hurried over to join her before Ryan could close him down.

'Nearly the weekend,' Bri said by way of greeting.

'Yay!' Charlie agreed weakly.

Bri didn't seem to notice his lack of enthusiasm. 'Anything nice planned?'

'Nothing in particular. You?'

Bri, it turned out, had lots special planned. It was Harper's birthday so she'd booked them a surprise night away and she was so keen to tell Charlie all about it that he was spared further questions on his own non-existent weekend. It was his father's birthday too. He'd received a curt email invitation home for the weekend, which he'd declined on the utterly false grounds that he was working. It would rob his family of the delights of asking him all about his new profession, but he was sure they'd have far more fun speculating about him being beaten up in the yard and struggling to lift baskets and generally being useless, so who was he to spoil things with the tedious truth? Mind you, Ryan was looking gleeful daggers at him so maybe the beating was yet to come. He steered Bri towards Sean.

'Paperwork ready, Sean?'

'And good morning to you too, Charlie.'

Charlie gritted his teeth. 'Good morning, Sean. Is the paperwork ready?'

'You're keen.'

'Feels busy out there. I'd like to get going and not be late for once.'

'Very commendable, I'm sure. Let's see . . . Ah yes, Hope Street.'

He held out the paperwork but Ryan cut between them and grabbed it.

'Still got Greg Sutton on your run then, Charlie boy?' he said, jabbing at the paper.

'I don't know,' Charlie said. 'I can't see the list.'

Ryan held it up high. 'Oh, he's here all right. He's going to the "Inspirational Blog of the Year" awards, you know.'

'I do know. He was being measured for a new DJ last week.'

'Was he? How sweet. Did you advise him on it? Did you check out his lines?'

Charlie frowned at him. 'No I did not. What are you going on about, Ryan?'

'Are you taking the piss out of disability?' Bri asked.

Ryan bristled. 'Course not. Just checking out Charlie here, hobnobbing with the stars. Still, no wonder with your . . . pedigree.'

Charlie made a grab for his paperwork but Ryan whipped it away, forcing Charlie to turn reluctantly to his boss. 'Sean, please. I want to get going.'

Sean looked panicked. He glared at Ryan, who released the sheet so that it fluttered to the floor. Pathetic. Charlie bent and picked it up then made for his van, his mind racing. 'Pedigree,' Ryan had said. What had he meant? What did he know? He shoved the paperwork on to the passenger seat, rammed the key into the ignition and turned. Nothing. He tried again. Still nothing.

Below him, Ryan was sauntering to his own van, swinging his keys from one finger. Charlie watched him go and tried his own key again, but still nothing. He banged his hands on the wheel in frustration. All around him, vans were pulling out of the yard as he sat here helpless. Typical! He swung back out of the van and stomped across to the warehouse to find Jack.

'Something up?' Bri asked, intercepting him.

'It's my van. It won't bloody start.'

'Odd. I thought Jack always checked them before loading up.'

'He does,' Jack said, coming up behind them.

'Well, it's not working now.'

'I'll have a look,' Bri offered. 'My dad's a mechanic and he's taught me the way around an engine. Flick her open.'

Charlie leaned inside to release the bonnet and Bri peered in, her slim body all but swallowed up by the big lid.

'I'll make you late,' Charlie said.

'Doubt it.' Bri reappeared grinning and holding a tiny device in her hand. 'Easy-peasy. Your fuel pump fuse has come out.'

'Come out?'

'Uh-huh. Here we go.' She dived into the engine again. 'Try her now.'

Charlie climbed inside and turned the key. The van shook obligingly into life and Bri leaped up to grab the bonnet lid and slam it back into place.

'Amazing,' Charlie said.

'That's me,' Bri agreed. She came round and stood on tiptoes to put a hand on his leg. 'Just one thing though, Charlie . . .' She beckoned him down, dropping her voice. 'Fuel pump fuses don't usually just come out.'

'They don't?'

'Nope. Tight-fitting little things they are, as you'd imagine.'

'So . . .?'

She shrugged. 'Dunno, mate. Just thought I'd say. Take care, right?'

She gave his leg a squeeze and then she was gone, leaving him staring after her. There wasn't much time to think about what she'd said, however, before someone else took her place – someone tall and thin and mean-looking.

'You got her started then?'

'Ryan, did you . . .?'

'Wanted a word, mate. You've been avoiding me all week.'

'Just getting on with my job.'

'Are you? Are you really? Just getting on with your perfectly ordinary job that you got in a perfectly ordinary way?'

'That's right.'

Ryan stepped on to the running board and snatched Charlie's keys out of the ignition.

'I know about you, Charlie "Sparrow". I know *all* about you. I wondered why you were so bloody absent from the internet. No one is that anonymous online these days, are they? No one! So why were *you*? No Facebook, no Twitter, no Insta, not even a local news article or a tag by a friend. You seemed to be a ghost, my friend. But you're not, are you? Oh no. You, Charlie boy, are all over the internet and it's not good, is it? It's not good at all.' He caught at Charlie's chin, jerking it upwards. 'Nothing to say, little sparrow?'

Charlie's throat felt as if he'd swallowed some dark poison that was slowly closing it up. He had been mad to think he could keep his former self secret. He had been bonkers to think it would burn with his passport, as if identity was nothing more than a piece of paper.

'What do you want, Ryan?' He forced out the words.

Ryan gave a slow smile. 'Hope Street,' he said. 'I want Hope Street.'

'No!'

'No? Oh dear. Well then, Charlie boy, I feel I must speak up. It's not ethical, you see. You can't be visiting certain people, not with your history.'

'I was proven innocent, Ryan.'

'Proven? What, like Michael Jackson was proven? The law's a funny business, Charlie, especially for those with money to spend on it.'

'I haven't got money. Ryan, please . . .'

Charlie was going to cry, he knew he was. What on earth had possessed him to come to work here? Or anywhere? What had made him think he could integrate back into normal life when he was nothing like normal any more?

'Hope Street,' Ryan growled. 'Tell Sean you don't want it any more.'

'But I *do* want it. It's the . . . the personal touch, remember? And I've got plans, Ryan. I'm making restitution.'

'Restitution!' Ryan greeted the word with the high-pitched scorn Charlie suddenly knew for sure it deserved.

He felt desperately for the plug in his pocket. The metal prongs jabbed callously at his fingers. Restitution indeed.

'Fine, Ryan,' he said wearily. 'I'll talk to Sean.'

Ryan's smile widened. 'Good. See that you do. Today.'

'The end of today,' Charlie said.

That, at least, gave him one more round. One more chance. He'd have to make the most of it.

Chapter Nineteen

Number 95 Hope Street:

Chicken thighs, boned
Basil
Shallots
Lemongrass
Rice noodles
Galangal root
Roasted peanuts
Green papaya
Jasmine rice
Lime leaves
Nam pla
Dried shrimp
Pork tenderloin
Pork liver
Mint
Spring onions
Tamarind paste
Spaghetti hoops, 2 cans
Cornflakes
Milk
Nail-tail Shiraz, 1 bottle

'Come along in, Charlie. Come right along in.'

Vik waved Charlie into his kitchen, peering hopefully into the top basket. He'd be needing the tamarind any minute now for his pad thai. He was a bit nervous about it, what with it being Greg's own recipe from Thailand, but he'd figured the young man might like a reminder of his happy trip on this drizzly day in England and just hoped he could do it justice.

'You're busy there, Vik,' Charlie said, indicating the pots bubbling on the stove.

'Yep,' Vik agreed. 'I've got a, er, friend coming over later. Thought I'd cook up an extra dish or two.'

Was Greg a friend? Sort of, he supposed. And, anyway, Charlie wouldn't know otherwise.

'It's a feast,' the delivery driver said mildly and Vik smiled and delved into his shopping.

He found the two jars of tamarind (it had been in a buy-one-get-one-free deal. Nika had always loved a 'BOGOF' – the word had made her giggle every single time), lifted them out and set them by the stove. Charlie, he noticed, was fidgeting and casting anxious glances around his kitchen.

'You OK, Charlie?'

'Me? Oh, yes, fine. Just want to, you know, be sure I've got everything right for you this week after the wine thing.'

'The wine thing? Oh, leaving the bottle here. Don't worry about that, really. It was a blessing in disguise.'

'It was?'

Charlie looked straight at him for perhaps the first time since he'd arrived. Vik should tell him how well he'd got on with Greg, thank him for the mistake that had brought the young man to his house, but he couldn't quite find the words. He felt a sudden shudder of unease and looked over his shoulder to the curries he'd been so keenly preparing for this stranger from across the road.

There was the pad thai, then a pork laap and a som tam salad. Classics, or so Greg's lovely blog assured him. He didn't know Thai cuisine very well but it was nice to have a new challenge. And a new guest too. He'd heard nothing from Sai this week and had sent no message either. A disturbingly large part of him was dreading a sudden text saying that his son was coming over and he hated himself for that.

He turned back to see Charlie edging along the side wall of the kitchen towards the lounge door and leaped forward.

'Not in there.'

Charlie jumped as Vik nudged past him and yanked the door swiftly shut.

'Sorry,' he stuttered and Vik felt bad again.

'No, no, don't worry. It's just, you know, a mess in the lounge. And cold.'

'You said before. Maybe you should get a fire?'

'A fire?'

'A gas fire. To sit by?'

'Oh. Oh, I see. Yes. Could do, I suppose, but, you know, I don't really go in there much. I prefer it in here. Cosier.' Vik snatched a packet out of the basket to cover his confusion. Lemongrass. Another Thai ingredient, unfamiliar to him. What on earth was he up to, making Thai curries as if this were some sort of weird date? 'Or in the garden,' he hurried on. 'I like it in the garden. I sometimes think I should grow my own herbs. Do you think I should grow my own herbs, Charlie?'

Charlie looked to the window. 'I don't know. Is it warm enough?'

'I think I'd need a greenhouse to be sure. And to stop Rickets eating them, of course.'

'Of course.'

'We had a little greenhouse when Sai was a lad but he kept kicking footballs into it so we gave up. Nika kept basil and coriander on the windowsill but it's not the same as a proper herb bed, is it? I think I'd like a herb bed – something to nurture.'

He was gabbling again, drunk on company.

'It's a great idea, Vik,' Charlie said, sidling away from the window again. What was with him today? He seemed to almost be clinging to Vik's walls. 'You can get plastic greenhouses now too.'

'Plastic? You sure?'

'Very sure. I spent two hours cleaning one the other day.'

'You did?'

'My neighbour's.'

'Right. Where d'you live, Charlie?'

'Hazel Avenue. The new flats. D'you know them?'

'I do. Sai looked at buying one a while back as a . . . you know, investment. They're nice.'

'I used to think so, yes.'

Vik looked at the lad curiously but he didn't seem inclined to elaborate.

'I might get a greenhouse then,' he said eventually. 'Do your lot sell them?'

'I don't think so, sorry. Perhaps you could ask your son to get you one for Christmas?'

Vik gave a little laugh. 'It might stop him buying me clothes. It wouldn't be so bad but he chooses such ridiculously tight fits that I can never wear them. Do I look like I have the physique for a figure-hugging shirt?'

He threw his arms wide to expose his skinny frame and at last Charlie smiled.

'At least you haven't got a gut.'

'I haven't got anything. Wasting away, I am.'

Now Charlie frowned. 'You do eat, Vik?'

Vik jumped. 'What does it look like?' he shot back, waving at his curries with a wooden spoon.

'It looks like you cook.'

The answer was so sharp it cut right through Vik. He glanced guiltily into the basket where the spaghetti hoops and cereal crouched apologetically.

'And why would anyone cook if they didn't want to eat?' he demanded.

The question hung awkwardly in the steam between them and, unable to bear the younger man's gaze, Vik turned to his curries, stirring diligently. He heard Charlie shuffle behind him and hoped he was gathering up the baskets to go. He'd felt so happy when the lad had arrived and now he was all out of sorts. He reached for one of the jars, hoping to restore his equilibrium with the ritual of cooking, but at that moment there was a little pop somewhere behind him and his glowing halogen hobs died beneath the pans. He looked round in confusion.

'What's happened?'

'Power cut?' Charlie suggested.

He looked very pink-cheeked. Probably worried that he'd be stuck here and go over his time limit. Vik peered out of the window.

'Next door's lights are still on. Fuse maybe?' He went to the box above the door into the hall and flicked it open. Charlie hovered behind him. 'Ah yes – the fuse.' Vik reached up and fiddled with the switch but every time he clicked it back into position it bounced out again. 'Funny. It won't go back.'

'Maybe you need to wait a bit for the, you know, surge to die away?'

'Maybe.' Vik looked to his curries. The laap would need to simmer for a good while to break down the pork and he hadn't even started the som tam yet. 'But what if it's not that?'

Charlie's eyes darted around the kitchen.

'Try it again,' he suggested eventually.

Vik did. Nothing.

'The bloody switch won't go up. I need an electrician.'

Did he know an electrician? Nika used to have a book with all that sort of thing in – a flowery address book, bursting at the seams with cards and notes that she collected off people and could never be bothered to transfer neatly into the correct section. Where had she kept it? If she was here now she'd have reached out and put her soft hands around it in an instant. She'd have opened it and rifled through the seemingly formless mass of papers and drawn out just the right one.

'I knew it was here,' she'd have said. 'I remember the colour of the card. Look, Vikram – isn't it a lovely shade of blue?'

And he'd have looked and smiled in agreement, though to him it would have seemed a perfectly standard shade of blue, and then she'd have been off to call and get everything sorted out. Nika had been amazing at getting things sorted out and suddenly the weight of having to do it without her felt almost unbearable. Vik sank into the nearest chair and fought to resist putting his head in his hands like some sort of stereotype of despair.

Charlie gave a strangled little cough. 'Do you know an electrician, Vik?'

'No.'

Vik stared at the floor. Where was Nika's book? Then he remembered – it would be in the drawer under the coffee table. She'd have kept it there so she didn't have to get up from her comfy sofa if it was needed. He glanced to the lounge door. He wasn't going in there, not until Charlie was gone.

'I'll find one,' he said, forcing himself to his feet. 'It's fine, Charlie. You get on.'

Charlie, however, was shuffling around in front of him. 'I do.'

'Do what?'

'Know an electrician – a woman just down the road. I've got to take her shopping next so I could ask her if she'd come and take a look?'

'Really?' Vik glanced to the lounge door. Even if he found Nika's book it might take him for ever to locate an electrician's number inside it. 'That would be a big help, if you think you could?'

'Course. I'll go now, shall I?'

'Would you? I'd be so grateful.' Vik felt peculiarly weak, as if his own energy had been switched off with the lights. 'It's the curries, you see . . .'

'I see,' Charlie agreed and scuttled out of the door.

Alone, Vik forced himself to his feet and went back to the stove. He put a finger to the nearest ring – it was still warm, though cooling rapidly. Nika had been like that. After. It had been the worst thing, that creeping cold, as if something evil was literally sucking the fragments of life out of her and leaving him nothing but a husk of a body. He'd rather that had dissolved too. It had felt like an insult to leave him this lump of something to be got rid of, instead of a body to be cherished. The still form had looked so like her and yet so totally unlike and for one horrible, violent moment all he'd wanted to do was shake and shake it until she came back and made it look right again.

He went back to the hall doorway and tried the fuse but it still wouldn't click back into place and let the electricity flow around his house. He sank on to the bottom stair and forced himself to breathe. It was just a little electrical problem, nothing more. Charlie would sort it. He'd be back and he'd sort it.

He hadn't shaken Nika, of course. He hadn't done anything but stare, lost in the vacuum of her passing, before some grain of common sense had sent him to the phone.

'It's my wife,' he'd said. 'I think she's dead.'

They'd asked him all sorts of questions. Very calm they'd been, very kind. Well, you would be, wouldn't you? They'd sent an ambulance but the moment the paramedics had seen Nika they'd stopped rushing and, instead, moved with steady gravity, handling him with care as if he, not Nika, was the patient.

'She's dead,' they'd confirmed, and even though he'd known it, though he'd faced the truth of it in the privacy of his own bed, it had still been a shock.

'I thought so,' he'd said, as calm as they were, and then he'd cracked and the tears had spilled out and they'd asked if they could call anyone and he'd wanted to shout 'Nika! Call Nika!' because it had always been Nika, but that would have been silly so he'd asked for Sai. He'd listened as the older of the two medics had used his phone to call the number and had heard him use his calm to field Sai's impatience and then his confusion and finally his shock.

'Dead?' he'd heard his son shriek – most unlike him, especially if he was at work. 'She can't be dead!'

He'd loved him then for shouting the words he'd wanted to shout himself, but by the time Sai had arrived at the house he'd been composed and had joined the medics in look-after-the-old-man mode, as if Nika's passing was nothing more than a symptom of Vik's own shaking body.

'You came,' he'd said like a fool.

'Of course I came, Dad. Of course I did.'

He'd even held his hand and Vik remembered noticing that now his son's fingers clasped around his own instead of the other way round. It had been strange, but good-strange. That had been over a year ago, though. Sai didn't come any more. However much curry Vik made, he didn't come any more.

Keep cooking, Vikram, Nika's voice said in his head, but how could he keep cooking with his electricity gone? He put his head in his hands, fixed his eyes on the door and waited.

Chapter Twenty

Number 112 Hope Street:

Value wholemeal bread
Baked beans, 4 cans
Value ready salted crisps, 6-pack
Bacon bits
Pasta
Value pasta sauce
Chocolate
Jelly babies
Lemons, 3
Vodka, 1ltr
Tonic, 2x 1ltr
Clan James blended whisky, 70ml
Paracetamol x1
Cold and flu tablets x1

'I've got a favour to ask you,' Charlie said.

Ruth looked at him bleary-eyed. She'd not slept well last night, or at least not until dawn had broken and the piercing blue eyes had let her go, dropping her, perversely, into a sleep so deep that the alarm had invaded her dreams as a wail for far too long before she'd torn herself out of them. *Mummy, Mummy, Mummy!* it had screeched and even now it seemed to bounce around her head, pinging off her brain cells and making it hard to work out what the delivery driver was saying.

'A favour? From me?'

Charlie moved forward. 'It's the old man across the road at number ninety-five. His electrics have gone and he's very upset.'

Electrics? Ruth's brain, or part of it at least, fought its way past the wail. She had a cold, that was part of the problem; she was all clogged up with snot.

'Fuse?' she suggested.

'He tried that. It won't go back on.'

'Something must be disrupting the circuit.'

'Well, yes, but what?'

'I don't know.'

Ruth lifted this week's vodka bottle out of the basket and nudged it on to the side. Damn. She'd forgotten to decant the remains of Sanjeed's spirit into the Turner's bottle. She shoved it behind a four-slice toaster and hastily unloaded a large bar of chocolate in front of it. She had a stinking cold; she needed treats.

'Might you come and have a look? It would mean the world to him.'

Charlie's words jarred against her weary mind.

'The world, Charlie? Really?'

'Well, OK, not the world, but a lot. He's cooking, you see, and his hob has died.'

'He should have gas.'

'But he doesn't.'

'Right.' Ruth unloaded more shopping. Whisky as well as vodka this week, but purely medicinal. She sat it on the side, pointedly sticking a jar of honey alongside it. 'Hot toddy,' she said, holding up a net of lemons. 'See.'

Charlie put his hands up. 'It's none of my business what you order, Ruth.'

'Correct. Just like this man's electrics are none of mine.'

'Except that they are. That is, you *do* run an electrical business.'

'Did.'

'You've sold Sparkly Sparkies?'

Ruth tugged at her dressing gown. Hayley had sent her more messages asking when she'd be coming back but she'd ignored them all.

'No, but I might.'

'You'd still be an electrician though. I bet it's something really simple. Wouldn't take you long.'

'I'm not sure, Charlie.'

'And think what a help it would be for Vik.'

'Vik?'

Damn – now the man had a name. That made him harder to ignore. She'd used to love collecting names when she was first working as a sparkie. A lot of people's names just seemed spot on the minute they said them but occasionally someone confounded you. Like the mousy little woman in the shapeless cardigan who'd introduced herself as Candice, or the hulk of a gym-stud who'd told her, without missing a beat, that his name was Malcolm.

Ruth's eyes drifted towards the little door under the stairs and Charlie leaped forward. 'Are your tools in there? Shall I fetch them for you?'

Ruth glared at him. 'Persistent little shit, aren't you?'

Charlie flinched but stood his ground. 'I just feel sorry for Vik. His wife died so he's all alone.'

'Diddums!'

Ruth glared at Charlie again but he didn't shift. There was something different about him this morning; something more assertive.

'Maybe just a little look?' he pushed.

He bent and unhooked the understairs door. It swung open and there, seeming almost to be shuffling forward in its eagerness to be used again, was Ruth's toolbox. Her fingers twitched. How long had it been since she'd stepped out of the door with that magic box in her hands? A year and a half almost to the day. Too long for sure.

'Fine,' she snapped and made for the stairs before she could change her mind.

'Where are you going?' Charlie called after her.

'Give a girl a minute to dress, can't you? If you're bored you can unpack the rest of my shopping.'

She shot into her room and looked around. Clothes lay all over the floor, rumpled and creased. Her eyes were drawn to the central drawer that she'd barely opened since the dreadful day Libby had died. The uniforms in that drawer were smart and purposeful and she just hadn't felt able to inhabit them. Now, though, it seemed she had little choice. She couldn't go to a job in baggy leggings; it just wouldn't be right.

Yanking the drawer open, Ruth pulled out a pair of navy combat trousers, bristling with useful pockets. She pulled them on beneath her dressing gown and looked again. The cheery yellow polo shirts smiled up at her, embroidered with the silver logo of a spanner turned into the female symbol and the words *Sparkly Sparkies*. Her own design, intended to catch attention. Far too much attention, it seemed now.

Ruth started to shake and glanced longingly to her bed but there was no time for foolish fear. Charlie was waiting. So, grabbing the top shirt, she shook it open, flung off her stained dressing gown and pulled it over her head. The cotton felt crisp and clean against her skin and she stretched out her back and rolled her shoulders beneath its sharp lines.

A glance in the mirror showed her half-dyed hair like a mockery of a wig above the smart clothing and she grabbed a scrunchie from the dressing table and pulled it hastily back. The band divided the grey roots and the red ends into something approaching a style and she almost smiled. Furious with herself, she tumbled out of the room and down the stairs to find Charlie waiting in the kitchen, her basket unloaded and clutched in his hand.

'Wow,' he said. 'You look good.'

Ruth jumped and tugged self-consciously at the yellow polo shirt. 'I didn't want pink.'

'Isn't your dressing gown pink?' She shook her head. 'But . . .'

'It isn't *my* dressing gown. It's Tony's, or it was. It was a joke, back when we did jokes.'

She resisted the memory but it clawed at her anyway: Tony standing in M&S modelling the dressing gown to the giggles of the shop lady nearby.

'I think it suits me better than the stupid checked ones in the men's department,' he'd said, flicking back the hood and prancing up and down between the lines of silky nighties. 'It's longer too – hides my knobbly knees. And look, if I get the extra-large, there's room in here for two.'

Then he'd grabbed her, wrapping the edges of the dressing gown around her and tying her tight in against him with the belt. She'd had to buy it just to get him out of there but, oh, she could still remember that shop assistant's giggle – an indulgent, 'aren't they in love' type laugh that she'd barely even noticed at the time because . . . well, because she'd been so blinking in love.

Shaking off the rogue memory she strode to the understairs cupboard, lifted out the big toolbox and set it on the table. She flicked open the catches, the familiar click snagging on her heart, and looked inside. Spanners, screwdrivers, wire-strippers, volt-testers – all present and correct. She sorted through, digging out confidence from among them, then clamped the lid shut and lifted it up before she could change her mind.

'Lead on, McCharlie!'

'It's Lay on, actually, and . . . Doesn't matter. Let's go.'

In the event, though, it was Ruth who led, keeping herself moving for fear of grinding to a sparkly yellow halt. She glanced momentarily at her van but it was crazy to take it just across the road and, besides, after all this time it probably wouldn't start. Instead, she set one work boot in front of the other and marched up to number 95, then paused before the flower beds.

'I always admire these flowers,' she said to Charlie, crouching down to look at them before feeling uncomfortably like a tourist and straightening hastily back up.

Charlie knocked and a man answered as quickly as if he'd been right there on the other side. He latched straight on to Ruth.

'Thank you so much for coming. It just went – poof! I was cooking, you see, and one minute everything was bubbling away nicely then the next, not. Did I overload the cooker, do you think?'

'Oh no,' she assured him, on safe ground here. 'They're designed to all run at once. Fuse box?'

Vik showed her and she pulled a torch from her box and shone it along the switches, checking the labels, looking for signs of trouble. It was like stepping back in time, not a slow path back but a drop-off-the-cliff immersion. And it felt good.

'Socket problem,' she said, tapping the label beneath the recalcitrant fuse. 'Very common.'

'Fixable?' Vik asked.

'Once we've found the source, yes. May I?'

She indicated the amazing kitchen, nearly as cluttered as her own but with the sort of stuff that actually belonged – jar upon jar of spices and pulses and different sorts of rice.

'Please.'

Vik waved her forward as Charlie sidled past them and made for the far wall. Ruth looked at him curiously but she had a job to do, so she took her volt checker from her toolbox and applied herself to the sockets one at a time.

'OK there, Charlie?' she heard Vik ask.

'Fine,' came the reply. 'I'm fine. Just getting in the way, really. I should head off.'

'It was very kind of you to fetch . . .' Vik turned to Ruth.

'Ruth,' she supplied. 'From Sparkly Sparkies.'

It tripped naturally off her tongue, surprising her. For so long she'd felt as if her work self had died with her daughter, but maybe it hadn't; maybe it had just been hibernating. Coming out into the sunshine again was terrifying, but she had to admit it felt warm on her skin.

'I really must go,' Charlie was saying behind her.

She moved on the next socket. No problems showing up yet.

'I didn't sign for my shopping,' Vik told him.

'Never mind.'

'But what about your records?'

'I'll do it for you, shall I?'

'Is that allowed?'

'Oh yes.'

Charlie sounded strangely panicked and when Ruth looked round to see if there were any more sockets he made an odd little noise.

'There,' Vik said, 'behind the bread bin.'

'Thanks.'

Ruth stepped up to the final socket and Charlie squeezed round her, making for the door before, somehow, he seemed to fall over his own feet. He stumbled and reached out a hand to support himself but caught at a jar of paprika that tumbled to the floor and burst open, sending the red spice everywhere.

'Oh no! Sorry. I'm so sorry, Vik.'

Vik looked from the splattered tiles to the dark hob, panic in his eyes. Ruth tested the socket.

'Odd,' she said, 'there doesn't seem to be any obvious fault on any of the sockets in here. What about in . . .?' She indicated the closed door at the back of the kitchen but Vik jumped in front of it.

'Doubt there's a problem in there.'

Ruth looked sideways at him then back to Charlie, still staring at the paprika with his hands to his mouth.

'OK then. Maybe try flicking the fuse again will you, Charlie?'

'The fuse?' Charlie stuttered.

'Above your head.'

Ruth pointed at the box and, after only a moment's hesitation, Charlie reached up and pushed it. It clicked into place and, as if by magic, the lights came on. Vik clapped delightedly and spun to the cooker, where already the halogen rings were starting to glow.

'You did it, Ruth!'

Ruth looked around, a little startled herself. 'I didn't do anything.'

'You made it work.'

'I really didn't,' she said.

Something odd had happened here. Electricity might seem mysterious to a lot of people but not to Ruth. It was a logical system of connections and reactions that didn't simply cut out without explanation. Something had been blocking the circuit in Vik's kitchen and then it hadn't been – the question was what? She had to suspect Charlie, but then the question became why? He'd been very worried about Vik and very keen to help him, but maybe he was just a nice person. Or maybe electricity had got temperamental since she'd last worked with it. Any which way, Vik didn't seem to care.

'I'm so grateful, truly,' he said, grabbing her hand in his and shaking it up and down. 'What do I owe you?'

'Nothing.'

'Don't be silly. You came over here specially and you made it all work again.' Behind Vik, the curries started to bubble and a delicious scent crept into the room. 'How much?' he insisted.

'Free. Really. Call it a taster.'

'A taster, ha ha!' This seemed to tickle Vik no end and he slapped his thigh in high glee. 'Then how about I offer you a taster in return?'

'Of what?'

'Curry!'

'Oh.' Ruth was stunned.

'You do like curry?'

'Very much,' she said. 'It . . . it smells delicious.'

'Good, good. Shall we say six o'clock then?'

Ruth stared at him. 'Tonight? Here?'

'That's right. I have a friend coming over and I'd be honoured if you'd join us. He's from Hope Street too. It'll be a street party!'

He slapped his thigh again, pleased with his own joke, but Ruth still couldn't quite believe what she was hearing.

'I've got a cold, I—'

'All the more reason to come – nothing better for a cold than a nice, spicy curry.'

Vik seemed supercharged suddenly, as if Ruth had sent electricity into him as well as the house. The curry point was a good one, mind you; Tony had always used to make her a super-hot madras if she'd had a cold. She shivered, coughed. 'But I don't know your friend.'

'You soon will.'

'Strangers are just friends you haven't met yet,' Charlie said from somewhere behind them and both Ruth and Vik turned to stare at him where he stood beneath the fuse box, paprika scattered, scarlet, around his feet. 'Greg's very nice,' he added, even pinker in the face than he'd been before.

'You know him?' Ruth asked.

'I deliver to him.'

'That's how I got to know him,' Vik agreed delightedly and then added, 'the same way as I now know you. Say you'll come, Ruth. There's lots.'

Ruth looked to the bubbling pots as a delicious smell rose from them. 'I've never done a job for curry before,' she said.

'There's a first for everything.'

She supposed Vik was right, but she'd thought she was done with firsts. That's what too many lasts did for you. She stared at the kind-eyed older man, feeling as giddy as if she'd drunk half a bottle of vodka. No, better. It felt the way vodka used to feel before it became a chase to nothingness. Tipsy, that was the word, and with not a drop to drink.

'Thank you,' she heard herself say. 'That would be lovely.'

'Fantastic! See you later then.'

'See you later,' she agreed numbly, then she let herself out and made her way back across Hope Street.

Charlie trailed behind her to retrieve his van, his phone buzzing madly in his pocket.

'Someone's keen to talk to you,' she said to him.

'It'll be my boss. I'm a bit behind schedule.'

'It was kind of you to help Vik.'

'Kind of *you*.'

'Not really. You should be the one going for curry.'

For a moment, Ruth thought she saw longing in Charlie's eyes, but then they reached his van and he turned to shove the side up with a grind of metal and a disconcerting flash of giant banana.

'Not me,' he grunted into the van. 'You have fun, OK?'

It came out almost as an order.

'OK,' Ruth agreed. 'Thanks, Charlie. See you next week.'

But the delivery driver just gave a grunt, leaped into his cab and jerked away so fast that he almost collided with a smart little convertible. The girl at the wheel shook her fist and Ruth caught a final glimpse of Charlie bowing his head apologetically, before he was lost down Hope Street. She looked back to number 95 then turned slowly indoors. Her nose was running and her eyes crept to the whisky bottle but there was no time for that, medicinal or otherwise. If she was going out tonight, she needed a bath and some clean clothes.

Chapter Twenty-one

Number 80 Hope Street

Sausages
Bacon
Small beef joint
Potatoes
Frozen Yorkshire puddings
Battered cod
Oven chips
Mushy peas
Best bitter, 4 cans
Nail-tail Shiraz, 2 bottles

Greg's phone beeped and he looked down to see yet another message from Turner's telling him that his driver was held up and would be with him in the next twenty minutes. He checked the time – well past five o'clock already.

'Bloody hell, Charlie,' he muttered, 'what are you up to out there?'

He'd only booked the later slot because Marcus had been delivering his new DJ this morning and he'd felt rather self-conscious about it. He'd looked up the cost of a bespoke suit on the company website and been stunned – it was more than his lift. Mind you, it made him look a hell of a lot better than the lift so perhaps it was worth it!

Marcus had certainly been very pleased. He'd brought a photographer with him and they'd spent for ever setting up a white screen and adjusting the lighting and capturing his 'interesting shape' from all angles. He'd felt quite the model! Marcus had gone off muttering about *Esquire* magazine and Greg had only just remembered to ask him to send copies through for his own website. This whole thing was becoming increasingly surreal but for now the only way to cope seemed to be to ride the PR wave and hope it didn't send him crashing on to a stony shore.

To be honest, it was making him feel quite giddy with nerves. He'd ordered himself solid English food this week, the sort of stuff his mum had used to make, as if that might in some way root him, but it wouldn't do that if Charlie didn't turn up soon. He glanced to the DJ, hanging in the corner, raring to go. The awards were a week tomorrow. Next Wednesday someone from the production company was coming to do his 'VT'. His parents had called him to say they were being interviewed for it and his sister's flight from the States was booked for Friday. Rachel was staying a whole week and he was torn between longing to see her and dreading the weird new Greg she'd be presented with.

She'd seen his 'interesting shape' before, of course, but not since it had been buffed to such a slick shine. It had felt more honest when he'd been properly broken but, then again, he'd been a mean git back then and none of his poor family or friends had deserved that.

'Hey – Greg, old lad. Good to see you.' He could hear his friends' voices now, all gruff and matey as they'd crowded around his hospital bed, bearing packs of pork scratchings and smuggled-in beer, as if the party could somehow continue as if nothing had happened.

They hadn't got it when he'd refused to play along. But then, he hadn't explained it very well, he knew. He hadn't told them that even a sip or two of beer hit the myriad drugs in his veins like the strongest skunk and made his head spin and lose control of what was left of his body. He hadn't explained that his stomach was so delicate that it was hard to get porridge to stay in it, let alone pork fat, and he hadn't said that he'd spent weeks staring, paralysed, into such a vast abyss that pub jokes and banter felt like lemon juice on an open sore. It just wasn't the way he and his mates spoke. He hadn't had the vocab for it and so, like a dickhead, he'd gone for grunting and gruff criticism instead. Worked a treat, that had!

One by one they'd stopped visiting and although a couple of the more persistent ones had tried again once he was home, he'd been stuck with his parents in his retro thirteen-year-old self and soon seen them off. Every so often, he was sure one of them would say 'Pity old Greg's not still here', but then another would retort 'Off round the world with his new mates, isn't he?' and they'd order in another round and put him out of their thoughts for another month or two. And rightly so.

Greg sighed and looked at the time again. No point dwelling in the past, however tempting. He was due over at Vik's at six and if Charlie didn't hurry up he'd be late. He'd had such a nice time last week. It was only when he'd finally limped home that he'd realised that for several lovely hours he'd not really thought about himself at all. Or, rather, he'd not thought about his former self. He'd not spent the whole time looking around and thinking '*before* I could have done this' or '*before* he would have thought that of me'. He'd been far more his travel self than his home one and all week he'd been wondering uncomfortably if maybe he didn't have to send himself quite so far from his own front door for release from his past.

He caught a flash of purple outside the window and looked thankfully out to see a giant banana pulling up. Grabbing his stick, he made for the door, opening it just as Charlie stepped up to knock. The delivery driver visibly jumped.

'Sorry, Charlie, I was a bit over-keen there.'

'No, I'm sorry. I'm very late.'

'Bad traffic?'

'Not really. Just . . . stuff.'

'Stuff?'

'Hmmm. Can I come in?'

Greg realised he was blocking the way and stepped hastily aside. 'Course. Sorry. Again.'

Charlie made straight for the breakfast bar. He looked a little out of sorts, but no wonder if he was running over.

'Hot date to get to?' Greg asked, but Charlie shook his head vehemently.

'No date.'

'Shame.'

'You?'

'Nah – though I am off to Vik's for another of his hot curries.'

'It's Thai.'

'What is?'

'Your curry. At least, that's what Vik was cooking this morning so I assume . . . Sorry. None of my business.'

He was definitely ill at ease. His hands were flickering over the goods in Greg's basket as if they might nip at him and his eyes looked dark around the edges.

'Course it's your business,' Greg told him. 'After all, it was your trick with the wine that got me over there last week.'

'Trick?' Charlie looked up sharply. 'It wasn't a trick.'

'Course it was. And a good one. I'm grateful.'

'It *wasn't* a trick.'

Poor Charlie looked almost tearful and, for the first time in what felt like for ever, Greg found himself in the curious position of being the stronger one.

'OK,' he agreed hastily. 'Let's call it a happy accident then, for both Vik and me. I discovered his amazing curries and he discovered Shiraz.'

Charlie raised a weak smile.

'That's great. I'm glad you're meeting up again. And I, er, I think there might be someone else there too. Ruth Madison from number a hundred and twelve.'

'More matchmaking, Charlie?'

'I didn't—'

'Course you didn't. Sorry. I'm teasing. Sounds like quite the party.'

He kept his voice light, tried to ignore a tug of nerves.

'I'm sure you're used to eclectic groups,' Charlie said.

'I am?'

'From your travels.'

'Oh, right. Yeah. It's weirder, though, on your own doorstep. It's more . . . exposed.'

Charlie looked at him curiously.

'Is that why you travel? To hide?'

'Hide?' Greg felt his face flare. 'Maybe. I tend to think of it more as having two selves. You know, my travel one, all outgoing and daring, and my home one who's more, well, real.'

'Real?'

'Angry and bitter and permanently trying to drown in my own past glories.'

'Right.' Charlie paused and then said, 'But you're doing good things now. At least with your blog you've got a way to move forward. Forgive and forget and all that.'

'Not forget,' Greg said. 'I don't think that's possible. Not bloody forgive either. If I could see that bastard occupational-health idiot again I'd have a few things to say to him, I can tell you. But no doubt he's off earning some stonking salary somewhere, with a flash car and a beautiful wife and a gym membership to keep himself in shape. And to blank out the shape he put *me* in.'

'I doubt that.'

'Why?'

'Well, you don't just "blank out" a thing like, like . . .'

'Like permanently disabling someone?'

'Yeah,' Charlie agreed, his voice small. 'Like that.'

It took the wind out of the sails of Greg's anger and he sighed. 'I'm sure you're right. Don't let disability disable your life, hey?'

'Even if that disability is guilt?'

'Guilt?' Greg looked at Charlie, stunned, but the driver was making for the door. Why did Greg always seem to chase him away? 'Charlie,' he called. 'Charlie, stop. It's fine, really.'

Charlie did stop, as suddenly as if someone had put comedy brakes on him. He nodded to the DJ on its hook. 'Very smart.' He turned back to Greg. 'I do hope you enjoy the awards.'

'Er, thanks, but they're not until next Saturday. I'll see you before that.'

'Maybe.'

'Charlie? Is everything OK?'

'Fine, fine. Great, in fact. It's Friday night, right?'

'Thank God!'

They exchanged matey eye-rolls that were as fake as they were awkward. For a moment, Greg remembered Fridays *before*, when he was home with his bulging new pay cheque. He'd sweep Tia up and head out the door to all the swankiest bars and restaurants he could find to throw it away. So proud of himself he'd been, so uncomplicatedly happy. And now, *after*, he was getting excited about limping across a busy road to eat home-made curry with a lonely old man whose son was too busy leading Greg's old life to bother coming.

'You going out, Charlie?'

'Me? Nah. Work tomorrow.'

'You should . . .' He stopped himself. Who was he to invite Charlie over to Vik's? 'You should look after yourself,' he finished lamely.

'Right. OK. Er, thanks.'

'And I'll see you next week, so . . .'

But Charlie was gone.

Greg watched him get into his van, bump on to Hope Street and head off past number 95. The sun was shining on Vik's pretty flowers and Greg swore he could see steam curling around them from the open window. Curry time. It might not be the high life but he was looking forward to it all the same and he wasn't going to let his stupid paranoias spoil that.

Aromas of coconut and lemongrass hit Greg's nostrils the moment he walked into Vik's kitchen.

'Thai?'

'Just for you.'

'Charlie said as much when I saw him just now.'

'Just now?'

'He was running late. He's not long left.'

He gestured down Hope Street and Vik leaned forward to see, but, in truth, it had taken Greg for ever to juggle his stick and the wine and get across the Friday-night traffic, and Charlie's purple van was long gone.

'You should have brought him with you,' Vik said.

'You know, I thought of that but I didn't want to presume.'

'Oh, the more the merrier as far as I'm concerned. Back in the day, Nika used to invite anyone and everyone – parents from Sai's school, people from her choir, my staff, waifs and strays she met on the street. "Company is good for the soul, Vikram," she'd say, and you know what, she was right. It's not good for us to sit around alone.'

Greg nodded, set the wine on Vik's big table. 'She *was* right. I've spent far too much time alone since my accident. It turns you in on yourself – in and in until there's nowhere left to go. No new ideas, no different perspectives, no jokes or stories or other people's problems, just a spiral of your own.' He realised Vik was staring at him and clamped his mouth shut. 'See!' he said with a sheepish grin.

Vik smiled back and clapped him gently on the shoulder. 'But you must meet loads of people on your trips?'

'Yes. Yes, I must. I *do*. It's not the same, though, as people who are always there. People you don't mind seeing you first thing in the morning, people you can be grumpy with, people you can eat baked beans on the sofa with. People who know the crap TV programme you secretly love, or where you're ticklish, or the silly things that scare you.'

He thought of Tia. She'd been that person for him, but he hadn't realised how important she was and now she was gone. She'd come to see him in the hospital, full of remorse, but he'd been as horrible to her as he had to everyone else and chased her away. And he was glad: no way had he wanted her life to be dragged down to the state of his just because he'd been too much of an idiot to appreciate her. Last thing he'd heard she'd got engaged, but there'd been no wedding invitation. No

surprise, really – he was just a ghost from her past now. Just
. . . Greg stopped himself.

'Sorry, Vik. I'm very maudlin tonight. Let's get that wine
open, shall we?'

Vik smiled again and reached for the bottle but was stopped
by a tentative knock at the door.

'That'll be Ruth from a hundred and twelve. She rescued me
when I had a power cut this morning.'

'Rescued you?'

'She's an electrician. Charlie suggested her.'

'Course he did.'

'What d'you mean?' Vik was heading for the door but he
looked curiously back at Greg.

'Just that I don't think my wine got left at your house by
accident, so maybe this Ruth was engineered too?'

'You can't fake a power cut, can you?'

'Dunno. Ask Ruth.'

Greg watched curiously as Vik opened the door to reveal a
woman of around forty, clutching a bottle of vodka in one hand
and a large carrier bag in the other. She was very tall, maybe
six foot, and well built, but she looked elegant in plain black
trousers and a Shiraz-red top to match her glossy hair. She also
looked terrified.

'I nearly didn't come,' were her first words.

'Well, thank heavens you did,' Vik said smoothly, ushering
her inside. 'Greg and I need a woman to civilise us, right Greg?'

Ruth glanced over to Greg looking even more nervous, and
for the second time that evening he found himself having to
support someone else.

'Dead right,' he agreed, dredging up his best smile, the one
his mother said still made him look handsome, as if that was
some sort of blessing to be counted.

'This is Greg,' Vik said, 'from number eighty.'

'Hello, Greg.'

Ruth came forward, hand outstretched. There was something
very vulnerable about her, a wariness behind the eyes that Greg

recognised from the rehabilitation clinics he'd spent far too much time in. Despite her strong body, she looked as broken as he was, and he pushed himself up to shake her hand.

'Hello, Ruth. Nice to meet you.'

'Hmm.' She looked around her. 'Bit weird, this. I mean, nice weird, obviously. The food smells amazing, Vik, and I'm very grateful for the invitation, really I am. It's just . . .'

'A bit weird,' Greg finished for her. 'I guess it is. Does that matter?'

She gave a hoarse laugh. 'I don't suppose it does. I brought vodka.' She set the big bottle down next to Greg's slim Shiraz and grimaced. 'It was all I had. I've got tonic too.' She dug in the bag to produce a bottle of tonic and then suddenly spun round to Vik, holding the bag out to him. 'And this is for you.'

'For me?' Vik came forward uncertainly and peered into the bag. 'Wow, Ruth!' He lifted out a beautiful food processor, then a succession of attachments. 'This is amazing. Really. But you can't give me this.'

'Why not?'

'It's too much. These things cost a fortune.'

'Not for me. I get them from the tip and mend them. Then I have no idea what to do with them. Take it – you'll be doing me a favour.'

'Really? Well then, thank you.'

Vik began putting the different bits together, exclaiming 'Ooh, dough hooks' and 'Look – a veg shredder.' Ruth watched indulgently and Greg saw her shoulders relax a tiny bit.

'I'll make vodkas before we open the wine, shall I?' he suggested.

'Please.'

It was a strangely comfortable moment, Greg assembling drinks as Ruth sank into a seat and watched Vik test his new machine. It felt . . . nice. OK, so this wasn't a swanky bar and he wasn't a flash scientist, but it was still nice. And if he wanted flash, he had the awards ceremony to look forward to next weekend. His gut twisted.

Candy Drew was going. She'd tweeted him this afternoon: *Can't wait to meet my hero #inspoawards #dontletdisability #soexcited*. Even by the time Greg had seen it, it had been retweeted 173 times. He'd had no idea what to reply and in the end had settled for a picture of his DJ on the hanger and the brief message *All set*. It had apparently been the right thing to do as he'd got a *So cool* back and retweets were well into the thousands, with a worrying amount of speculation added in. No way was Candy Drew interested in anything more than Greg's PR value. Handsome he might be, but broken he definitely was. He had nothing for her.

'You OK there, Greg?' Vik asked.

Greg blinked and realised he'd been stood frozen, tonic bottle in hand. 'Fine, yes. Just thinking about next weekend.'

'Greg's been nominated for an "Inspirational Blog" award,' Vik told Ruth.

'That's amazing.'

'It isn't,' Greg assured her. 'It's just cos some pop star's decided I'm good for her image. It's all fake.'

'In what way?'

She had a very frank stare. Greg hastily poured tonic. 'It's a game – a Twitter game. She decides I'm "inspirational" so thousands of other people do too.'

'But you must have done something for her to pick you?'

'Well, yes. I have a blog about travelling for the less able-bodied.'

'So you *are* inspirational.'

'Not really. I mean . . . I don't feel inspirational. I don't deserve that sort of label.'

Ruth laughed. 'Who does? If it's a game, Greg, why not just play it?' He stared at her and she rose and came to take her vodka and tonic off him. 'Well – why not?'

He shifted. 'Maybe because the stakes are too high.'

'Why?'

She was looking intently at him and he didn't like it. Is this how it would be at the awards, everyone watching him, questioning him?

'They just are, OK?'

It came out horribly aggressive but it didn't seem to faze her. 'OK. Then don't go. You don't have to, do you?'

'No, but . . .'

She smiled. 'But you want to.'

'I don't.'

'It's allowed.'

'It's not that. There's this little girl who wants to meet me and this company who've made me a special DJ and my family are coming and . . .'

'And you want to.'

Did he?

'If I knew it was going to go well, I'd want to,' he admitted.

'And why shouldn't it?'

But why it shouldn't Greg was not prepared to admit, not to a woman he'd known barely ten minutes. Not to anyone.

'Why indeed,' he managed as lightly as he could. He handed Vik his vodka and raised his glass. 'Cheers.'

'Cheers,' they both echoed back and Greg pushed thoughts of next weekend away. Why shouldn't it go well? As Ruth had said, he just had to play the game and pray the dice fell in his favour. And if they didn't, well, he'd been to rock bottom already, hadn't he? Surely there was no further to drop?

Chapter Twenty-two

Charlie drove slowly into the yard and eased his van on to the end of the line. The place was deserted, the day shift long gone and the evening shift out already. Good. He couldn't face any more people today. He just wanted to go home to his blank, empty little flat, curl up and try to block out the rest of the world. His bike was sat in the rack waiting. All he had to do was cross the yard, get on it and cycle the twenty minutes home. He looked to the van door, then back to the bike. He was desperate to go but his limbs felt heavy, his head too fuzzy to issue the command to move.

'One last push, Charlie,' he muttered to himself, but still he sat there.

'Charlie!' The shout juddered through him. 'Charlie, where the frig have you been?'

The door flew open and there was his team leader. Charlie looked down at him, feeling curiously detached. 'Hello, Sean.'

Sean gave him a furious frown. 'What on earth are you doing?'

It was a good question and one for which Charlie had no answer. He reached across to the passenger seat to get his ruck-sack, removed the keys from the ignition and slowly climbed down, forcing Sean to step back.

'Charlie?' He sounded uncertain now. 'You're late.'

'I am,' Charlie agreed, making for the depot.

Sean ran past and squared up in front of him. 'Very late.'

Charlie stopped. 'I am very late, yes.'

Sean folded his arms. 'Why?'

'Why?' Charlie repeated.

That was a good question too but it was taking all his energy to reach his bike and he couldn't find an answer for it either.

'This is a disciplinary matter, Charlie, do you understand that? I've already had to give you a verbal warning. If you can't explain yourself, I'll have to go up to a written warning and if you offend again after that, well . . .'

'I'm out?'

'That's right. And all your fancy connections won't help you then.'

That jolted Charlie into life at last. He reached out and grabbed Sean's arm. 'What did you tell Ryan, Sean?'

'What?' Sean tried to pull away but Charlie held on. 'Let go of me. This is assault.'

'No it isn't. It's a perfectly fair question about my personal data. What did you tell Ryan?'

'Nothing. I told him nothing, Charlie. Let go!'

He yanked away just as Charlie released his grip and he staggered backwards, arms flailing as he battled to keep on his feet. It almost made Charlie laugh, then tears pricked instead and he saw the idiot he was making of himself. He sucked in a deep breath.

'I'm sorry, Sean. It's been a long day. Tricky customers.'

That wasn't really true. The design lot had been so pleased with themselves this week that they'd pressed a bottle of Prosecco on Charlie as a tip, pants-man had been wearing jeans, and he'd got Ruth out of the house. Even now she might be eating curry with Greg and Vik. How good was that? He should open his Prosecco to celebrate, right? If he could ever actually get home. And if he could trust himself with the everyday luxury of drinking.

Sean had, thankfully, stayed on his feet. He brushed some imaginary dirt off his trousers and tugged his thinning hair into place.

'It happens,' he said, eventually. 'We'll, er, keep this one between ourselves, hey?'

'Thanks, Sean.' Charlie suspected his boss wanted more gratitude for his great magnanimity but it wasn't in him. 'Oh, and Sean . . .'

His boss had turned for the depot but now he looked back.

'Charlie?'

'I think maybe it's Hope Street. It's a bit . . . busy for me. Maybe it would be best if Ryan took it on. He's much more . . . experienced, you know, on the road.'

Sean flicked at the imaginary dirt again. 'I didn't tell him anything, Charlie.'

'It's nothing to do with that. I just don't want to be late again. I know there's the personal-touch thing . . .' The words caught in his throat; Hope Street had become far, far too personal. 'But I think maybe I'm not up to Hope Street yet.'

'Right.' Sean looked like he'd ask more but then, thankfully, changed his mind. 'Well, we'll see on Monday. It's training week next week anyway so everything will be shifting around.'

'Training week?'

'New tablets. Enhanced customer service. Everyone's got to learn about it.'

'About enhanced customer service?'

'That's right.'

'Seems a shame.'

'What d'you mean?'

'That we have to learn it rather than just, you know, doing it.'

'I don't think you understand, Charlie. This is a new system.'

'Oh I understand. Here.'

He pulled his clipboard out of his rucksack and handed it over. It was starting to rain and big drops fell on the words Hope Street written at the top. Seeing them, he almost snatched it back, but it was time. What Ryan had said this morning – 'It's not ethical, you see. You can't be visiting certain people, not with your history' – played on a loop inside his mind.

Your history.

Two little words, one great wealth of meaning. With a history like his, how on earth had Charlie thought he could have a future? Yes, he was much better away from Hope Street and if the thought of not seeing Vik or Ruth or Greg dug painfully at his heart, well, tough. It was only what he deserved.

Chapter Twenty-three

'I'd like to propose a toast,' Vik said, swinging round from the stove and thrusting his glass in the air.

Ruth looked at her host. He was flushed from cooking and quite possibly from the two vodka and tonics he'd sunk as the rice cooked. He didn't look like a man who was used to drinking.

'Go ahead,' she encouraged.

Her own two vodkas had done their work and she felt marginally more relaxed in this strange kitchen with these strange men. Well, not strange – they both seemed lovely – but unknown. Vik had a quiet sadness about him and Greg had clearly been in some sort of horrible accident, but what business of hers was that?

'To Charlie,' Vik sang, 'the man who brought us all together.'

'To Charlie!' Greg echoed.

Ruth looked from one to the other, confused. 'The Turner's driver?' she asked.

'That's him,' Greg agreed. 'He linked us all up. Matchmade us, if you like.'

'He's our friendship cupid.'

Vik almost giggled and Ruth looked at him enviously, wishing vodka still affected her like that. She shrugged and raised her glass.

'Then here's to our friendship cupid.' They all drank, save Vik whose glass was empty. He reached for the red wine and Ruth felt a rush of protectiveness that she never felt about her own drinking. 'Perhaps we should eat, Vik?'

He looked over, surprised. 'We should. Of course we should. Look at me, neglecting my duties.'

'Not at all. I'll help. What can I do?' She moved to the pots and he fell back a little. 'Is this OK?'

He nodded. 'It's OK. Thank you. I just . . . I've not seen a woman at the stove since Nika.'

'Your wife?'

'That's right. She died just over a year ago.'

'I'm so sorry.'

He gave a funny little nod. 'Yeah. I am too. But, hey, if she'd been here, she'd have batted that spoon at me and told me to stop gabbling on and feed my damn guests, so that's what I should do. It's Thai food, Ruth. I hope you like it?'

'Certainly do. I went to Thailand on honeymoon with my husband. My, er, ex-husband.'

'Ah. Sorry.'

'No, it's OK. It was a happy time.'

She stopped, caught in memories, and the two men stood awkwardly watching until Greg asked, 'Where's your husband now?'

She looked at him. 'He's in a flat above his hardware store just down Hope Street.'

It sounded so odd when said like that. She glanced towards the window as if she might somehow catch a glimpse of Tony but all she saw was rain flinging itself against the pane. He'd lived in that flat when they'd first been dating. She'd still been with her parents and his three private rooms had seemed like the ultimate luxury. They'd kissed in there, slept together in there. Eventually, she'd stayed the night, then weeks at a time. She'd bought curtains, saucepans. They'd been like little kids in a Wendy house, high on how grown-up they were. She sighed.

'We split up after . . .' She stopped herself. 'We split up.'

'I'm sorry,' Greg said.

'For good?' Vik asked.

She stared at him. 'I think so. I don't think he'd want me back. I mean, look at me.'

She was met with two blank stares.

'What's wrong with you?' Greg asked eventually and, looking down, she realised with something of a shock that they were seeing the buffed-up Ruth she'd created this afternoon.

She'd been hunting for bubble bath when she'd found the hair dye – old, but apparently still effective. And once she'd done her hair, it had seemed logical to shave her legs, dig out some make-up to cover her cold-red nose, and even iron her clothes. And it had worked – they saw the surface, not the bag lady underneath.

If she'd looked like this last week, would she have stayed to talk to Tony? she wondered. Would he have listened? The thought was unbearably seductive but what the hell would she have said? How long did it take to feel the surface shine underneath as well? Too long.

'Thanks,' she managed gruffly. 'Now, food – it smells amazing.'

She bustled about transferring curries to the table, the men falling into step around her and soon they were all sitting down. Ruth fought to focus on the colourful dishes, but pictures of Tony in his flat not far down Hope Street kept intruding. She picked up a serving spoon. 'What's this one?'

'Pad thai,' Vik said. 'I made it in Greg's honour.'

Ruth looked to Greg. 'Oh? Why?'

'I got back from Thailand a few weeks ago.'

'It's all on his blog,' Vik supplied. 'You should take a look – it's very good.'

'You've read it?' Greg asked him, looking weirdly uncomfortable.

'Of course. Silver surfer, me. Nika was very up on all that stuff. Made me buy her a computer years ago. She had a little blog herself at one point. Not a blog, a vlog. That's it. A sewing one, showing people how to sew on buttons, that sort of thing. It was Sai's idea. She was going to be a "YouTube sensation", or so he said, and she might have been too. Very good she was. Very clear. Very smiley. People like smiley, don't they?'

'They do,' Greg agreed. 'I should probably be more smiley.'

'Oh no, no, no. You're cool instead.'

'Hardly.'

'You *are*. All posh photos and super-dry stories and wise words. Nika was an amateur next to you, but people liked her.'

'What happened?' Ruth asked, digging into her curries. They were all delicious and they were certainly helping her cold; she felt miles better already.

'Oh, Sai lost interest. He got a new job that took up all his time and then he met Hermione and decided to make vlogs with her instead.'

Greg's eyebrows raised. 'Oh yes?'

'Not like that! Investment advice. She's a merchant banker. Very clever. Very pretty. It does well. "Nika's sewing bee" didn't stand much chance by comparison. People still watch them, though; I check sometimes. And *I* watch them. I could sew a button on in my sleep, I've watched them so many times.' He glanced to the door at the back of the kitchen but it was firmly shut and he yanked his eyes away again almost immediately. 'Silly, hey, living in the past like that?'

He reached again for the wine and Ruth leaned over and touched his arm.

'It's not silly, Vik. Sometimes the past can be the nicest place to live. I keep Libby's – that's my daughter's – bedroom exactly as it was. My counsellor told me it wasn't healthy. She said I should choose a few precious items to keep in a special box and then clear the rest. Clear it – imagine!'

'Your daughter died?' Vik asked.

Ruth nodded. *Don't offer boring personal information,* she reminded herself, but Vik was asking. He was actually asking.

'Aged thirteen.' She gave a hoarse little laugh. 'You can imagine the room. Typical teen – it's a state. But it's *her* state. I'm not stupid. I know she's not coming back but somehow, in some little way, with her room like that, she's still there.'

Vik pressed a warm hand over hers. 'Do you go in it often, Ruth?'

'Never. I keep the door firmly shut. But I know that I could.'

'Well, for what it's worth, I think that's lovely.'

'You do? Really?'

'I do. You should be able to do what you want with your own rooms. And, in my experience, grief is a minefield. It can explode in your face at any time and you need all the tools you can arm yourself with to get through.'

He gave a little sigh but when his eyes met Ruth's she saw nothing but kindness in them.

'You do,' she agreed quietly. 'Thank you, Vik.'

She glanced to the vodka bottle but it didn't seem the right thing to drink with Vik's subtle dishes and in the end she just grabbed a glass of water from the sink.

'Your son not around this week?' Greg was asking Vik.

'Nah. This ballet show seems to be taking up all his time.'

Ruth jumped. 'Your son does ballet?'

Vik laughed so hard he almost choked on his som tam.

'Sai! Doing ballet! That I'd love to see. No, it's his daughter.'

'Daughter?'

Ruth felt her heartstrings twang the way they always did when people mentioned their children.

'Aleesha,' Vik said. 'She's three years old and, oh, she's the cutest thing. Here, let me show you.'

No, Ruth wanted to say, but the word got lodged behind a mouthful of pork laap and, besides, Vik was already leaping up and making for the closed doorway at the back of the room. He opened it a crack and slid rather self-consciously through, shutting it carefully behind him. Ruth looked curiously to Greg but already Vik was returning, bearing a framed picture like a trophy before him. She fought to swallow a suddenly enormous lump of pork and made herself look at the photo as Vik set it down before them. It showed a little girl with a heart-shaped face and a mass of dark curls playing on a swing. Caught on the rise, she was laughing merrily into the camera.

'She's lovely, Vik,' Greg said.

And she was. Ruth stared and stared, as if the little girl might leap off the swing and out into her arms.

'She's such a livewire,' she half heard Vik saying. 'Always looking for the next tree to climb or toy truck to ride. And she loves swings, as you can see.'

Ruth stretched out a tentative hand and touched the silver frame.

Mummy!

'She's beautiful.'

She sniffed and dug hastily around for a tissue. Vik sank down into the seat next to her and proffered a beautifully clean hanky.

'You look sad, my dear.'

'It's just a cold,' Ruth mumbled, gratefully hiding her face in the crisp cotton.

'Of course. And perhaps, also, my Aleesha reminds you of *your* daughter?'

Ruth peeked out of the hanky to consider the picture. She drank in the little girl's laughter, the kick of her feet, the way her eyes were turned so merrily to the eye-blue sky above her.

'It's more,' she admitted, 'that she *doesn't* remind me of her. Libby was never like this, Vik. You see the pure, easy joy your granddaughter has here; Libby never had that.'

'How do you mean?'

Ruth looked from him to Greg. They were both sat quietly, waiting for her to speak. And she wanted to, she so wanted to. She'd said it out loud now: Libby died. She'd said it several times and the world hadn't imploded, but she'd managed no more than those two simple words. The facts of Libby's death remained locked painfully inside her.

Once, not long after, she'd gone into a Catholic church and got as far as the confessional box before she'd lost her nerve. It wasn't so much that she'd wanted forgiveness – she knew she could never have that – as that she'd wanted to tell someone what had happened, to speak the dreaded words out loud in the desperate hope that it might stop them clawing eternally at her insides. The church had been too intimidating and she'd fled, but these two simple men, sat in a cloud of curry steam, were now offering her the chance she'd so long craved. She reached for her vodka, tasted water, and liked it. It was time.

'The best way I can describe it is that Libby never had this light.' She moved the photo around, analysing it. 'Life was always troublesome for her. She'd have happy phases, yes, but they were manic, as if she'd watched other people and was copying them rather than just being naturally content.' She dared a look up but both men just continued to watch her. 'It took us ages to realise it. She'd have these awful bouts of anger but we just thought the terrible twos were going on and on. And on. It took us until she was ten to seek proper help.'

'And then?'

Ruth put the picture of Aleesha on the table, face down. 'You don't want to know.'

'We do,' they both said, quiet but sure.

'Depression.' Neither of them flinched. She rolled the word around her tongue. 'The doctors said she had depression. I was stunned. And Tony – Tony was angry. I watched him rant and rave, blaming himself, the doctors, the school, everyone but Libby. He was red in the face with fury and I hated it.'

Greg grimaced. 'Maybe it's a guy thing, Ruth. After my accident, I found anger very much the easiest emotion.'

'Me too,' Vik said. 'I was angry for ages after Nika's death. I clung to it. Like you said, Greg, it's easier. Anger is hot and sharp. It has a language. It's not a very nice one but that's what's so good about it. It strikes out. Not like grief; grief burrows inwards and that's much more painful.'

Ruth looked from one to the other, intrigued. Is that all Tony's rage had been – grief?

'Who were you angry at, Vik?' Greg asked.

'Everyone,' Vik said fiercely. 'I was angry at myself for not waking up when Nika took the tablets and I was angry at Nika for taking them.'

Ruth stared at Vik. The curries seemed to swim between them as his face came into super-sharp focus.

'Your wife . . . your wife committed suicide?' she stuttered.

Vik looked at her with a sad little smile. 'She'd have called it self-euthanasia as she was dying anyway – cancer. But, yes, effectively she committed suicide.'

Ruth stared at him. All the hurt and pain of the last year and a half seemed to be rising up inside her, fighting to get out.

'She committed suicide,' she repeated. Vik flinched and she grabbed at his hands. 'Sorry. I'm so sorry to repeat it, Vik, but you see . . .' She swallowed again. 'You see, Libby committed suicide too.'

It was the first time she'd said it out loud to anyone. The endless counsellors had known already so she'd never had to speak the actual words. They sounded hard and shocking, but somehow less hideous than she'd imagined.

'Can you tell us about it?' Vik's voice asked, unspeakably gentle.

'Do you want me to?'

'Yes.'

One word. So straightforward, so certain. Ruth drank her water, letting the cool simplicity of it open up her throat. Then she nodded. 'OK, I will. We were on holiday. Hay-on-Wye. Libby wanted to go to the literary festival and Tony and I were delighted because it was the first time she'd shown an interest in anything other than watching horror films and listening to weird music. She'd got this new English teacher, you see. Some young man who'd told her she had a talent for literature. I think she had a bit of a crush on him. I don't know. I didn't care.

'Suddenly she was asking for a library card and spending all her pocket money on Amazon. Books came through the door every second day and she devoured them. I'd find her stretched out on her bed reading at all hours of the day and night and she'd talk about the characters avidly, as if they were her friends. It was like she'd found a key to another world and I didn't know whether to be sad it wasn't *our* world or just glad she'd found somewhere she felt at home. And loads of people read, right?'

'So I've heard,' Greg said, an edge to his voice. Ruth looked at him curiously. 'The occupational therapist on my boat liked to read. Liked it better than treating real people.'

Vik huffed loudly. 'Much like the carer at Nika's home. Mr Bloody Bookman. Full of fictional characters, he was – not so good at real people. I know which *I* think is more important.'

Ruth looked from one to the other, curiously comforted. 'Tony and I, we'd never been reading types. The odd newspaper, a comic or two when we were young, but not novels. Not fiction. I did try, we both did, but the books this teacher was recommending to Libby were such big, heavy things and at the end of a long day wrestling with people's electrics the last thing I wanted to do was wrestle with words too. Tony was the same. "It's all bollocks, if you ask me," he said one night and we laughed. Oh God, how we laughed. We dismissed it all so lightly. "Intellectual bollocks," we said. "Made-up stories with no use or power." How wrong we were.'

Ruth thought back to the first days of that terrible holiday a year and a half ago. It had all seemed to be going so well. Libby had taken a pile of books with her and after a few half-hearted attempts to get her to come walking with them in the Brecons, they'd just left her to it. It had been easier. Or it had seemed it at the time. God, if she could go back now, she'd prise her daughter off those books and take her kicking and screaming up every damn mountain in Wales. She'd listen to her whinge and moan and drag her teenage feet for hours on end because she'd be alive. The wind would be in her greasy hair and the dirt on her ripped jeans, and her hands – even if she only ever used them to push her mother away – would still be warm.

But she hadn't. Neither of them had. They'd left her in her books and gone walking just the two of them and, God, it had been glorious. They'd walked miles and truly got on with each other for the first time in far too long. They'd stopped in pubs and ordered second pints because Libby wouldn't notice whether they were there or not. And she hadn't. She'd had no idea where they were. But they'd had no idea where *she* was either. It had been just two days later that she'd walked herself out of their lives.

'Virginia Woolf,' Ruth said. 'Have you read her? Have you read about her?'

'I have,' Greg said. 'That is, Tia used to like her. She'd go on about her to me.'

'Then you'll know how she died.'

Greg looked at the floor. 'She drowned herself.'

'How?' Ruth demanded. 'Do you know *how* she drowned herself?'

Greg swallowed audibly. 'I believe she put stones in her pocket and just . . . just let herself go.'

Ruth nodded. 'She did. She had depression, you see, bouts of darkness, just like our Libby. She called them "glooms". I read about it. Afterwards. Stupid. What use was it to me then? I should have read it first. I should have seen Libby's obsession with this strange woman with a death wish and I should have battled those tangled words with every ounce of my strength because they were battling with my daughter. They were seducing her with promises of rest and solace and some sort of heroic end. As if sinking to the bottom of a cold river, alone and lost and in the grip of merciless stones, was heroic!'

Ruth paused and blew her nose self-consciously but still they waited. She put the hanky down.

'It all went wrong the day of the festival. Tony and I were dreading it – we'd much rather have gone out into the Brecons again – but it was only one day and she was so manic with excitement that a bit of boredom seemed a small price to pay. But we should have seen the signs. She was too excited, too wound up in her own visions. I think she was expecting some sort of soulful communion with her literary heroes and what she got was rain and mud and crowds of noisy people. What she got were seats behind a pillar and inane interviewers asking anodyne questions and not one of the bouncy microphone-holding festival helpers noticing a desperate girl waving her hand in the air to ask just one of her own.'

Ruth closed her eyes, remembering the way Libby's excited little face had closed up as her mood had got darker and darker. She and Tony had looked at each other and known without speaking that they had to get her away. They'd been heading out of the marquee when one of the volunteers had stepped up and asked if she'd like to fill in a feedback form. They especially liked to hear from younger visitors, she'd said – big mistake.

Libby had let rip. She'd gone on and on at her about how no one had been keen to hear from her in the question time, how no one had paid any attention to someone with an actual intelligent question to ask because they were so busy scrambling over themselves to hand the microphone to fat middle-class people who wanted to know 'where your inspiration comes from' and 'do you write every day', as if it was the author that mattered and not their creation. And, God, Ruth had been proud of her then. She'd stood there watching her daughter, her Libby, give the most eloquent, thoughtful argument they'd heard in that damned marquee in all of the fancy festival and what had the woman done?

'They called security on us,' she told the others. 'Libby got angry with them and they called security on us. And, of course, then Tony bundled in and that only made things worse. We were marched out of there like criminals and we took Libby home to the holiday house, raging and fuming. When she said she was going to bed to read we let her. We just let her. She ran into the arms of bloody Virginia Woolf and we . . . we sat downstairs and opened a bottle of wine and tried to forget all about it. The path of least resistance, let me tell you, leads to hell.'

Ruth paused for breath as memories swirled around her like the devil's own flames.

'What happened, Ruth?' Vik finally asked.

She sighed.

'D'you know what, Vik, I don't know. I can guess, but I don't know. And why don't I know? Because I was asleep. I was tucked up with half a bottle of red inside me, snoring off the embarrassment of being thrown out of a stupid literary festival I hadn't even wanted to go to in the first place.'

She clutched her hands tight around her water glass as if it might somehow tether her to the world so the memory couldn't pick her up and take her, screaming, to the dark places where it found her so many times in the night. She hadn't woken up when her daughter left her bedroom. She hadn't heard her go downstairs and so she hadn't gone out and stopped her. She hadn't asked her what was wrong so she'd never, ever know exactly what had been going through her mind.

She only knew that she'd been reading *Mrs* Frigging *Dalloway* and Michael Cunningham's *The Hours* and she could only pray with every fibre of her being that her little girl had still been in that literary world, that she had somehow imagined she was Virginia Woolf or her character or both – that she'd walked to that river in a trance and picked up those stones wanting to end some imaginary life she'd hooked into and not her real one with Tony and her, because if it wasn't like that she simply couldn't bear it.

She closed her eyes and straight away there they were – Libby's big, blue eyes. Scared. Definitely scared, staring at her through the darkness of the water. Pleading with her. And there was her daughter's hand, reaching out for help, and now she opened her mouth to cry 'Mummy!' and the black, cold water rushed into her poor little lungs and claimed her.

'If she went into that water hating me,' she burst out, 'then I hate myself one hundred times more. And if I think that when those stones pulled her to the bottom and she opened her poor little lungs and the water poured in, she looked for me, her mother, to rescue her and died knowing I hadn't been there for her, I want to die myself. I *deserve* to die myself.'

'No!' Vik leaped up. 'No, Ruth, you mustn't think like that. It wasn't your fault.' He grabbed her arms, shook her. 'You mustn't blame yourself.'

'Why not?' she asked him. 'Why mustn't I?'

'Because she chose to die, Ruth, just like my Nika did. Have you thought that maybe she went happily? That mortal life was just too much for her? That there was a sort of ecstasy to her passing?'

'Ecstasy?' Ruth stuttered.

'I'm not saying this right. I don't mean she wanted to leave you, just that life was too big a burden for her and that, in casting it off, she maybe went happily, at peace.'

'With water in her lungs?'

'They say it's a very dreamy way to die,' Greg said. 'The brain, starved of oxygen, goes into a hallucinogenic state, similar to being on drugs.'

'It does?'

He nodded keenly. 'There are people who've been rescued at the last minute that have said so.'

'And, any which way,' Vik added gently, 'there's no point sending your life after hers, is there?'

Ruth grabbed his arms. 'But I see her, Vik. I see her all the time. I see her beautiful blue eyes in the dark water and her little hand reaching for me. And I hear her calling me, again and again and again. *Mummy!*' She clapped her hands over her ears. 'I should have pulled her out. I should have pulled her out long, long before she waded into the river. I was her mother.'

'And she was ill.'

Vik's calm voice pulled her back from the brink of those terrible, sucking waters. She dropped her hands slowly to the table.

'Which is why I should have been reading her books before her. Do you know how they found her?'

The two men shook their heads.

'It was a young policewoman, barely out of school. She asked if she could look in Libby's bedroom and within just a minute or two she was dashing out of the house with *The Hours* in her hand shouting "Search the riverbank" into her radio. She knew how Virginia Woolf had died, you see, and so she knew where to look.

'If I'd known, if I'd seen that book and gone running to the river, I might have been in time to stop her. They reckon she'd not long been in the water. I could have grabbed her hand and held her back and told her that I'd do everything I could to make this world, *our* world, bearable for her. I could have told her that I loved her, that I thought she was wonderful. I could have told her how proud I was of her for standing up to that volunteer and how far that ferocity and belief would get her in life. But I didn't know and so I only got there in time to see a man in a wetsuit bringing her up out of the brown water, limp and pale and dead.'

She stopped, overwhelmed by memory. The words sat there, between them. Ruth could almost see them shimmering in the steam. She focused on them, not daring to meet either man's eye. And then, from somewhere through the messy fog of guilt and grief and horror, Greg said, 'It's not your fault.'

She looked at him. 'I was her mother.'

'And she had depression. You said it yourself. Clinical depression. That's hard, Ruth. I know, I've been there. It grinds you down, cuts you up; it breaks you. It can be fought, yes, but it can't always be defeated. It's as much a disease as cancer.'

'Rubbish!'

'It's not rubbish. Depression is like a growth in the brain – a hard, determined physical growth, swelling up and forcing out the other, healthier bits that can resist temptations like suicide.'

'Temptations?'

'Haven't you been tempted?' Ruth bit at her lip. 'Haven't you?' She nodded. 'Vik?'

Vik nodded too. 'Horribly tempted. They left Nika's morphine here after she died. No one thought to take it away. It's still here, still locked up in the cupboard. I still have the key. Many's the night I've thought about taking it, about joining her. She was allowed, after all, so why aren't I?'

Ruth squeezed his hand. 'Because,' she said slowly, 'if you did, who'd make us curries?'

And then Vik was laughing and Greg was laughing and somehow, some crazy, messed-up, glorious how, she was laughing too. Suicide wasn't funny and yet still the laughter came, tinged with tears but all the better for it.

'Oh Ruth,' she heard Vik gasp, 'God bless you.'

And somehow it felt as if he actually did. Not that she believed in God, not a religious almighty-type God anyway. But here, creased up with guilty laughter with two men she'd never met before today, she felt like there was some sort of deity of collective consciousness, a greatness made up by the meeting of human minds that was, finally, worth being blessed by.

Chapter Twenty-four

Charlie was soaked by the time he got home. His Turner's waterproof had protected his top half but the water running off his cycle helmet had channelled straight down his neck, forming an icy line along his spine, and his trousers were wet through. He'd forgotten his gloves and had to physically peel his frozen fingers off the handlebars to lift the bike up the steps.

He squelched into the lobby, one shoe full of water where a lorry had splashed a puddle straight into it, and the other equally so where a car had turned left in front of him, forcing him to put his foot down on a blocked drain. His fingers were still too cold to undo the combination on his padlock and with a grimace he slid both hands under his coat and into his armpits to warm them up. The sensation of cold flesh against warm was both agony and ecstasy and he was standing there with his eyes closed, waiting for them to even each other out, when he heard someone coming down the stairs and caught the distinctive nasal tones of Mr Graham.

Hands still shoved into his dripping coat, he shuffled into the alcove behind the stairs and prayed he wasn't seen. He'd heard nothing more on the blasted seedlings but the last thing he needed was to jog his neighbour's memory.

'Do you think Lucy will be there?' he heard Mr Graham say, and then a woman's voice in reply.

'I do hope so. I want to ask her all about her geography trip. Such fun things they do in school these days.'

Charlie blinked and risked a peep out. Mr Graham was coming down the stairs in a very smart suit, his white hair brushed and a high shine on his well-worn shoes. On his arm was an attractive older lady, presumably his wife, wearing a floral dress and a big coat. She was smiling up at him as she talked and he was looking indulgently down at her.

'Mandy said it was snowing at the top,' he said. 'Good job we got her that thermal sleeping bag for her birthday.'

'Worth the extra twenty quid?'

Did Charlie detect teasing?

'It was. You're always right, my love.'

He did! He couldn't resist leaning out a little further.

'Surely she'll be there,' his wife went on, smoothly returning to the original subject. 'It's her mum's fortieth after all. Teens these days, though, they . . . Oh!' Mrs Graham spotted Charlie and stopped. He tried to draw back but it was too late. 'Oh, my dear, poor you – you're soaked through.'

Charlie looked sheepishly down at the puddle at his feet and fought to extricate his hands.

'It's raining hard,' he said, rather needlessly. 'I hope you have an umbrella?'

'Of course.' Mr Graham produced a large, stripy one. 'Can't have my Madge getting wet.'

His Madge batted at his arm then turned back to Charlie. 'You get yourself in a hot bath, young man, or you'll catch a terrible chill. Do you live here?'

Mr Graham gave her arm a little tug. 'Charlie lives on the top floor, remember?'

'Charlie?'

'The one who, er, had the bonfire.'

'Oh, of course.' Madge Graham turned back to Charlie and he felt a far greater chill than rain run down his spine, but as she came towards him she reached for his hands. 'I did feel for you, Charlie. Such a terrible thing to happen. I do hope you're looking after yourself.' Charlie gaped at her. 'Are you eating properly?' she went on. 'Young men need to eat properly. And not all that McDougall's stuff.'

'McDonald's,' Mr Graham said behind her.

'That's what I said, Justin.'

Justin! Charlie almost smiled.

'I do my best,' he told Madge.

'Good, good. Life throws stuff at us, Charlie. The thing is not to let it knock us over. I remember . . .'

But at that Mr Graham – Justin – came up and took her arm again. 'Charlie needs to get warm, love.'

She shook herself. 'Of course he does. Silly me. I go on something terrible, Charlie. Have that bath, yes?'

'I will. Thank you.'

Charlie stood in the shade of the steps and watched as the couple made for the door, Mr Graham solicitously leaving his wife inside as he stepped out and raised the umbrella for her. And then they were gone, off to their daughter's fortieth birthday party in all their finery. And still Charlie stood there, shaking from the wet and the cold and, above all else, from the fierce shock of such unexpected kindness.

Eventually, he remembered himself and, fumbling the bike lock into place, headed up the stairs at a soggy run until, at last, he was inside his flat. He shed his clothes right there in the hall and went naked into the empty lounge. On the shelves sat the little jar of ash with George Sand's words wrapped around it: *We cannot tear out a single page of our life, but we can throw the whole book in the fire.* He'd thrown the book in hoping to rise up out of its ashes, but men like him didn't rise.

He lifted the jar, unscrewed the lid and slowly, deliberately, turned it over. The ash came out in a grey clump, clouding out around him, but if he'd been looking for some sort of ephemeral release, all that actually happened was that it clung to his wet skin in dark little clods. Of course it did. Life wasn't poetry; he'd learned that the hard way.

Dropping the jar, Charlie made for the bathroom. He glanced at the bath, Madge Graham's words echoing softly in his ears, but he hadn't had a bath since the incident and he daren't start now. Water was too tempting. It wasn't like fire – fierce and bright. Water lapped and soothed and drew you under.

And killed you all the same. No, the shower was safer. Charlie dived under the cascade, letting it run over him, clear and hot and cleansing. And if the tears flowed with it then nobody, not even Charlie, could tell.

Chapter Twenty-five

'To curry!' Ruth said, raising her water glass to the other two.

'To curry!' Greg echoed, grabbing his wine.

They both looked to Vik but the tremors of laughter were still running through him and swift on the back of them came more, less happy shakes. Watching Ruth talk about Libby had sent all sorts of slimy emotions worming around his gut. He could feel them crawling through his innards, looking for bits of him to chew on, and he couldn't bear it any more.

'He doesn't come,' he said.

Ruth slowly lowered her glass.

'Who doesn't, Vik?'

'Sai. My son. He doesn't come to see me any more. He left home, got his own life. I understand that. But he doesn't live very far away and he always says he's going to. "Next week," he always says. "I'm very busy but next week I'll be there, Dad." But he never is. I think . . . I think he blames me for his mother's death.'

'Why?'

'Because I was here, wasn't I? Because I should have known, should have stopped her. He blames me and so he doesn't come.'

'Are you sure he isn't just busy, like he says?'

'No one's that busy.'

'But . . .'

'Here.' Vik leaped up. He had to make them see. 'Come in here and I'll show you.'

He saw Ruth look uncertainly to Greg, but it was time.

He had to show someone. He edged around the table and made for the lounge door.

'Is it rude?' Ruth asked nervously behind him.

He looked back. 'No! It's . . . Oh, just come and see.'

He yanked open the door and followed them as they edged forward, trying to see the room through the eyes of strangers. There was all the usual furniture – the sofa Nika had sat so happily on; the coffee table with its drawer full of her magazines and books; the big TV she'd so loved – but they'd been compressed into the far end where they huddled so close to each other as to be of little use. And hogging most of the once-happy space, staring blankly at them all like something out of *Doctor Who*, was the enormous grey freezer Vik had spent the last months hiding from view.

Greg put out a tentative hand. 'What is this, Vik?'

'It's a freezer.'

'Well, yes. I can see that. But what's in it?'

'And are you sure you want to show us?' Ruth added, her voice shaking.

Vik stared at her. Her big brown eyes were as wide as the saucers Nika had insisted on using for 'smart guests'.

'Why? What do you think I've got inside?'

'Your wife?' she replied, half in a whisper.

'My wife? Oh good Lord, no. I'm not some madman keeping poor Nika frozen to draw out for a quick cuddle each night before she defrosts.'

Greg gave a snort of laughter and nudged Ruth. 'Glad you asked. I wondered myself. So if it's not your wife in there, Vik, what is it?'

In answer, Vik lifted the lid to reveal basket upon basket of Tupperware containers, neatly stacked and clearly labelled.

'Is that . . . curry?'

Vik nodded. Every Friday for the last year he'd made curries for Sai and every Friday for the last year Sai had found an excuse not to come.

'"Keep cooking, Vikram," that's what my Nika said to me. "Keep cooking and he'll come." So I've kept cooking, every

Friday, but he hasn't come. Oh, he appears occasionally, but never to eat and never for more than an hour. He's always got somewhere better to be.' Cold air was billowing out of the open freezer in an icy mist that seemed to creep towards Vik as if the truth was materialising before him. 'He hates me.'

'No!'

Ruth reached for his hand but he shrugged it off.

'He does. He hates me. He thinks I was neglectful and selfish. He thinks I didn't look after his mother and that's why she . . . why she killed herself. He thinks that and he's right.'

'Rubbish!' Ruth said crisply. 'That's total balls, Vik. Come on, I thought you were an intelligent man?'

'You thought wrong. Why would she have gone if she thought I cared?'

'Why would she have stayed when she knew how much you cared?'

'What?'

'You loved her and she knew that. Did she shout at you? Did she tell you she couldn't take it any more?'

'No! I wish she had. If she'd shouted, I could have shouted back. I could have reasoned with her, explained it all to her. I had no idea she was planning it. None. We didn't have secrets, Nika and I, so why did she keep this one from me?'

'You didn't have any idea?' Greg asked.

Vik looked at the curries. 'Not one single clue. Not that night, anyway. I knew she'd been finding it hard. She was dying, and dying fast. She knew it was just going to get more painful and harder work and, above all else, less dignified. She hated that.

'"I don't want you to have to wipe my bottom, Vikram," she said to me once.

'"I wouldn't mind," I told her.

'"But I would," she said. "I would very much. It's not what I want for our last times together."

'And I got that. I could see how it might go at some point, but not then. Not that night.' He banged the freezer lid down in fury. 'We were happy. Or, at least, I thought we were happy.

That night when she came back from the care home we had such a lovely time.'

'What did you do?' Ruth asked.

Vik looked at her. 'Oh, nothing special. That is, nothing grand. No hilltop sunsets or fancy meals or romantic gestures. We just went home together and sat here, in our own kitchen, and drank tea and ate butter chicken and talked.'

He stepped back into the kitchen to run his hand along the grain of the dear wooden table where they'd sat together that night. They'd talked of when they first met and of getting wed. They'd talked of Sai when he was little, of holidays and first days at school and silly Sundays in the garden with the tortoise. They'd talked of him growing up and of the last years as just the two of them again, the circle closing but bigger now, fuller. That's how Nika had described it. She'd told him that he was her sun. She'd told him that he'd made her warm and light and full of life and he'd believed her because that night that's what she'd been.

'That's why I couldn't believe it when, the next morning, she was gone. All gone. No more life.'

'Except that there was,' Greg said, reaching out to put a hand on Vik's arm. 'There was still the life you'd shared.'

Vik nodded slowly. 'She'd made sure I remembered it all before she went. She left me in love. I didn't want her to, but when did she ever listen to me? And she was probably right, she usually was.' He looked round through tears. 'After all, I never did have to wipe her bottom.'

'Oh Vik!' Ruth suddenly flung her big arms round him. He pulled away a little but the hug was so strong and so caring that in the end he leaned into it and let himself fold against her. 'She wasn't cross with you,' Ruth said. 'And she didn't think you were neglectful. Quite the reverse. She knew how very much you cared and she wanted to spare you. You must see that?'

Vik drew in a shaky breath and thought about it. 'Maybe. She always saw things more clearly than me. I think she spent that week in the bloody care home planning the whole thing. Not just the tablets. She saved up the morphine, yes, but she also saved up her energy, her love. She poured it all into our last night together to make it perfect. And it was. It was so perfect I thought it was a new start, a sign that she was well enough for us to have weeks, maybe even months, more. But it wasn't, was it? It was one big, final gift of a night to end everything in style.'

He pulled back and looked from Ruth to Greg. They both nodded.

'It was a gift of love,' Ruth said. 'You have to believe that.'

'I do?' Vik asked, but it was a knee-jerk response for, in truth, the questions were gone.

Nika hadn't left him a note but she'd whispered her love into his ear as he'd gone innocently to sleep that night, and he still replayed it in his head every single evening. It should be enough. He should be able to accept her final words, to respect the decision she'd made even if he didn't like it, even if it had deprived him of the only thing he'd wanted – her. But still, it niggled at him.

'We're not the ones to convince you,' Greg said.

'You've been great. Amazing. I've never really told anyone before.'

'I know. And it's good that you have but we're not the ones who really need to know.'

'Greg . . .'

'You know who you have to talk to, don't you?'

'No, I . . .'

'You know who you have to talk to about that night.'

'I don't . . .'

Vik stopped himself. He did know. Of course he did. He glanced back at the huge freezer and felt the pulse of a hundred uneaten curries emanating from it. 'Dead?' he heard Sai shriek from down the phone, from down too much lost time. 'She can't be dead!' He'd been every bit as shocked as Vik. He probably still was. But they hadn't talked about it. Not once. 'You came,' Vik had said to him. And the reply had been immediate: 'Of course I came, Dad. Of course I did.'

'I need to talk to Sai.'

'Spot on.'

'But he hates me.'

'Like Nika hated you?' Ruth asked. 'Do you not think that maybe, just maybe, he doesn't know how to talk to you any more than you know how to talk to him? Do you not think that maybe all your lives you relied on Nika to do the talking and that without her you're just a bit, well . . .'

'Lost?'

'Directionless, certainly. Go and see him, Vik. Go and see him and his wife and your lovely granddaughter.'

Vik looked from Ruth to Greg. They made it sound so simple but it wasn't. A year of uneaten curries surely told them that.

'I'm scared,' he admitted. 'I'm scared of what he'll say.'

Ruth nodded slowly. 'I get that. I'm scared to talk to Tony for exactly the same reason.' Vik looked at her and she offered him a watery smile. 'Tell you what, if I talk to Tony will you talk to Sai? A pact?'

'A pact?' Vik let out a long, shaky breath. It made sense. He could see from Ruth's eyes how much the offer had cost her and he appreciated it, he really did. But . . . 'Sai's house is massive, Ruth. I never look right in it.'

'What the . . .?!'

'It's true. He outgrew us. We sold our family home so that we could release some money for him to buy his first place. We moved here to Hope Street and he bought a little flat. He was so excited but within the year he was selling it and moving into a fancy apartment block with a security guard and its own swimming pool. Two more years and he was into a four-bedroomed house and then he met Hermione and went scrambling on up the property ladder. And we were pleased, really we were. It's just . . . well, I think maybe he's so far up the ladder now that it's impossible not to look down on us folks at the bottom.'

'But it was you taking that step down that got him going!' Ruth said indignantly.

Greg put a restraining hand on her arm. 'And maybe,' he said, 'it's because you think you're looking up that it feels that way.

You need to talk to him, Vik. Is there somewhere other than his house you can find him? His work, maybe?'

'Goodness, they'd probably think I was a tramp if I turned up there.'

Greg shook his head but now Ruth was jumping up and down. 'The ballet show!'

'What?'

'Didn't you say your granddaughter has a ballet show?'

'I did, yes, next Wednesday, but it's all sold out.'

'Surely they could squeeze you in? You're her grandpa.'

'You'd have thought so, but I guess there are a lot of grandpas out there. Hermione tried but it was impossible. It's in some fancy theatre with proper seats – guess it's hard to just squeeze people into a place like that.'

'A three-year-old's ballet show in a theatre?'

'Only the best for Sai.'

'It doesn't seem the best to me if there's no room for family to attend,' Ruth retorted, then clapped her hand over her mouth. 'Sorry, Vik. Shouldn't have said that. I'm sure it'll be great for Aleesha.'

'Maybe. But you're right – I should be able to go to my own granddaughter's show, shouldn't I?'

'So do,' Greg said.

'What?'

'Just turn up.'

'Yes,' Ruth agreed, 'just walk through the door.'

Vik looked from one to the other. 'Won't they send me packing?'

'Nah,' Greg assured him. 'There's bound to be a no-show or two. And if there's not, play the disability card. It works a treat.'

'I'm not disabled, Greg.'

'They don't know that. Tell them you're dying.'

'Greg!'

'What? You are. We all are. You don't need to say you've only got a few months left, just imply it. Take a stick. It's magic, is a stick.' He waved his own with a funny grimace and Vik looked uncertainly at it. 'Look, you don't have to go for the trickery but you should certainly turn up in case there's a seat free. What have you got to lose?'

'Nothing.' Vik examined the idea, turning it over and over in his mind. From every angle it seemed like a good one. 'Just turn up. That's what I'll do. I'll go to the show and talk to Sai.'

'And I'll go to the hardware shop and talk to Tony,' Ruth said. They looked at each other. Ruth stuck out a big, capable hand and, with another deep breath, Vik slotted his own into it. 'A pact!'

'It seems to be.' He clung to Ruth's hand and she didn't draw away. It gave him courage. 'And if it goes horribly wrong I'll . . . I'll have a bloody heart attack and be done with it!'

Ruth laughed. 'Me too.'

'And I'll feed you both to a polar bear,' Greg told them.

Vik stared at him. 'You'll what?'

Greg gave a funny little shrug. 'There was a polar bear on the ice just before my accident. A lone female, just sitting there staring out across the Arctic. I remember thinking as the winch started chewing on me that I hoped they'd feed me to her. Sometimes I still wish they had. I'd have liked that – for my final act to be nourishing such a beautiful creature. So much better than being burned in a box, don't you think?'

'It's a little macabre, Greg,' Ruth said.

'Is it though? Why should other animals be eaten and not us? Wouldn't I be completing the circle of life? Isn't putting ourselves back into the food chain better than veganism?'

'But surely it would interfere with the natural order?'

Greg snorted. 'And we haven't done that already? Without humans, the bears wouldn't need any help. They'd be happy on their plentiful ice with their plentiful seals. We've taken those things away with our greed for light and heat and endless communication devices, so why shouldn't we have to sacrifice something in return? And it wouldn't even be a sacrifice if we were dead already, just an efficient use of our bodies.'

Vik nodded slowly; what Greg said made a strange kind of sense. 'Nika's body wasn't her. She'd gone from it.'

'Libby's too,' Ruth said. 'When they brought her out of the river it just looked as if the diver was carrying a doll. I reckon she'd have liked being fed to some starving creature.' She shook herself. 'God, I can't believe I'm saying this. Isn't it disrespectful somehow?'

'To pass your flesh on to something that needs it?' Greg asked. 'I don't think so. It's like organ donation, isn't it?'

Ruth nodded. 'Libby was on the donor register. I made sure of it. My cousin had a kidney replacement that saved his life and I'd talked to her about it. She'd agreed.' Ruth picked up her glass, turning it round and round in her hands. 'They were too late for her heart, but somewhere in Britain there are children with her lungs and her liver and her kidneys. She's helping people survive.'

Vik stepped closer to her. 'That's amazing, Ruth.'

Ruth looked at him. 'I guess. It's hard though. When someone out there cuddles their child, a little bit of that cuddle goes around Libby and that makes me feel both proud and very, very jealous.'

She gave a sad smile and Vik put a tentative arm around her. She leaned into it straight away and he felt her relax just a little and was honoured that she trusted him to comfort her.

'Every cloud and all that,' she went on. 'As we stood in the hospital weeping over Libby, someone else was getting the most joyous phone call and whisking their baby in to take life from her death and that has to be a good thing. It *has* to. So, yes, Greg, why not feed our flesh to the polar bears. Why the bloody hell not!'

'I'll drink to that,' Vik agreed, grabbing his glass. 'Cheers, folks – to the ultimate recycling!'

'The ultimate recycling!' they chorused and clinked glasses vigorously.

And, yes, it was a bit weird, Vik thought as he sipped at his red wine. But good weird and that was all he really needed right now. And, besides, the polar bears weren't having him yet, no way; he'd got a family to reclaim first.

Chapter Twenty-six

For the third time in as many minutes the tinkling FaceTime chimes rang out from Charlie's phone. He groaned. They wouldn't give up until he'd answered so he might as well just get it over with. He glanced at the time: 9.05. They'd be at least two bottles of Prosecco and God knows how much claret down the line by now and bristling with their own self-importance. No wonder they wanted to speak to him – the contrast would serve as a blissful reminder of their superiority to the rest of the world, the ranks of which Charlie had so amusingly joined.

'Let's call little Charlie,' they'd be saying, all super-jolly.

That's what they always called him, Little Charlie, with a sort of coo, as if it was a term of endearment rather than the dismissal they truly meant. They might even start out nice, or at least pseudo-nice, with drawn-out 'how-aaare-yous' and carefully sympathetic glints in their bright eyes, but it wouldn't take long for the digs to start. They just couldn't help themselves. He reached for the phone, assuming what he thought of as the crash position: nervous system as desensitised as possible, patience notched up to max, heart hardened.

'Mum. Hi.'

'Charlie, darling.' She was slurring in that way she thought was endearing. At least being a hundred miles away, he was spared her pawing at his arm. 'We miss you.'

'Are you all there?'

'Of course.'

The screen waved wildly past the others – his father with

his paunch wedged into his favourite armchair, his big brother and sister on the sofa, George leaning back, legs spread in his I-own-the-world way, and Annabel sat up neatly, tucked in tight even this far into an evening at home.

Who's judging now, Charlie, he admonished himself as they all gave genial waves. He waved back and his mother leaned forward, cleavage astonishingly bouncy for her sixty-two years. Charlie tried not to look.

'Where have all your books gone, Charlie?'

'My books?' Charlie glanced behind. Damn, he'd answered with his empty shelves in the background. 'Spring cleaning.'

'In October?'

'October is the new March.'

She laughed far louder than his poor wit deserved and then George leaned into the picture.

'So you'd rather "spring" clean than come and celebrate Father's birthday?'

Charlie gripped the phone a little tighter. It had taken even less time than usual.

'I told you, I'm working.'

'Of course, yes – your high-powered job. Silly me.'

'Hush, George,' his mum tried, but it was half-hearted at best and she turned away to pour herself more wine.

George took the phone from her. 'Going well, is it?'

'Yes, thank you.'

'Interesting work?'

'It's fine.'

'Made any, er, exciting deliveries?'

George's lips, stained with expensive wine, made it clear how unlikely he found this to be.

'No, George, no exciting deliveries.'

Charlie thought of the design lot and of pants-man. He thought of Greg and Vik and Ruth and felt a little as if he'd betrayed them with such an easy dismissal, but his brother wouldn't understand and would care even less. There was only one topic that really interested him.

'How are you then, George?'

'Exhausted. Daddy works me like a demon.'

'Hardly,' Annabel said. The phone swung to her. 'Georgie's gone into marketing, or so he calls it. Seems to mainly involve going to parties and dinners.'

'You're just jealous,' George crowed from off-screen.

'I am not.' Annabel turned to him, Charlie forgotten. The phone dropped to show their knees. 'I'm loving finance. It's the heart of the business.'

'The bowels, more like – where all the shit gets processed.'

'George! That's horrible. Daddy, you won't let him get away with that, will you?'

A rumble in the background made it clear that their father would absolutely let George get away with it, as he always did. Annabel was the more intelligent of Charlie's siblings and by far the harder worker, but George dazzled. He always had. Life was effortless for him.

'So learn from that,' his mother had once told Charlie when he'd complained about it. 'Don't take things so to heart, darling. The only person you hurt is you.'

If only that were true.

Charlie looked to his plain white ceiling to avoid the sight of his siblings' knees jiggling about as they continued to bicker, before suddenly his father grabbed the phone, holding it so close to his face that Charlie could see every individual pore. He tried not to lean back.

'Happy birthday, Dad.'

'Thanks, Charlie. OK there?'

'Fine.'

'Good, good. How's life on the road?'

Goodness – his dad could join Sean and Ryan in their B-movie.

'Pretty straightforward, thanks.'

'Excellent. You'll have to tell me about it. Or, I know, I could maybe come up and see you there sometime?'

'No! I mean, best not. I have a rather hectic schedule.'

'You might be right. Lunch then. Or dinner. What about dinner? Delivery drivers still eat, right?'

Charlie sighed. 'Right, Dad.'

'Good. That's settled then. I'll let you know when I'm in the area. Or Mummy will.'

'Great.'

The screen flashed past the arm of his dad's chair, across the log burner and round to the beautiful oak bookshelves that had so fascinated Charlie as a child. For the first time, he felt a pang of longing for home.

'Are you really working all weekend, Charlie?' his mum asked, suddenly appearing on the screen, her head tipped pleadingly sideways.

She sounded wistful, almost sincere. For a second, Charlie considered admitting that he was free on Sunday but then, behind her, George said, 'Little Charlie has a very important job, Mummy,' and he came to his senses.

''Fraid so. Sorry.'

'You could just jack it in, couldn't you? I mean, at that salary, surely it's hardly worth the effort?'

Ouch! However much he prepped himself they still managed to wound – him and most of the population besides. She had no idea. No doubt their wine bill for this evening would be about his monthly salary but that wasn't the point.

'I can't just give up, Mum. I've signed a contract. Imagine if everyone went back on their contracts?'

'Good point,' he heard his dad grunt in the background.

His mum glared in his general direction. 'But, Charlie, I'm sure—'

'I can't just give up, Mum.'

Quiet but firm, that was the best way to deal with his family. And, sure enough, she drooped and grabbed for her wine.

'Quite right, Charlie,' she said, tight-lipped around the edge of her glass.

'Thank you.'

'But if you change your—'

'Mum!'

'Fine, fine. If your stupid delivery vans are more important to you than your own family then who are we to stand in your way?'

Uh-oh – she'd tipped over from wheedling to accusatory.

'So,' he said quickly, loudly, 'have a lovely weekend and I'll see you all soon, right?'

'Very soon,' George called. 'I think we've ordered a delivery for tomorrow, haven't we, Pater?'

He and Annabel roared with laughter. Their mum looked across and, obviously remembering where her affections lay, laughed with them.

'Bye, Charlie.'

'Bye, Mum. Bye all.'

The phone wavered around the room, everyone half-waved and he heard his dad say, 'Lord, I need a whisky,' before the connection clicked off and they were gone.

The sudden silence was a huge relief.

Wasn't it?

WEEK FIVE

Chapter Twenty-seven

Vik twitched nervously at the lapels of his suit. Was it too formal? Not formal enough? He had no idea what was appropriate for a three-year-old's ballet show and had stood in front of his wardrobe this afternoon for longer than was dignified for a man of his years.

'What shall I wear, Nika?' he'd asked, as he'd done so many times when she was alive and, as it always had back then, the answer had bounced straight back to him: *Dress smart and you'll feel smart.*

So, with a quiet nod, he'd released his old workwear from the wardrobe in the spare room. It had come out with the smell of the office and a different era of his life: of leaving the house first thing in the morning with a coffee and a kiss and returning several number-filled hours later to tea and, of course, a kiss. Always a kiss. Even if they'd had an argument, he and Nika would always kiss each other hello and goodbye and goodnight.

'What if you had a horrible accident and died?' Nika would say. 'How would I ever forgive myself if a cross word was the last thing you'd had from me?'

Wise words and a wise practice too – a kiss took the sting out of any dispute. No one kissed him hello or goodbye any more though; maybe that's why he hardly ever left the house. He hadn't realised quite how much of a recluse he'd become until he'd caught the bus into town on a busy Wednesday afternoon and been bewildered by the crowds and the traffic and the sheer logistics of getting from A to B. The bus had been packed and when a young man had got up to offer him his seat he'd almost wept with gratitude, not so much because his legs were tired as because the bumping and jostling of so many other humans had been almost too much to bear.

But here he was, outside the theatre and it seemed, from the number of families heading through the big doors, that he'd come to the right place. He'd googled it on Nika's computer and it had been remarkably easy to find. Links had come up straight away to the dancing school's website, Facebook page and Twitter account. On Facebook, he'd found a picture of the rehearsals that had supposedly kept his family from him and he'd scanned it eagerly for Aleesha. He thought he'd spotted her crazy curls among the mass of little girls but the photo was artistically blurred and it had been hard to tell. Surely, though, he'd be able to pick her out on the stage?

Vik felt a shiver of excitement, almost like the long-forgotten thrill of going on a date, and took a few steps forward. The theatre was a smart little Georgian building with a pillared porch at the top of curving steps, people milling around beneath it. It wasn't yet five but already it was almost dark and the lights of the theatre made them all look very glamorous. And at least there were other men in suits. OK, so theirs said 'Daddy's come dashing from work', rather than 'Grandpa feels uncomfortable among all these fancy people', but so what?

Dress smart and you'll feel smart, he told himself, then put his head up and made for the entrance.

'Good evening, sir.' The girl behind the ticket desk was young and smiley. 'Are you picking up tickets?'

Vik looked nervously around but could see no sign of Sai or Hermione. He leaned over the counter. 'I don't actually have a ticket. I was hoping there might be some returns?'

'Returns?' She gave a little frown and Vik's hopes plummeted.

Who would give up the chance to see their little sweetie in a tutu? He'd been mad to come and now he'd have to face that packed bus home again for nothing.

'It doesn't matter. I just thought—'

'We don't have any returns, sir, but there are seats available.'

'There are?'

'Oh yes. Quite a few.' She leaned in too. 'It's quite a big theatre, you know, for a kids' production.'

Her eyes were friendly, almost conspiratorial.

'I was told it was sold out,' Vik said.

She shook her head. 'Oh no. Perhaps the dancing school just said that to look, you know, successful.'

She gave him another complicit smile and he returned it, though the cogs in his brain were turning and he didn't like the grooves they were falling into. It wasn't the school who'd told him it was sold out, but Sai. He hadn't wanted him here. Why not? Was he that embarrassing? He'd had a shave, his shirt was clean, he was even in a damn suit.

'So how many tickets would you like, sir?' the girl was asking.

'What? Oh, just one, please.'

'That's great. I have a single seat free on the front row. You'll be so close you'll almost be able to touch their little dancing feet.'

'Perfect.'

Vik took his ticket with a grateful smile and tucked it into his suit pocket, then looked nervously around the foyer, teeming with parents braying to each other with ultra-smooth vowels.

'There's a bar to the right,' the girl said in his ear.

'Good idea. Thanks.'

He gave her a final smile and dived through the crowd. Buying a drink would at least be something to do until it was time to go in and a glass of red wine would be very welcome. He'd got quite a taste for it since sharing that first bottle with Greg.

It struck him as he waited his turn that this was the first thing he'd actually embraced as a new pleasure for himself, a thing to savour – a reason, if you like, to still be alive. It sounded a rather overdramatic thing to say about a glass of red wine but it was still true, and although a little bit of Vik hated that he had to find Nika-free things to enjoy now, he knew she'd be pleased and tried to feel proud of himself for this step. He reached the front of the queue.

'A glass of red wine, please.'

'Certainly, sir. We've got Shiraz, Grenache, Merlot or Cab Sauv.'

Vik blinked but tried not to panic. What was that nice kangaroo wine of Greg's? He ought to know – he'd ordered the damn thing himself last week – but his stupid old mind wouldn't call it up.

'Which would you recommend?' he asked eventually.

'The Merlot is very good,' the waiter replied in the sort of patronising tone that made Vik want to order one of the others, save that he couldn't remember what they were.

'Fine.'

The price of it made Vik's eyes water. He could have had a whole bottle delivered by Charlie for that, but it tasted good and he felt better armed for cultural combat with it in his hand. He found a spot against the wall and stood sipping and watching the crowds milling around, looking for Sai and Hermione and wondering what on earth he'd say when he found them. 'Surprise!' seemed the best option, and the thought of Sai's thunderstruck face gave Vik a moment of dark pleasure before he remembered this was his son and sadness drowned it out.

He watched a group of women stood just in front of him, all drinking something pink and bubbly from fluted glasses and fighting to praise each other's outfits.

'Such darling shoes,' he heard.

'And such a pretty top. Peach can be so flattering, can't it?'

'Especially at our age.'

It was clear, even to Vik, that the woman in the peach top was considerably older than the others and that the claim of communality, much like the praise, was designed to separate as much as to join. He watched the perfectly taloned hands on the long stems of the glasses and wondered how any man these days ever dared to approach such terrifying creatures. But then suddenly there was Sai, diving through the crowd, phone in one hand, briefcase in the other, wearing a suit at least five times more expensive than Vik's old thing. He seemed to know everyone and greeted them all with charming smiles and nods as he carved his way through to stop, not far from Vik, with a loud 'Darling!' As she turned, Vik realised that his daughter-in-law was one of the group of women.

'Sai!' she cried. 'At last. Honestly!'

It was a showy telling-off and Sai grinned.

'I know. I'm sorry, darling. I just couldn't get away.' He kissed her loudly and added to the crowd as a whole, 'Bloody board meeting went on and on. In the end, I had to say, "Look, sir, I know this deal is worth several million pounds but I'm afraid my little girl is more important."'

Sighs of pleasure met this undoubtedly nonsense tale and Vik felt a little bit ashamed of his son's shallow crowd-pleasing. He sipped more wine and wished Nika was here to swoop in and kiss Sai and say hello to all his smart friends. Red wine made things easier, yes, but it wasn't a patch on how easy his wife had made them. He was trying to figure out how to slide up to Sai when the doors to the theatre opened and there was a surge forward.

Relieved, Vik stood finishing his drink and let them go, watching incredulously as so many of them carelessly ditched only half-empty glasses as if they hadn't cost the sort of money on which a frugal housekeeper could easily feed a family of four. He watched as Hermione, immaculate if a little pale in a slinky black dress, went to put her flute down and saw Sai take it from her and, as she turned away, finish it in two elegant gulps. At least something of his upbringing had gone in then!

Once his son and daughter-in-law were safely through into the auditorium with their gaggle of friends, Vik made his way to the doors.

'Row A, sir? Lovely. You must have booked early.'

Vik gave the woman on the door what he hoped was an affirmative smile and made his way down the steps to the front. It was indeed a proper theatre with painted balconies and a big proscenium arch, although, to be honest, Vik would have just as happily watched Aleesha in a creaking village hall, sat on a plastic chair and with warm drinks served from a trestle table by smiling mums. Ah well, he was here now and he was going to make the most of it for himself, for Nika who would have loved it, and for Aleesha.

He could hear the chatter of overexcited children in the wings and pictured his granddaughter with her friends. Who'd made her costumes? he wondered. Probably some fancy dressmaker, though they'd never find one as talented with a needle as Nika. Vik reached for his red wine but, of course, he'd finished it in the foyer. He folded his hands in his lap, sat back and waited for the curtains to open.

All around him, people were fiddling with phones and cameras, desperate to capture their little darlings. Vik wanted to point out the great big, professional-looking camera sat ostentatiously at the back, but it seemed everyone wanted their own, immediate record. People were passing a hashtag – #littledancers – between them like some sort of magic code and Vik reminded himself that he really must get up to speed with social media before Aleesha was old enough to use it. He didn't want her thinking he was some duffer.

But now the curtain was parting and a teacher was sliding out. To Vik's surprise, it was a young man, slim and nice-looking in an angular sort of way, wearing unbelievably tight black trousers and a dark orange shirt. To Vik's mind, it was spoiled by the addition of a curious multicoloured scarf, but he supposed it was all part of the theatrical look the lad was being paid too much to project.

'Thank you all so much for coming tonight,' he said, his voice warm and surprisingly low, given the scarf. 'The girls and boys have worked very hard for this and can't wait to show you their dances – though do please remember that they are quite young and one or two may be a little overawed by the occasion.'

The audience gave a polite titter and Vik suspected they were all secretly hoping theirs would be the one to keep dancing after the others had stopped, or to refuse to leave the stage, or all the other potentially viral acts three-year-olds were prone to.

He just wanted to see Aleesha dance. He leaned forward as the teacher left and the curtains swooshed back. Tinkly music filled the auditorium and one by one children came tripping out on to the stage dressed like woodland sprites. And there she was, Aleesha, up on her tippy-toes, her gorgeous face creased in such perfect concentration that it took Vik's breath away.

He watched, rapt, as the sprites skipped and pranced and finally curled up into the cutest little shapes among crepe-paper leaves and pretended to sleep. Slightly older children came out to skip and prance slightly more expertly around them before waking them for a grand finale all together, and then the sprites were gone and Vik was clapping fit to burst. Oh, he was so glad he'd come.

The programme said he had three more dances until Aleesha's year was back on as sugar-plum fairies. He enjoyed them all but when Aleesha returned his heart filled and the stage-space seemed to take on new light. She was in a white tutu this time, the skirt frilling out in exuberant layers above her chubby little legs. Her curls were held back by a deep purple headband and a matching sash was tied around her little middle. She looked wonderfully young but there were hints, too, of the woman she would one day become, and as she came tiptoeing towards the front of the stage Vik half rose in his seat.

She was so close. Her hands were above her head and then, as they all stopped, one toe pointing perfectly forward, she brought them demurely down to rest on her frothy skirt. Vik stared at her, drinking her in. When had he last seen her? He fought to remember back through the run of 'busy tonight' texts to the ring of his doorbell bringing his family to call but it didn't come. Sai didn't come.

Already, though, as he stared up at the little girl, Vik knew that it wasn't all Sai's fault. Here, in front of him, was Aleesha, his granddaughter, Nika's granddaughter – a flesh-and-blood little girl who he could perfectly easily go and visit at any point instead of just sitting behind a freezer full of curries.

'Aleesha,' he mouthed and now on to the stage came the bigger girls, slotting themselves between the littlies as they stepped and

233

spun. Aleesha, with the others, looked up to the girl at her left then reached out and slotted a little hand into hers, and in that moment she looked so utterly like Sai as he'd reached for Vik's hand on the trip to nursery every single weekday morning of his young life, that he gasped. The people either side of him looked round, nudged each other. Vik felt a tear drop out of his eye and then another and suddenly they were streaming down his face. He lifted a hand helplessly towards his granddaughter and, as if she'd felt it, she suddenly looked down.

'Grampie!'

Dance forgotten, she leaped up and down on the spot, giving him a huge wave. An indulgent 'aaah' ran around the room. Cameras whirred. Vik hastily wiped the tears away as Aleesha beamed and waved again. He gave her a self-conscious wave back but then a teacher gave a little cough from the wings and the girl next to Aleesha tugged her back into line. She went happily, totally unabashed, and as Vik gave her a big thumbs-up the dance, thankfully, went on again, #littledancers lit up social media and Vik's heart swam with joy.

He needn't have worried about how to approach Sai as his son pounced on him the moment the curtain fell. He was at Vik's side within the space of maybe just ten 'she was so adorable's, clapping him on the back and hugging him tight.

'Dad! You made it. What a wonderful surprise. Aleesha was so pleased to see you.'

'So it seems. Sorry about that, Sai.'

'Not at all, not at all. They're only little, aren't they? These things happen.'

He was glowing with pride and his friends were crowding round to be introduced to Vik as if he were some sort of minor celebrity. Vik was polite for as long as he could be but finally seized a chance to grab Sai's arm and ask, 'When can I see Aleesha?'

'Oh, any minute, any minute. Hermione's gone to fetch her. She'll bring her straight to you, don't you worry.'

Vik didn't doubt it. Little girls and boys were tripping off the stage into their parents' waiting arms and Hermione would be picking her moment carefully. But so what? He looked keenly to the stage and finally there his granddaughter was, bursting free of her mum's hand and flinging herself bodily into Vik's arms. He staggered, but Sai was there to keep him upright. More cameras flashed but Vik didn't care. Aleesha was warm and wriggly in his arms. Her curls were tickling his cheek, the still-baby smell of her was filling his nostrils, and her laughter was joyous in his ear.

'I didn't know you were coming, Grampie. Daddy said you couldn't make it.'

Vik absorbed this, let it go. 'It was a surprise.'

'It was a good one. Are you coming for tea? Please come for tea. There'll be burgers!'

'Burgers! Oooh, your granny Nika loved burgers.'

Vik looked to Sai, who shuffled his feet. 'A few of us are popping to a local place for a quick bite before the little ones run out of steam. It's nothing much and it'll be very noisy.'

Could he have been any less encouraging? Vik met his son's eyes and saw a coldness inside them. Had he done that? And how did he undo it? He had no idea, but Aleesha was tugging eagerly at his lapels and that was as good a place as any to start.

'Of course I'll come,' he said and was rewarded by a yelp of delight from Aleesha.

'Lovely,' Hermione sang. 'Isn't that lovely, Sai?'

'Lovely,' Sai agreed tightly.

The little ones, in the event, ran out of steam far more quickly than suited their parents. Despite agreeing magnanimously to forgo starters and only have a 'very quick cocktail', the five little girls and one boy in the party were grizzling long before their burgers came out. Some food revived them briefly but then they hit a manic phase that had other diners looking crossly round, the waiters pulling on their iciest politeness, and the parents very grumpily having to rush their confit duck.

Vik had had the burger because Aleesha had assured him it was the 'very best thing here'. Sai had protested that it was a kid's meal, but Vik had said that was fine as he didn't have much of an appetite these days and it wouldn't be a kid's meal with a glass of red. Sai had looked surprised but poured him a glass and as the burger had come with the other kids' meals, it had left Vik free to look after Aleesha as the 'grown-up' mains arrived. It didn't take Sai long to spot the joy of this and he became very expansive as he and Hermione ate at leisure while others battled to keep little Avas and Alfies quiet long enough to enjoy a few bites.

'Aren't grandparents marvellous,' one man said loudly as he tried to spoon risotto into his mouth while fending off a hyperactive monster.

'Bloody fantastic,' another agreed, 'if they don't live in sodding Spain.'

'Or spend most of their time on the golf course. Do you play golf, Vikram?'

'I don't.'

'Perfect! You're so lucky, Sai.'

Sai gave another tight smile and didn't answer. Hermione picked at her green salad. Aleesha, blissfully unaware of any tension, bounced up and down on Vik's lap.

'I want to see you more. Why can't we see you more, Grampie?'

Her voice seemed to carry all the way up the chaotic table and faces turned their way.

'Grampie's very busy, sweetie,' Hermione said.

'I'm not,' Vik retorted. 'I'd be happy to have Aleesha any time.'

'Any time!' someone echoed in something like awe.

Hermione coughed. 'That's very kind of you, Vikram. I didn't realise. I thought . . .' She ran out of words, looked to Sai.

'We were worried it would be too much for you, Dad, you know, without Mum.'

A little sigh went round the table. Somehow, Vik's son had reclaimed the high ground. He was smooth, Vik had to give him that. But then he remembered this was his family, his grandchild.

It was no business game and he should be ashamed of himself for ever getting into this situation.

'That doesn't matter,' he said firmly. 'I know how to look after a child even without Nika here. I'd be delighted to have her.'

'Hooray!' Aleesha cried, bouncing again. 'Can I go, Mummy? Can I go to Grampie's? Can I go for a sleepover?'

'No, Aleesha.'

'Now? Can I? Please.'

'No, Aleesha! It's nursery tomorrow.'

'Grampie can take me.'

'I don't have all your things, Aleesha,' Vik said. Her face fell. 'But tell you what,' he rushed on, 'what about Friday? You could come and stay with me on Friday. Mummy and Daddy as well, if they like?'

He turned his eyes on to Sai; let's see him get out of that.

'Friday?' Sai hedged. 'No can do, Dad, sorry. I've got a work thing.'

'Hermione?'

'She's coming with me.'

'So what were you doing with Aleesha?'

'Babysitter, Dad. What did you think – that we'd leave her alone? We do care for her, you know.'

The words felt laced with dark meaning. Vik swallowed, but he wasn't going to give up now.

'Of course you do, Sai. But, look, this way you don't have to pay a sitter . . .'

'That's hardly an issue, Dad.'

'Well, it should be. Money should never be wasted.'

'But—'

'And, besides, this way you can stay out as late as you like and have a lie-in as well.'

Hermione's eyes lit up. 'A lie-in?'

She looked tired, Vik noticed suddenly. Her perfect make-up was fading a little and he could see bags under her pretty eyes.

'Why not? You deserve it. And I'm sure I can cope.'

'She gets up very early.'

'So do I.'

Hermione looked to Sai.

'He does,' Sai admitted begrudgingly.

He was staring at Vik as if he longed to get him in a dark corner but now one of his friends was leaning in.

'Good God, Sai, why are you hesitating, man? A night out and a lie-in with your lovely wife? It's a dream come true. Snap his bloody hand off.'

Aleesha looked uncertainly to Vik's hands and he wrapped them around her.

'He just means it's a good idea,' he told her.

'Oh.' Her eyes lit up again. 'It *is* a good idea. Does that mean we can do it, Mummy? Daddy?'

Vik saw Hermione look to Sai with something like desperation in her eyes and wondered what was going on in his ever-competent daughter-in-law's mind, but clearly Sai had weighed his options and decided that the most beneficial move at this point was to submit.

'Course you can, sweetheart. Sounds fantastic.'

'Sounds like a morning shag to me,' the other man muttered mournfully and Vik turned hastily to Aleesha to hide his laughter.

'I'll teach you to make curry, Leesha.'

Sai looked alarmed. 'I'm not sure she'd like curry, Dad.'

'Not a hot one!'

'Even so. We tend to eat more, well, European food.'

Sai had the grace to look a little ashamed but Vik wasn't going to let a silly thing like the menu upset his opportunity.

'Fine. European food. I can do that. I eat pasta.'

He pictured the spaghetti hoops in his pantry, knowing Sai would not be impressed, though Aleesha probably would and that's what really counted. He hugged her again and she giggled happily, her easy laughter flowing through Vik like the finest wine.

'Till Friday then, sweetie,' he said, standing up and easing her off his knee.

'Friday,' she echoed happily. 'I'll bring Ted and my Barbies and my blankie. Ooh and my books and maybe my Lego and—'

'Not too much stuff,' Hermione said, picking her up with a fond smile. 'Grampie's house isn't very big.'

'His table's bigger than ours,' Aleesha retorted and Vik smiled and glanced to the ceiling in case Nika was watching.

The family that eats together stays together. Well, that hadn't been happening recently but he was determined to sort it out. He had a freezer full of curry to eat up and he wasn't going to let Sai's reluctance stop him any more.

Chapter Twenty-eight

Ruth put the cloth down. The damn deep-fat fryer was shinier than it ever needed to be and all she was doing now was wearing out the cloth. It looked good though – as good as new. She really ought to put it on eBay like Charlie had suggested but the effort of selling her poxy collection of rescued appliances felt far greater than the sum they might ever earn. And it had been so nice giving them away. Vik had been so pleased with his food processor and Maureen still clucked her thanks for her light-up kettle every Sunday.

Not that Ruth had needed vodka this week. Vik had insisted she take her bottle home with her on Friday but it had proved singularly untempting. Every time she'd fancied a drink, she'd remembered the cool taste of the water on her tongue as Vik had told her about Nika taking her own life, and gone straight to the tap.

She wasn't the only one.

She wasn't the only one whose love hadn't been enough to keep someone in the world and that knowledge was like a balm, soothing at least some of the red-raw wounds of losing Libby. Her daughter's eyes had peered less into the darkness of Ruth's sleep this week and she felt so much better for it.

Vik was a lovely man. Anyone could see how kind he was, how generous, how very much in love with his wife. If he hadn't been able to persuade Nika to stay alive then maybe it was true what counsellor after counsellor had told her – that, at the end of the day, it wasn't about the people around the sufferer but the suffering itself.

'Depression is like cancer.' That's what Greg had said. No one expected you to beat cancer. Sometimes people did and that was cause for great celebration, but if you lost the battle it was a tragedy not a failure. Was it possible that it was the same for Libby's illness? Or was that tantalising belief the true temptation? She had no idea any more but someone might – Tony might.

And, in all fairness, she had to talk to him about the house. Another mortgage demand had landed on the mat this morning, scarlet and fat with its own importance, and she had no idea how much time she had left. She'd put it on the growing pile of unopened mail, but she knew that it would be full of words like 'final demand' and 'repossession' and 'bailiffs'. Actually, she wasn't sure whether bailiffs were a real thing, but she was starting to torment herself with what they might look like if they did exist.

Would they just turn up one day, all muscles and tattoos, and bundle her stuff into a van? Would they let her choose which things they took first? Might they be appeased by her collection of appliances and kept from going upstairs? It seemed unlikely, so her new plan was a big lock. She'd fix it to Libby's room to stop the men (or women; no doubt women would deprive people of all their worldly goods in these days of gender equality) going in. Besides, if nothing else it gave her a valid excuse to go to the hardware shop. Right inside this time. How hard could it be?

She'd been reading Greg's blog this last week. She loved all his tales of travel, though she could only take so much of it before it made her feel pathetic and useless. He'd been broken by the teeth of a giant winch, not just the loss of a daughter who had been half-lost before, and he could still get out there and do so much. She'd told herself sternly that going down the road to visit her not-quite ex-husband was nothing compared to trekking a Thai jungle on walking sticks, and had determinedly set today as the day. Now that the moment had come, however, it didn't seem such a good plan.

'Don't let disability disable your life,' she told herself firmly and picked up the fryer. 'Come on,' she said as if it were some sort of curious pet. 'Let's just get on with it, shall we? Let's just go.'

The fryer did nothing as obliging as wagging its tail or running to the door to help propel her forward. Ruth stared at it, forcing herself to remember Maureen's delight in her kettle and the look on Sanjeed's face when she'd taken in the fixed-up scooter yesterday.

'For me?' he'd asked.

'For your grandchildren. To play with.'

'They will be very excited. They will be . . . King of the Road, yes?'

'I hope so, Sanjeed.'

'I know it. You are very kind lady, Ruth. Very kind.'

It wasn't true but it had been nice to hear all the same. And it proved one thing: people liked getting presents. Besides, she'd made a pact with Vik to speak to Tony and she had to have something to report when she went for curry again on Friday, even if it was a disaster.

She fetched her coat, trying not to think of Tony the last time she'd seen him almost a year and half ago. He'd been red in the face and screaming at her. 'Do you blame me, Ruth? Is that the problem? Did I do something wrong?'

'No,' she'd told him. 'I don't blame you. I blame *us*.'

But he hadn't got it. He hadn't seen that their genes must be toxic together.

'You've not got a monopoly on grief, Ruth,' he'd raged. 'It's not your own personal hell, you know. It's mine too. Why can't we at least live in it together?'

'What would be the point in that?' she'd demanded. 'It'd still be hell.'

'Not in time. Just because we've lost Libby, doesn't mean we have to lose each other too.'

But Ruth hadn't agreed. It had all gone wrong when they'd left Libby alone, when they'd looked to each other and, in doing so, had looked away from her. Ruth had been safely in Tony's arms when Libby had got out of bed, put stones in her pockets and walked into the cold, dark river alone. It was hard to get away from that, however irrational it might be.

But maybe it was time to try.

*

The route to the shop was so familiar she could have done it with her eyes shut, which was just as well as they nearly were. The faint sound of kids playing drifted down Hope Street from what had once been Libby's primary school and Ruth felt their happy laughter like icy mist from the grave. Not that Libby had ever really laughed like that; Libby's laughter had always been either manic or mocking.

Ruth clutched the fryer close, wishing she had a box for it. Looking down, she saw her reflection in the stainless steel and stopped dead, staring at it in horror. What had she thought she was doing, brushing her hair into a high shine and putting lipstick on as if this were some sort of date? Her mouth looked ridiculous, all pearly pink, and she scrubbed so hard at it that she almost dropped the fryer. A man and his dog crossed to the other side of the street; she didn't blame them.

It was almost a relief to get to the solidity of the shop, with its display buckets and brooms, plant pots and pesticides. Hardware stores were so reassuringly useful. They spoke of comfort and care and a world in which everything could be mended. You took your house problems to a hardware shop and they dug you out something to fix it. If only, she thought as she tucked into the safety of the wire shelving again, there was a hardware shop for life too.

Broken heart, madam? Don't worry about that, I've got some extra-strong tape that should seal it up in a jiffy.

Money a bit short, sir? Here's some fertiliser to help you grow more.

Feeling a bit depressed, young lady – here's a new bulb that will put the light back into your eyes.

Ruth swallowed. They'd never found the right bulb for Libby and now they were all in darkness. Or maybe Tony wasn't. Maybe Tony was doing just fine, thank you very much. Maybe he had a nice new flat with a nice new fryer and even a nice new woman to eat chips with and the last thing he needed walking into his shop was Ruth and her tip-salvage. Well, tough!

Sticking her head up, Ruth pushed on the door and went inside, hearing the familiar jangle of the bell. It was louder than she remembered and as Tony looked up from behind the counter, she froze.

'Ruth?' He stared at her. 'Oh my God, Ruth! It is you. Come in, come in.'

He was round the counter and ushering her into the heart of the shop before the bell's jangle had died away and Ruth sucked in the familiar musky smell of a thousand household substances and tried not to notice the undertone of Imperial Leather soap that Tony had used in all the time she'd known him.

'It's good to see you,' he said and Ruth looked up into his kind face, desperately wanting to believe him.

Tony was a tall man – six foot three in his bare feet and with shoulders broad enough to carry two children if they'd ever managed to produce a second. He'd been pretty broad in the belly too at one point but he was as skinny as one of his own rakes now and looked disconcertingly like the eighteen-year-old she'd been so dazzled by in this very shop.

'It's good to see you too, Tony.'

They stared at each other. A man examining paints in the corner looked curiously over but they both ignored him.

'Is, er, is that broken?' Tony asked eventually, pointing to the fryer she was still clutching against her chest.

'This? Oh, no. No, it's fine. I just . . . I thought you might like it. For chips. Do you still like chips?'

'I love chips.'

'You've probably got one, though. Silly idea really.'

'No, it's not. It's a great idea. I haven't got one. I have to make do with oven chips.'

'Not the same at all,' they said as one, then looked at each other again and blushed.

The man with the paint came noisily forward with his chosen tub. Cherry-blossom pink, Ruth noted as Tony went to serve him with a hurried instruction not to go away. Ruth stood listening as he chatted to the man about his purchase. A new baby on the way. Scan said it was a girl. Wife very excited. Got two boys already and this was one last throw of the gender dice. Desperate for a pink nursery and this looks about as pink as it gets. Tony smiled and agreed and managed to also sell the man white gloss for the skirting, some stick-on butterflies and a pink and yellow roller blind. Ruth watched, amazed.

'How did you do that?' she asked when he'd seen the man out and come back to her.

'Do what? Sell him all that stuff? Oh, he wanted it really, I just helped him to think of it.'

'Not that so much. More talking about, you know, babies . . .'

He shrugged.

'Well, he was having a baby so it seemed an obvious thing to talk about.' Ruth nodded and he looked at her with such concern in his eyes that she had to look away. 'Shall I take that then?'

He pointed to the fryer and she nodded and bundled it towards him.

'Please. Yes. It's for you.'

'Thank you.'

'It should work. I've tested it.'

'I'm sure you have. I'll have chips tonight and think of you.'

'You will?'

'Of course. I think of you anyway but now I'll have something specific to focus on.'

'Chips?'

'Yeah.' He put the fryer down on the counter. 'Did you want something else, Ruth?'

Did she? She was sure she did but her brain seemed to have turned to mush. She looked around the shop for inspiration. 'A lock. I want a lock, please.'

'A padlock?'

'A bolt and padlock, yes. Please.'

'What's it for?' She hesitated. 'I mean, for a box or a door or . . .?'

'A door. A bedroom door.'

'You need to padlock your bedroom door? Ruth, are you OK? Is someone—'

'Not *my* bedroom.'

'No?'

'No. Libby's.'

Her voice squeaked on the name. Tony put a tentative hand on her arm and she felt a sharp yearning to fling herself against his still broad chest. He'd wrap his long arms around her as he always had and she'd feel as if someone had padlocked her in, safe and secure from all the ills of the world. She leaned towards him then remembered lying in those very arms as Libby tiptoed past in search of rocks and water and oblivion and took a hasty step back.

'Ruth?'

'Yes.'

'Why do you want a lock on Libby's door?'

'So no one can get in and . . . and take anything.'

'Who would want to take anything?'

His voice was so gentle and so, so familiar. It felt so natural to be talking to him like this that again she longed to step up and press herself against him, but it couldn't be that easy.

'Bailiffs.'

She waited for the explosion but Tony just looked down at her for what felt like ages. 'Are you struggling for money, Ruth?'

His gentleness was worse than criticism.

'I've fallen behind with the mortgage,' she admitted to the scrupulously clean floor.

'Why? Is work not good? I thought Sparkies was going well? I seem to see the vans all the time.'

'You do?'

'They're hard to miss.' That much was true. In canary yellow and silver, they certainly stood out in a traffic jam. 'I'm always looking to see if it's you driving.'

'It won't be.'

'Why? Ruth, why won't it be you?'

She shuffled her feet across the floor. 'I've not been working.'

'Since when?'

'Since, you know . . .'

'Since the accident?'

Her head flew up. 'It wasn't an accident, Tony.'

'You know what I mean.'

'No. No I don't.' She stepped back. 'I don't know what you mean at all. It wasn't an accident. It was negligence, neglect, cruelty!'

'Sssh! Ruth, please.'

Another customer had come in, a woman with a toddler in a pushchair. Christ, did everyone have children around here?

Ruth backed away. 'Forget it. I was silly to come.'

'No! Please, Ruth, you weren't silly. It's good to see you, really. I miss you.'

That stopped her. 'You do?'

'All the time.'

'Then why did you leave?'

He stared at her. 'Because you made me.'

'Right. Yes.' Ruth scuffed at the floor. This was hopeless. 'I should go.'

'Rubbish!'

It came out as a shout and the woman steered her pushchair hastily around them and made for the relative safety of the garden section. Ruth watched her bend to check her little girl, fuss with her cutesy blanket, find her a snack from a Tupperware container. What would that baby be like ten years from now? Would her mother be standing rolling her eyes to friends over teenage antics, or would she be facing her one-time husband, trying to figure out how on earth she'd died?

In front of her, Tony was breathing heavily.

'Sorry.' His voice was calmer now, lower. 'I'm sorry, Ruth, but it *is* rubbish. You must have come here for a reason so let's talk properly. Please?'

'I'm sorry too, Tony. Things remind me, you know?'

He nodded. 'I do know, Ruth. I know more than anyone. That's why we need to talk.'

'She's not here any more.'

'But *we* are.'

Again she saw herself locked in his arms. *Mummy!* Libby's voice called, thick with black water, and she turned, fighting for the door to try and escape it. But now Tony's big hand was on her arm, holding her back.

'Don't go, Ruth. Let me help you.' She shook her head furiously, fighting to escape. 'What about the lock? I can get you a lock.'

'I'll order one online.'

'And what about the bailiffs?'

Ruth glared at him, yanked her arm away. 'I'll sort it, Tony.'

His eyes narrowed. 'How? How will you sort it? By locking them out, like you've locked everyone else out?'

'This is you helping me?'

'Trying to.'

'Then you're not very good at it.'

He put his hands up. 'Apparently not.'

She shook her head and swung round to the door but at that moment an older man came in, blocking her escape route. He gave Tony a cheery wave.

'Morning, Sam,' Tony choked out.

'Morning, Tony. Glad you're here.' He came bustling forward, stepping carelessly in front of Ruth. 'My drains are blocked up something rotten, lad. Every time I run the kitchen tap, the yard floods.'

'Have you tried clearing them?' Tony asked, his eyes still on Ruth.

'Course I have, but whatever it is must be deep down.'

'Have you been putting fat down the sink perhaps?'

'Fat? Like butter?'

'Or oil.'

'Oil? Like from a chip pan?'

He looked at the fryer Tony had placed on the counter and Tony looked again to Ruth. *Don't go*, his eyes were saying and they held her there more effectively than any strong arm.

So many years she'd looked into those eyes, so many years they'd been all that mattered to her. She moved away from the door and he gave her a grateful smile.

Two minutes, he mouthed to her and turned to the old man.

'Exactly that, Sam.'

'Maybe once or twice, but so what? It's liquid, isn't it? What's the problem?'

'The problem, Sam, is that it solidifies if it gets cold enough. But don't worry, I have just the thing for you. You pour it down the sink and it fizzes everything away. Your drains'll be clear in no time.'

Ruth watched him fetch the product for the old man. Wouldn't it be wonderful if there was something she could pour into herself that would fizz away her grief – something other than vodka, that is. She watched Tony reading Sam the instructions and felt sadness bite. Tony wanted to help her. He'd been kind to her, patient, gentle, and all she'd done in return was bite and spit at him. Just like last time. Tony wasn't the problem, she was, and as her husband took his customer to the till she turned, let herself out, and ran.

'Ruth!' she heard him cry but she couldn't go back, not until she was a better person for him.

A van drove past, canary yellow with silver lettering glittering in the low sun: Sparkly Sparkies. It was like a message from the universe: work, that was the answer. She had to pick up her toolbox and go back to work. No grief de-fizzers, no tape around her heart, just good, old-fashioned graft. And maybe, somehow, someday, she'd work her way back to Tony.

Chapter Twenty-nine

'So, if we could just get you walking up the ramp into your house . . .'

Greg looked sceptically at Kirstie, the perky reporter who'd been bouncing around his house for the last hour 'assessing potential'. Her eyes clouded beneath her blue fringe.

'Does it hurt you?'

'No. It's just . . . I can't walk very well.'

'I know. That's kind of the point.'

She gave him a rueful little smile and he nodded reluctantly.

'I suppose it is. Fine. Which stick then?'

'Sorry?'

Greg gestured to the stand by the door where his selection of sticks lived.

Kirstie's eyes lit up. 'OMG! You have so many. We can *so* get that. Dec, over here – get the sticks.'

The cameraman came running over as if the sticks might gambol off if he didn't hurry. The poor lad was probably desperate to get on a David Attenborough shoot and instead he was stuck filming Greg limp up a ramp.

'Why so many?' Kirstie asked.

'Why not? I was spending every day with them so it seemed fun to have a choice.'

'Fun!' Kirstie clasped her hands together delightedly. 'I love that. You're so positive, Greg. Now, can you say that again, just the same, for the camera?'

Greg did so. Kirstie clapped again.

'Marvellous. Just marvellous. Oh this is going to be so cool! I see a montage, Greg, of you in different places with different sticks.'

'A montage?'

'Like in a pop video. Oh, oh, and I know – we'll put a Mardy Cows track over the top. How cool is that?'

'Almost as cool as Gene Kelly in *Singing in the Rain*,' Greg said, deadpan.

'Exactly!'

He laughed. He had to admire her enthusiasm. 'If you say so, Kirstie. I'm new to all this.'

'Hardly. You've been blogging for ages.'

'A year.'

'Exactly – ages!'

'But I'm just a shy scientist at heart.'

Kirstie gave a little shriek. 'I love that. Say it again. Dec, get him saying that again.'

So Greg did.

It felt ridiculous in one way but he had to admit that it was kind of fun. Kirstie was so unflaggingly excitable and there was something rather hypnotic about the camera. Its big eye was so openly curious that you found yourself telling it things you'd never normally say and in ways you'd never normally say them.

'Now,' Kirstie said, positioning him on the lift, 'do your catchphrase.'

'My what?'

'You know – "don't let disability disable your life".'

'Ah. That.'

'It'll make the perfect end. You say it and the lift carries you upwards. Dec will pan in from your poor body to your gorgeous smiling face and bang, right on message for the audience. Not to mention the judges.'

Greg looked up. 'It isn't decided already?'

'Oh no. There's a panel who choose on the night.'

'So you, Kirstie, could be my ticket to an award?'

251

She giggled. 'I certainly could. And you, Greg, could be my ticket to a promotion. There's a job going on *Kids'll Eat Anything* that I'm up for. If this is good, it might seal it for me.'

Her focus narrowed a little and Greg caught a glimpse of the steel beneath her relentlessly bubbly exterior.

'Well, in that case, let's get filming.'

It was exhausting but invigorating. Kirstie threw idea after idea at him and Greg tried them all. They must have filmed at least two hours' worth of footage for what would be a two-minute VT but Kirstie assured him it was 'all in the edit', so he just went with what she said and eventually she declared it a 'wrap'. They both collapsed at the breakfast bar while Dec bustled around putting his camera away.

'Beer?' Greg suggested.

'God, yes please.'

'Could you . . .?'

He indicated the fridge. His leg was aching now and his spine was on fire but it had been worth it. For a morning he'd felt alive, important. Only now, as the adrenaline of filming drained away, it hit him again what a game it all was.

'These ones?' Kirstie asked, pulling out the Einstok.

'Perfect.' He saw her examining the label. 'They're Icelandic. I'm getting in practice.'

'For your next trip? Cool. I'd love to go to Iceland. You can bathe in hot springs beneath the earth, you know.'

'I know.'

'Course you do. Sorry. You're the adventurer, not me.'

'Hardly.'

'You *are*. I think it's so cool what you do.'

'What, go on holiday all the time?'

'No! Travel. See the world. It would be so easy, I imagine, just to sit inside all day feeling sorry for yourself, but not you. Don't let disability disable your life!'

She raised her can and he clunked his against it.

'My "catchphrase".'

'It's a good one.'

'I guess.'

'Greg? Are you OK?'

He took a deep swallow of his beer. It still tasted of nothing. 'I'm fine. Just tired.'

'Of course. It must be hard for you.' Greg tried to smile but it came out a bit crooked. 'I forgot cos you were so good at it. You should vlog, Greg. Why don't you do that? Your blogs are all stills, right?'

'Right.'

'Why?'

'Dunno. Easier to pose, I guess.'

'Pose?'

'Vanity, Kirstie. I can make myself look . . . not good, as such, but at least kind of interesting in stills. Video is merciless.'

'But truer?'

'Exactly!'

She considered this, head cocked on one side. 'Well, for what it's worth, Greg, I think you're very interesting both still and on the move. And you know why?' He shook his head, shifted his weight on the stool. 'Because you're warm and natural and funny and cool.'

'Rubbish!'

'You are. And that's nothing to do with the shape of your spine. That's just you.'

He shook his head. 'It's not me, Kirstie. It's a construct, a character for the camera.'

She shrugged. 'Of course it is, but a camera is like wine. You know − the whole "*in vino veritas*" thing. Being drunk only enhances your true characteristics and the camera is the same. It magnifies you but it doesn't turn you into someone new.'

Greg closed his eyes, drained his beer. God, he was exhausted. 'Shame,' he said.

But as he saw Kirstie out and she kissed both his cheeks and told him how 'bloody marvellous' she'd make his VT, he felt a surprising shiver of excitement at the thought of seeing it. Maybe the awards ceremony would be OK? Maybe he'd even enjoy it? And maybe, just maybe, she was right and, however fake it felt, he was more the 'inspirational' blogger guy than he'd thought he was. After all, not all the tweets he got these days were from Candy Drew wannabes. Every day he got one or two from people who were genuinely touched by his blog, who'd contacted him to let him know it had made a difference to them.

Today I went to the seaside for the first time in two years, one had said yesterday. *Never would have dared until I read @gregsutton's amazing blog. Had the BEST time. #dontletdisability*.

Had the BEST time.

He'd done that. And maybe, if he just got on with it, he could keep doing it. He must call North Face and get that Iceland trip properly planned out, then get on that plane and head out there. Adventuring.

Chapter Thirty

Charlie looked around the big room and felt whatever was left of his soul shrivel at the unrelenting blankness of it all. It was a classic conference centre – beige walls, stackable chairs and mediocre art. Which git in the world of venue decoration, he wondered, had decreed that people in conferences would far rather look at untalented swirls of colour than actual, heartfelt pictures? Who'd gone, 'I know we could have reproductions of great masters but where's the fun in that? Let's have asinine crap instead'? Perhaps it was so that there was half a chance of people looking at the equally asinine course leaders? And some poor people spent their whole lives in these insidiously average rooms. No wonder they became more puppets than human beings. Talking of which . . .

'Charlie! Great to have you along.'

'Morning, Sue.'

'Looking forward to seeing the new tablets?'

'Very much.'

'Good, good. They're going to offer such enhanced customer service.'

'So I've heard.'

'Yes, well . . . You saw them here first!' It was like a warped sofa advert. 'Have you had a coffee? There's biscuits too.'

'Lovely. I'll get one now.'

Charlie extricated himself and joined all the other poor purple people at the big urns on the side. Had they really needed to come in uniform? They looked like a load of overripe plums. He shuffled forward to take his white cup and saucer and squirt brown liquid pretending to be coffee into it. He wished Bri was here but Turner's couldn't have all their drivers off the road at once so she'd come to yesterday's extravaganza. She'd texted Charlie a series of bored, vomitous and finally murderous emojis throughout the day that hadn't exactly filled him with excited anticipation.

Still, at least it meant he didn't have to watch Ryan driving gleefully off to deliver to Greg and Ruth and Vik this morning. Last Monday, Sean had made the route switch, much to Ryan's crowing delight, and all week Charlie had taken the Chestnut Hill route without complaint, but Friday would have been hard. He was dying to know how their dinner had gone, dying to know how Greg was feeling about the awards tomorrow, and if Ruth had given machines to anyone else, and what Vik was cooking and for whom. Had they got on with each other or had they just washed their curry down with Turner's wine and awkward small talk and gone back to their separate houses wondering what on earth that had all been about? He'd never know and maybe that was for the best. It wasn't as if he was their friend.

'You're just a delivery driver, Charlie,' he reminded himself under his breath.

'Just?' Oh Lord, it was Sue again, bouncing up at his side. 'Don't underestimate yourself, Charlie. You're bringing food to the masses.'

He squinted at her. Did she really believe Turner's was some sort of glorious community service?

'The *paying* masses, Sue.'

'Well, yes, obviously. You don't get anything in this life for free.'

'How very true.'

Sue beamed smugly and took her brown water off to the long table at the head of the room where she greeted a thin man dressed to blend perfectly into the walls, complete with swirly pattern tie. These, then, were the course leaders – goodie!

Charlie took a seat at one of the round tables, supposedly designed to be friendly but actually too large to comfortably talk to anyone, and helped himself to a couple of mint imperials.

At the front, Sue gave an ineffectual cough. No one paid any attention, though others did start to slide into seats.

'Dudley,' the man next to Charlie introduced himself, flicking his phone on to silent and hiding it in his lap. Charlie wasn't alone, it seemed, in expecting to be less than riveted by Sue and her sidekick.

'Charlie,' Charlie replied, taking a sip of pseudo-coffee and bracing himself for the fun to come.

He wasn't ready, however, for the sudden sideswipe of memory from his old job as Sue faced the room. There'd been nothing bland about that. There had, perhaps, been the same level of plasticky fittings and wipe-clean walls, but at least it had been full of life, of people rich with quirks and stories. Every purple person here was already glaze-eyed with boredom and they hadn't even started yet.

Sue coughed again, then her colleague gave a nervous tap at his glass. A few people looked over and a resigned sigh rippled around the tables. Then an all-too-familiar voice said, 'This place taken?' and Charlie looked up to see Ryan Sharp sliding into a seat dead opposite.

'Aren't you working?' he demanded.

'I was meant to be,' Ryan agreed, 'but Sean found cover. He wanted me to come today to meet Colin.'

'Colin?'

Ryan gestured to Sue's sidekick. 'Area manager. Important chap. In charge of promotions, know what I mean? Oh, but of course you do . . .'

Charlie's fingers tightened on his pen.

'Who's got Hope Street?' he snapped.

Ryan shrugged carelessly.

'Dunno. Sean didn't say.'

'But how will they know . . .?'

He stopped himself and Ryan offered him his most patronising smile. 'It's hardly rocket science, is it?'

'No.' Charlie drew a series of circles on his notepad to calm himself. It didn't work. 'I thought you were desperate for Hope Street, Ryan?'

'Hardly *desperate*, Charlie.'

Ryan gave him a sly smile. Charlie drew bigger circles. Dudley looked curiously at them but, thankfully, Sue started into her opening spiel and all eyes turned reluctantly her way. And, Lord, it was dull. Sue had the charisma of a goldfish as she took them through a cardboard welcome full of fire exits, platitudes about their worth to the company and exhortations to turn off mobile phones, before finally she lifted up the new tablet.

'Well,' she announced, leaving an excruciating *X Factor*-style pause, 'this is it!'

She waved the device and everyone squinted at it.

'It's hardly the Holy pigging Grail, is it?' Dudley growled and Charlie smiled. Maybe this wouldn't be so bad after all?

An hour-long PowerPoint presentation of the magic device's 'enhanced customer service features', however, soon ground any optimism out of him. Heads drooped, phones were surreptitiously played with, biscuits were scoffed and still Sue went on, doggedly bright-eyed as she ran through menu after tedious menu. It was excruciatingly pointless. It seemed Turner's could afford no money to do anything more than send their drivers dashing in and out of people's houses like robots on speed, but endless amounts of it to bore them with empty presentations. The economics were all skewed.

Charlie was just wondering if he could get away with a quick snooze when his phone buzzed in his lap. He snatched it up guiltily and glanced down to see a text on his screen. It was an unknown number:

Hi Charlie. Hope you don't mind me using . . .

Curiously, Charlie slid his finger across to open the rest:

your Turner's number like this but I wondered if you'd like to come for curry tonight. It's Vik, from number 95 Hope Street.

Vik! Charlie felt a funny little skip in his heart.

Greg from number 80 is coming and so is Ruth from number 112 and we'd love you to join us if you can. But not if you don't want to. Anyway, let me know. Thank you. Vik.

Charlie stared in astonishment at the endearingly wordy message. Curry with Vik. And Greg and Ruth. It must, then, have gone well last week. Had they talked about him? Had they guessed what he'd done to get them together? Were they cross? Surely not. They'd report him if they were cross, not ask him for curry. A smile crept over Charlie's face and he listened to the rest of Sue's nonsense with new serenity.

'And so,' she finally concluded, 'we'll take a bit of a break.' Heads came up. 'And after that you'll all get a chance to experiment with a tablet yourselves.'

'Yippee!' Dudley said, scrolling through Facebook beneath the table.

'But for now – any questions?'

Sue looked eagerly around the room. Charlie had a question. *Don't ask it,* he told himself.

'Anyone?'

It's not worth it.

'Ooh, I must have been very clear. Excellent. Well then . . . Ah yes. Over there at the back.'

Charlie stood up. 'Will we get five minutes now then?' he asked.

Sue stared blankly at him. 'Five minutes for what?'

'Will we get five minutes per house in order to provide the enhanced customer service?'

He just about managed to say it without irony but a small ripple of amused appreciation ran around the drivers.

Sue's face tightened. 'That will not be necessary. It can be done within the time already allocated.'

'Alongside getting the baskets out of the van, carrying them up long drives and into blocks of flats, waiting for the customer to empty them, getting signatures, sorting returns and then taking them back to the van?'

Sue's eyes narrowed. 'Are you being facetious, young man?'

'Charlie,' he reminded her, touching his name badge. 'And no, Sue, not at all. I'm genuinely keen to know.'

All the other drivers nodded that they, too, were fascinated to hear Sue's answer and Sue shuffled her mid-heeled feet and consulted her notes. They clearly offered her no help.

'The time is an average,' she said eventually. 'Some houses will take more, some less.'

'And occasionally,' Dudley muttered, just loud enough for all to hear, 'one will even take the four minutes allowed. If you're very lucky.'

Sue looked cross. 'I don't think any of you are appreciating what we're trying to do here. Your upgraded tablets offer you the chance to interact with customers in a more meaningful way.'

'Not as meaningful as a few more minutes would allow,' someone else called and Sue looked panicked as people shuffled chairs and turned to murmur to each other. It was a far cry from a rebellion but it certainly hadn't turned out the way Sue had wanted and she glared at Charlie as the noise in the room rose. Colin got to his feet.

'Breaktime,' he said masterfully and the roomful of plums jumped up and stampeded for the doors.

'Good point you made there, Charlie,' Dudley said to him.

'Yeah,' Ryan agreed. 'Way to go! Mind you, old Sue doesn't look so keen on her little pet now.'

'I'm not her pet, Ryan.'

'Not any more you're not.'

Charlie didn't give a fig about Sue's opinion but far too many people were heading his way.

'Well said, Charlie.'

'They've got no idea about real customer service, Charlie.'

'Have you thought about union work, Charlie?'

Suddenly everyone knew his name and he found himself covering up his badge as he made a hasty dive for the toilets. He bundled into a cubicle and, shaking, pulled out his phone. Vik's message was still there, long and inviting, and he read it three times before putting his fingers to the keys.

Thank you, Vik. I would love to come for curry.

The reply was instant.

Wonderful. Come at six. Just bring yourself.

Just bring yourself – what welcoming words. Charlie sat for some time on the beige loo, staring at them until he heard a bell calling the Turner's workers back to the conference. Reluctantly, he unlocked the door and returned to the fray. The next session would be tedious, he knew, but at least he had something to look forward to at the end and he smiled at Dudley as he retook his seat.

'Magic tablets are here.' Dudley waved to the table where a little device was, indeed, squatting at every place.

Charlie picked his up, pressed the perfectly self-explanatory buttons Sue had spent the last hour explaining and called up the menus.

'Charlie, right?'

Charlie looked up to see Colin at his shoulder. Great. Why hadn't he just kept his bloody mouth shut? Meddling, you see, he just couldn't resist it. *You're a sparrow,* he reminded himself. *A harmless little sparrow.*

'That's right, sir.'

'Call me Colin, please. Everyone does.'

Not, Charlie suspected, behind his back, but he said nothing. Colin leaned closer. 'I believe you're—'

'Eager to try this out. Yes I am, Colin.'

Colin jerked back but nodded tightly. 'I see. Right. Good.' He stood back and addressed the whole table. 'Well, these babies are live so you can put in a real customer and call up their Turner's account. Go on – try it!'

'You want us to put in a real name?' Dudley asked.

'That's right.'

'What about data protection?'

'They're your customers so you're authorised.'

'If you say so.' Dudley tapped away. 'Ooh, look – Mrs Jackson's yoghurt preferences for the last six months right before my eyes. Super!'

Charlie hid a smile.

'Well, I think it's very useful,' Ryan said, sanctimoniously. 'If a customer asks me if I've brought their usual brand I'll be able to reassure them that I have.'

'If you had the time to work through the menus,' Dudley retorted.

At Charlie's side, Colin audibly ground his teeth. 'Have you all done it?' he asked tightly.

Charlie called up the customer box and tapped in the first name that came to mind – Greg Sutton. Would some anonymous driver be taking Greg his groceries right now? Had he even placed an order if he was off to the awards tomorrow? His magic tablet had the answer – yes, he had. Due in the next hour. More Icelandic food, by the look of it. More wine too. And even a bottle of Prosecco. Perhaps he was looking forward to the awards more than he'd let on? Charlie hoped so.

'If you press "past orders",' Colin droned on, 'you can call up all their—'

'Past orders?' Dudley suggested.

'That's right.' Colin's patience was clearly wearing thin.

Charlie glanced to Dudley, who rolled his eyes. Charlie grinned and pressed 'past orders'. A long list came up in front of him.

'Wow, that's a lot of information.'

Colin beamed proudly. 'Information is power, Charlie.'

Charlie looked again to Dudley. Had Colin really just said that about shopping? What on earth sort of power did someone's food choices give you, bar the power to sell them more food? Though, to be fair, if you were a supermarket that was power enough. Charlie scrolled desultorily through, wishing Colin would go away and wondering what was for lunch. Dates whirred across the screen, helpfully marked with week numbers: Week 30, week 29, week 28. A little worm of unease crept into Charlie's stomach. Week 27, week 26, week 25.

He glanced around. Everyone was playing with their own machines. No one was looking at him. He scrolled faster: Week 24, 23, 22, 21. Week 16, 15, 14. Week 3, 2, 1. Greg hadn't missed a single week. Not one. But surely that wasn't possible if he'd been away travelling?

'What happens if a customer doesn't order one week?'

'Great question, Charlie.' Colin jumped back to his side. 'It appears as a blank line, like . . . Oh. Seems your guy is one of our favourites – lovely, regular ordering, week in, week out.'

He looked a little closer. 'Not even a week off in the summer. Who . . .?'

Charlie snatched the tablet away. 'Doesn't matter.'

Across the table, Ryan looked up. Hastily, Charlie scrolled back to the start and plugged in Vik's name.

'He's old,' he said loudly, 'and widowed. Guess he doesn't get out much.'

'There's a lot like that,' Dudley agreed. 'Always want to chat, don't they?'

'But you've only got four minutes,' the woman on his far side said. 'Right, Charlie?'

Charlie swallowed and looked nervously around. The beige walls seemed to be closing in on him, the swirly paintings sucking him into their blank hearts.

'I suppose,' he stuttered, 'that we have to remember we're delivery drivers not social workers.'

'Quite right, Charlie,' Colin agreed. 'Quite right. Now, let's consider the "returns" feature. Main menu, folks, and select—'

'Returns?' Dudley sniggered.

'Well, I can see you clever lot don't need me.'

Visibly bristling, Colin moved away and Charlie pulled his phone into his lap, calling up Greg's blog. There was a menu down the side – 'pick a trip' – and the drop-down bar for this year offered him five options: *Thailand – September, Russia – August, Vietnam – June, Chile – April, India – January.* Five trips, five different months, any number of Turner's delivery weeks. How on earth had Greg been able to receive deliveries? And why had he wanted them? Was someone else living there with him? Someone that he, for some reason, didn't want seen?

Hastily, he keyed Greg's name in again, jabbed at orders:

Week 38: Lemongrass, Prawns, Noodles, Peanuts, Coconut milk, SangSom whisky

Week 33: Beetroot, Potatoes, Dill, Beef, Mushrooms, Sour Cream, Blini, Caviar, Vodka

Week 4: Coriander, Cumin, Garam masala, Lentils, Paneer, Naan breads

He stared at the information, not wanting to believe it but with no idea how not to. Greg had told him he felt a fake and he'd meant it. He didn't just feel a fake; he *was* a fake. *Information is power*, Colin's words mocked him, but Charlie didn't want this sort of power.

'What you so engrossed in, Charlie boy?' Charlie started and his tablet jumped from his hands and landed at Ryan's feet. He scrambled to reclaim it. 'On your phone as well, hey? What did Sue say? All mobiles off.'

'Get lost, Ryan.'

Charlie fumbled for the tablet, juggling it with his phone in a desperate attempt to shut off the screens.

'That's Greg Sutton's blog, isn't it?'

'No,' Charlie snapped, but it was too late. Already Dudley had looked over.

'You deliver to Greg Sutton? Cool. My lad's best mate's got cystic fibrosis and he loves that blog. Says he's going to be an adventurer when he grows up, just like Greg. So he's from round here then?'

'Can't say,' Charlie said stiffly.

'Course you can't. Data protection, right? It's still cool, though. The man's a total star, if you ask me. D'you know, he made it down the Vietcong tunnels despite that poor spine. Astonishing.'

'Isn't it?' Ryan agreed. 'He's an inspiration. And now I can look at his shopping on my—'

'OK, folks, time's up, I'm afraid.' Charlie swore he'd never thought he'd be so glad to hear the grate of Sue's voice. 'If you could put your tablets into the baskets in the middle of the table, we've got a little team-building exercise for you.'

And he'd never been happier to hear the words 'team-building exercise'. Hastily, he wiped his tablet and placed it in the basket, watching the others to be sure they did so too before the devices were all whisked away and replaced, ominously, with four rolls of toilet paper.

'Oh God, here we go!' Dudley moaned, but Charlie could only be grateful for the distraction and didn't even put up a protest when Ryan nominated him to be their team's 'Mummy'.

It was only as he stood, arms out and legs akimbo while grown men and women wrapped toilet roll around him, that it really struck home what he'd seen. Greg Sutton hadn't left his house once this year. His fancy blogs were a Photoshop creation, his motivational words a farce, and tomorrow he was up for an award for the whole damn thing. No wonder he'd been so reluctant to go. And, worst of all, tonight Charlie would see him for dinner. What on earth would he say?

He looked around the blank room full of men and women being forced to make fools of themselves in the name of team-building and suddenly he knew exactly what he'd say – nothing. So what if Greg's blog was faked? It was still inspirational; it still made others get up and out. And that, surely, was what counted? Greg's secret was safe with him and, looking down at Ryan as he pulled bog roll as tight as he could around his hips, he could only pray it would stay that way.

Chapter Thirty-one

Charlie approached number 95 Hope Street shredded with nerves. He couldn't remember when he'd last been out on anything that might count as a social occasion and was worried he'd forgotten how to act, especially around Greg after all he'd just learned. He felt as terrified as if he were fourteen again, going to his first proper party. Matt Jenkins' fifteenth birthday it had been, in a village hall with an actual DJ and girls. No one had talked of anything else for weeks and anticipation had reached a fever pitch that stood a very poor chance of being matched by the event itself.

Charlie had been a bag of nerve endings as he'd waited for the hour to finally kick round and now he hesitated before Vik Varma's immaculate flower beds and tried to remember what Matt Jenkins' party had actually been like. A blur of girls in glamorous dresses looking suddenly like alien creatures and boys trying to chat them up through swigs of stolen booze. Most people had managed to relieve their parents' drinks cupboards of their more eclectic bottles and Charlie's only distinct memory was of a girl swigging so much curaçao that it turned her lips blue.

His own offering had been a half-bottle of a sixty-year-old malt that he'd only realised the value of years later. All he'd noticed at the time had been the burn as it went down his throat and the strange look on Mrs Jenkins' face when she'd clocked it. She hadn't said anything though. No one ever had back then, other than clamouring to be his friend. Or, at least, to be seen with him.

Charlie shivered and tugged on his coat, feeling a strange stab of longing for the purple fleece he'd left behind in his flat.

He hated it, he reminded himself, but the sad fact was that he also felt safe in it. He could hide behind its shapelessness, behind the logo, even behind the name badge. With it on, he was Charlie-the-delivery-driver; without it he was, well, just Charlie. And he didn't much like just Charlie.

Quit the self-pity, he told himself and pressed fiercely on the doorbell. It was answered almost immediately by a beaming Vik.

'Charlie! Come in, come in, come in. Wait till you see who I've got here!'

But Charlie didn't have to wait as a little girl, all big eyes and dark curls, came rocketing into the hall.

'Hello,' she said. 'Who are you?'

'I'm Charlie,' he told her, crouching down and holding out his hand.

She giggled and took it, shaking it vigorously.

'Charlie is the supermarket delivery driver,' Vik told her.

'Is he?' She looked Charlie up and down with that open fascination he'd forgotten children had. 'He doesn't look like a delivery driver.'

'That's because he isn't in uniform at the moment.'

'Why?'

'Because tonight he's our guest.'

The word, spoken in Vik's kind tones, warmed Charlie's heart. Quickly, he reached into his bag and pulled out a bottle. He'd been to a supermarket on the way over. Not Turner's. He was sick of Turner's.

'Wine,' he said foolishly. 'It's red. Shiraz. I think that's what you like, isn't it?'

Vik took it and clapped Charlie on the shoulder with a low chuckle. 'I think it might be. I'm no expert, Charlie. I only started drinking it when you left Greg's bottle here.'

'That wasn't me as such. There was—'

'Whatever, Charlie. It doesn't matter. It introduced me to wine and, more importantly, to Greg. Lovely young man, isn't he? So brave.'

'Yes,' Charlie agreed, fighting to swallow the lump that formed instantly in his throat. 'Is he, er, coming tonight?'

'Yes, yes. Should be here any minute.'

'Good.' The word came out a bit squeaky but luckily Aleesha was speaking to Vik and he didn't notice.

'Aleesha wants to know if you'd like a cocktail, Charlie?' he asked.

'A cocktail? Oh no. Thank you. That is, I don't drink.'

'Oh, that's fine. We have – what did you call them, Leesha?'

'Mocktails,' the little girl said pertly. 'For the drivers.'

'And for you too?' Charlie suggested and was rewarded with a big smile and a little skip.

'And for me, yes. And really, Charlie . . .' she tugged on his T-shirt, 'they're much nicer than the burny adult ones.'

Oh, how Charlie wished that were true. But he nodded and let the little girl pull him into the kitchen, where Vik had set up a veritable bar of drinks and mixers at one end of his big table.

'Wow, Vik!'

Vik looked a little sheepish.

'Aleesha wanted to do cocktails like her mummy and daddy do for guests so we looked up a few on the internet and went out and bought the stuff. It's not from Turner's, I'm afraid.'

Charlie smiled. 'Neither is the wine, Vik.'

'Charlie!' Aleesha tugged on his T-shirt again. 'Can I make you a drink now? We have all sorts of colours. What colour would you like?'

'What colour's yours?'

'Pink.'

'Then I'll have pink too, please.'

'Yay!' She ran round the table and perused the myriad bottles. 'How do we make the pink one, Grampie?'

Charlie sat down and watched Vik and his granddaughter marshalling ingredients. Several Barbie dolls were lounging among the bottles, including one with a long piece of string tied around her impossibly tiny waist. He picked her up.

'Are these your dolls?' he asked Aleesha.

She looked up from a cocktail umbrella she was trying to unfurl. 'Yep. This one is Princess Barbie and this is Going-to-the-shops

Barbie and that one you've got there was Party Barbie but today she's Climbing Barbie.'

'Quite the transformation.' Charlie lifted her up by the string. 'Where does she climb?'

'Up the big cliff.' Aleesha pointed across the kitchen. Charlie looked behind him but all he could see were shelves of spices. 'In there,' Aleesha said impatiently, waggling her umbrella at the lounge door Vik always kept so carefully closed.

'In there?' Charlie repeated, not quite looking at Vik.

'Yes. On the big, grey freezer. It's just like a cliff. Climbing Barbie loves it. Shall I—' But before she could show Charlie, the doorbell went and she was instantly distracted. 'Another guest, Grampie!'

She ran to the door.

'I can't reach the handle,' came a frustrated little cry and, with an indulgent smile, Vik headed after her.

Charlie stood frozen. He glanced to the lounge door but it felt rude to go in by himself and he put Climbing Barbie slowly back down. He wondered if it was Greg arriving and tried to push all he'd learned today out of his mind. There might yet be a logical explanation. Greg might have a housesitter or a relative who came by – a relative who ordered foods to match their host's travels. It was, he had to admit, highly unlikely and the other man's apparent secret wormed in his gut. Greg seemed so together, as if he'd got over his accident – in as much as you ever could – and was moving on. But if what the stupid enhanced customer tablet suggested was true, he wasn't recovered at all. Quite the reverse.

Charlie shifted his feet nervously but then heard Aleesha call, 'It's a lady!' and breathed a momentary sigh of relief.

'Charlie!' Ruth gave him a broad smile as she walked into the kitchen. 'How lovely.'

The lump in Charlie's throat returned as she came forward to shake his hand. Not nerves now, so much as complicated, tearful gratitude. When had anyone last said it was lovely to see him?

Quit the self-pity, he told himself again, as Aleesha dragged Ruth to the cocktail bar, where Vik mixed a lurid red drink.

Ruth took a loudly grateful swig and Charlie tried not to watch too closely.

'Is *my* drink ready?' he asked.

Aleesha turned to him. 'Nearly, Charlie. How many umbrellas do you want?'

'Erm. How many fit in the glass?'

'Let's see.' Aleesha stuck her little tongue out in concentration as she picked the rubber band off an umbrella and carefully opened it out. 'One,' she announced, slotting it into the glass and turning to the next one.

'Charlie's got to be able to drink it, Leesha,' Vik warned, but Aleesha was too focused on her task to pay any attention.

'Two.' She picked up a third, her cheeks flushed. 'Three!' She looked at the glass. 'One more?'

'Oh yes,' Charlie said and she beamed at him and picked up umbrella number four.

He'd never be able to drink it, but so what? She was having so much fun. Then he noticed Ruth watching Aleesha avidly and suddenly it was as if someone had closed up all the little cocktail umbrellas just like that. There was a fierce longing in her dark eyes and Charlie wondered if she was remembering her own daughter at Aleesha's age and, worse, imagining what she'd be like now.

'Four! Look, Charlie, you've got four umbrellas.'

'Lovely. Thank you.'

Charlie took the drink, wishing it had at least one measure of alcohol in it. He turned the glass, looking for a way in, and Vik leaned across and slotted a straw into the centre of the spinning umbrellas.

'There you go.'

'Thanks.'

It solved the drinking issue, though not the vodka one. Charlie took a long, cold, alcohol-free sip.

'Nice?' Aleesha asked eagerly.

'Very nice. Thank you.'

Still Ruth was watching Aleesha and Charlie put down his drink and turned to his bag. 'I brought you something, Ruth.'

'Me?'

'Her?' Aleesha echoed, her eyes narrowing a little.

'Er, yes.'

'What about me?'

Charlie swallowed. 'I'm sorry. I didn't know you'd be here. But I bet Ruth will share her present. Why don't you give it to her?'

He drew out the box and Aleesha took it carefully in both hands. 'It's quite big,' she said. 'Oh! It's a jigsaw. I like jigsaws.'

'Me too.' Ruth knelt down to look at it with her. 'It's a very big one with, look, lions and tigers and a zebra.'

'And a giraffe.' Aleesha pointed.

'And a giraffe, yes. Lots of animals. Charlie's right. I will need help.' She looked up over Aleesha's dark little head. 'Thank you, Charlie. That's very kind.'

'Least I can do.'

'Why?'

'Why?' He panicked a moment, then remembered. 'Because of my coffee machine, of course. It works brilliantly.'

'Of course! I'd forgotten all about that. I'm so glad. But it cost me nothing, you know.'

'It cost you time.'

'Mmm. My time isn't worth much though, is it?'

But at that Vik leaped in. 'It *is* Ruth. Don't be like that. Did you go and see Tony?'

Ruth flushed. 'I did, Vik. Took me ages to pluck up the courage but I did.'

'And?'

She gave an awkward shrug. 'It wasn't the best. There's a . . . a long way to go there. We couldn't really talk.'

'I'm sorry.'

'It's OK because, guess what – I *did* talk to Hayley at work and I've arranged to go in next week.'

'That's fantastic! You can get that lovely uniform out again.'

'I can. And get the poor old van going too. D'you know . . .'

Charlie watched them chatting away as if they'd known each other for ages and marvelled. He'd done that. He'd brought them together. Surely, then, he wasn't all bad?

'Ruth,' Aleesha asked, tugging on her arm to drag her from the dull grown-up conversation, 'do you want to see Climbing Barbie scale the great cliff?'

'Cliff?' Ruth asked Vik.

He rolled his eyes. 'The bloody freezer. At least it's good for something, hey?'

They both laughed and Charlie looked again to the open lounge door.

'What freezer?' he asked, but the doorbell was ringing once more and this time it could only be one person.

As if in answer the cooker pinged out and, turning to it, Vik said, 'Could you get that, Charlie?'

Charlie swallowed. 'Er, yeah. Course. Right.'

He heard the words scrape out of him and turned to the door. He sucked up his pink mocktail but it was no use to him at all. God, he needed a drink. This, he remembered, was why he chose not to go out any more. At home, in his blank, cleared-out flat, he could resist with the fierce ascetism of a hair-shirted monk. Out here in the world, though, it was a mass of confusions and difficulties and temptations. The bell rang again and he forced himself to the door and pulled it open.

'Hi Greg.'

'Charlie! Hey, you look different in civvies. God, stupid thing to say. I mean, you look great. Purple's a tricky colour to pull off, right?'

He gave Charlie a lopsided grin and Charlie relaxed a little. It was just Greg, just a person. And if he had a secret, well, so what? Who didn't? Charlie was a mass of bloody lies so he, of all people, should be able to look past it.

'You mean a Turner's fleece isn't the height of sophistication?' he asked.

'Not quite, mate. A medium peak, perhaps.'

'Well, you should know, adventurer!'

Too much? Charlie felt the jocularity grind but Greg didn't seem to notice.

'Perhaps you can lend it to me for my next trip? It'd look very fetching against the Northern Lights.'

Charlie watched Greg limp past him into the kitchen and again questioned the evidence he'd seen today.

'When do you go to Iceland then?' he asked, following him inside, but his question was drowned out by Ruth and Vik.

'Hey, it's our local star! All ready for the awards, oh inspirational one?'

'As ready as I'll ever be, Ruth.'

'Did they come to do your VT?'

'God, yes. This super-enthusiastic girl called Kirstie was at my house for hours. I needed the patience of a tortoise! Ooh, cocktails, Vik, fantastic. And who's this?'

'Aleesha! I'm Aleesha!'

Charlie stood back and watched as Greg was introduced to Vik's granddaughter, who bossed him into a green cocktail as they all chatted like old friends. Charlie sipped his mocktail and tried not to eyeball the array of liqueurs on the table just three short steps away.

'So, I'm guessing, Vik,' he heard Greg say through the fug of temptation, 'that you made it to the ballet show?'

'Certainly did. Aleesha was brilliant.'

'I was,' Aleesha confirmed happily.

'And you saw your son?'

'I did. My daughter-in-law, too.'

'And that went well? It must have done if Aleesha's here?'

'Well enough,' Vik agreed. 'For now. We still need to talk but, hey, this is a start.'

'It certainly is. Well done.' Greg patted him on the back.

'Maybe,' Ruth said, 'Aleesha could show us her dance?'

'Now?' Aleesha said. 'Here?'

'Why not?'

'I'm not sure there's space,' Vik started, but already Aleesha was pushing back chairs to create a 'stage'. Greg, Vik and Ruth all watched as she started dancing and Charlie watched them, trying to be pleased. His plan had worked. These people didn't need four pathetic minutes of Turner's time now; they had each other. Great. Well done him.

Aleesha finished and everyone clapped. Charlie joined in, hard and loud and for far too long. The others looked at him.

'Great,' he said, dropping his hands self-consciously. 'Wasn't she great?'

'Fantastic,' Ruth agreed.

'I wish I could send her on stage instead of me tomorrow,' Greg said.

'Stage?' Aleesha asked eagerly.

'Greg's getting an award tomorrow,' Vik told her.

'Not necessarily,' Greg said. 'I mean, I won't win. At least, I'd better not.'

Charlie saw a shadow cross his handsome face and looked away.

'I dunno, Greg,' Ruth said. 'That Candy Drew's been filling Twitter with pictures of you and they're pretty cool. That one of you on the beach with your scar looking like some sort of exotic snake is amazing. Where is that?'

'What? Oh, Thailand. Railay Beach. You can only get there by boat.'

'Beautiful.'

'Thanks.'

She nudged him. 'Not you – the beach!'

He managed a smile. 'Cheers, Ruth! Now, are we eating or what? I'm starving.'

They took their places at Vik's big table and he proudly brought all manner of curries to the middle, helped by an over-excited Aleesha.

'Daddy says I don't like curry,' she told Vik once they were sat down too. 'But it looks very pretty.'

'Doesn't it,' Ruth agreed, leaning over. 'Just try a little bit, sweetheart. I bet you'll like this lovely fluffy naan. And this chicken. See how soft it is.'

Aleesha obediently tried it and her dark eyes lit up. 'Nice.' A mischievous twinkle entered them. 'Daddy was wrong!'

'Yes, well, daddies are wrong sometimes. Mummies, too.'

'Really?'

Aleesha looked entranced by this information and Ruth gave Vik an apologetic grimace. He smiled back and poured wine.

'Charlie?' He proffered the bottle then hastily pulled it back. 'Oh, no. Sorry. Stupid.'

'It's fine. I've got this delicious mocktail.'

Charlie sipped it again. It hadn't got any better. In fact, the too-sweet fruit clashed with the curry. He could smell the rich tang of the Shiraz in the others' glasses and his taste buds itched for it.

'So,' he said, 'did you all get your deliveries OK today?'

'Oh yes,' Vik told him. 'Some tiny little girl with the most beautiful hair. Wasn't it beautiful, Aleesha?'

'It was a rainbow,' Aleesha agreed delightedly. 'Just like a My Little Pony mane.'

'Praise indeed,' Greg said. 'It *was* pretty cool, mind you. She seemed very nice. And strong. Like Vik said, she was tiny, but she carried three baskets in no bother.'

'That'll be Bri,' Charlie said. 'She's great.'

'Very friendly,' Ruth said. 'I gather she's soon to be a mum?'

'Er, yes.' Charlie looked round, thrown. Bri had been chatting to Ruth about Harper then? Well, of course she had. She told everyone about Harper. And why shouldn't she? It was nice. Even so, these were *his* people, *his* customers.

Ryan's customers, he reminded himself and his heart lurched. Perhaps he should stand up to Ryan. Tell Sean the truth, ask for Hope Street back. They couldn't sack him. He'd been proven innocent. He'd done nothing wrong.

He knew, though, that wasn't true. He had been proven innocent but he *had* done something wrong. Very wrong. He looked across the table and felt a rush of scalding-hot guilt. What was he doing sitting here pretending to be these people's friends when he'd caused such hurt to one of them? A few paltry tricks with wine and plugs was hardly 'restitution,' was it? Who was he kidding? He was a life-wrecker and didn't deserve this welcome, this food, this friendship. Greg wasn't the fraudster here; Charlie was.

He stared at the table, unable to help noticing Ruth's half-drunk cocktail just a finger's-reach away. She'd abandoned it in favour of the wine and God it looked good. He could just imagine the taste of it, the kick of the spirits, the rush of the alcohol across his body and into his poor, tired mind. He could just . . .

He stood fiercely up, pushing his chair back. 'I should go.'

'What?' The others looked at him, horrified. 'Why? It's early.'

'I know, but it's dark and I've got my bike and—'

'And you've got lights,' Ruth said, pointing to them in his open bag behind. 'Relax, Charlie. There's loads still to eat.'

'And,' Vik said, 'we've got pancakes for afterwards.'

'Pancakes?' Greg asked. 'Damn. I knew I should have worn an elasticated waistband!'

Everyone laughed and Aleesha began telling them all about how they were doing Susie's craps, which made them laugh more. Charlie watched Vik explaining that they were crêpes Suzette and wondered if he was slowly becoming detached from reality. God, he hoped so. Ruth's glass was still there, the red cocktail like a fantasy potion inside it. He put his hand on the table.

'A toast,' Greg proposed suddenly, thrusting his wine glass in the air. 'To our amazing chef, Vikram!'

'Vikram!' Ruth echoed instantly, raising her own.

Charlie pushed his hand forward, gripped. 'Vikram!'

He lifted his glass with the others and if it was Ruth's abandoned red drink and not his own innocuous pink one, no one seemed to notice, no one save Charlie himself as the long-resisted alcohol hit the back of his throat and sprinted, like a kid on Christmas morning, around his bloodstream. Oh God, that was good. It was like the finest medicine, chasing down the pain and anaesthetising it, not exactly driving it away but loosening it so it floated above him instead of anchoring itself deep into his bones. He took another sip and another. The taste was sickly, unpleasant even, but the burn! The burn was better than any damn bonfire.

One, he told himself. *I'll just have this one. Just for the toast.* He put the glass down, edged his fingers away. It was still there, still half full. He could have more. Soon. He'd take his time, control it. He could, he was sure he could.

'You're too kind,' Vik said, blushing. Then he was up and clearing curry away to make space for a little one-ring camping stove. 'Ready for fire?' he asked Aleesha and she jumped madly up and down. 'Thought so.'

Vik put a match to the camping stove and the flames danced up in a delicate blue circle.

'Oh!' Aleesha gasped. 'Pretty!'

'You wait,' Vik said proudly. 'I've been on YouTube and I've got a cool trick. If it works. Charlie, can you watch the pan?' He'd placed a frying pan on the flames and now he brushed a little oil on to it and turned the handle towards Charlie. Charlie took it with some trepidation.

'Why me, Vik?'

'Because you're sober.'

Charlie looked guiltily to the red cocktail but even now, Ruth, her wine finished, was picking it up again. Charlie felt a desperate desire to jump over the table and snatch it back. He looked down at the pan.

'I think you're trusting the wrong person, Vik. I'm at my limit at scrambled eggs.'

'Didn't you help your mum make pancakes as a kid?'

Charlie laughed mirthlessly. 'She wasn't that sort of mum. I think we had a Polish nanny at one point who did them for us.'

'Nanny . . .? Oh, don't worry. It's very much the same idea as scrambled eggs, you just stir less. Now, here's the pancake mix. When it looks hot enough, pour some in.'

'Right.'

Charlie looked back to the cocktail glass but Ruth had emptied it. Good. It was gone. Temptation dismissed. He focused on the pan. A little smoke started to rise off the puddles of oil and when he tipped it, they ran joyously round as if chasing each other. Vik had picked up an orange and was carving the skin off it in one long, elegant twist. Aleesha crawled on to Ruth's lap and they both watched, mesmerised.

'Pour,' Vik said to Charlie.

'OK.'

Nervously, Charlie lifted the jug of pancake mix and poured it carefully into the pan. It spread out rapidly, chasing towards the edges.

'It's working!'

'You're a natural, Charlie. That's plenty.'

Charlie obediently put the jug down and watched in satisfaction as the batter closed up a small gap in the middle and settled into a perfect circle.

'Now what?'

'Wait until you see it all cooking through and we'll turn it.'

'Flip it, surely,' Greg said.

Charlie turned to him. 'You want me to flip this? Up in the air?'

'Of course.'

'What if I mess it up?'

'You won't.'

'And even if you do,' Vik added, 'we can just make another. There's loads of mixture.'

That much was true, but Charlie had been brought up not to make a mess. Mind you – look how well that had gone! He waited for the usual rush of bitterness and self-loathing but it didn't make it through the absurdly simple thrill of throwing a pancake in the air. Maybe it was the hit of the alcohol, maybe it was the hit of simple pleasure, but either way he liked it.

'It's almost cooked,' Vik said. 'Are you ready, Charlie?'

Charlie looked around at the little group who'd welcomed him in so readily and tried to ignore the crushing feeling that he was imposing on their friendship.

'I'm ready.'

He lifted the pan off the stove, squared his feet, then dipped it a little and flicked it upwards. The pancake jolted into the air. Charlie watched it lift and turn, held his breath as steady as the pan, and then there it was, flopping back in like an obedient pet, brown side upwards. Everyone burst into applause.

'You did it!' Aleesha cried.

'I did it,' Charlie agreed, staring at the perfectly aligned pancake. 'I really did it.'

'Well done,' Vik said, clapping him on the back. 'Now pop it back on the stove and let's get to the really fun stuff!'

Charlie did so. His skin was actually tingling with his success. Silly really, but so what? He was here, with friends, in the warmth and light, with a lingering fug of curry being chased away by the childish smell of batter and orange juice, and it was perfect. Simply perfect.

'Right,' Vik said. 'Almost there.' He fetched a bowl from the fridge and spooned some fruit – peaches and raspberries and pieces of orange – on to the centre of the pancake, watching it carefully. 'Now, Charlie, you're going to have to hold your nerve here. Are you good with fire?'

For a moment the flames of all his possessions wafted past Charlie's mind's eye, but he pushed them aside. Nodded.

'You got Aleesha safe?' Vik asked Ruth.

'Very safe,' she assured him.

'Good. Here goes then!'

Vik spiked one end of the orange peel on a knife then held it up so that the rest spiralled down over the pan until the tip touched the sizzling pancake. He took a bottle of Grand Marnier from his cocktail selection and very, very slowly poured it on to the tip. The liqueur slid, honey-coloured, down the peel and when it hit the pan, it burst into a blue flame that licked straight back up so that the whole thing was a river of flame.

Everyone gasped. And now, as the liquid ran into the pan, the flame spread into a blue haze across it so that the pieces of fruit seemed to shimmer and dance. Charlie held the pan steady and gazed in wonder as the flames whirled round on themselves and then, with a whisper, went out.

'Perfect!' Vik said, his voice awed. 'That was bloody perfect. Oops, sorry Aleesha. But it was! Plate, please.' Ruth passed him one and he held it out to Charlie, who eased the pancake on to it. 'Who's first? Aleesha?'

Aleesha, though, was still staring. 'It was on fire, Grampie!'

'It was, sweetheart. Wasn't it pretty?' She nodded dumbly. 'Would you like to try it?' But at that she shook her head. Vik laughed. 'Here, let's all try it.'

He carefully turned the stove off and put it on the side, then handed out spoons. Ruth set Aleesha down and she tiptoed up to the table as if the pancake might magically flame again. Vik drew her in against him.

'Try it, Leesha.'

Again she shook her head. 'You try it, Grampie.'

'With pleasure.' Vik dug his spoon into the pancake and lifted up a section, cupping his hand under the spoon as he lifted it over Aleesha's head and up to his lips. 'Delicious! Dig in everyone.'

They all reached for a spoon, Charlie as eager as the rest. The pancake was delicious – the batter buttery, the fruit warm and sweet with a gloriously heady kick of spirit at its heart. Charlie closed his eyes for a moment, letting the flavours sing across his tongue and down his throat, but a sudden series of irritable beeps made him open them again.

'What's that?'

'Sorry,' Greg said as they all looked around. 'It's my bloody Twitter alerts. I'll put it on silent.'

He reached for his phone but even as he did so more beeps came through, almost falling over each other in their rush to make themselves heard and sending the device buzzing across the table. Greg snatched it up and turned it sideways to switch it to silent but then froze.

'What the . . .?'

He sank into his chair, his eyes flicking across the screen, his spoon hanging limply from his other hand.

'What is it, Greg?' Ruth asked. 'What's happened?'

Greg didn't speak but Charlie knew. Greg's phone was still bleating in his hand like a lost lamb and he was staring at it with utter horror and all Charlie could think was that he'd done it again. This was his fault. All his bloody fault.

Chapter Thirty-two

Greg stared at the endless little boxes of bile flashing across his screen. Words hit out at him, right hook, left hook, again and again – *cheat, fraud, liar.* Then the defences: *How do we know? Who's the liar here? Let Greg defend himself. Let him speak. Greg will tell us the truth.*

There were thousands of expectant tweeters just waiting for him, wanting him to refute the rumour, to tell the truth. Or, rather, to keep up the lie. Greg dropped his phone on to the table and sank his head into his hands. One more day. That's all he'd needed – one more bloody day and he could have got through this ceremony and sorted himself out.

'I was going to go to Iceland,' he cried.

He'd signed the contract with North Face this morning, decided it was his chance to actually make it on to a plane and do what he'd been telling the world he'd been doing for the last year, to step into his carefully constructed cocoon of a lie and actually live it. But now the cocoon had been smashed.

'What? Greg, what's up? What's happened?'

He could hear the voices but not see the people. All he could see was blackness. It was like the accident all over again – a gaping hole before him where once his future had been.

'I was,' he insisted, louder now. 'I *was* going to go to Iceland. I was going to get on the plane.'

'Greg, please.' Someone shook him and he tried to focus. It was a woman, a woman with red hair and big brown eyes brimming with concern. 'Is it true, Greg?'

She nodded her head to the phone. A man was holding it. An Indian man with soft grey hair and a curly-haired girl pinging up and down at his side. Where the hell was he? He felt as if someone had taken every molecule of his broken body and shaken them up and he couldn't claw them back into any sort of shape.

'Of course,' he groaned. 'Of course this was going to happen. Of course they were going to find out. I was mad to think I could keep it a secret. Mad to ever start the whole bloody thing.'

'Greg, stop it!'

Someone loomed close and Greg felt two big, warm hands either side of his face. He pulled back from the touch and pain exploded across his spine, but the dark edges receded a little.

'Ruth,' he said.

'Sorry.' She swallowed and slowly removed her hands. 'I'm sorry if I startled you, but you looked lost in there.'

'I was. That is, I *am*.'

'So it's true? You haven't been travelling?'

Greg looked again to his phone, buzzing away like a self-important insect in Vik's hand as a steady stream of Twitter-bile poured from it.

'It's true,' he admitted heavily. 'I'm no bloody adventurer, not unless you count the armchair kind. Travel by Photoshop, that's me. Every last pretty picture gloriously created with screens and effects and Turner's most exotic foodstuffs.' He looked around at Ruth, Vik, Aleesha and Charlie. They'd been so nice to him, so welcoming. 'I'm a fraud.'

Ruth frowned. 'Not to me you're not.'

'I lied.'

'Not to me.'

'Ruth, I lied to the whole world.'

She gave a little tilt of the head. 'Well, that's true but it's easily done. And you lied about what you did, not about who you are.'

'Aren't they the same? I can't be the brave adventurer if I don't do the brave adventuring. I can't tell people to get out there and take on the world when I never leave my own house.'

'You've come here,' Vik said quietly.

'Yes. And the first time it nearly killed me.' He looked to Charlie, stood back from the others. 'You've no idea how hard it was to walk those few steps down Hope Street.'

'I'm sorry.' The delivery driver looked as sick as Greg felt.

'But you did it,' Vik said gently.

'I did.' Greg sighed. 'I did and I'm glad of it. But . . .' Behind them, Vik's clock struck the hour and Greg glanced up at it as a new thought struck him. 'Shit – Rachel! She'll be landing at Heathrow any minute now. Mum and Dad have gone to fetch her. They're coming to the awards. They're so excited. Mum's got a new dress and Dad sent his suit to the dry-cleaners and Kirstie interviewed them. Oh God, Kirstie! She was relying on my VT to get her a job. And my sister's come all the way from the States and I . . . I . . .'

He fought for breath as it all overwhelmed him. Ruth lifted a hand and for a moment he thought she was going to slap him, but instead she rubbed his back in strong, sure circles until his lungs filled. The panic, however, did not recede.

'How will I tell them?'

'The tweeters?'

'No! I don't care about them. I mean my family. They've done so much for me. Been so supportive and I've let them down.'

'No, Greg!' Ruth's voice was firm.

'But I have. I didn't mean to. I only started this to protect them.'

'From what?'

'From *me*. From having to look after me. I was such a miserable bastard and they were so kind. I didn't want to be a burden so I told them I was going abroad. And I was going to go. I had the plane tickets, I'd booked accommodation. They dropped me off at the airport, clucking and fussing and saying how proud they were. I sent them off, determined I could manage on my own, but . . .'

Still his phone was buzzing away and he was grateful when Charlie snatched it from Vik and flicked it off. The sudden silence made him realise just how frantic the room had grown. So many people after him.

'Thank you,' he said to Charlie, then remembered something. 'Oh, but my parents – they might be trying to contact me.'

Reluctantly, he switched it back on and a dawn chorus of tweets filled the room.

'I could turn off your notifications,' Ruth suggested.

Greg stared at her. Just turn them off! That would be so wonderfully easy and yet it wouldn't make the problem go away, would it? He shook his head and let the world tweet on.

'Are we making another pancake?' Aleesha asked, looking around them all, confused.

'Course we are,' Charlie agreed, pulling her away from Greg.

The stove flared blue again, the pan hissed excitedly. Aleesha gave a little giggle and Greg envied her with a ferocity he hated himself for.

'I never got on that first plane to India back in January,' he told the others dully. 'I . . . I couldn't face it.'

It hadn't been quite that simple. He could remember it now, clear as day. It was the bag drop that had been the problem – virtually the first thing he'd done. The woman operating it had been one of those heavily made-up types with red nails. She'd swung his bag on to the belt with surprising strength and then asked him if he had anything else to check in.

'No thank you,' he'd said.

'What about the stick?'

'Sorry?'

'Your stick, sir. You'll have to check it in.'

That's when the panic had started to tick inside his head. His stick had been a walker's pole, rugged and strong, and he'd come to think of it as his third leg.

'It doesn't fit in the bag.'

'Oh that's fine. We can tag it separately. It'll be quite safe. Going trekking, are you?'

She hadn't even bothered to look at him. She'd only been thinking about her precious baggage allowances.

'Yes.'

'Fantastic.'

Her voice had had a sing-song tone, the words a refrain not a conversation. And then she'd reached for his stick with her blood-red nails and the panic had ticked stronger within him.

'You can't have it.'

'I beg your pardon?' A little frown had creased her foundation.

'I'd rather keep it with me, thank you.'

'No can do, I'm afraid, sir. It could be classed as a weapon, you see, and we can't condone weapons on the airline, can we?'

'Weapon?' The tick-tick of panic had pushed through into anger, coursing through Greg's veins, strong and sure. 'You consider me a threat?'

'Of course not, sir, but we have to be very careful these days.'

'Look at me.'

'Sir, I . . .'

'Just bloody look at me. This is not a weapon. It's a walking stick. A stick that I need for walking.'

Her lips had been pursed, lemon-sour, but she had looked and she had seen and a blush had crept across whatever skin she'd had hidden beneath the Max-Factor mask.

'Oh God, I'm sorry.' For a moment she'd been human, but then she'd tugged her corporate neck-scarf into place and composed herself. 'You should have said, sir. I do apologise but, you see, it's company policy not to allow sticks on the plane. It's not you, you understand, but others.'

'All the terrorists that you allow onboard?'

'There's no need for sarcasm, sir. This is a serious matter.'

'I know, I—'

'But obviously we are here to do all we can to help.' Pause for a saccharine smile. 'We have a special wheelchair service that—'

'Wheelchair service?'

'That's right.' She'd beamed as if offering him a business-class upgrade. 'If you just wait here, sir, I'll fetch Darren and—'

'Don't bother.'

'But, sir, we're here to help.'

'I don't want Darren and his bloody wheelchair.'

'Can I ask you not to swear, sir. It's disrespectful and our charter says—'

'I don't care about your charter. Where's *my* respect? Six months it's taken me to fight my way out of a wheelchair and I didn't come here to have you push me straight back into one.'

'Well, now—'

'I just want to keep my walking stick with me and all will be fine.'

'But, sir, it's company policy—'

'You are refusing me my disability aid?'

Greg had seen panic behind the woman's super-dark lashes and been glad. Maybe now she knew how he felt. People had been looking over, nudging each other, pointing. A young man had drawn out his phone and pointed it in Greg's direction in case he did something YouTube-worthy. Greg had clutched his stick tighter as the whole airport had seemed to close in on him in a swirl of faces and noise and perfectly functioning bodies. And in that moment, he'd known he couldn't do this. He'd swung away and made for the exit, with the stupid red-taloned woman calling, 'Sir, sir,' after him, like a bleating bloody sheep.

'I left,' he told the others. 'I called a cab and went home and hid out there.'

He'd probably overreacted. He'd checked since and either she'd been wrong or the airline had changed their policy shortly afterwards as sticks *were* allowed for those that clearly needed them. Perhaps if he'd been calmer, just asked to see a manager, it would all have been fine, but the damn woman had backed them both into a corner and he'd fought his way out of it, snarling like a wild dog. That airport had been the start of a journey all right, but not a good one.

'I cooked up a few photos to send Mum and Dad so they wouldn't worry and it worked. They came round to see me once I was "home" and I cooked them Indian food and talked about Indian places and it was such a relief to have something to say that wasn't about physios and drugs and rehab. And my mum said over and over how proud she was of me and how much better I looked and that's when I said it. That's when I said, "I think I might go somewhere else," knowing full well this time that I'd got no intention of flying anywhere other than into cyberspace. The next day, I ordered the all-singing, all-dancing Photoshop suite with some of my company pay-off and, well, the rest is history. Or, rather, fiction. Sordid or what?'

The others looked at each other as shame crept through Greg's body, far more painful than any winch's teeth.

'You made it up?' Vik asked. 'All of it? But you know so much. I mean, you write about the places in so much detail.'

Greg gave a rueful grimace. 'I've always been good at research.'

They fell into silence again until, eventually, Ruth cleared her throat. 'Well, it's hardly the worst crime, Greg. And, anyway, how do people know?'

Greg stared at her. 'Good point. Who started all this?'

Across the table, the pancake pan clattered. Vik leaped forward, pulling Aleesha back. 'Careful, Charlie.'

'Sorry. Slipped.'

He steadied the pan, then lifted the orange spiral and began to pour Grand Marnier down it.

Greg reached for his phone. The screen was filled with tweets, uppermost among them one from the *Daily Mail*.

INSIDE SCOOP. GREG SUTTON: INSPIRATIONAL LIAR. READ IT NOW.

Hands shaking, he clicked on the link and there it was:

> For weeks Twitter has been going mad over the adventures of handsome disabled traveller Greg Sutton. His slogan – don't let disability disable your life – has inspired thousands, including pop star Candy Drew whose own little sister is a wheelchair user. 'Greg made me see life could still be an adventure for my beautiful Chloe,' Drew tweeted recently. But it seems that Greg Sutton's adventures are a fraud and a sham for the man hasn't left his house in a year. And how do we know? Because he's had a Turner's supermarket delivery every single week. We spoke with. . .

Greg stopped reading. He looked across the kitchen to where Charlie was still pouring spirits down a damned orange spiral as if it was the only thing that mattered in the world.

'You!' He leaped up and Charlie jumped. 'You're the one who leaked it, Charlie. You're the one who told on me.'

'No! I'm not.' Charlie put the pan down. 'That's not true, Greg. I've said nothing.'

'You came into my house, all nice and kind and helpful. All "let me unpack for you, Greg", "take a load off, Greg". And all along you were, what, spying on me?'

'No! I wasn't. I didn't.'

'Is that why you took the Turner's job?'

'No.'

'Is that why you came to Hope Street?'

'No, Greg. It isn't. I wasn't spying.'

'How much did they pay you? Thousands, I bet. You won't have to deliver groceries any more, will you? Nice work, Charlie. A few weeks' grind and a fat pay-off. And why not, really? I deserve it after all.'

'You don't. Please, Greg. That's not how it was. I found out your secret today, with our stupid new system, but it wasn't me who went to the press. I wouldn't do that.'

'Why? Because you're too nice?'

'No! Because I know what it's like to keep secrets.'

Charlie was shouting now. Vik had moved the hot pan away but he was still waving the spiralled orange skin in front of him like some manic weapon.

Greg shook his head. 'I don't believe you, Charlie.'

'Well, you should. You must.' Charlie looked around, drew in a juddering breath. 'I was sent to Hope Street by fate. I knew it the minute I saw the name on the list – the name of the person whose life I wrecked. But it wasn't you, Greg.'

He looked desperately into the spiral of orange, glowing syrupy gold. Greg looked to Vik and then to Ruth, but they were both fixed on Charlie as he spoke again.

'I didn't mean to kill her. I didn't mean her to die.'

'Die?' Aleesha's little voice quavered. 'Who died? I don't want anyone to die.'

'I didn't want that either,' Charlie said. 'You have to believe me, I didn't want her to die.'

'Who?' Vik demanded. 'Who didn't you want to die, Charlie?'

Charlie turned sad eyes to him, blew out several times, and then swung round to Ruth.

'Libby,' he said. 'I didn't want Libby to die.'

Chapter Thirty-three

'You!' Ruth stared at the delivery driver, unable to believe what he was saying. 'You killed Libby?' Instantly, the eyes were back, peering through the darkness of her daughter's unknown death. 'How?'

'How you said – by poisoning her with dark books, by encouraging her to read above her years, by giving her Virginia bloody Woolf.'

Mummy! Libby called to Ruth, her little hand reaching out. She tried to grab it but it was too late. It had always been too late.

'I don't understand,' she stuttered.

Charlie looked straight at her. 'I was her English teacher, Ruth. I taught Libby. I thought she was remarkable. I was excited to have found a student of so much potential. She understood what great literature was all about. She was a thinker, a questioner. She was the sort of student teachers like me dream of.'

'But . . . but you're not a teacher.'

'Not any more.'

'You were sacked?'

'No. I was proven innocent, remember?'

'Yes, but . . .'

'But it was still my fault. I know that, Ruth. It torments me every single day. For months it was the only thing I could think about. I told Libby to emulate her heroes, but I didn't mean by putting stones in her pockets and . . . and . . .'

'Enough!'

Anger swelled inside Ruth, filling her veins and sending her blood pulsing and screaming through her. And with it came clarity. This was the smug bastard who'd stolen Libby from her. He was right here in front of her. She couldn't reach Libby's poor, flailing little hand but this was the next best thing.

She'd been unable to face an inquest full of strangers discussing her little girl's death so, like a coward, she'd left Tony to go alone. Afterwards she'd regretted it, had longed to confront the bastard and make him see what he'd done but it had been too late. Or so she'd thought. Now, however, it turned out he'd been blithely walking into her house for these last few weeks.

'You brought me jigsaws!'

'I wanted to help.'

'Jigsaws, Charlie! You thought a couple of charity-shop puzzles would make up for my daughter?'

'No!'

'Ruth . . .' Vik said at her side but she was past hearing anyone but the bastard in front of her.

'I talked to you. I told you about Libby and you . . . you just sat there and said nothing.'

'I know. I'm sorry. I couldn't find the words to explain.'

'Couldn't find . . . Oh, that's rich! That's fantastic, that is. The bloody English teacher, the one who told my Libby that words were the answer to everything, couldn't find the ones to tell her mother what he'd done. D'you know what word you needed, Charlie? Do you know what *one* word would have done? It's not even a difficult one. Little kids can manage it. Sor—'

'Sorry,' Charlie said. 'I know. And I am, Ruth. I am sorry. Very, very sorry. It wrecked me. Really. I gave up my job because of it – my job that I'd fought my family all my life to be allowed to do.'

The absurdity of this stopped Ruth. Had she misunderstood what Charlie was telling her? She blinked and looked around for help. Vik came forward.

'You had to fight your family to become an English teacher?'

Even Greg looked up from where he was hunched over his phone.

291

Charlie sighed. 'I did. They wanted me to do economics or accountancy or marketing. They wanted me to go into the family business.'

'Which is?'

Charlie rubbed a hand across his eyes. 'Turner's,' he said gruffly. 'Turner's supermarkets.'

No one spoke. Aleesha, bored, fiddled with the cutlery, but the three adults just looked at each other.

'Your family run Turner's?' Greg asked eventually.

'*Own* it,' Charlie said wearily. 'I am a "Turner". Or I was until I changed my name. Dad got me the delivery job to "get me back on my feet". My siblings think it's hilarious. They take the piss out of me all the time. But, you know what, I don't care because my life fell apart after Libby died. I started drinking and couldn't stop. I was a mess.'

'Oh boohoo,' Ruth snapped, furious again.

How dare he claim her hurt? It wasn't his daughter who had died. It wasn't his family – his rich, frigging family – who'd fallen apart at the seams.

'I just meant . . .' Charlie closed his mouth, looked down. 'I should go.'

He placed the still gleaming orange peel on the table in front of him and took a step towards the door.

Ruth moved instantly to block him. 'Oh no. No way. It's not that easy.'

'But there's nothing I can do. You're right, Ruth – jigsaws and petty tricks with electrics can't help.'

'That was you?' Vik said.

Charlie looked at him. 'Clever, hey?' he scoffed at himself. 'Aren't I doing good? Aren't I making restitution?'

'You're trying,' Vik said.

Ruth glared at him. 'It's not enough, Vik.'

'So what *would* be enough?'

'Why are you defending him?'

'Because it seems to me that everyone's hurting here and—'

'Ooowww!'

Vik stopped dead at Aleesha's cry of pain. Ruth looked down and saw, like something out of a garish horror film, the glistening hot orange peel wrapped around her tiny hand.

'Oh my God!' Vik ran to the little girl, clasping her in his arms. He tried to pull the peel away but she'd grasped it firmly and it was burned to her skin. He looked furiously up at Charlie. 'Why did you put it there, Charlie? Why did you put it right in front of her?' Charlie's mouth opened and closed but nothing came out. 'Look at her little hand. Oh God, look at it. The peel's still hot. We have to get it off her.'

Ruth looked round in panic, spotted a water glass still half full and, picking it up, threw it over Aleesha's hand. The little girl gasped in shock but the peel, at least, shifted and Vik was able to prise it off. The skin beneath was raw and already blistering.

Aleesha looked down at it and burst into sobs. 'It hurts. It really, really hurts.'

Vik held her tight, sobbing too. Ruth watched helplessly.

'Want Mummy!' Aleesha cried and the word battered around Ruth's head: *Mummy, Mummy, Mummy!*

She put her hands up to try and block it but her mind was racing. Charlie was Mr Turner. Charlie was the traitor teacher who'd sent Libby into the watery arms of Virginia bloody Woolf. She could picture it all too clearly – the policewoman finding the book, the way she'd rushed past Ruth, shouting, 'Search the riverbank' into the radio.

Something nudged at her shoulder, pulling her out of the nightmare, and she looked back to see Greg had pulled himself away from his phone and grabbed the bowl of pancake fruit. He dumped it in the sink and filled it with water, which he handed to Ruth.

'Get her hand in that to keep the air off the burn.'

Ruth fought to concentrate, to look past the bright blue eyes of her own nightmares into the one before her.

'How do you know that's the right thing to do?' she demanded, but Greg just raised a sardonic eyebrow at her and she stopped herself. 'OK.' She bent down to the little girl. 'Here, Aleesha, put your hand in the bowl. It will help, I promise.'

The water was pink from the berries and Aleesha eyed it suspiciously. Ruth glanced uncertainly back to Greg, but he nodded her on so she took a quick breath then grabbed Aleesha by the wrist and plunged her hand into the water before she had time to pull back. Aleesha gasped again and looked furiously at Ruth but she didn't let go and moments later her sobs eased slightly.

Mummy, Mummy, Mummy!

Libby's poor, limp, lifeless body had been brought from the water by a man in a black wetsuit just like something out of one of her blasted novels. Ruth imagined her daughter's sky-blue eyes taking in the scene and wondered if they would have rather liked what they saw, then cursed herself for a fool and forced her focus back on to Aleesha.

'Does that help?'

Aleesha gave a tiny nod. Vik looked gratefully at Ruth. Greg hovered. Behind them all, Charlie gave a strained cough.

'I should go,' he said again.

'You should,' Vik grunted, but now it was Greg who stepped in Charlie's way.

'Aleesha needs to go to hospital.'

'Hospital?' Vik gasped.

'Just to be sure. That wound needs professional dressing.'

'Yes. Yes, of course. Hospital. But how—'

'I've got my van,' Ruth said, looking to the door, keen to help, to do something, anything, to avoid the swirl of her own thoughts. 'I'll drive her,' she insisted. 'I'll get the van now and—'

'You've been drinking, Ruth.'

She froze. 'Only one cocktail.'

'And at least one glass of wine, and how much before you came?'

Ruth thought with shame of the three vodka and tonics she'd sunk earlier. She'd done so well all week but it was Friday and she'd wanted a treat, not to mention the courage to come over. What an idiot.

'Too much,' she admitted.

Listen to her. She'd drunk too much to take a little girl in pain to hospital. She'd drunk too much to go back to work and too much to have a proper conversation with the man she loved. It had to stop. It *would* stop. Tomorrow. But that still left today.

'Can you drive?' she asked Greg.

'Like hell!'

He lifted his twisted leg and she grimaced. 'Course. Sorry. Vik?'

'I've been drinking too. Cocktail, red wine. Oh God, why? What an idiot. I had Aleesha here. I should have been more careful. I should . . . Shit, Sai! He's going to kill me. Should I call him? I should, shouldn't I? I should call him.'

He was working himself into a frenzy and, conversely, it calmed Ruth's own thoughts. She put a hand on his back. 'First things first, Vik. It's not like she's in a critical condition is it, so let's get her seen by a medic and then you can call him.'

'But we can't get to the hospital!'

'Course we can. We'll call an ambulance.'

'It might take ages though. She's not critical, right? But she's hurting and she's my responsibility and—'

'I can drive,' Charlie offered.

They all looked to him.

'I thought you'd gone,' Vik said coldly.

Charlie's eyes narrowed. 'I can. If that's what you want. Or I can drive you to the hospital first.'

Vik looked to Ruth. Ruth looked to Greg. Greg looked to his phone.

'Bloody hell,' he said, 'what choice have we got? Let's go.'

'All of us?'

'Yep. It's your van, Ruth, it's Vik's granddaughter and I . . . I need to keep an eye on Turner's-boy here.'

'I didn't tell them,' Charlie protested.

Greg shook his head. 'You didn't tell a lot of people a lot of things, it seems. But right now the best thing you can do is drive.'

*

Ruth took Charlie to her van in stony silence.

'Here.' She handed him the keys to the incongruously jaunty yellow vehicle. 'I hope she starts. I've not used her in . . . in too long.'

Charlie slid into the driver's seat and turned the key. The van spluttered, then juddered into life.

'Thank God,' Ruth said, getting into the passenger side. 'Go!'

Charlie backed the van on to Hope Street and turned it into Vik's drive. The other three came out, Vik holding Aleesha on his hip with Greg stumblingly trying to balance the bowl of water in front of them so that the little girl's poor hand stayed covered. They pulled open the side door and clambered awkwardly into the back of the van.

'Do we sit on the floor?' Aleesha asked, momentarily diverted from her injury.

'That's right,' Greg said through gritted teeth.

Ruth looked back at him and gave him a sympathetic grimace.

'Go!' she ordered Charlie again.

He did as instructed, heading west up Hope Street. They flashed past the hardware store and Ruth glanced across. There was a light in the window of the flat above. Tony must be in there. Was he alone? Was he, maybe, eating chips from his fryer and thinking of her as he'd said he'd do? And meanwhile here she was, driving past with someone else's child and the man who'd taken their own from them.

It wasn't just him, a tiny voice said in her head, but she quashed it, looked again for the anger. It was easily found.

'Is that why you wanted to be a teacher?' she demanded of Charlie. 'To have control over young lives?'

'No! I just loved books and I loved what a difference they'd made to me and I wanted to . . . to share that with others.'

'Aaah. Sweet. So, you turned down a job in your multi-million-pound family business – bully for you. You told a girl she had talent – how kind. You gave your time and energy to "nurturing" that talent . . .'

'I tried. I—'

'And then you killed her.'

The van swerved and there was a collective squeak from those in the back. Charlie swiftly corrected it.

'Ruth, I—'

'You're sorry. I know. Not half as sorry as I am. Hospital – there.' She pointed and Charlie swung the van into the big entrance. Under the glaring street lights, Ruth saw tears on his cheeks, but she didn't care. She refused to care. 'Drop us at A&E. You don't need to come in.'

Charlie followed the signs silently. In the back, Aleesha's sobs had given way to little hiccupping gasps and Vik was keeping up a low monotone of comfort. Greg was still shifting around trying to get comfortable while jabbing at his phone.

'Don't answer it,' Ruth suggested. 'Switch it off.'

'But they're talking about me. The whole world is talking. About *me*.' His phone rang. 'Oh God, no . . .' He sucked in a breath, answered. 'Mum? Hi. Yes, I know. I've seen it. I'm OK, yes. I'm with friends . . . well, mainly friends.'

He glared at Charlie's back. Charlie flinched but drove on, turning round the huge hospital to the A&E department at the rear. Greg paused, listened. A woman's voice reached into the cramped van.

'Is it true, Greg? Darling? Did you . . . did you make it all up?'

Greg gave a huge sigh. 'It's true, Mum. I'm sorry. I didn't mean to deceive you. It just . . . What? Now? Really? That's very kind and it would be lovely but I'm not at home. I'm at the hospital. No! No, not me. It's a friend's granddaughter. She . . . Oh God, it's a long story, Mum. Can I tell you tomorrow? Yes. Yes, thank you. Thank you, Mum, and give them my love too, will you? Yes. Night then. What . . .?' He listened again as Charlie swung into A&E. 'Do I know who told them? Oh yes. Yes, I believe I do.'

Charlie jerked to a halt alongside an ambulance. The water in Aleesha's bowl sloshed over her lap and she squealed.

'Charlie!' Vik shouted. 'Haven't you done enough?'

'I didn't . . .' Charlie started, then he clamped his mouth shut. 'Yes, I have. I've done more than enough. To all of you. Sorry. Again. And, er, good luck.'

Ruth looked at him as the others began to clamber out of the back and something within her shuddered at the sight of him. His shoulders were hunched over the wheel, his hands gripping it so hard the knuckles were white.

'Charlie . . .' she started.

'I'll leave your van on your drive. I'll put the key through the letter box.'

'Right.' Vik, Greg and Aleesha were out now and heading through the big doors. Ruth reached for the handle, hesitated. Something about Charlie nagged at her; a suggestion of the worst memory of all. 'Perhaps we can talk another time?'

Charlie gave a weary laugh. 'Is there any point, Ruth? It's like you said, there are no words to make this right, not even from a smug, self-important bastard like me.'

The words didn't fit on his lips. Ruth remembered Charlie bringing her that first jigsaw, flushed with shyness but still urging it on her. He hadn't needed to do that. He hadn't needed to reach out to her. He hadn't needed to come to her house at all. She looked into herself for Libby's blue eyes but they were obscured by swirling water.

'Charlie . . .' she started again, but another ambulance came screeching in behind them, cutting across her.

'I need to get out of the way, Ruth.'

'Right. OK. Er, thanks for, you know, driving.'

'Yeah.'

He didn't look at her, just sat with his red-rimmed eyes fixed on his rear-view mirror as she got slowly out, and the moment she closed the door he was gone. She stood there, in the raw glare of the ambulance's flashing lights, watching as he disappeared.

'Mr Turner . . .?' she muttered, shaking her already spinning head. But then a little voice called 'Ruth' from inside the hospital and she turned to see Aleesha being helped across the lobby by a young nurse. She headed after her, banishing Charlie from her mind. Libby was gone but Aleesha was here and asking for her and that was all she needed to focus on for now.

Chapter Thirty-four

Vik rushed after the nurse as she led Aleesha across the waiting room, desperately trying to shade the little girl from all the unpleasant sights. To his left, a man sat holding a large wad of bandages to his temple, blood soaking through them. To his right, a young woman was being sick into a bucket, and ahead of them, nurses were rushing to someone fitting on the white floor. Oh God, this was no place for a three-year-old. It was no place for *him*. He felt weak and old and feeble. He knew he had to call Sai, but he couldn't face his son's inevitable anger – his son's *justifiable* anger. All he truly wanted was Nika. She'd always been so calm in situations like this.

'Don't worry, Vikram,' she'd have said. 'Our little girl is in the right hands. The lovely doctors and nurses will sort her out in a jiffy.'

He looked to the nurse and, sure enough, she was shielding Aleesha with her body and talking away to her in a low, soothing tone.

'We'll soon have this right, Aleesha. We'll just get you into a nice little room all of your own and I can have a look and get it all mended for you. OK?'

'OK,' Aleesha said, looking trustingly up at the nurse, her fingers still swirling around in the bowl of water the woman was holding for her.

'You did very well to get in this quickly,' the nurse said to Vik. 'That will help us.'

'Charlie drove me,' Aleesha said.

The nurse looked to Greg, who shook his head vehemently. 'I'm not Charlie.'

'He's, er, gone,' Vik said.

'And good riddance,' Greg growled.

'Greg,' Vik warned. 'We're here for Aleesha now.'

Greg dipped his head. 'Yeah. Right. Sorry Vik.'

'It's OK. I know how you feel.'

Frankly, Vik was boiling with rage at Charlie. He'd seemed so nice, so friendly and open and kind, but it had all been a front. He'd all but killed Ruth's poor daughter, had dobbed Greg in to the national press and then been so wrapped up in his own stupid concerns that he'd put a boiling-hot piece of peel down right in front of a curious three-year-old. Bastard.

But as Vik followed Aleesha and the nurse into a curtained cubicle, he couldn't hide a squirm of unease. Charlie had sounded so vehement when he'd insisted he hadn't said anything about Greg and he'd been so distressed when he'd confessed to Ruth. Was it any wonder he'd been a little distracted? And who, after all, should have been keeping an eye on the curious three-year-old faced with a jewel-bright piece of peel? Who but her own grandfather? He glanced to the door, wondering if Charlie might follow them in, but saw Ruth instead.

'How's she doing?' she asked.

Aleesha looked up at her. 'It hurts.'

'I know, sweetie.' Ruth bent to her. 'But the nurse will soon make it better, won't you?'

'I'll do my best,' the nurse agreed. 'Now, Aleesha, can you lift your hand out of the water for me?'

Aleesha, her eyes red and swollen with pain and tiredness, gave a nod and let her hand be drawn out of the water, but as soon as it hit the air she wailed and tried to shove it back. The nurse held on tight and it was clear she didn't like what she saw. She let Aleesha put it back in the water and looked up at Vik.

'Is that blood?' she asked, indicating the pink water.

'Raspberries,' Vik said foolishly.

'Right. OK. Good.'

'How is it?'

She bit her lip. 'It doesn't look great, I'm afraid. Don't panic,' she added as Vik swayed. 'I'm sure we can sort it. I'm going to get a dressing on so we can get rid of the water and make her comfortable but I'd like the consultant to see it.'

'Why?' Vik asked.

'Just so we do everything possible to ensure there's no lasting damage.'

'Lasting damage?' Vik's knees buckled and it was only Ruth's strong arm shooting around his waist that kept him upright.

'I'm sure it will be fine,' the nurse soothed. 'Young skin heals very well, really it does. I just want to take extra care of her, OK? OK, Aleesha?'

Aleesha nodded. 'Want Mummy,' she whispered.

The nurse looked to Ruth.

'You're not her mother?'

'No. I'm a friend. But Vik here is her grandfather.'

'OK, great. You might want to inform her parents though?'

'Really?' Vik asked. 'Do I have to?'

'I'd say so,' came the uncompromising reply.

'Right. Yes. Oh God.'

She gave him a kind smile. 'Accidents happen all the time, sir. Don't blame yourself. Now, I'll be back in a minute with that dressing.'

She bustled off and Vik sank on to the seat, gathering Aleesha into his lap and rocking her.

'Grampie! The water's spilling!'

The sudden clarity of her voice made him stop. He kissed the top of her curls and looked over them to Ruth and Charlie.

'I have to call Sai.'

He longed for someone to contradict him, but how could they? Aleesha was in hospital. She had to see a consultant and her parents deserved to know. He looked to Ruth and she gave him a grim nod of assent.

The nurse returned and Vik handed Aleesha into her care and trudged heavily up the corridor, holding his phone in his hands as gingerly as if it were the damn orange peel. Leaning back against the wall, he dialled.

'Dad?' His son answered on the first ring. 'Everything OK?'

Vik looked to the skies for help from Nika but found nothing more than the blank hospital ceiling.

'It's OK,' he said, fighting for words. 'It's just that Aleesha, well, she's had a little accident.'

'What?'

The word cracked down the phone. Vik's knees buckled and he put a hand to the wall to hold himself upright. 'She picked up a hot bit of orange peel.'

'A hot . . .?'

'And it stuck to her hand. And it's burned it a bit. Not a lot. But, well, we're in hospital. Just to get it checked. Just to be sure. We got here very quickly, the nurse says. There's no need to panic, she says. The consultant's just going to have a look at it to . . . to . . .'

He ran out of words. At the other end, he could hear Sai filling Hermione in and her cries of distress. He came back on the line.

'I can't believe this, Dad. I can't bloody believe it. One night. Just one bloody night and—'

Hermione interrupted him, babbling something about getting the car.

'OK, OK. I'm going now, Dad, but I've got a lot more to say. We'll be there very soon. Don't go anywhere.'

'No. Of course not. Sai, I'm so sorry.'

But his son had hung up. Vik stood against the wall, staring at the blank screen. In front of him, the poor young woman was sick into her bucket again. Vik wanted to snatch it off her and throw up himself. All his lovingly created curries were churning in his stomach with the stupid cocktail he'd let Aleesha talk him into making. He'd been so high on having friends over, so excited to have Aleesha there. He'd been like a stupid, giddy kid and now look what had happened. He deserved everything Sai had to say to him and more.

'Nika,' he murmured to the ceiling, but she wasn't there. She was never there any more and somehow he'd have to face this one on his own.

He looked back to the nurse wrapping a light gauze around his precious granddaughter's burned hand and felt a single tear run down his face. He put up a hand to wipe it away, but someone was there first, holding out a crisp hanky.

'Come on, Vik,' Greg said. 'Don't worry about them. They're just shocked. They'll be OK when they see her, when they know it's not that bad.'

Vik looked at him. 'She said "lasting damage", Greg. What if there's lasting damage? You know what that's like. You know what it could mean to her.'

'She also said young skin heals well. Try and be positive. For Aleesha.'

'For Aleesha,' Vik agreed and let himself be led back to his granddaughter, but he had one eye on the entrance, braced for Sai's arrival.

If only he could turn the clock back. But then, who didn't wish that? They all had things they'd have done so very differently given a second chance but life didn't work that way. All you could realistically hope to do was to deal with the fallout of your own mistakes. If only that fallout hadn't involved his precious little granddaughter.

Sai whirled into A&E twenty minutes later on turbo charge. The consultant had just arrived to look at Aleesha's hand and the curtains had been drawn around the cubicle but Vik would know his son's commanding tones anywhere, and he edged out from Aleesha's bedside to see Sai stood at the desk, demanding to see his daughter.

Distress suited him, Vik noted, taking a few extra moments before he would have to call out and let him know where he was. His son's athletic body bristled beneath his expensive clothes and the darkness around his eyes brought out the natural smoulder in his handsome face. Hermione was doing less well. Her perfect

303

make-up was smudged with crying and her eyes, as she scanned the motley crowd in the waiting room, were wild with distress.

'Sai,' Vik croaked. A woman holding the hand of a sleeping man in a wheelchair just a metre or so away looked curiously up but no one else heard. 'Sai!'

Sai was too busy fighting his way to the front of the queue at the desk, but Hermione heard. She tugged on her husband's arm and Sai zoned in on Vik instantly. He came striding across.

'Where is she, Dad? Where's my little girl?'

Vik swallowed. 'She's in here. The consultant is just checking her out and—'

He was almost knocked over by Typhoon Sai as he whirled past him, Hermione in tow.

'Mummy!' Aleesha cried. 'Mummy, Daddy, I've hurted my hand.'

'I know, darling. Poor you. You're being very brave. Silly Grampie.'

The little girl frowned. 'Grampie didn't do it. It was the hot orange.'

'But who put the hot orange there?'

'Sai,' Hermione said. 'Now's not the time . . .'

'Charlie did.'

'Charlie? Who's Charlie?' Sai looked around the cubicle, taking in Greg, sitting uncomfortably in a chair, and Ruth hovering behind. 'And who are you?'

'We're your father's friends. We were with him when Aleesha had her little accident.'

'Little!'

'Sai, please,' Hermione begged, tugging on his sleeve. 'You're scaring Leesha.'

Sai swung back to his daughter, all softness, but not before he'd given everyone else in the cubicle a glare that made it more than clear that he was not done with them yet. Vik could see why his son was doing so well in business. All the energy in the little room had focused around him the moment he'd walked in and now the consultant turned instinctively his way.

'The good news is that I've had a long look at Aleesha's hand and I'm confident that with care the skin will mend fine.'

'There'll be no lasting damage?' Vik gasped.

The doctor looked over at him. 'No lasting damage, sir. Correct. But you did right to bring her in so promptly. And to keep her hand in the water. It made a big difference.'

Vik glanced gratefully to Greg.

'Charlie drove us,' Aleesha said again.

Sai looked round as the consultant slid away with the nurse. 'Who the hell is this Charlie?' No one said anything. 'And why was he at your house, Dad? This pair too.'

'Excuse me—' Ruth protested, but Vik shook his head quickly at her. Sai was not in the mood to be interrupted. And no wonder.

'We were having dinner,' he told him.

'Dinner? You had Aleesha over for a sleepover – a sleepover you begged me to let you do – and you asked friends around too? Could that not have waited?'

'It could,' Vik agreed. 'It should have done. It was just that I'd already invited them and Aleesha was keen.'

'I was,' Aleesha agreed. 'We did cocktails for them, like you and Mummy do, and I did the umbrellas. Charlie had four umbrellas in his.'

Sai raised an eyebrow. 'How jolly. How many cocktails exactly, Dad?'

Vik frowned. Sai was staring down his handsome nose at him as if he were the father and Vik the son and he didn't like it.

'Now, Sai, I know you're upset but—'

'Never again, Dad.'

'What?' Panic coursed through Vik. 'Wait a minute, son. It was a mistake, a tiny lapse in concentration.'

'Not so tiny, Dad. We trusted you. You said you could look after her and we trusted you and we were wrong. So I tell you – never again.'

'But it was an accident.'

'Oh, was it? Why were you burning fruit in front of a three-year-old?'

'You said she liked European food and we found this recipe for crêpes Suzette and—'

'Crêpes Suzette? Good God – you're her grandfather, not her personal chef. It's ridiculous, Dad. Pathetic and irresponsible and ridiculous. Mum would never have allowed it!'

The words hit Vik like a hammer and he crumpled, collapsing against Greg, who stood up and faced Sai. 'That's not fair!'

Sai looked at him and gave a little snort. 'This is nothing to do with you, whoever you are.'

'Yes it is, because I was there. Your dad is a very devoted grandfather.'

Sai looked from Greg to Vik and shrugged. 'Devoted isn't enough. We need committed, responsible, careful.'

'He isn't an employee,' Greg fumed. 'He was all those things and more – loving and tender and kind.'

Vik looked gratefully at Greg. He saw Hermione glance uncertainly his way but Sai was having none of it.

'He was foolish! End of.'

Now Ruth stepped up. 'We're all a bit foolish sometimes, though, aren't we?'

Vik's heart rose at his new friends' defence. Sai seemed to waver for a moment but then he gathered Aleesha and Hermione majestically under his perfectly honed arm and swept his gaze around them all.

'Not in my world,' he said coldly, then he turned his family firmly away.

'You will let me know how she is?' Vik called after him.

He got a tiny wave of acknowledgement in return.

'I'll visit her. Please let me visit her.'

Not even a wave this time. Sai glided out of A&E without looking back and Vik was left in an empty cubicle with a bowl of raspberry water and his two friends.

'Are you OK?' Ruth asked nervously.

Vik felt so battered that he had to resist physically patting himself down for bruises. 'I'm OK, I guess. Thank you for standing up for me.'

'Hey, we all need someone to stand up for us at times. Shall we call a cab?'

Vik looked nervously to the doorway. 'Maybe in a while. Greg?'

Greg looked every bit as nervously to the doorway. 'I'm in no hurry.'

Ruth gave a tight little smile. 'Can't say the world looks a very enticing place to me either right now. So then – cup of tea?'

'Cup of tea,' Vik agreed wearily.

He couldn't hide in here for ever but right now he couldn't face going home to the wreck of his stupid dinner party, and the end of his happy night with his precious granddaughter, and the ghost of his furious wife. It wasn't a time to be on your own. He frowned.

'Do you think Charlie's OK?' he asked the others.

'Charlie?' Ruth echoed, more a growl than a word.

'Charlie,' Greg said at her side, 'can go to hell.'

Chapter Thirty-five

'The Talisker, sir?' Charlie nodded dumbly. 'A fine choice. Special occasion?'

'Something like that. Oh, and two packets of paracetamol, please.'

'Planning the hangover already, hey? I like it!'

'Ha, ha.'

Charlie handed over his card, wincing automatically at the price of the malt whisky. It was the brand his father chose as his 'everyday tipple' but the most expensive one available in this Hope Street offie. It cost nearly a whole day's wages – not that that mattered now. Nothing mattered now. Soon he would be as free of worrying about money as he would about anything else.

Mind you, he hadn't ever truly worried about money, had he? He'd been like that Pulp song about always being able to call your dad if you'd had enough. Charlie could pretend to be as independent as he liked but Daddy Turner had always been there with his golden chequebook. Not that it had done any good.

Sue had known who he was, hadn't she? That's why she'd come smarming round to check up on how he was doing so that a good report would go back to the big boss. She'd probably thought it was some hearty learn-the-business-from-the-bottom management exercise and not what it had truly been – a helping hand with a built-in slap on the arse to amuse the troops.

Oh, they would have used him as a 'spy', of course they would. The Turners never wasted anything. To be honest, when he'd gone crawling to ask his father if he could set him up as a driver he'd thought he'd seen a glimmer of respect in his eye for the first time ever, but at the end of the day the purpose of Charlie's job, from his family's point of view, had been solely about emphasising how not-one-of-them he was any more. Well, fine. He didn't want to be one of them anyway. He'd changed his name, hadn't he? He'd sent Charlie Turner into the flames and brought Charlie Sparrow out.

Problem was, Charlie Sparrow had turned out to be rubbish too.

Had he always just been playing at it? Charlie asked himself as he took his whisky and headed back out to his bike. Had even becoming an English teacher just been a finger up at his money-obsessed family? It hadn't felt that way. Quite the opposite. The moment he'd discovered reading, it had been like nothing else mattered. The real world – the world the rest of his family cleaved to with such relish – had paled into insignificance for Charlie next to Narnia and Hogwarts and Mordor and he'd dived as eagerly into them as if they'd been created just for him.

But it hadn't just been escapism. Almost from the start he'd been fascinated by the craft of these amazing creations. He'd loved the building bricks of the novels as much as the transcendent creations they became. He'd been intrigued by the way that words, so insignificant on their own, could be melded together to conjure magical sights and sounds and tastes. Even now, it amazed him that the same words that could be hammered into an ugly little tweet attacking someone's looks or values or choices in life could be rearranged to draw forth a beautiful foreign country for the reader to step lightly into.

Words, he had understood from a very early age, were a tool. And, it turned out, a weapon.

The iron claw that had been tightening around Charlie's heart ever since that first flurry of indignant tweets on Greg's phone gripped harder and he welcomed it. If he was lucky, it would simply squeeze the life out of him before he got home and save him a job. He calculated his route. With a detour he could pass six stores. At two packets from each he should have enough, especially with the ones he'd taken from Ruth's house.

Her keys had been on the same ring as the van one and he'd let himself in without a qualm. It was stealing, maybe, but he was sure Ruth would have handed the little pills over with her blessing – or, rather, her curse. And quite right too. An eye for an eye, a tooth for a tooth, a life for a life. It was the restitution he had always owed her. He'd known it the moment he'd seen poor Libby's limp body being brought up from the river on the news a year and a half ago; he'd known it when he'd put all his books on the bonfire two months back; he'd known it when he'd seen her name on his delivery list that first day in the yard of his family's bloody supermarket. Jigsaws and cups of tea! Cheap tricks with electrics to find her a friend! How patronising. How cheap. How undignified.

Libby's room had been exactly as he'd imagined it would be. Ruth had kept it utterly intact, down to the jeans on the floor, the uncapped mascara on the dressing table and the open book on the bedside table. *Tess of the d'Urbervilles.* One of Charlie's favourites. He'd stood there and remembered the girl's face in school the week before her death. It had been the last day of term and all the other kids had been impossible, babbling about holiday plans and paying not the blindest bit of attention to the romantic poets, despite him picking Wordsworth's 'I Wandered Lonely as a Cloud' to fit the spring mood. But Libby . . . She'd come up to his desk and put that same copy down on it and said, 'Shit, sir, this Hardy bloke was good!'

He'd heard her voice so loud in his head as he'd tiptoed across her room and lifted up the book. Page 172. She'd never got to Tess stabbing Alec d'Urberville then, never had the chance to relish the poor girl's revenge. Or, indeed, to see her hung for it. Why hadn't she taken this book away with her? Why had she switched to Virginia Woolf? Why hadn't he given her another Hardy instead?

Because they were such positive books, he mocked himself. *Jude the Obscure* would have really knocked her out of depression, right? What had he been thinking? He'd known she was different. He'd seen that she had few friends, noticed the strange intensity about her, as if she was always halfway over some edge, but like an idiot he'd viewed that as a passion for literature. Like a pompous fool he'd felt that there was something of his younger self in her and yearned to help her let it free. Instead, it had trapped her in darkness and trapped Ruth and her lost husband with it. He'd lined up his fancy books before that family, taken aim and fired . . . Bang! Taking the paracetamol from Ruth's room had felt fair. Poetic justice. Ha!

Charlie stopped his bike outside the next shop, snatched the whisky from the basket, screwed off the top and, without a second's hesitation, took a deep swig. The spirit hit the back of his throat like the bullet he craved and sent blessed fire shooting around his body. A man heading into the shop gave him a disapproving look and he raised the bottle to him in a toast. He didn't care what this random stranger thought of him. He didn't care what anyone thought of him. He was released from care now. He hastened inside and snatched up two packets of paracetamol.

'Going to be a big night, is it?' the lady behind the counter joked with a wink.

Is that what everyone assumed? Was an excess of joy the only pain people were prepared to imagine?

'Very big,' he agreed.

'That's one pound thirty-two, please.'

A princely sum for oblivion. Charlie handed over a two-pound coin. 'Keep the change.'

He heard it clatter into the charity box as he left and hoped it was for a good cause. He hadn't made a will, he realised, but, really, what did he have to leave? He'd burned all his books, even the rare ones he'd collected with such love at university; even the leather-bound works of Shakespeare he'd requested from his parents for his twenty-first and received wrapped up in a sports car he hadn't given a toss about; even the first edition of *Sons and Lovers* he'd bought with the proceeds of selling that car. DH Lawrence – another gloomy writer. Why hadn't he gone for Austen or Wilde or Wodehouse? They would never have sent Libby Clarke to the bottom of a river.

ANNA STUART

Two more shops, two more fiery swigs, four more packets.
They filled the pocket of his coat as the whisky filled his stomach,
chasing away the remnants of the disastrous curry and filling him
with purpose. He thought of George Sand: *We cannot tear out
a single page of our life, but we can throw the whole book in the
fire*. George Sand had turned out to be a woman, and a French
one at that, hiding behind a false identity every bit as much as
Charlie but with far greater wisdom.

Charlie had tried to throw all his books on the fire. He'd tried
to tear out the Libby page of his life, but it hadn't worked. It
hadn't been enough. It was *him* the flames wanted.

Two more shops, four more packets, half the bottle gone.
Charlie was unsteady on his feet now. The ground moved inter-
estingly beneath him. Trees and walls stepped out in front of him
as if, perhaps, trying to stop him. But no, that was fanciful. He'd
always been fanciful. He swayed around them and pressed on.
His legs tangled in his bike pedals and he battled with it before
remembering it didn't matter any more. Nothing mattered any
more. He cast it into a side alley and left it on its side, wheel
spinning furiously.

Last two shops. So many packets that he had to stick the final
two in the back pockets of his jeans – a modern-day gunslinger.
He reached for the bottle again, then remembered he'd need
co-ordination to manage all the little foil bubbles and stopped.
He could control himself. He could wait. He had time. He had
all the time he wanted to make it to no time at all.

Charlie let himself into the flats and made for the stairs as
someone came in behind him.

'Evenin', Mr Graham.'

'Charlie. Are you . . . drunk?'

'No.'

'You are.'

'Oh yes. Yes, I am.'

'I thought you'd sworn off alcohol, young man, after the fire.'

'I had. But I've . . . lapsed.'

'So I see. The Residents' Association won't like this, Charlie.'

312

'Don't worry. It won't happen again.'

'So you say, but—'

'No, really. It won't happen again. I won't bother the Residents' Association again. I won't bother anyone again.'

'Charlie?' Mr Graham looked at his bulging pockets. Charlie glanced down and shoved the packets deeper in. 'Charlie, are you OK?' The kindness sideswiped him. He staggered and clutched at the banister. 'Let me get Madge,' Mr Graham said, coming a little closer. 'She'll help.'

'Madge? No, I . . .'

'She could make you a cup of tea. How about that, Charlie? Would you like a nice cup of tea?'

'No!'

Mr Graham recoiled. Well good. Charlie didn't need kindness, not now, not when he was so close.

'I just . . .'

'Well, don't. I don't want your bloody tea, you interfering old busybody.'

'Fine then, forget it. I was just trying to be nice but I can see it's not worth my time. You're trouble, Charlie Turner – trouble. You need to sort yourself out, and fast.'

'Oh I will,' Charlie promised him, but he was gone, fussing up the stairs and banging into his apartment to find his precious wife and doubtless indulge in a nice rant against the youth of today. Well, good riddance.

Charlie sank on to the step, sucking in deep breaths. The iron claw squeezed.

'Go on then,' he muttered, 'take me.' But it wasn't that kind.

Trouble. That's exactly what he was. Hadn't tonight proved it? He'd been asked out for a nice, friendly dinner and wrecked it for everyone. Even before the meal had been finished Greg's precious secret had been exposed to the world. He suspected Road-man Ryan of the actual story-selling, but the creep would never have picked up the clues without Charlie giving them away so blatantly. Then he'd gone on to drop poor Ruth right back into the horror of her daughter's death just as she was starting

313

to pick herself up again, before finishing off with burning Vik's precious granddaughter with, of all things, a honeyed orange peel. The surrealists couldn't have done a better job.

Charlie was shaking now. He fumbled for the whisky and a packet of tablets fell out and flopped down on to the step at his feet. It stared up at him, pristine white against the dirty concrete. Charlie swiped it up, pulled himself back to standing and headed up the stairs. It was one of the packets from Ruth's house – a Turner's packet. He'd probably delivered it himself. Well, good. That was justice, at least.

'I'm so sorry,' he muttered to the ghostly shape of her furious pain. 'I really am so sorry and I'm going to make it up to you. Now.'

His key fought him but he wrestled it into submission and forced his way inside his flat, his sanctuary. He'd worked so hard in his first year as a teacher to save up for the deposit on this place. His father had laughed, kept trying to write him a cheque, but he'd refused.

'This is fool's pride,' his dad had said. 'What's the point of me if I can't help my own son?'

You could help, he'd wanted to tell him, *if you just asked me about my job, if you just sat down a minute and let me tell you about the school and the kids and the books*. But his dad only sat down in boardrooms and didn't see the point in listening when he could talk instead. Briefly, Charlie wondered what it must be like to have such confidence in your own opinions, and then he remembered that he had done. He'd had fierce, absolute certainty in his vocation to be an English teacher. And he'd been wrong. So very, very wrong.

He sank to the living room floor and, spilling all the packets out of his pockets, began popping the little white pills on to the blank wooden boards. Some fired out and had to be stopped from rolling away, some flopped on to the growing pile and others got stuck in the foil and had to be worked out with his nail, but eventually they were all there – a wonky little pyramid of death.

'You didn't tell a lot of people a lot of things,' Greg had told him.

'Haven't you done enough?' Vik had shouted.

'You killed her!' Ruth had screamed.

It was Aleesha, though, who'd put her finger on it: 'It hurts. It really, really hurts.'

But not for much longer.

Charlie looked to his phone. He hadn't been going to say anything, hadn't been going to bother anyone with last words, but, God, he loved words. Always had. That had been the problem. And, really, did it matter any more? He picked up his phone and tapped out a text: *I'm sorry about the jigsaws. They could never make up for Libby. I hope, in some small way, this does.*

Then, lifting the whisky bottle and raising it in a final toast to the books that had once graced his shelves, Charlie put down the phone, picked up the first pill and sat it on his tongue. The books were ash on the wind and, by the bottom of the pyramid, Charlie would be too. He couldn't wait.

Chapter Thirty-six

I'm sorry about the jigsaws. They could never make up for Libby. I hope, in some small way, this does.

'This?' Ruth said. 'What does he mean by "this"?'

She looked at Greg and Vik, sat across a plastic table from her, nursing cups of over-stewed tea and picking at a Danish pastry no one actually wanted. They squinted back at her and she shoved the phone across to them.

'"I'm sorry about the jigsaws,"' Vik read. '"They could never make up for Libby." Poor lad. I think he really is sorry, Ruth.'

Ruth tore a strip off the pastry.

'"I hope, in some small way, this does,"' Greg read. 'Odd. Is there a picture coming?'

They all stared at the screen but it remained resolutely fixed on the words.

'No picture,' Ruth said.

An uneasy feeling was worming through her gut. The sort of uneasy feeling she remembered all too well. She saw blue eyes pleading with her, a hand reaching out. She'd known. The moment she'd walked into Libby's bedroom in that cutesy little holiday cottage and seen her daughter's bed empty, she'd known. Not exactly what had happened, but she'd known it was bad.

'Virginia Woolf,' she said.

The two men stared at her.

'Virginia who?' Vik asked, but Greg remembered.

'You don't think . . .' He paled. 'Shit, Ruth, you *do* think.'

'I told him to leave us alone. He drove us here and I told him to leave us alone. I told him it was his fault Libby had died.'

Vik stared at her. 'And I told him it was his fault Aleesha was hurt.'

'And I told him it was his fault my stupid lies had been exposed to the world. I . . . I said he could go to hell.'

'He didn't hear that, Greg.'

'But he knew it all the same.'

They looked at each other. Ruth saw blue eyes – Charlie's blue eyes. She saw his hand reaching out.

'We have to go!' she screamed at the other two. 'Now!'

As one they shoved back their plastic chairs and began to run.

'But where?' Greg gasped out. 'How on earth do we know where he lives?'

'I know,' Vik said. 'He told me once. Hazel Road. The new flats.'

Ruth jabbed at buttons on her phone as they made for the entrance at as much speed as they could manage with Vik's old legs and Greg's twisted one.

'Taxi,' she shouted into it. 'We need a taxi from the hospital. And fast.'

Hold on, Charlie, she willed him, reaching across the city for his hand. *Please hold on.* She couldn't be too late. Not again. Not this time.

Chapter Thirty-seven

Flames danced, scarlet and amber, their hearts blue, their edges flecked with violet as they licked their way like lovers across Charlie's chest, around his neck, into his throat. He looked for demons but saw none, bar the patterns of his own errors fanning the fire with gilded phoenix wings. There was Libby, her body white through the orange light. There was Ruth, facing him across a pancake pan, pain raw across her face. And there was whisky, pouring on to the orange-peel flames to send them higher and higher so that the images grew and moved and danced before him – a winged eternity of pain.

'No!' he screamed, putting up his hands, but the flames just licked across his nails, painting them blood-red. And then . . .

'Charlie. We're here. We're here for you.'

Voices babbled through the flames. Demons perhaps, taunting him with the promise of a rescue he knew could never be possible.

'Charlie, don't go. You mustn't go. We need you. We love you.'

Lying demons! That's what they did, didn't they, demons? That's what they did in Dante's *Inferno*, wasn't it? Charlie closed his eyes. He couldn't remember; didn't want to remember.

Something rose up out of the heart of the fire and whacked him. His eyes opened in shock and he looked for a damn golden bird and saw instead a book, a great big book flapping crazily in the swirling air. *Paradise Lost*, perhaps. Or *The Exorcist*. No, not *The Exorcist*. The demon was inside Charlie and there was no getting him out. He'd given himself to the flames so why wouldn't they just take him?

'Charlie!'

Something tugged on his hand, fighting to pull him from the fire. For a moment the flames receded, sucking upwards into a sun, bright in an achingly beautiful blue sky.

'No!'

He tried to pull away but the something was holding him still and the sky was swirling inwards, sending sweet, fresh oxygen up his nostrils and into his lungs, filling them so full that he had to take a breath. He flapped his hands despairingly and the flames sucked back further and the sun shone clearer and the demons were dropping away into the depths. He wanted to shout them back, to beg them to take him with them to where he belonged in the heat and the fear and the searing pain of death.

'Charlie! Please stay, Charlie.'

He couldn't place the voice. It wasn't his mother. Of course it wasn't his mother. And now another, deeper voice. And a third – older, more wavering.

'Don't die, Charlie. Please don't die. We'd miss you.'

He was hallucinating; he had to be.

'And who'd deliver our groceries, hey?'

That voice was forcibly light but it hit through the ashy air around Charlie. Groceries? Deliveries? His eyes flew open. He was in a hospital bed and stood at his side, like a very strange pair of angels, were Vik and Greg.

'What? How . . .?'

'Charlie!' They all but flung themselves forward. 'You're alive!'

Charlie groaned. 'How did I get here?'

'We got talking, Charlie. After Sai had gone with Aleesha and—'

'Aleesha! How's Aleesha?'

'She's fine,' Vik assured him. 'That is, she's going to be fine. Sai's furious with me. He said all sorts of horrible things about how careless I'd been, about how I'd broken his trust. Oh.'

He stepped hastily aside as a nurse came rushing up, pressing her hand to Charlie's forehead, checking the machine behind him. Charlie looked past her.

'But you weren't careless, Vik. It was me. You said it yourself. I put the peel down. I put her in danger, I—'

'I *was* careless, Charlie. I'm her grandfather, not you. I was in charge of her safety and I only got it wrong for a moment. I tried to tell Sai that but he wouldn't listen. He was so caught up in his own anger and fear that he wouldn't listen.' He paused. 'Like I wouldn't listen to you.'

'And like *I* wouldn't listen to you,' Greg put in.

Charlie looked at him, struggling to work out what was going on. The nurse slid away and they were alone again. His throat ached terribly, his head was pounding and he felt horribly sick but he was alive. He could still sense the flames around the edges of his consciousness but it seemed that maybe they weren't real, maybe they wouldn't get him. He wasn't sure yet whether to be sad or glad.

'I know it wasn't you, Charlie,' Greg told him.

'How? How do you know?'

'Because some tit called Ryan Sharp is all over social media boasting about it. He's done interviews for every newspaper under the sun.'

'Ryan,' Charlie groaned.

'You know him?'

'Oh yes.'

'Thought you might, because he's doing interviews about you being an "undercover Turner" as well. He's having a field day.'

'He would.' The words rasped out of Charlie's throat and he put a hand tentatively to the skin.

'They put a tube down your throat to pump your stomach,' Vik explained gently.

Charlie retched but, perhaps not surprisingly, nothing came up. He looked around him. There was a needle in his hand, attached to a drip by the side of the bed and sensors on his chest attached him to a monitor behind it. It all spoke of care and a strange determination to keep him alive.

'How on earth did I get here?' he stuttered.

'I told you, we got talking.'

'Yes, but . . .'

'And we realised what it's like not to be listened to. And we realised, well, we hadn't listened to *you*. And then . . . well, then we worried. So we hopped in a taxi and came to find you.'

Charlie turned his head into his pillow. Pain was pounding through his skull as the realisation that he had failed played the drums across his brain. He had failed even at killing himself. He was still here, still Charlie.

'You shouldn't have.'

'Charlie . . .'

'I didn't ask you to. I didn't want you to. I'm not worth saving.'

'Bollocks!' Greg said loudly. Somewhere outside the curtain, a nurse called 'Hush' and he bit his lip but leaned in to say it again. 'Bollocks, Charlie. You're more worth saving than most. You're a good, kind, open-hearted man.'

Charlie shook his head. 'I'm not. I'm a smug, self-important, deluded . . .' He struggled to remember all the other criticisms. 'I'm a git. No, worse, I'm a killer. A murderer. Ask Ruth. I bet she didn't want to save me.'

Vik gave a low laugh and took Charlie's hand in his. 'Who d'you think thought to come and find you, Charlie?' he said gently.

He frowned. 'Ruth?' he rasped, unable to believe it.

'Ruth,' a voice confirmed from his other side, soft and feminine; the voice he'd heard when he'd first surfaced from the flames.

Charlie jerked his head towards it. 'Ruth!'

Libby's mother stepped forward and took his other hand.

'You're not a killer, Charlie. I see it now. I saw it the moment I got your text offering your life for Libby's as if that would make it better. As if I was some sort of blood-sucking grief vampire, thirsty for more. All this therapy and time on my own and bloody vodka and it took just one sharp moment of facing a second death to put it all into perspective.' She shivered but pressed on. 'I'm so glad you made it, Charlie. And, more than that, I'm so glad Libby met you. The books gave her joy, peace, a place to escape. And she needed that. She needed that so badly.'

'But I should have realised. I'd read *Mrs Dalloway*. I'd read *The Hours*.'

'And I hadn't. And I should have done. But it was too hard for me. No, not even that, just too boring. I couldn't be bothered. But you – you bothered.'

'And I fucked up. You said it yourself – you blame the twat of an English teacher who gave her Virginia Woolf.'

'Well, of course I said that. It's easier, isn't it, to blame some faceless fool than to face up to your own inadequacies. Charlie, Libby was ill. She had been all her life. She was on a collision course from the moment she was born and if she hadn't crashed into Virginia Woolf it would have been something else.'

Charlie stared at her. His head was aching, his throat was sore and all his limbs felt leaden. He felt as if he'd gone ten rounds with a heavyweight boxer. The nurse was heading back, looking all set to throw his visitors out, and a huge part of him wanted them to go so he could sleep, but this was important.

'You're just being kind.'

'I'm not! I'm being truthful.'

'She is,' Greg said. 'It was the same with me, Charlie. I was messed up in the head and if I hadn't been hauled into an Arctic winch I'd have been ground up in a back-street bar instead. I was spoiling for a fight and I didn't care who it was with. It was the motivation, not the means.'

'With Nika too,' Vik said. 'We had enough morphine in the house to kill her. Had done for ages. I knew, deep down, that she'd wanted to take it, to die peacefully, but I'd been too cowardly to let her. Too cowardly and too selfish. I wanted every last drop of her, so I refused. I kept it locked up and the key close. I thought I was so clever but she found a way anyway. She wanted to go.'

'But Libby was a child,' Charlie protested.

'*My* child,' Ruth said. 'Mine and Tony's. We were the ones who failed to look after her. If it was anyone's fault, it was ours, but you know what, Charlie? I don't even think that any more. Not since I've met you lot and had a chance to talk properly, to look at it from all sides instead of just through the prism of my own pain and guilt. I'll always wish I could have stopped her, Charlie. I'll always wish we'd been different, *she'd* been different. And, yes, I'll always wish she didn't decide Virginia bloody Woolf was her heroine, but she did. She did and she's gone and that's it. And we're here. You're here.' She squeezed his hand tight. 'I forgive you, Charlie. I forgive myself and I forgive Tony and I forgive you.'

Charlie stared up into her broad face and her big eyes. The nurse hovered but didn't intrude and now the flames were clearing from round the edges of his consciousness. The blue sky was expanding, pushing them away and there, sweeping and soaring and twittering busily in and out of the trees, were sparrows. Happy, ordinary little sparrows. A book rose up, brushing gently against him and he flexed his fingers, longing to catch it. He looked to Ruth, who held his gaze as firmly and kindly as she held his hand. Then he turned to Vik and to Greg, both looking weary and dishevelled, but here. Here for him. A demon tugged at his toe and he kicked out against it.

'Thank you,' he said. 'Thank you so much.'

They all moved a step closer so their shadows fell on him, soft and warm and protective.

'What are friends for, Charlie? What are friends for?'

Chapter Thirty-eight

Madras, jalfrezi, tikka masala, tarka dhal. Vik looked at the curries bubbling on the stove. He had all the classics for his guests, but was there enough? He glanced through to the big grey freezer in the lounge. Maybe a bit more dhal? Ooh, and there were samosas in there too. Might as well get them out. There would be a lot of people after all and Nika would be furious with him if anyone went hungry.

He went through, lifted the lid and peered inside, smiling to see the space at the top where he had, for the first time in a year, taken curries out instead of putting them in. What a fool he'd been, shutting himself up in his house, his imagined resentments freezing with his food, instead of taking the damn Tupperware to Sai's house and sorting things out. What had he been afraid of? It had been easy.

The doorbell rang and, yanking out two more Tupperware of dhal and a big bag of samosas, Vik shoved the lid down and ran to answer.

'Leesha! How are you doing?'

'Good, Grampie. I'm good. I brought Teddy.' She waved a blue bear almost as big as herself.

'Yeah, thanks for that, Dad,' Sai laughed, giving him a quick hug. 'She made us put the baby seat in the car for him and everything.'

'I see. How did it look?'

Sai and Hermione exchanged shy glances. 'Nice,' Hermione admitted. 'Weird but, you know, nice.'

Vik kissed her and ushered them inside, taking coats and fussing over drinks and thanking every god there was that he'd plucked up the courage to go and see them this morning. He still wasn't sure how he'd made it up that big driveway with the pebbles that crunched luxuriously beneath the car and the landscaped bushes and the soaring porch curving over a giant front door. But sitting watching Charlie struggling for life last night had changed things in his head.

All he'd been able to see as the poor young man had lain there rasping for breath had been Sai, and he'd thought how he'd feel if his own son had been dying and he'd wasted all this precious time shilly-shallying around him. Then he'd thought of Aleesha bounding around his kitchen and of Sai as a boy, clinging to his hand as they walked together to nursery, and he'd steeled himself and knocked.

'Grampie!' It had been Hermione who'd opened the door but Aleesha who'd come hurtling into him. 'Grampie, look at my new bandage. It's pink! And the nurse said I was really brave. I was, wasn't I, Grampie? I was really brave.'

'You were, Leesha. You were amazing. This is for you.'

He'd held out the giant teddy he'd found in the toyshop on the way over and she'd squealed and danced around with it before coming bundling back, jumping up and down with her arms raised, begging to be lifted. Vik had looked to Hermione for permission and, to his astonishment, had seen tears in her elegantly made-up eyes.

'Please,' she'd said and, as he'd gathered Aleesha up, she'd added, 'you better come in.'

It hadn't been the most gracious of invitations but Vik had snatched at it all the same, and followed his stiff-backed daughter-in-law across the parquet hallway and into a beautiful airy living room. Sai had come out of a door to his left and frozen.

'Sai,' Hermione had warned and, to Vik's surprise, he'd said nothing, just followed them into the room.

Sai and Hermione had sat on one duck-egg sofa and waved Vik into the other. He'd almost expected them to ring a bell for a maid, but they hadn't. They'd just sat there, Hermione staring at Aleesha playing with the teddy on Vik's knee and Sai staring at the floor.

'I know you don't want to see me,' Vik had said to Sai. 'And I get that, really I do. But I just had to see you to say how sorry I am. I was being so careful, honestly. It was a matter of moments. I just . . .'

'I know.' It was Hermione. 'I know, Vik. It terrifies me. Every moment I'm with her, I'm terrified I'll hurt her. It's exhausting.'

Vik had stared at her, but not half as hard as Sai had.

'Kids don't break easily, Hermione,' Vik had said eventually.

'But they do. Look at her poor hand.'

'Which is healing.'

She'd bitten her lip. 'It is. This time. But what if it happens again? What if I let something happen? Sai would be furious.'

'No, I wouldn't,' Sai had said. 'Hermione, I wouldn't. Not with you. With myself, perhaps, with the world, with the way we run our lives, but not with you, never with you.'

Then she'd looked at him and burst into tears and Vik had quickly suggested that Aleesha show him the garden.

They'd come to find him a little later.

'Dad.'

'Sai. Hermione. Are you OK?'

'Fine, Vik, thank you. Much better, actually. Hey, Leesha, is that a butterfly?'

The girls had moved off after the pretty creature and the two men had stood, staring intently at a flower bed neither of them, Vik had been sure, were really seeing.

'You blame me, I know,' Vik had said eventually.

'Blame you, Dad?'

'For your mum's death. For her, you know . . .'

'Suicide?'

Vik had nodded and looked down, fighting tears, but suddenly Sai had been in front of him, grabbing him by the arms and forcing him to look into his handsome face.

'Is that what you really think?'

'Of course. And you're right to. I didn't look after her properly. I didn't take enough care. I didn't keep her safe.'

'Oh, Dad, no one could have done more.'

'What?'

He'd seen compassion in his son's brown eyes, so very like Nika's.

'You cared for her brilliantly. You loved her and she knew that. That's why she wanted to go. She wanted you to remember her as "her", not as some deteriorating burden.'

'How do you know?'

'Because she told me. She told me when I visited her in the respite home.'

'You knew what she was planning?'

'No! God, no. She kept all that to herself. I was shocked, horrified, but underneath I knew it was what she'd wanted at some point, so I was OK with it.'

'You don't blame me?'

'No. I told you. And you shouldn't blame yourself, either.'

'But then why . . . Why did you stop coming?' Now it was Sai who looked down. 'Sai?'

'You need to tell him, Sai,' Hermione had said gently, coming over, and Sai had looked up again and nodded.

'I stopped coming because all you ever did was talk about Mum, about how much you missed her, how much "we" missed her. And it hurt. Cos I did, Dad, I missed her so much. I still do, but talking about it just made it worse.'

Vik had stared at him, astounded.

'And . . .' Hermione had prompted, putting a slim hand on Sai's shoulder.

'And,' he'd said on a sigh, 'I thought I wasn't enough for you. I thought having me around made it more painful because, well, because I wasn't her.'

'More painful?' Vik reached up and clasped Sai's arms where they held his own. 'Oh Lord, son, what a pair of prize prats we've been.'

It was Hermione who'd laughed first, then Sai. It had come bursting out of him like water from an unblocked pipe in a stream of childish joy.

'So you don't blame me for your mother's death?' Vik had spluttered.

'No! And you don't wish I'd died instead of her?'

'God, no!'

And then they'd been hugging so tight and Aleesha had come charging across the lawn to bundle in between them and even Hermione had joined the crazy huddle. And that's when the proper talking had begun. It had been clear from her earlier outburst that Hermione was finding things hard and Sai had reluctantly admitted that maybe their high-paced life was a little stressful.

'It's good, Dad, really. We never stop and we both like it that way, mainly, but it seems that sometimes . . . sometimes it's too much even for us.'

They wanted another baby, they'd admitted – a little brother or sister for Aleesha – but they were scared it would be too much. So that's when Vik had proposed that he have Aleesha over every Friday to give them a break, and then Sai had added that he could perhaps come to theirs once a week as well to collect her from nursery early, or maybe even have her all day. They'd both been cautious, keen to take it slowly, but Vik could see a new future opening up and he liked it.

'No cocktails,' he'd promised.

'Well, maybe just with us?' Sai had countered, and they'd both laughed again because it was better than the tears that were threatening. But it hadn't worked.

'Why are you crying?' Aleesha had demanded.

'They're happy tears,' Vik had told her.

'Happy tears?' She'd frowned and then, with the easy acceptance of her three wise years, said, 'Well, don't cry too many of them or you'll wet Teddy.'

Vik smiled at the memory as the three of them moved into his kitchen now and Sai produced a bottle of champagne.

'I thought we should celebrate.'

Vik looked at the bottle uncertainly. 'What if we have to drive?'

'We won't, Dad. It was a one-off. A lesson learned. Kids have accidents all the time.'

Vik remembered the nurse saying that in the hospital last night when all had been dark – though not as dark as two hours later when they'd screamed back in an ambulance with Charlie fighting for his life.

'Champagne,' he agreed, 'why not? There's a lot to celebrate after all. Oh, and look – here's Ruth coming.' He pointed out the window where Ruth was sidling shyly up the drive hand in hand with a giraffe of a man. 'Glasses are in the usual place,' he said to Sai. 'I won't be a moment.'

'Take as long as you want, Dad.'

Vik nodded his thanks and went back to the door. 'Ruth! Come in, come in. And you must be Tony?'

The man let go of Ruth's hand to take Vik's in a warm, strong grasp. 'I am. Thanks for inviting me over.'

'My pleasure.'

'And thanks, too, for telling this idiot woman to come and talk to me again.'

'Oi!' Ruth said, nudging him, but her face was glowing with love.

'You've, er, made up then?' Vik asked.

Tony chuckled. 'We've been making up all afternoon, mate.'

'Tony!' Ruth blushed furiously but didn't resist when her husband put his big arm around her.

'I'm glad,' Vik said. 'And I've been doing a bit of making up myself – though not, perhaps, in quite the same way.'

'You mean Sai . . .?'

'Why don't you come in and meet my son and daughter-in-law,' Vik replied, unable to keep the grin off his face as he ushered them through.

'Ruth!'

Aleesha came running down the kitchen to fling herself at Ruth, showing off her teddy and babbling about her bandages. Introductions were made and Ruth turned to Vik. 'Is Charlie coming?'

'I believe so, if he's up to it. He was discharged at lunchtime, so I hope so.'

'Me too. Tony wants to meet him. He wants to tell him that we don't blame him. God, Vik, I can't believe he nearly killed himself. And for me. I can't believe he'd think that I'd want that. Well, I can because I was a cow to him but – shit! Every time I think how close he came it makes me feel sick.'

Vik gave her a hug. 'We got there on time, Ruth.'

'This time.'

'Yes. And that's good. Let's move forward now, shall we?'

She nodded. 'That's what Tony says.'

'Then you should listen to Tony more often.'

Ruth smiled coyly. 'I intend to. Every day.'

'He's moving back in?'

'Not yet. We're going to date. Is that silly, do you think?'

'Not at all. It's a great idea. Take your time, Ruth. It's too important to rush.'

'And I've got some clearing to do in the house – though I've got a plan for that.'

'You have?'

She nodded keenly. 'There's a lad down the tip called Frank. He's saving up to train as a nurse, so I reckon he could do with the cash they might earn and he's bound to be a dab hand with eBay. Thought I'd pop them all in the van and take them down to him tomorrow.'

'That's a great idea, Ruth.'

'Yeah, well – the nurses last night saved Charlie so the more of those wonderful people we have in the world the better, right?'

'Dead right. And with your house clear of machines there'll be more room for the important stuff.'

'The important *people*,' she corrected.

She looked over to Tony and Vik saw him wink, making her blush again, and smiled to see it. But now she was turning to the big TV that he'd set up at the end of the kitchen. Nika would have been disgusted – no TV outside the lounge had been a key rule – but he needed a bit of time to get the freezer eaten up and cleared out and, for tonight, he figured she'd understand.

'What time do the awards start?' Ruth asked.

Vik glanced at the clock. 'Pretty much now. Shall I turn it on?'

She nodded. 'Do you know what he's going to do?'

'No idea. He went off to talk about it with his family. As far as I'm aware, he's not said a single word to the media and they're all but imploding with excitement as a result.'

Sure enough, as the TV switched on to BBC4, a reporter was stood in front of a red carpet, barely glancing at the celebrities arriving behind.

'Everyone,' she said, 'is waiting to see if Greg Sutton will arrive after the media storm over a report that his inspirational travel blog is a fraud. So far, Greg has maintained a dignified silence on the matter, but if he arrives here that surely cannot continue.'

Vik and Ruth looked at one another.

'I hope he knows what he's doing,' Ruth said.

Vik peered at the stream of cars, looking for Greg's distinctive shape to emerge from one of them, but there was no sign of him yet. There was a minor flurry of excitement as Candy Drew arrived in a bright red outfit, more bikini than dress, with her little sister, wide-eyed in a wheelchair, before her, but for once she wasn't the star attraction and the cameras roamed restlessly away as she strutted down the carpet and into the building. Back in Vik's house, the doorbell rang again.

'Charlie!' Ruth cried.

She paled a little but Tony was at her side in an instant, reaching for her hand.

'OK if we get this, Vik?' he asked.

'Of course.'

The couple headed for the hall together and Vik watched them, wondering how two such big, strong people could look so very fragile.

'Is Ruth OK?' Aleesha asked, peering after them too.

Vik hitched her up on to his hip. 'She will be,' he said. 'Now, where's Teddy going to sit for dinner?'

He fussed around his granddaughter, keeping one ear tuned into the murmuring voices in the hall, and looked up keenly when Ruth reappeared, followed by a pale-looking Charlie, in turn flanked by an equally pale older couple. Both were trying to look relaxed in casual trousers and jumpers, but both still exuded effortless style. Somehow, Vik doubted their clothes were from Turner's *True-You* clothing range, but he still felt for them as they edged nervously into the room.

'Mr and Mrs Turner – welcome.'

'Thank you,' Mrs Turner murmured and Mr Turner came forward and shook his hand, almost visibly pulling on a level of assurance Vik was sure he was normally very used to.

'You must be Mr Varma.'

'Vik, please.'

'Donald. And this is Cassie.'

'Nice to meet you both, and thank you for bringing Charlie tonight.'

'No. Oh no, Mr . . . Vik. It's my wife and I who should thank *you*. And Ruth here.' Donald Turner visibly squared his cashmere shoulders. 'We have been very neglectful parents to our precious boy. We have joked about his choices in life – his brave, strong choices – and we have belittled his attempts to deal with a very difficult situation. We have, in short, failed him.'

It was clearly a well-rehearsed speech but none the less sincere for it and when Vik looked to Charlie he saw his eyes shining with tears.

'Dad, please. You don't have to . . .'

But Donald Turner was clearly not a man who did things by halves.

'No, Charlie. It has to be said and who better to say it to than the people who saved you for us. Ruth, Vik – if you had not been thoughtful and caring enough to see Charlie's distress in time he would not be with us now. We would be without our son.'

Ruth looked to Tony, then back to Donald Turner. 'We all make mistakes. Tony and I know that better than anyone.'

'But few as callous as ours,' Donald shot back. 'No wonder Charlie wanted to change his name.'

'Dad,' Charlie said again, 'please . . .'

Vik stepped hastily forward. 'Thank you, Donald. That can't have been easy to say and Ruth is right. Everyone here knows about making mistakes and failing to communicate. But it's done now. We're here, together, and that's what counts. Shall we agree to forgive and forget?'

Donald Turner looked uncertainly to his wife, who looked uncertainly to their son.

'Charlie?' she asked.

'Yes,' Charlie said and though his voice rasped again, it did so with assurance. 'That is, we won't forget. We can't forget, for we can't tear out a single page of our life, but we will forgive. Yes?'

'Yes,' everyone chorused.

Vik saw the hesitation in Charlie's parents' eyes.

'Will you change your name back, Charlie?' Donald asked. 'Will you be a Turner again?'

Charlie blushed. 'I don't know Dad. I rather like being a Sparrow.'

'Why?'

'Dull, small, ordinary.'

'Cheerful, helpful, hard-working,' Ruth corrected.

Charlie smiled. 'That too, I hope.'

Donald Turner swallowed. 'Fair enough, son. Whatever you want.'

It was clear these were not words that usually came from this man's mouth. Charlie looked at him and gave a tiny shrug.

'Maybe I could be both.'

'Turner-Sparrow? Sounds quite good actually.'

'Sounds wanky to me,' Ruth said and then clamped her hand over her mouth.

Charlie gave a splutter of a laugh as his father looked at her, astonished, and Vik was very grateful when Sai stepped smoothly forward.

'Champagne?'

Donald Turner gave an audible sigh of relief. 'Lovely. Thank you. Charlie?'

'Water for me,' Charlie said and Ruth moved to his side.

'For me too.'

Sai poured and handed Donald Turner a glass, drawing him subtly aside.

'Here you go, Donald. I'm Sai Varma, pleased to meet you. You own Turner's supermarkets, is that right? I hear profits have been down a little this year. I might be able to help you with that.'

'You might?'

Vik looked to Charlie and rolled his eyes. Charlie smiled back, perhaps as relieved as Vik that some things were still as they'd been before the madness of the last twenty-four hours. But now squealing came from the TV and they all swung round to look. A big car had pulled up and a stick had emerged from the opened door – a garishly patterned, gold-topped stick – and now, leaning heavily on it, a distinctively twisted figure stepped out.

'Greg,' Ruth breathed.

Greg stood up and looked around, breathtakingly handsome in his new DJ. His eyes were shadowed and he did not smile but it only made him look sexier. The crowd went insane but he just stood there in the glare of a thousand flashes, as first his parents and then his sister emerged from the car and gathered possessively around him. They all began to move slowly up the red carpet.

'Greg!' voices called from all sides. 'Greg, is it true?', 'Greg, did you make it all up?', 'Greg, are you still competing for the award?'

Greg ignored them all until he reached the three steps up to the hotel. He eschewed the wheelchair ramp at one side and instead climbed heavily but determinedly up the middle, then turned and spoke one sentence, loud and clear: 'My VT will speak for itself.'

Then a girl in a sparkly dress came skipping up to him and, reaching out to take her hand and offer his only smile in her direction, he went into the building with his family forming a guard behind. The crowd went even wilder. The young BBC reporter looked as if she might wet herself with the mystery of it all. The programme was quietly set away on BBC4 but you could see the light of prime-time news in her eyes. Despite Greg giving her precisely nothing to go on, she launched into a summary of all anyone had ever said about him and Vik clicked the sound down to minimum.

'Shall we eat?' he asked his guests. 'There's a curry or two to get through.'

He was rewarded with a scraping of chairs and a babble of conversation, quiet yet but growing in confidence as his curious assortment of guests began to relax and get to know each other. He glanced to the ceiling. *Good job we've got this big table, Nika.* Then he noticed Charlie sat in the middle, still looking stunned to even be here.

'You did this, Charlie,' he said, leaning over to pass him a plate. 'You brought everyone together.'

'Nonsense,' Charlie muttered, but his eyes were shining again as he looked around the table and not, this time, with tears.

They were most of the way through their curries and all loosening waistbands when the TV reporter, barely able to contain herself, announced Greg's VT.

'There's Greg!' Aleesha squealed delightedly. 'Look, everyone – there's Greg.'

But everyone was already looking.

It was an impressive film, showing Greg in Thailand, in Moscow and in the tunnels of the Vietcong, intercut with pictures of him at home and overlaid with tweet after tweet thanking him for inspiring people to get out and tackle the world.

'He did good,' Ruth said. 'However he did it, he did good.'

Tony put an arm around her as the camera cut to Greg on his disability lift, heading upwards, while over the top his own voice said, clear as day, 'Don't let disability disable your life.' The TV camera opened out to show the fancy hall and the great crowd watching in silence as Greg moved up the screen and then suddenly there he was in the flesh, standing on some sort of platform above it as if lifted up there by his own VT. A gasp ran around the auditorium.

'What's he doing?' Vik asked, transfixed.

'I need to speak,' Greg replied from above the screen. 'It's not orthodox, I know, and I apologise to the organisers, but the world deserves to know who is speaking the truth – me, or the small-minded delivery driver who told everyone he believed my trips to be a fraud.'

He paused. Silence hang heavily in the auditorium and in Vik's kitchen. Then Greg smiled straight into the camera.

'Ryan Sharp told the truth.'

The crowd gasped; the cameras went mental.

'I made it up. All of it. I haven't been outside the UK since I was airlifted into it from my accident in the Arctic two years ago. Indeed, I've barely been out of my own home in all that time, until one very kind, very caring man talked me into it a few weeks ago and showed me the value of human company again.'

He looked slowly around. 'But human company is not without its dangers, as I have found in this last, distressing day. I deserve all censure. I am not an adventurer. I am not brave or daring or strong. I am weak and scared and lonely. Or I was. Standing up here is the hardest thing I have ever done and I've been throwing up for most of the day.'

A ripple of a laugh ran around the auditorium.

'But I had to do it to answer all the accusations and counter-accusations, to step into the morass of social media and speak the truth.

'I am a fraud. I did make up my travels and all you saw in that fantastic VT was a lie – all but one part of it: the tweets from other people, other people braver and stronger and more daring than me who did go out there and tackle the world. I take inspiration from them.

'I withdraw from these awards. I thank the organisers for including me and for accommodating this rather overdramatic confession. I thank Holly Adebayou, a truly wonderful individual, for accompanying me here. I thank Kirstie for making such a fantastic VT of my fictional life, and I thank my family for being at my side. I couldn't have done it without you.

'I do *not* thank Candy Drew who picked me out of a crowd of "special" cases to make herself look good and I do not apologise for failing to do so.' The camera spun gleefully around to Candy, her face as scarlet as her scrap of a dress. 'My mistakes are my own,' Greg went on and it swung instantly back to him. 'I also do not thank Ryan Sharp for outing me with such spiteful glee or all those who took up his salacious gossip with equal delight. We live in a society, it seems, that glories in people's failures. I fed that. I failed. But I promise you all that I will learn. I will not do it again.'

The murmurs in the crowd were growing louder now and Greg held up a hand.

'One last thank you.' He looked deep into the camera. 'To Charlie – who showed me that bravery is not in grand trips across the world or beautiful photos of scars or spouting wise words on the internet, but in reaching out a hand and giving someone weak a much-needed step up. Thank you, Charlie.'

And with that the stage went dark, the auditorium went mental and, in Vik's warm, curry-rich kitchen, all eyes went to Charlie. The one-time delivery driver looked back at them, bemused.

'What a fuss,' he said, rubbing at his eyes. 'I did nothing much. After all, I only had four minutes.'

'Four minutes to save a life,' Vik said, turning off the TV.

'To save several,' Ruth corrected him.

Charlie flushed and flapped his hand.

'Pudding?' he squeaked.

'Susie's craps!' Aleesha cried.

'Ice cream,' Vik said firmly. 'I've got loads in the freezer.'

Epilogue

Charlie stands, his hand on the classroom door, his senses afire. It might be a new school but it's all so familiar – the smell of disinfectant and adolescent sweat, the feel of the sticky lino beneath his feet, the sight of the kids scrabbling around their desks through the thin line of wire-chequered glass down the middle of the door. This is teaching. This is all he ever really wanted to do. So why is he so terrified?

Someone is coming down the corridor. He can't be seen hovering here, scared of his own class. Schools are mercilessly efficient rumour-conductors. News of it would be round before first break and he'd been done for before he'd even started. He puts his hand to the door. How hard can it be? It's his job, after all. Ruth has gone back to work and is loving it. Last time he saw her and Tony, she was talking about expanding the business. And Greg's done it too.

Charlie was with him the week after the chaos of the awards ceremony when an old friend from work called. He saw Greg's shoulders tense as he braced himself for the usual questions but it turned out this girl – Ellie – didn't give a toss about the blog stuff. Quite the reverse, in fact. She was delighted that he wasn't off 'adventuring' as they were desperate for scientists to co-ordinate a new project from their labs in Southampton. Greg was bricking himself about facing the world again, but he did it anyway. And, by all accounts, he's loving it now. And loving Ellie too, if his recent, rather coy texts are anything to go by.

Charlie smiles at the thought and puts his hand to the door. It's good to be back. Being a delivery driver was a hell of an experience but this is where he belongs. And he's still in touch with Turner's via Bri. Harper had their baby and they called him Neo because, so Bri told Charlie when he first went to visit, he's a new start for them both. Their little house was messy and chaotic and gloriously welcoming and he found himself returning time and again. Then, last week, Bri stunned him by asking him to be Neo's godfather. It's a responsibility that would have terrified him before but with his own relations with his parents, if not exactly cosy at least much improved, he bit the bullet and accepted the honour.

'I did consider asking Ryan,' Bri told him, straight-faced, 'what with him being such a great role model and all, but somehow I've lost touch.'

Charlie had laughed and it had been a relief. He'd been furious at Ryan for ages, but the man lost his job and now he's being sued for breach of confidentiality and it's looking like the damages will eat up all his readily snatched media payouts and more besides, so it seems karma has found him out and Charlie can afford to let his anger go. It's better that way; anger burns like a very satisfying fire but ultimately consumes yourself more than the target of your ire. And, really, why hang around looking back when forwards is so much more enticing.

Charlie gives himself a little nod and pushes on the door. It resists as the safety mechanism flexes its muscles and then it gives. Thirty faces turn, thirty pairs of young eyes look curiously at him.

They don't know, he reminds himself. *No one knows*. Well, the head does, but she's been lovely about it.

'Young people are very vulnerable,' she told him at interview, 'and dealing with them makes us very vulnerable too. As far as I'm concerned, you did nothing wrong and I would be delighted to welcome you back into teaching.'

Her words echo through him. She trusts him. She's put him here. Now it's up to him. He steps inside.

'Good morning, class, I'm Mr Turner and I'll be your teacher for the rest of this year. Do sit down.'

They do. Phew!

'I believe we're doing Virginia Woolf.'

There's a collective groan and Charlie smiles. He recognises this, feels it pulse through him.

'Oh, don't you worry. By the time we're through you'll love her. Well, maybe not love her, but you'll get her.' He pauses, looks at the curious faces, takes a deep breath. 'What you need to know is that Virginia Woolf was a very troubled woman. She had depression, full clinical depression. She knew it and she dealt with it as best she could but in the end it defeated her. We're lucky now. There's more we can do. Depression doesn't have to be a stone in your heart. There's help out there and if anyone needs it they should speak to someone. Anyone. Friend, parent, doctor, teacher.'

They gape at him and he smiles.

'But enough of that. Woolf was part of the Bloomsbury set. Quite the dudes of their time. Let me tell you about them . . .'

Acknowledgements

I would like to start by thanking the amazing Sam Eades and Kate Shaw, who sat and brainstormed my chaotic ideas about what eventually became this novel with such enthusiasm and energy. It was a new experience for me to create a plotline collaboratively and one that I very much enjoyed. The fact that I then failed to plan it out properly and so had to do the most massive rewrite ever was all my own fault, but again it was down to Sam's patience, great eye and continued enthusiasm for Charlie and his friends that I managed to do that, so thank you.

Thanks as well to the wonderful Phoebe Morgan who has stepped so beautifully into Sam's shoes whilst she has been off having her baby. It's been such a privilege to have another clever eye on my work and your advice has helped hone this novel in ways that would never have occurred to me alone. I'm very lucky to have been taken into the energetic, creative and supportive Trapeze embrace and have loved every minute of it so far.

A vote of thanks must go out to all the brilliant delivery drivers who've brought groceries to my house over the last few years, as they inspired this book. I was slow to get into online shopping but once I did, I never looked back. I find it amazing that I can sit in bed at 11 p.m. adding items to my list and some nice man or woman will bring them to my door the very next morning. And I've been very lucky with drivers. In my area, they are all cheerful, chatty, helpful souls and out of a combination of them all Charlie was born. I hope none of them have his problems, but I do suspect that they brighten up more than a few lonely days for customers and I salute them for it.

This book is dedicated to two of my very best friends – the girls I met in my first weeks at university and who have remained my amazing mates ever since and are also now lovely pseudo-aunties to my kids. I don't see as much of them these days as I'd like to – due to them living in the big smoke and me out in the rural sticks of Derbyshire – but whenever I do, it's every bit as easy and happy as it always has been and I know I could always rely on them if I needed to. Thank you, girls.

I must thank my beta readers for their absolutely invaluable help in the tricky drafting stages of my novels. An especially loud shout-out goes to my dad, to my Auntie Barbie, to Brenda and Jamie and to my lovely husband Stuart, who always takes his marriage in his hands when he dares to criticise and is always right (in his 'literary' critique, not in day-to-day life, obviously . . . !!).

And finally, of course, my alpha readers – all of you. A book is not a book until it is read, so thank you all very much for gracing mine with your time. Do please get in touch via my website – www.annastuartbooks.com, Twitter – @annastuartbooks, or Facebook – @annastuartauthor, as I would love to hear from you.

Missed out on Anna Stuart's first book?

After 50 years together Stan still adores
his wife... so why is he dating again?

**After 50 years together Stan still adores his wife . . . so
why is he dating again?**

Bonnie and Stan are soulmates. They met during the Swinging
Sixties, to the soundtrack of The Beatles and the Merseybeat
scene. Now they've grown up and grown old together, had
children and grandchildren. They are finally building their
dream home, when disaster strikes.

Stan is running out of time, and can't bear the thought of
leaving Bonnie alone. Alongside his teenage granddaughter
Greya, he forms a plan to find Bonnie a new love of her life.
And she must never find out . . .

Bonnie and Stan is a poignant, surprising love story
set during the Swinging Sixties and the present day.
Ultimately feel-good and full of emotion, *Bonnie and Stan*
will make your heart sing.

'A fresh, original love story, beautifully told.'
RUTH HOGAN, author of *The Keeper of Lost Things*

Credits

Trapeze would like to thank everyone at Orion who worked on the publication of *Four Minutes to Save a Life* in the UK.

Editorial
Phoebe Morgan
Ru Merritt
Rosie Pearce
Charlie Panayiotou
Jane Hughes
Alice Davis

Copy-editor
Justine Taylor

Proofreader
Jade Craddock

Audio
Paul Stark
Amber Bates

Contracts
Anne Goddard
Paul Bulos
Ellen Harber

Design
Rachael Lancaster
Lucie Stericker
Joanna Ridley
Nick May
Clare Sivell
Helen Ewing
Jan Bielecki
Debbie Holmes

Finance
Naomi Mercer
Jasdip Nandra
Afeera Ahmed
Elizabeth Beaumont
Sue Baker
Victor Falola

Marketing
Amy Davies